Bright

JESSICA JUNG

First published in USA in 2022
by Simon Pulse, an imprint of Simon & Schuster Children's Publishing Division
1230 Avenue of the Americas, New York, New York 10020

First published in Great Britain in 2022
by Electric Monkey, part of Farshore

An imprint of HarperCollins*Publishers*
1 London Bridge Street, London SE1 9GF

farshore.co.uk

HarperCollins*Publishers*
1st Floor, Watermarque Building,
Ringsend Road, Dublin 4, Ireland

Text copyright © 2022 by Jessica Jung

The moral rights of the author have been asserted

ISBN 978 0 7555 0029 1
Printed and bound in the UK using 100% renewable electricity
at CPI Group
1

To my Golden Stars
let's shine always and forever

✦ One ✦

Smile, they say. *You're living the dream countless girls would die for! Besides, you look so much prettier when you smile. Come on now. Softer. Sweeter. You don't want to be an Ice Queen, do you?*

"Rachel! Over here!"

"Give us a smile!"

Cameras flash in my direction before my champagne-coloured stilettos have even touched the ground. I subtly smooth down my outfit – a glittering wrap dress with a strapless sweetheart neckline – as I step on to the red carpet. Mina is close at my heels, and seven girls emerge from the limo behind us, lifting their hands in queenlike waves. Fans scream when they see us, clamouring to get closer through the wall of paparazzi.

"How about a group shot?" a photographer yells.

Like we've done a thousand times before, the girls assemble for the photo – each of us instinctively knowing where to stand so that our best features are shown off. We balance each other out, the tall girls and the shorter girls finding their spots in the formation so no one looks out of place. As we pose, the cameras start clicking in a frenzy, catching us from all angles. There's something about having all nine of us together that makes a certain kind of energy radiate. I once saw someone share a group photo of us on social media with the caption, *This is what power looks like!!* I think about that sometimes. Power. It's such a far cry from how I felt around these girls for so long, but a lot has changed in the past five and a half years.

The girls and I take our time walking down the carpet, pausing to pose, lips glossed, hands on hips, literally sparkling like the sun in brilliant rose-gold outfits. As we reach the glass doors of the Peninsula Hotel Shanghai, I look over my shoulder and wink at a camera flashing in my direction, giving them one last dazzling grin.

I've come a long way from the trainee girl who used to freeze like a deer in headlights at the first sign of a flash bulb. The cameras don't scare me any more.

Now I own them.

Smile.

The first time a fan told me that I changed her life, I cried.

It was a year after I debuted with Girls Forever, and we were promoting our comeback single, "Sweet for You." The music video hit fifty million views on the day it released, and the pastel bucket hats and pearl-frame sunglasses we wore in the video were sold out everywhere within a week. The fan was maybe eleven years old – the same age as me when I first started training with DB Entertainment – lanky and a little self-conscious, but all smiles to meet me, her eyes sparkling like the rhinestone studs on her T-shirt that spelled out my name: *RACHEL KIM*.

"Thank you so much, Rachel," she said softly, holding out a homemade poster for me to sign.

"Of course!" I smiled back, fumbling with my gold signing pen as I scribbled out my name in what would become my well-known autograph (big *R* – *ACHE* – and finally a loopy *L* with a star on the tail).

I handed the poster back to the young girl, and a yellow-vested usher began to guide her down the line, but she called out, "Wait!" The usher rolled his eyes but allowed the girl to say her piece. She took a breath and looked at me with serious eyes. "I just moved to Seoul from America – just like you. It's been hard," she admitted, "but when I watch you perform and see you doing what you love, I feel less alone. Like maybe someday I can find my own way to shine. You really changed my life." She smiled and thanked me for my signature. "Ahh!" she squealed, looking at it again. "You have no idea how much this means to me!" And with that, she hugged the poster to her chest and walked away. A big fat tear rolled down my cheek as I waved goodbye, swallowing the lump in my throat. Really, it was the other way around: she had no idea what her words meant to *me*.

Five and a half years in, I don't cry at the fansigns any more – I've learned how to keep a pleasant smile on my face through the events, to keep my emotions in check. Even so, sometimes I still want to pinch myself because it doesn't feel real. How did I manage to get here? To say that training wasn't easy would be a huge understatement. It was ruthless, demanding, and made me question my life choices more than a few times. And when we finally debuted, the pressure only amplified. Intense rehearsals, back-to-back live performances, and early-morning wake-up calls for music video shoots that lasted for two days straight, all with my eight Girls Forever groupmates, who I suddenly found myself with 24/7 (which, let's be real, was a whole *other* kind of challenge).

But at the end of the day, it's all been worth it. There really is magic in the music, and there's magic in meeting the people who connect to it. Being a K-pop idol means being part of something bigger than myself.

The energy from tonight's crowd was wild. Shanghai was the last stop on our multicountry Glow Asia Tour. Months of being on the road, a new city every couple of weeks. It's been a whirlwind, and there were times when I found myself missing my own bed. But up onstage tonight, I realised just how much I'll miss this once we're back home in Korea. It's January and we won't tour again this year until the fall, so this is our last big group performance for a while. And you could feel that in the air. We gave 110 per cent tonight, and the fans gave it right back to us. Now it's time to celebrate.

I look around the Peninsula Shanghai's ballroom. The promoters have really gone all out on this one. Brilliant teardrop-crystal chandeliers line the ceiling, shining down on the waiters in glossy tuxedos weaving through the crowd with silver trays of champagne flutes, music pulsing against the walls as people dance and mingle. They've converted part of the ballroom's dance floor into a miniature roller rink. Electric pink and fluorescent yellow cocktails surf by me on glow-in-the-dark platters – an homage to the title track off our latest album, "Glow." It's a true bop, and it dominated the charts this past summer. For the party tonight, they've rigged a projector to display themed images from the music video against the walls: glow-in-the-dark bowling alleys; fields of fireflies; a Ferris wheel riding to the top, with the twinkling city lights spread out below like candles on a birthday cake. Honestly, it's enough to make you forget that it's the dead of winter and currently a whopping three degrees Celsius out tonight.

Just as I'm reaching for a champagne flute, a voice behind me calls out my name.

"Rachel Kim!" A wiry man with red square-rimmed glasses and a warm smile walks towards me, extending his hand for a handshake. "I'm Park Hyunbae, VP of programming at SOAR Drama and Entertainment. I was hoping to run into you tonight."

SOAR is one of the biggest media broadcasting companies in Korea. We've appeared in a few of their TV programs, but DB always handles the business side of things, so I've never met one of their executives in person. "So nice to meet you," I say, shaking his hand.

"I hope you don't mind." He reaches into his pocket and sheepishly produces a pen. "My daughter is a big fan of yours and she'd kill me if I didn't at least ask. Could you sign this for her? Her name is Park Miyoung."

"I'd be more than happy to." Even after the thousands (could it be millions?) of autographs I've signed over the past few years, I still have a hard time saying no.

He smiles as I hand my signed cocktail napkin back to him. "I'll be guarding this with my life tonight." He folds the autograph and places it in his breast pocket, patting it securely. "You know, Rachel, Miyoung's not your only fan. My wife and I are big fans too. You have a fantastic voice."

Now it's my turn to smile gratefully. "Thank you so much, Mr. Park."

"You'd be great on radio." He raises his eyebrows curiously. "Would you ever be interested in hosting? SOAR is launching a new radio show that focuses on one-on-one conversations with artists from all different walks of life. You'd be a great host."

I immediately perk up. "That would be amazing," I tell him with another smile. "If you connect with DB, I'm sure they could set up a meeting for us," I add with more confidence than I actually feel. But why shouldn't DB be interested? SOAR's radio shows have a huge audience, and if I can use it to promote Girls Forever while also enjoying deep, intimate conversations about the creative process, isn't that a win-win?

"Excellent," Mr. Park says. "I'll be in touch!"

We toast and then he's swept away by a group of other

media folks eager to speak with him. I'm debating between checking out the dessert bar or hitting the dance floor when Mina sashays towards me, grabbing my free hand.

"There you are!"

Mina must have a radar system that alerts her anytime someone else is getting special praise or attention – I had barely finished my toast with Mr. Park when suddenly she was at my side. But she's bright and beaming, her eyes shining with the high of the music, exuding charismatic energy, the kind that makes you want to join in on whatever she's doing. So when she says "Come on, let's dance!" I take a quick swig of my drink and then let it melt away on to one of the many passing trays as she leads me to the dance floor, spinning me under her arm.

She looks chic in her shimmering wide-leg pantsuit, her ash-brown hair twisted away from her face in a loose, elegant updo. We dance, laughing, me following along with her moves. She's undeniably magnetic and even more so when she dances, totally effortless and buoyant, and all the cameras in the room have already started pointing in our direction.

For a second, I let myself believe that they're capturing something real, a moment of true friendship between girls who used to be enemies. *Look how far we've come*, I imagine myself saying. *Remember how much we used to hate each other? How about that time you drugged me at the trainee house and filmed me dancing drunk on the table? Ha! Doesn't that feel like a lifetime ago?*

But then, some things don't change, even in a lifetime.

It took ages for the rumours about our so-called love

triangle with DB Entertainment's most popular K-pop idol, Jason Lee, to die down. In reality, the "love triangle" was nothing but a publicity stunt pulled by DB themselves before Mina and I debuted. They wanted to boost Jason's solo career after he left his group NEXT BOYZ, and we were the perfect promotional tools. After all, what could make the already-adored Jason Lee seem even more desirable than having two up-and-coming K-pop stars fighting for his love? Of course, Mina knew it was a setup the whole time. I was not clued in to that little piece of information until *after* I had already fallen in actual, real, head-over-heels love with the guy.

As for me and Mina, after our debut DB decided they'd got all they could out of our love-triangle feud and decided to stage a reconciliation between the two of us. We hugged and cried in a "leaked" video and swore we'd never let a man come between us again. Since then, we've had nothing but good press, and I'm determined to keep it that way.

Still. In moments like this, I can't help but enjoy playing make-believe, pretending that the fun we're having isn't just for show or publicity but because we really, truly like each other.

"That dress is *so* brave of you, fashionista," Mina shouts over the music. "Look at those cute thighs!"

Yep. Moment shattered.

The night passes in a happy haze of dances and champagne glasses. The ballroom is filled with familiar DB faces and hosts of new people I've never met before, all of them eager to greet me.

"Wonderful job at the concert tonight, Rachel!"

"Your voice keeps getting lovelier and lovelier."

"Absolutely phenomenal! You were born to be a star, there's no doubt about that."

After hours of dancing and mingling, I'm ready to call it a night. Some of the more introverted girls of the group like Youngeun, Jiyoon, and Sunhee have already made their graceful exits to their hotel rooms, while Mina, Lizzie, and Eunji have somehow found themselves on the roller rink, squealing and laughing as they spin around in their skates, shimmering outfits fanning out like sparkling parasols. Ari and Sumin are sipping cocktails by the dessert bar and, as usual, are arguing about something or other. Being the same age and having started training at the same time, the two of them are constantly jumping back and forth between being best friends and roasting each other until one of them cries. Honestly, they're like a dysfunctional old married couple. It's actually kind of adorable.

I'm dreaming of going up to my hotel room and soaking in the Jacuzzi tub. As much as I love these strappy Jimmy Choo stilettos, I'm dying to take them off and sink my toes in a bubble bath. Ahh yes. An aromatherapy soak plus a face mask sounds like the perfect way to end this tour.

Just as I'm heading out of the ballroom, I hear my name called again. I turn and spot a figure leaning up against the wall where our music video is being projected, colours and lights dancing playfully across his face.

"Jason?" I say in surprise.

His lips curl up into an impish smile, and he cocks his head to the side. "Has it been so long that you don't recognise me?"

Of course I recognise him, in that slick white suit and those bright-green and gold sneakers. How could I not?

After the love-triangle debacle with Mina, Jason and I had a falling-out. I just couldn't trust him any more. But slowly, over time, the ice between us started to thaw. A text here, a secret coffee date there. Eventually, we were able to make up and pick up where we left off. Or at least, we tried. But between Girls Forever's launch, and his successful career as DB's hottest solo artist, we barely had time to sleep, let alone date. Eventually, things fizzled between us because of our busy schedules. And Jason doesn't know it, but it was also a little bit because of the secret video Mina had threatened to leak of Jason and me kissing backstage. With her threat looming over my head, I could never quite relax when I was with him.

The thing is, Mina never did end up leaking that video. And even though the threat of it was often on my mind during the year and a half Jason and I dated, ultimately, we had the chance to give our relationship a fair shot without any tabloid frenzy. Maybe Mina never intended to hurt me as much as I thought she did.

"The Orange Music Awards six months ago," Jason says, snapping his fingers. "That was the last time we saw each other, wasn't it?"

"I think you're right." These days, our paths only seem to cross at crowded events like this one or some award show.

I notice that he's grown his hair out in the last six months. It's long enough now that he could tie it in a mini ponytail, but he has it slicked back, looking like the epitome of a fresh-faced K-pop idol, all smiles and twinkling eyes. "I wasn't expecting you to be in Shanghai," I tell him. "You look great."

He smiles. "You do too. And are you kidding? I wouldn't miss a party like this." A waiter walks by with a tray of pink champagne and Jason grabs two, passing one to me. "Have a moment to catch up with your old friend?"

My feet protest, but it is nice to see Jason. Not that I have any romantic feelings for him any more, but I do still care about him and I'm curious about what he's been up to. I take the champagne and let him lead me out on to the balcony. The January night air makes our breath puff out in little clouds, but there are heaters placed around the deck for warmth, and anyway, the coolness is a welcome change from the heat of the crowded ballroom.

"I heard that the tour was a big success," Jason says, leaning against the balcony railing. "That must feel great."

"Thanks," I say with a smile. "It was our best yet." Around anyone else this might seem like bragging, but I know Jason gets it. I take a sip of champagne, feeling nostalgic. "When we first debuted, everything was so exciting and new, but half the time I felt like I had no idea what I was doing. Training is one thing, but when you're really out there with all these eyes on you . . ."

"It's different," Jason finishes for me. He laughs. "Yeah, I remember."

I look up at the moon, thinking fondly back to the days when Jason called me "Werewolf Girl." God, the butterflies I felt around him then. Is there anything more intoxicating than first love?

"I'm happy for you, Rach," Jason says, squeezing my shoulder. "So what's next for you? I saw you talking to that exec from SOAR – do we have a new Rachel Kim–hosted quiz show to look forward to? Launching a new side gig as a presenter? Must be about time you started working on whatever's next, right?"

I laugh and tell him about the radio show opportunity. Girls Forever is still in its prime, with hopefully many years still ahead of us, but we all know that this career doesn't last forever. What will my life be like after K-pop, I suddenly wonder? It seems like too big a question to ponder right now, as the music from the ballroom blasts on, filtering out through the balcony entrance.

"What about you?" I ask Jason, deflecting the conversation away from my minor existential crisis. "What's going on in your career?"

He grins, straightening his shoulders. "Well, since you asked, you happen to be looking at the second male lead in Kim Haeyoung's newest movie."

I gasp. "Are you serious? Kim Haeyoung's movies always make me sob! She's like the best screenwriter in Korea. That's amazing."

"Thanks," he says, shining with excitement. "Sena has

been helping me prepare for the role, but I'm still nervous. It'll be my first time acting in a production this big."

"You'll be great," I say. "Will Sena be in the movie too?"

Jason and Won Sena publicly announced their relationship over a year ago. Being a popular K-drama star since she was a teenager, she has just as much star power as Jason, if not more. They're a cute couple with a great, supportive fanbase, and the media has basically dubbed them "Korea's Sweethearts."

It's been a while since I've felt that way for anyone, and even though I know it's just as well – my life as an idol does not lend itself easily to romance – I can't help but miss it.

"No. She's already been tapped for a new drama," Jason says, breaking my reverie. "They're still looking for female leads for this one, actually, so if you're interested . . ." He raises his eyebrows meaningfully.

I laugh. "I'll keep that in mind. I'm sure my third-grade teacher would give me a glowing recommendation. Did I ever tell you I played a piece of toast in the school play about food groups?"

"A piece of toast? Whew, Rachel, I don't know. I think you may be too qualified for a Kim Haeyoung film."

We both laugh, and I feel a wave of emotion come over me. After everything we've been through, I'm grateful that Jason and I can still be friends. It could have ended in so many other ways, but I'm glad it ended here.

As if he's thinking the same thing, Jason says, "I'm so happy I caught you tonight."

"Same. But it's time for a foot bath – these heels are killing me."

Jason chuckles. "How about we cheers to end the night? Since I hear you're an expert on all things 'toast.'"

I roll my eyes at his cheesy dad joke but hold up my champagne flute. "To the next heartthrob of Hallyu."

He smiles and raises his glass. "To both of us. And whatever our futures may hold."

We clink our glasses and drink.

A fresh wave of determination courses through me as I return to my room to pack for the trip back to Seoul. When I get home, I'm going to start thinking more deeply about what I want and make some plans. Jason was right about one thing. It *is* probably well past time to start thinking about what comes next. With any luck, I can build a career with DB's help that lasts beyond Girls Forever, though at the moment, it's hard to imagine anything following forever.

⭐ *Two* ⭐

The CIA should hire +EVER to work for them. Our fans' tracking skills are seriously on another level. As soon as we step out of the arrival gate at Incheon International Airport, we're met with a crowd of fans screaming our name.

Our fanbase has affectionately named themselves +EVER, pronounced *and ever*. It's a play on the "Forever" in our name, but also meant to signify that they'll be by our side for eternity. Sometimes +EVERs will buy plane tickets on the same flight as us just so they can be close to us. Most of the fans who do this are really sweet. If they see us, they're totally respectful and mindful of our space. They don't even need to talk to us. They're just happy to be in our presence, a silent signal of support.

In fact, I'm pretty sure when I got up to stretch on our flight home, I saw a couple of +EVERs through the half-open curtain between first class and coach. I smiled, and could see their faces light up before I returned to my seat.

But now that we've landed, and are surrounded on all

sides by more fans, our bodyguards try to keep everyone at a distance, clearing enough space for us to make our way out of the airport. Even so, it doesn't deter our fans from snapping photo after photo and yelling out to us.

"Girls Forever, forever!"

"Unni, I love you!"

"Rachel, you're a style icon!"

"Fashionista Forever!"

I grin at that. I'm especially pleased with my outfit today: a classic fitted blazer by Nell Kramer, paired with raw-hem boyfriend jeans and high-heeled ankle boots. I topped off the look with circular black sunglasses perched on top of my head, my hair in natural curls down my shoulders.

Airport fashion is a big deal in Korea. Most of the time, our fans only get to see us in concert where we're wearing our performance clothes. The airport is where they can see us in our personal styles. There are entire Pinterest boards and Instagram accounts dedicated to K-pop airport fashion, and I know that among those photos, mine circulate widely. The rest of the girls look nice, but no one puts in as much time as I do in styling my outfits – or has as much fun doing it. I basically treat the airport like a runway.

As we walk out of the airport and into the three vans waiting for us, I adjust my camel Prada boho over my shoulder and inwardly grimace. The shoulder bag was my first big purchase for myself after our very first number-one hit, which feels like a century ago now. I still adore it, but it's the one thing that I *don't* love about my outfit today. I've been meaning to get a new carry-on bag for forever, one that has caught up to my aesthetic now, but I haven't found *The One*.

Leah says I'm pickier with bags than I am with guys. It's possible.

In the van, Sunhee starts reading aloud from her book. It's an over-the-top period romance about a count and a scullery maid, but despite the flowery language, I actually find myself getting into the story of the star-crossed lovers. Even as the world tries to tear them apart, they are drawn to each other with the unstoppable force of true love. If only that's how romance worked in real life.

"Sasha quivered as Francisco led her to the bedchamber . . ."

"Ugh. Sunheeeee," Youngeun groans.

In the rearview mirror, I catch our driver's eye and we both suppress a laugh. Jongseok is one of six managers who usher us from place to place and organise our schedules. Unlike our head manager, who packs our days as if we have thirty-seven hours, not twenty-four, Jongseok is always advocating for us to have time to rest and entertaining us with stories about his daredevil Australian shepherds. And he can be counted on to share a good-natured eye roll with me when the other girls are being silly.

A few turns later, we pull up to our villa in the posh neighbourhood of Cheongdam-dong, just as a few flakes begin to drift lazily from the sky.

Winter in Seoul is nothing short of magical, bringing

with it the excitement of new beginnings. Or maybe I just feel that way because it was winter when we first moved here. I remember my mom, up to her eyes in cardboard boxes, asked my dad to take me and Leah out for the day so she could try to get us unpacked and settled without two kids running around the house, wreaking havoc. So Appa brought us to the outdoor skating rink downtown. I remember looking up at the buildings that rose up around the rink – City Hall, the Metropolitan Library, the Plaza Hotel – all gleaming white and silver against the grey sky. I felt like I was inside one of Umma's snow globes from her prized collection. In that moment, all my nerves about moving here, starting a new school, and beginning my training at DB melted away. I felt safe.

These days, when I think "snow globe," it has an entirely different meaning. It's what the media calls the Girls Forever villa. A perfect little world in the heart of Cheongdam-dong. Real life, of course, is not quite so idyllic, but the name has stuck anyway. And on days like today, with the sky bright blue and the sun glinting off the thin layer of snow coating our front walk, it actually does feel kind of appropriate.

"Ugh. I am so ready for spring," Sumin says, pulling her hood tighter around her as she exits the van. "I can barely feel my face."

Mina taps the code into the keypad on our front door, and the rest of us follow in behind.

Finally. Home sweet home.

Well, kind of.

"Home" used to mean an apartment full of familiar little comforts like vegetable-shaped magnets on the fridge. Walls lined with family photos. Umma sitting cross-legged on the living room floor, folding laundry while watching the news. The sound of Appa singing in the shower at the crack of dawn, getting ready for his day at the boxing gym, or of my younger sister, Leah, padding into my room in bunny-toed slippers, snuggling next to me in bed so we can stay up and gossip all night.

Now home has floor-to-ceiling windows in the living room, an enormous balcony where you can see the Yeongdong Bridge, casting its twinkling lights over the Han River at night, and a walk-in pantry that our managers keep stocked with gourmet snacks and drinks. It's luxurious, for sure, but even after five and a half years, it doesn't fully feel like *home*. Maybe it's the fact that there are only two bathrooms. Two bathrooms. For nine girls. Who did the maths on that?! Had to be a man.

While Mina, Lizzie, and Eunji rock-paper-scissors for the first post-flight showers, I make a beeline for the kettle to heat up some water for hot cocoa, while Sunhee and Youngeun start brewing some tea. "Wait, did you guys hear about N&G?" Ari asks, flopping down on one of the stools at our kitchen island.

I love the guys of N&G. They debuted a couple of years ahead of us, and we've got to know them pretty well. They're like our collective big brothers, or older cousins. "No, what's going on?"

Ari scrolls through her phone and reads out loud: "'N&G – or Namil and Gangmin – a former subunit of K-pop boy group ROYALBLU, announced today that they will be participating in an upcoming multigroup show this summer. This will be the duo's first performance since parting ways with their agency, DB Entertainment, last year.'"

Jiyoon rolls her eyes as she fishes for some matcha-mousse Pocky in the pantry. "That's not news. Gangmin Oppa told me about that last week when we saw them in Taipei."

It may not be news to Jiyoon, but it's definitely news to me. Namil and Gangmin have been really quiet over the past year – no music releases, no TV appearances, no performances. I guess they've been working really hard to hone their new sound as a duo. I'll be excited to see them perform this summer.

What happened with N&G was major. Last year, they sued DB over the thirteen-year contracts that they were forced to sign. That we were *all* forced to sign. Shockingly, the boys actually won their case against the company, and as a result, all of DB's artists got to re-sign new, shorter deals. Now we're only on the hook for seven years at a time. Though, with the "optional" three-year extension we're also required to agree to up front, it still ends up being a ten-year commitment. When year seven comes along, DB will put out a simple press release and make it look like we've all just decided to remain a happy family for three more years – when in reality, that "decision" had been made long ago, when we were trainees and had no say in the matter. Even so, what N&G were able to achieve was huge. I mindlessly stir milk into my cocoa as I think about how much we all owe to Namil and Gangmin.

"Rachel!" Ari gasps, still looking down at her phone.

I nearly spill my cocoa down my blazer. "You're on Nell Kramer's Instagram!"

Nell Kramer?! With those two words, all thoughts of N&G evaporate from my brain. I've been obsessed with Nell Kramer's fashion designs since I first saw that two-page spread in *Elle* of her all-cerulean line. "Is that – am I on her weekly inspo post?" I ask, my voice a reverent hush.

"Yes!" she says, turning her phone around to show a picture of me at Incheon Airport this morning.

"No freaking way," Jiyoon says in awe, a green biscuit stick hanging out of her mouth like a cigar.

I squint at the phone screen. *Loving Rachel Kim's casual look in my blue blazer!* the photo caption says. *Perfect for travelling. Rachel, how about you make your next trip my spring fashion show in Paris?* ☺ *Consider this an invitation!*

Holy shit. She's even tagged me in the photo. Is this real life?

"What's going on?" Mina asks, walking over with wet hair to see what the commotion is about.

"Rachel's airport photo went viral, and Nell Kramer posted it on her Instagram!" Sunhee gushes, looking possibly even more thrilled than I am.

"She invited me to her spring Paris fashion show!" I say.

"Wow. Congrats," Mina says mildly. "Bathroom's free."

After my shower, I find Mina, Lizzie, Eunji, and Sunhee sprawled out on the sectional sofa, watching a variety show on

TV. It's an episode of *Let's Go Camping!*, where celebrity guests go on short camping trips around Korea, usually involving a lot of hijinks and not enough socks packed.

"Rachel, come watch!" Sunhee says. "It's a rerun of the episode Mina was on."

Mina groans. "Do we have to watch this one? I swear, I still have nightmares about how they made us fish for our dinner. Do you know how many worms I had to touch that day?"

She shudders at the memory and grabs for the remote, but Lizzie holds it over her head, out of Mina's reach.

"You look so cute here, though," Lizzie coos, pausing the screen on an unflattering angle of Mina, eyes half-closed and face pulled in disgust as she slaps a mosquito on her arm. "Look at you! Next album cover?"

"Very funny," Mina growls, grabbing for the remote again while Eunji and Sunhee laugh. She whirls on Sunhee with a glare. "Yah, are you really going to be so disrespectful to your unni?"

Sunhee stops laughing, her cheeks turning red, but before she can reply, Youngeun enters the living room wearing low-slung sweatpants and a faded Greenpeace T-shirt. "Ugh, that looks like me the last time my mom made me come to her café," she says, nodding at the screen, which is now showing Mina gobbling a hot dog. "She made me sit there for three hours and eat six bowls of patbingsu so that customers would get to see their Girls Forever bias go into a sugar coma."

The parents of K-pop idols sometimes try to capitalise on

their children's fame to boost their family businesses. All of our biggest fans know that Youngeun's mom runs the place, and it's not uncommon for crowds of +EVERs to visit the restaurant hoping to catch a glimpse of the Yoons' famous daughter and her friends.

My phone dings in my hand. *Speaking of family.* My own family group chat has been buzzing since I turned my phone off airplane mode.

Umma: Did you eat enough while you were away? Come by our place this week if you have time. I bought some ginger lemon tea. I heard it's good for your voice.

I smile. We've come a long way since the days when she threatened to pull me out of DB's training program. I text back, telling her I ate plenty – the xiaolongbao in Shanghai was incredible – and promise to try to come visit this week. But I know the chances of that actually happening are pretty slim. They live all the way across the river, near Ewha Women's University, where Umma works, and even though we just got back, I'm sure DB will have our schedule jam-packed. I feel the familiar tug of guilt and wish that being a good idol didn't so often come at the expense of being a good daughter.

But just the thought of my DB schedule also has my mind spinning. I can't say exactly why that fleeting conversation with Jason got under my skin, but I still can't stop mulling over what he said. That it's probably time to start thinking about what comes next. The idea feels so big and vague. But if he's right, then maybe I should follow in Jason's footsteps and give songwriting a try. If DB supported him in that way, they might see it as a path for me one day too. And I haven't even *tried* writing any lyrics in the past few years. My little blue notebook is probably growing mould in my nightstand.

I go back into my room and close the door, knowing I probably only have a few minutes of privacy left before my roommate, Jiyoon, joins me. Opening the drawer of my bedside table, I pull out my blue notebook and flop on to my bed.

Flipping past outfit sketches and the relics from my brief attempt at bullet journalling, I open to a fresh blank page and wait for the creative juices to start flowing.

I uncap my fine-tipped ink pen and jot down:

When I see you from across the street, my heart already knows that you're the one I wanna meet.

Too cheesy.

Your lips on mine, that would be so fine, I think that you would taste like the sweetest of wines.

Okay no. No no no. I cringe and stop writing. All of these lyrics feel wrong. And not just because they're cheesy. They feel wrong because *I* feel wrong, trying to write a love song when I'm not even in love. And haven't been in a very long time.

God. I severely need to get my mojo back. I open my closet and start pairing my outfits for the week. Nothing like styling my clothes to get my mind back into its happy place.

There's a knock on my door and Sunhee pokes her head in, hair damp from showering. Her pixie cut is growing out, curling naturally around her ears. A few months ago, Sunhee's parents demanded that DB cut off all her hair, saying that it'd help set her apart from the rest of us. We may be international superstars, but sometimes our parents still see us as eleven-year-old little girls who need their careers managed. After the haircut, the girls called her "Pororo" for weeks, referring to the helmet-wearing cartoon penguin. I can tell she still feels self-conscious about it by the way she's always playing with the ends, but I think it looks cute on her. It totally goes with her cherublike face.

"Can I come in?" she asks.

"Sure," I say. "Don't mind all the clothes on the bed. I'm just getting my outfits ready."

Sunhee steps in wearing her fluffy bathrobe and looks down at my bed, lightly touching the vintage Vuitton mint floral dress that I laid out for tomorrow. "I loved your airport outfit today," she says wistfully. "No wonder Nell Kramer tagged you. I wish I was as stylish as you. My photos never come up on airport fashion watches."

I feel another thrill when I think about it. Will I really be able to go to Paris Fashion Week this spring? It sounds surreal.

"What are you talking about?" I pat a free spot on my bed for her to sit down. "Everyone was raving about that cute little shift you wore at Narita." I can tell that Sunhee needs some hyping up. She's always visiting my room when she needs a pep talk. "You know, the Burberry shirt dress? I'm dying for one, but they're much better on you."

"You think so?" she says, perking up a little.

"Definitely. Here." I rummage through my closet and pull out white lace-up ankle boots. "These would look hot with that dress. You can borrow them if you want."

"Really?" Sunhee squeals. She takes the boots and then throws her arms around me. "I die! Thank you!"

In a lot of ways, she reminds me of Leah. Their personalities are totally different, but in age they're only two years apart and I find myself automatically slipping into the older-sister role around Sunhee.

It's not just her I see as a sister either. For better or for worse, all the Girls Forever members are like my sisters. We argue and bicker, but we also live life together and we know way too many intimate details about each other, like how Youngeun can recite every single line of the movie *Tangled* or how the only thing that will soothe Sumin's killer cramps are Lotte Happy Promise custard cakes. I spend more time with them than I do with my actual family, and while I might not be as close with them as I am with Leah, the least I can do is be there for them when they need me.

"Seriously, you are the best, Rach," Sunhee says, already putting on the boots, which look slightly ridiculous paired with her bathrobe.

"No worries." I smile. "What are sisters for?"

The next day, we all head to DB's gym for our mandatory workout sesh. I almost wipe out on the treadmill twice thinking about having to ask Mr. Noh for permission to attend Nell Kramer's fashion show. Finally, our trainer cuts us loose and I make my way to the DB boardroom, where I know that Mr. Noh and the other execs will be finishing up their regular Wednesday meeting. I wait outside the door, trying to steady my breath – ragged from the two hours of cardio, and from the nerves that are coursing through my body.

"Don't worry, I'm sure he'll say yes," Sunhee says encouragingly.

I jump at the sound of her voice, then turn to realise that all eight Girls Forever girls are lingering in the hallway, waiting to see what DB's answer will be. Besides Mina's solo stint on *Let's Go Camping!*, none of us has really done any kind of solo promotion or event. While some of the girls, like Sun, are clearly rooting for me, I can tell others are torn between hoping he'll say no, because they're jealous of the trip, and hoping he'll say yes, because of what it could mean for them going forward.

Then, the doors open, and various DB execs stream out. We bow as they pass, but they're so deep in conversation that they don't notice us.

". . . would be an amazing opportunity," one of the execs, Ms. Shim, is saying.

"Mm-hmm," another one, Mr. Lim, says. "It's not every day you get interest from *Vogue*."

I pause. Did I hear *Vogue*? I'm dying to know what they're talking about, but my moment has come. The conference room is now empty except for Mr. Noh sitting at the head of the mahogany table, reviewing some documents in a sleek leather folder, as Mr. Han looks over his shoulder and jots down notes on a pad.

I smooth my ponytail and do a quick check for BO, then knock on the open door. "Excuse me, Mr. Noh."

He looks up from his papers. "Rachel," he says with surprise. "And hello, what's this?" he says, noticing the crowd of girls behind me.

"I was wondering if you might have a minute to discuss something?" I ask.

"Of course. Come in, girls, come in." He adjusts his glasses and exchanges a glance with Mr. Han. "In fact, this is perfect timing – we were just about to call you all in for a meeting."

They were? Why? Could it have something to do with what the execs were talking about as they left the meeting? Has Girls Forever been offered an opportunity with *Vogue*?

We step inside, bowing in greeting to Mr. Han and Mr. Noh, and assemble ourselves around the table. There's a pause. I'm not sure if I should start or if I should let Mr. Noh tell us whatever it was he was calling us in for, but then Mr. Noh says, "Now, Rachel. You had something to discuss?"

I explain about the invitation from Nell Kramer, showing Mr. Noh the Instagram post. I wrap up by saying it would be an honour to attend the fashion show, and that I would of course make sure it doesn't conflict with any currently scheduled Girls Forever commitments.

I fold my hands and wait. Moments pass, and my heart clenches. I can see the back and forth on Mr. Noh's face, his brow furrowing deeper by the second.

"What a lucky day, Rachel," he says at last. "Looks like you're going to Paris." He smiles stiffly. "We'll have the managers add it to your schedule."

I release the breath I was holding in one big gush. "Thank you, Mr. Noh! I can't tell you how – "

"Now," Mr. Noh says, cutting me off. I swallow the rest of my words midsentence. I guess we're done talking about this, then. "I have some exciting news for you girls." He leans forward in his seat. "You've all been invited to be on an episode of *1, 2, 3, Win!*"

Oh. So not *Vogue*.

I've seen a few episodes of *1, 2, 3, Win*. It's this show where celebrities come on to compete against each other in a bunch of games that are either super intense or super embarrassing or both super intense and super embarrassing at the same time, like having to eat a double pack of Buldak Ramen, then run a 5k race in inflatable dinosaur costumes. Fun to watch but not exactly something I dream of doing myself.

"It'll be a special two-part destination episode filmed in Singapore early next month," Mr. Han adds.

I perk up as the girls immediately start buzzing with excitement. Singapore? Now that changes things. I *love* Singapore.

"You'll be competing against three other girl groups on the show, including DB's newest group, SayGO," Mr. Noh adds.

I brighten up even more. Not too long after I debuted, Leah joined DB Entertainment as a trainee. After only a few years of training, she debuted with her own girl group, SayGO. If Leah's going to be there, then I'm sold. Bring on all the game-show contests!

Mr. Noh dismisses us, and the girls start exiting the room, already chatting about Singapore's famous chili crab restaurant and the rooftop infinity pool at the iconic Marina Bay Sands Hotel, but I hang back. I just have to know.

"Um, Mr. Noh," I say, clearing my throat. He looks up from his papers again, as if surprised to still see me standing there. "Did I hear Mr. Lim mention that *Vogue* is interested in working with us?"

Almost immediately his eyes narrow behind his mirror-tinted glasses as he shakes his head. "No," he says curtly, going back to his papers. "There's no opportunity at *Vogue* for the group."

"Oh, but I thought I heard – "

"Rachel, you got your Paris trip. I advise you to be satisfied with that and leave the promotional opportunities to me," he says coolly. Then he nods to Mr. Han, who gets up from the table and walks towards where I'm standing in the doorway. For a moment, I think I see the slightest hint of sympathy in Mr. Han's eyes, but then the door is slammed in my face.

Three

"Did you know these beaches are artificial?" Youngeun says, peering through her sunglasses at the pristine white sand. "The sand is imported."

"How could you possibly know that?" Sumin asks.

"I read about it on the flight over."

Sumin lets out a low whistle. "Not bad for a man-made beach."

As soon as we arrived in Singapore, we were whisked off to Sentosa, an island off the southern coast. It may only be early February, but the climate in Singapore is basically endless summer. I'm praying that my skin comes across on camera as naturally dewy, not like I'm drowning in humidity.

As the camera crew gets set up, I scan the beach, taking in the blue-green water, dotted with cargo ships off in the distance. Further down the sand, there's a group of people playing beach volleyball, hurling the ball back and forth like pros. Then my eye lands on the best sight of all –

"Unni!"

Leah and her four SayGO groupmates are clustered under a sliver of shade from a nearby palm tree. I grab my own groupmates and rush over to Leah, giving her a big hug.

"Hi, everyone!" Leah says, giving us all a quick bow and friendly wave.

"Nice skirt," I say, bumping hips with her, and she gives me a playful eye roll. Her mini neon daisy-print skirt, which she's paired with a simple yellow baby tee, was looted from my closet last summer.

Most of the girls wave back, then start mingling with the other groups we'll be competing against, but Mina and Lizzie just stare at Leah with tight-lipped smiles. I pull Leah aside and start to ask about her flight over, but then Lizzie mutters loud enough for us to hear, "Did you see the way she bowed to us? That was barely even a bow."

"Yep," Mina says. "She's a year younger than Sunhee too. She really doesn't know how to respect her sunbaes."

This happens every time Leah interacts with Girls Forever. It's no secret that some of the girls resent how quickly Leah was able to get into DB and debut, especially when some of them have been hoping to get their own sisters on the same track. Lizzie's sister is only a year younger than Lizzie, and Lizzie's been trying to get her into DB for years, but for some reason or another, DB won't sign her.

Leah just smiles and rolls her eyes at me, showing that Lizzie and Mina's comments haven't fazed her.

"Did you remember to put on sunscreen?" I ask her.

"Trust me, after that one family trip to Haeundae Beach, I'll never forget again." She makes a face.

"Red as a lobster," we say together in Umma's signature concerned tone.

"We were just talking about that trip the other night," Leah says. "Umma picked up fish cakes for dinner. They were good, but not Busan-level good. I still dream about those ones we got at Haeundae Beach."

When Leah debuted, I made her agree to live at home with Umma and Appa instead of moving in with her groupmates right away. She was even younger than I was when I debuted, and I wanted Leah to still get to be a kid – to have someone tuck her in when she's sick, fuss over her when she's stressed. Now, hearing her describe their cosy night at home, reminiscing about our favourite family vacation over yummy takeout, I feel a swirling mix of nostalgia, jealousy, and guilt. I never did manage to get over to their place for a visit. As I suspected, our post-tour schedule was packed with welcome-home appearances and recovery sessions with our vocal coaches and physical therapists. It felt like I had barely unpacked my bags, when suddenly I was packing them again to come here to Singapore. Of course, my parents said they understood, but I can always tell when they're disappointed. Appa's last text to me only featured two emojis – No problem, daughter. Hope to see you soon ☺ 🌴 – instead of his customary dozen.

"Anyway," Leah says, shaking me from my thoughts, "I better rejoin SayGO. Can't let them think I'm fraternising with the competition."

I laugh and Leah gives me a wink before heading back to her own group.

And then I see them. TeenValentine. An eight-member group that debuted three years ago. My gaze slowly drifts over to a familiar face, and my breath catches in my throat.

It's Akari Masuda. My former best friend and fellow DB trainee. That is, before she was traded to another label and I never saw her again.

Okay, not never. I saw her from afar at the RARA awards ceremony in Tokyo not too long ago, and I know we've been at a lot of the same events, but we've never crossed paths. Not like this. Not so close.

She's definitely changed, but it's unmistakably Akari. I can tell from the gracefulness in her steps, a ballerina walk I used to be able to recognise in the DB halls from a mile away, and by the way her eyes widen in surprise when she sees me here on the beach. It's the same look she used to get when I'd tell her horror stories about my encounters with Choo Mina in our trainee days.

"Okay, ladies, gather around!" The host of the show is MC Yang, a famous comedian who's been hosting popular reality shows since I was a kid. Appa and I love him. He's basically all of Korea's uncle. We gather as he starts explaining the rules of the game. Something about a series of competitions around the island and how points will be distributed. Honestly, I'm only half paying attention. All I can think about is what I'm going to say to Akari if I get the chance. What *can* I say? *Hey Akari, sorry I was a shit friend to you when we were trainees and haven't been in touch at all since you were traded, but it's so good to see you now!*

Even thinking the words inside my head makes me cringe. I wish I knew exactly how to make amends and tell her how guilty I feel for the way our friendship fell apart, but so much time has passed between us that I hardly know where to begin.

"Are you ready?" MC Yang asks, pulling my focus away from thoughts of apologising to Akari and back to the task at hand.

"Yes!" all the girls shout.

"Just what I like to hear," MC Yang chuckles at our enthusiasm. "Then here we go: One. Two. Three. Win!"

As much as the girls and I were more excited to be in Singapore than to be on the game show itself, now that we're playing, we're determined to claim victory. I can feel the competitive fire spreading through our group.

"Stop cheering for the other team!" Mina yells at me every time Leah and I high-five each other during a game or cheer each other on. Just because I want to win doesn't mean I can't hype up Leah while I'm at it. MC Yang smiles at our display of sisterhood, shouting, "Go, Kim sisters! You two could form your own two-person team!" The cameras also love it. They zoom in on every interaction between me and Leah. It's been so long since we've had the chance to spend any time together. I'm sure joy is radiating on my face each time we pass each other in a relay race, or make eye contact during a game. When it's time for the durian-eating contest, we try to stop ourselves from gagging as they present the slices of fruit. MC Yang explains that the smell is so strong, and so notoriously bad, that it's actually banned on the MRT, Singapore's mass-transit system. I catch Leah making a grossed-out face behind MC Yang's back and throw a hand over my own face to hide my giggle, but I'm sure the cameras catch it anyway.

The cameras are eating up Mina's competitiveness, too. I'm pretty sure they think she's exaggerating for television, but I know Mina. That's 100 percent real. She hates losing more than anything, no matter how small the stakes are. It must be in her blood. When Ari falls behind in the egg-and-spoon race because she can't run fast enough in her four-inch wedge espadrilles, Mina shouts at her to just take them off, saying, "Come on, Choos don't lose!" before blushing and correcting herself – "I mean Girls Forever. *Girls Forever* doesn't lose. Come on, Ari, just go barefoot!"

By the time we get to the beach volleyball competition, our fire is at an all-time high. We may not be nearly as good as the people I saw playing on the beach earlier, but we move like a well-oiled machine. I pass the ball to Mina, who's perfectly positioned to bump it over to Jiyoon, who spikes it over the net with a loud, satisfying *slap!* The ball bounces from Ari to Sumin to Youngeun, never once touching the sand. What we lack in athleticism, we make up for in synchronisation. Just like photo ops on the red carpet, we know exactly where to position ourselves relative to the rest of the group – shifting our formations seamlessly just like we do in our choreography. The other groups don't stand a chance against us. Maybe we can get on each other's nerves sometimes, but we're always able to come together when there's something on the line, even if it is just a silly game show.

Finally, after a full day of nonstop challenges, and a big show of tallying up the points, the judges officially declare Girls Forever the winner of *1, 2, 3, Win*. There's star-shaped confetti and party music, and MC Yang hands us a big trophy with a number one on it. The whole thing is kind of ridiculous, but I swear it feels almost as sweet as the first time Girls Forever won Artist of the Year at RARA. With filming complete, we decide to celebrate our victory with drinks in our suite at the Capella Hotel, which has a private outdoor Jacuzzi with views of the water. Our managers tell us we have the rest of the day off here in Sentosa, and then tonight, we'll be heading back into the city and spending one last night in Singapore before flying home to Seoul tomorrow morning.

TeenValentine is heading for the airport now, loading their shuttle van with dejected faces. I watch Akari go, guilt and sadness pressing against my chest. Today's shoot was such a whirlwind – constantly moving between filming locations, crew members shouting instructions at us every time the cameras stopped rolling – that we never did get a chance to connect. I feel the pang of another lost opportunity as their van pulls out of the hotel parking lot. I guess there will be no apologies today.

"I could sit here forever," Eunji sighs, sinking deeper in the water. The hot tub is surrounded by lush greenery with a mini waterfall flowing down one of the stone walls. It really feels like we've found a little corner of paradise.

"Same," Sumin says blissfully. "Ugh. Just leave me here. I don't want to get back on the plane tomorrow. It's so cold at home." She makes a face. "I can't wait for the day when technology is advanced enough to make teleportation a thing. No more flying."

"How are you going to backpack around the world one day if you hate airplanes so much?" Ari teases.

"I told you, teleportation," Sumin says pointedly.

Lizzie plucks a piece of pineapple off the edge of her glass and pops it into her mouth, raising an eyebrow. "Since when did you want to backpack around the world, Soom?"

"Um, since always," Sumin says. "It's been on my bucket list since I was a kid."

I had never taken Sumin for a world-traveller type since she hates flying so much, but now that she mentions it, I can totally picture her trekking around the globe with nothing but a big backpack on her shoulders. "I can see that," I say.

"My bucket-list item is performing on Broadway or in the West End," Ari says wistfully.

"Really?" Youngeun says from underneath the waterfall, the water massaging her shoulders. "But you always tell the fans that you never want to do anything other than K-pop."

Ari shrugs. "I don't want to disappoint them. But I really love musicals. It would be dreamy to be in one, wouldn't it?"

I've never thought about it before, but I can picture that, too. Ari always has the most dramatic facial expressions in our music videos. She would be great in theatre.

"My dream is to start a dance school back in my hometown," Jiyoon says. Originally from Daegu, she moved up to Seoul to live with her aunt when she started training at DB. Her parents are still in Daegu, though, and I've always got the impression that she'd like to visit more often. It's been ages since she's last been there.

"I want to get married and have a big family," Eunji says.

"How big are we talking?" Sumin asks. "Like three kids or seven?"

Eunji shrugs. "The more the merrier. I'm an only child, so growing up, I always wished I had a house full of other kids to play with. I want to make sure my kids have that in the future."

"As the middle child in a set of five, I should warn you that bigger is not always better," Youngeun says, making Eunji laugh.

I lean back in the hot tub and take a sip of my drink. I find myself a little envious of how clear a vision they each have for their futures. When I try to picture myself pursuing some specific creative dream outside of K-pop, all I see is a blank page. Like the empty pages of my blue leather notebook every time I try to write some lyrics.

"How's the songwriting going, Rachel?" Mina asks.

I lean forward so quickly, I almost spill my entire passion-fruit margarita into the water. It's spooky how well we all know each other. Sometimes it's like we can literally read each other's minds. I look to where Mina sits on the opposite end of the hot tub, with just her toes in the water, her huge sunglasses masking her eyes.

"Songwriting?" Eunji asks.

"Yeah. The songs she's been working on lately. In that blue notebook."

I continue to look at Mina in surprise. I didn't think anyone knew about that.

"Please. I notice everything." She smirks, answering my unasked question. Then her face softens into a thoughtful ponder. "You know, I actually admire your hustle and independence."

Wait. Is Choo Mina complimenting me? I blink at her, my brain not fully processing this conversation. "Thanks," I say finally.

"I mean, Paris . . . A solo album . . . You're so active about going after what you want."

I see some of the other girls exchange glances. When

you're part of a group – especially a hugely successful one like Girls Forever – the words *solo album* are loaded. While one of us might occasionally sing a solo song for a movie's original soundtrack, idols rarely do entire albums on their own when they're still part of the group. That's usually reserved for when you launch a solo *career*. And when one person breaks away, it's often like pulling out a Jenga block. That one missing piece can send the whole tower crashing down.

"Oh, I'm not looking to do a solo album or anything," I say, staring hard at my own reflection in Mina's dark sunglasses. I need her to know I'm being honest. And I need her to stop making trouble where there is none. "Those lyrics were just for fun. A creative outlet. Like Youngeun's baking," I say, even though so far "fun" would be a strong word to describe the experience. More like *slightly better than going to the dentist*. It's more about making sure I practise and try to get good at the writing piece of it.

"Mmm, Youngeun, can you make some of your *creative outlets* when we get home?" Jiyoon asks. "I'm dying for more of your chocolate croissants."

"Actually, I think one day I'd like to go abroad to study fashion," I say softly, surprising myself. "And maybe even design my own line someday."

I seriously don't know where that idea just came from . . . or if anyone's even listening any more. They seem to have moved on to debating whether Youngeun's chocolate croissants are better than her vanilla cream-stuffed donuts, but even so,

I can't stop myself from saying it out loud for the first time.

Maybe it's not *such* an outlandish idea. Every time I open my blue notebook to try to write some song lyrics, I flip past all the outfit sketches I used to draw. I used to love sketching, but somewhere along the path to becoming a K-pop star, that hobby fell away. And between how excited I got when I thought there was a possibility of doing something with *Vogue*, and how excited I get every time I think about my upcoming trip to Paris, maybe this – fashion – could be my *thing*. But just because fans like my airport style, or one designer gave me love on Instagram, that doesn't necessarily mean I have the chops to try it for real someday.

"You would be great at that, Rachel," Sunhee says, giving me an encouraging smile.

"I can totally see you in London somewhere, studying fashion," Jiyoon adds.

My heart glows. So they did hear me – and they think I would be *good*. "Really?"

"Would DB allow something like that, though?" Mina says, swirling the straw of her strawberry mojito. "Studying fashion? Designing your own line? They'd probably say it would take too much time away from your Girls Forever schedule."

Sigh. Leave it to Mina to ruin the mood. Again. "We're talking about the *future*. What's your bucket-list dream anyway?"

"Mine?" Mina blinks. "I don't have one."

"I thought you said you wanted to act in Hollywood one day?" Lizzie says.

"That was just between us," Mina says, shooting her a look. "Besides, I didn't mean it like a bucket-list dream or anything. It's just something that I thought might be fun."

"Sorry. I didn't know it was a secret," Lizzie says, biting her lip. "But for what it's worth, I think you'd totally fit in in Hollywood."

"Me too," I agree. And I mean it. I've never heard Mina talk about Hollywood before, but she's definitely got the glamour for it. And the ambition.

"Me three," Ari adds.

A corner of Mina's lip quirks up in a smile. "I think so too." Her smile fades. "But my dad would never go for it. He wants me to stay in Korea forever, where he can keep an eye on me." There's a deflated note in her voice, but she quickly shrugs it off before any of us can comment. She lifts her sunglasses, her eyes shining with a wicked grin. "So I guess I'll just have to settle for a more achievable bucket-list dream."

"Oh yeah? What's that?" Eunji asks.

"World domination, obviously."

"So cheesy," Lizzie says, rolling her eyes.

Mina splashes water at Lizzie with her foot, making Lizzie scream and splash her back. Soon all the girls are splashing each other, yelling and laughing and trying to protect their drinks. I laugh along, but my mind keeps circling back to what Mina said.

I know I said I was talking about the future, but truthfully, I've been imagining a future that's sooner rather than later.

Would DB really not support me if I wanted to do something fashion-related now?

By the time we leave Sentosa and head back into Singapore to check into our hotel for the night, I'm beat from a long day in the sun. It's a perfect evening to turn in early, order dim sum from room service, and try out some new sheet masks. I'm just deciding between the Pearl Serum and the Aloe Soothing when Leah shows up in my room, bursting with energy. I swear this girl never gets tired.

"We're sneaking out," she says, holding a pair of sunglasses. "You have your sunnies, right?"

"Sneaking out?" I laugh. DB does keep us on a tight leash, and curfews are not unheard of, even for idols. But it's only four p.m. and we're not children. We can leave the hotel if we want to, without whatever cloak-and-dagger scheme Leah seems to be concocting. "By the way, you know that people can actually still identify you, even with sunglasses on, right? I can see like seventy-eight per cent of your face."

"Please, Unni," Leah says, lowering her sunglasses so I can see her puppy dog eyes. "When are we ever going to get an opportunity like this? Me, you, in Singapore with free time on our hands – even the bodyguards have the night off! Besides, everyone knows that paparazzi are basically illegal in Singapore, so we'll be fine!"

It's true, Singapore has very strict laws about photographing celebrities, so we're usually able to fly under the radar pretty easily when here. Still . . . I think longingly of my plans to snuggle up in a big fluffy bathrobe for the rest of the evening . . .

"We'll only go out for a couple of hours and then we'll come straight back to the hotel. I have to get back by then for a little practice time with the SayGO girls tonight anyway," Leah says, bouncing on the balls of her feet. "We have a show as soon as we get back to Seoul tomorrow, and Yebin is feeling totally underprepared."

I think about how long it's been since Leah and I spent any real time together. Seeing her today has been great, but running all over Sentosa competing in wacky challenges doesn't really make for quality sister bonding. And with Leah now on her own path to success, moments like this where we have overlapping free time will be harder and harder to come by. We could just cuddle up and do face masks here in the room, but then again, Singapore does have an incredible shopping scene. It would be a shame to let that go to waste . . .

"All right, all right," I say. I grab my own cat-eye sunglasses and slip them on to my face. "Just for a couple of hours."

"A couple of hours," Leah agrees. She slips her arm through mine and points toward the door. "Let's go!"

⭐ *Four* ⭐

Orchard Road is the definition of shopping luxury. The long boulevard is lined with brand-name shops and futuristic neon-lit department stores. I feel like I've dropped right in the middle of my very own paradise.

We browse souvenirs at Tangs, Singapore's oldest department store. We get lost in ION – a massive, dazzling shopping complex with eight levels of stores – trying on sunglasses at Celine, shoes at Chanel, and scarves at Hermès.

Leah laughs, her face tinted with purple neon light pulsing from the LED walls of the shopping mall as we leave Dior and head toward Prada. "Aren't you glad I made you come out?"

"Yes!" To think, I almost chose room service over this. "Come on, let's go!"

The evening passes in a blur of stores and lights and laughing with Leah, trying on everything and taking a million selfies together. Leah was right. There aren't any paparazzi waiting around the corner to bombard us with photos, and the longer we stay out, the more relaxed I feel.

As we enter our tenth (or maybe hundredth – who's counting?) store, my eyes immediately zero in on the display of bags against the wall. Specifically, one bag: a robin's-egg blue Balenciaga goatskin satchel with stitching detail on the straps.

Drawn like a magnet, I gravitate towards it, feeling my pulse race.

The leather is soft to the touch and smells impossibly like fresh starts and second chances, almond ice cream and gardenias. It's big enough for a book, phone, makeup bag, and handheld mini fan – which are all I really need in life – and it's sturdy without feeling heavy. The strap slings snugly over my shoulder like it was meant to be there. I've read articles about this sweet thing, but it's my first time seeing it in person. And now I know: This is it. The perfect complement to my airport look. My heart in handbag form. Aka, *The One*.

"Unni, j'adore! I'm obsessed," Leah says, coming up behind me. "It has you written all over it."

"Right?" My voice comes out hushed, like we've stumbled into a church, which we basically have, since I'm pretty sure what I'm experiencing is a spiritual awakening. I flip over the price tag. It's . . . well, what you'd expect from a religious experience in the shape of a satchel.

"Are you going to get it?" Leah asks.

"I'll . . ."

Not be able to sleep at night until I own it . . .

Regret my entire life if I don't buy it . . .

Never have these feelings of true bag love again . . .

". . . think about it," I finish reluctantly as the rational five per cent of my brain reawakens and begins screaming alarm bells. My mother bred good saving habits in me – *never spend more than you've made in a month all in one place* – and as much as I'm a shopping addict, there's always a voice in my head tsk-tsking. I put the bag down.

For now. Either my iron will and impeccable self-discipline will triumph, or I'll be back in the morning for this baby – it's a win either way, I figure.

We exit the shopping complex and stand on the wide sidewalk that lines Orchard Road, and I feel that same sense of disorientation that you get after an afternoon movie. Only this time, instead of going from a dark theatre to the bright daylight, it's the opposite – after the neon lights of the plaza, I'm shocked to find that the sky is streaked with pink and purple and the sun has nearly set. Leah checks the time. "Should we start heading back now? The girls will kill me if I miss our practice."

I can't believe it's already been three hours. "Yeah, we should go," I agree, but I can't hide the regret in my voice. It feels so good to just be out and about, exploring the city. Our night out feels like it was way too short.

"Or . . . I can head back first, and you can enjoy some more solo shopping time," Leah says. She grins. "I can tell by your face. You have the Rachel's-still-in-it furrow."

"Ugh, I do *not* have a furrow!" I swat her playfully, then hesitate, rubbing smooth the supposed furrow in my forehead while looking wistfully down Orchard Road. "You sure you're okay to go back on your own?"

"Of course. It's like a ten-minute walk back to the hotel." Leah blows me a kiss and says, "Just don't party too hard without me, okay?"

I laugh and blow her a kiss back, waving as she heads toward the hotel. Wow. When's the last time I got to hang out by myself like this? Sure, I travel around the world for work, but I'm always surrounded by my groupmates, a security team, and usually a DB exec or two. Being on my own in a foreign city, no less, is kind of exhilarating.

Just then my phone buzzes with a Kakao message.

Are you in Singapore right now?!

For a second I'm startled, checking behind myself for someone lurking. But it's just my group chat with the Cho twins, my best friends since middle school. Honestly, I wouldn't be surprised if the twins were here. They're both always jet-setting for their jobs, Juhyun to different fashion and beauty events (she took her YouTube channel full-time) and Hyeri to various conferences about eco-friendly engineering and design practices (she's working as an engineer for Molly Folly, her family's makeup corporation).

Our busy schedules mean we don't get to see each other as often as we'd like, so a group chat is vital to help us stay in the loop with each other's lives. It's basically a constant stream of updates from the small – like the time Hyeri finally found a baked potato–flavoured Kit Kat at 7-Eleven – to the huge –

like when Juhyun's channel hit five million followers, or when Hyeri got engaged to her longtime boyfriend, Daeho. It's not the same as seeing each other every day at school or having our regular Baskin-Robbins-fuelled sleepovers, but it's the best we can manage and I'm grateful for it.

Hyeri: We saw online that Girls Forever is there filming an episode of 1, 2, 3, Win!

Ahh, that explains the text.

Me: Yes! LOVING it here. We wrapped shooting, so I'm at Orchard Road killing time and my bank account. Two birds, one stone, right?

Juhyun: Best!! Get me some chili crab and airmail it!

Hyeri: Lol. Same plus I miss you. PS How long are you there? One of our bffs from uni is visiting Singapore right now too. You gotta meet up!

Juhyun: Yesssss! Remember Alex? DO IT. You two will love each other, we kid not.

The name rings a vaguely familiar bell in my mind. Oh right, Alex. She was one of Juhyun's floormates freshman year, I'm pretty sure. I remember it was the end of my debut year, and Girls Forever finally had a few days off, so I met up with the twins at Stanford. For forty-eight hours I lived the California college lifestyle – afternoons on the quad, nights in the sticky-floored frats. If I remember correctly, Alex was the girl who wore a Twister mat wrapped around herself like a toga for the ABC (Anything But Clothes) party and killed it at flip cup.

I quickly type back.

Me: Sure, I remember Alex! But I'm leaving early tomorrow morning. I don't know if I'll have time.

There's a pause. I can imagine Juhyun and Hyeri next to each other, heads bent close, debating over what they'll say next before typing out their message.

Hyeri: Too late, already arranging it. Alex can meet you at Petal in 20 mins. It's got a really cute café!! In Gardens by the Bay, not too far from Orchard.

Twenty minutes? But my solo exploration time . . . As much as I love the Cho twins and would genuinely like to remeet their friend, chances for me to hang out on my own like this are rare to come by.

Juhyun: Come on, Rach, do it for me! Aren't you always saying you wish you had more friends outside of the BIZ?? Alex is hella chill and you need more of that in your life, no offence. Love you babe!

She's not wrong. At this point the Cho twins are basically my only friends outside the industry. It *would* be nice to meet some new people . . .

It turns out when it comes to Leah or the Cho twins, I'm a complete pushover.

Me: Ok ok ok. You guys are completely extra, but I love you too. Tell Alex I'll be there in 20.

Petal's not too far away, but I can't wave down a car to save my life. An MRT station looms across the street, and I decide to take a leap and try it. DB managers usually chauffeur me wherever I need to go, so it's been a while since I did the whole public-transit thing. I laugh at myself thinking about nine-year-old Rachel, who used to duck under the turnstiles with confidence at the West 4th station on her way uptown to spend an afternoon with Umma at the Museum of Natural History. I used to know those eight stops like the back of my hand, counting down each one as we passed through the stations on our way to the big blue whale. Come on, Rachel, you may be a K-pop star, but you're also a New Yorker. You can handle this.

Luckily, like most things in this city, the MRT station is bright and clean and easy to navigate. I grab a ticket from a kiosk and make my way down the escalator. So far so good. Just gotta make the next train . . .

. . . that's already at the platform!

I rush down the last few steps of the escalator, careful not to collapse in my espadrilles. Back in New York, harried commuters will jam an arm between the doors to halt the train, but here, there's a double layer of doors – the second one divides the platform from the tracks – and it makes forcing yourself on to the train near impossible. But I manage to leap through them both just as the train doors slide closed behind me. I let out a breath of relief. Success! That was close.

I move to take a seat, but suddenly I find myself tugged back. *What the fu –*

My bag – the ancient Prada boho – is wedged between the inner set of doors. I try to yank it free, but it's stuck tight. The train starts to move. I tug desperately at the bag, trying to ignore the people on the train staring at me. In Singapore, where even drinking a sip of water isn't allowed on the train, metro manners matter, and I'm making a spectacle of myself. If only this was my Manhattan commute, where a mariachi band could board and start playing, and no one would bat an eye.

"Excuse me, do you need a hand?" A tall guy with clean-cut hair, in jeans and a pale blue button-down, rises from his seat and makes a move towards me. He's probably a few years older than me, with warm brown eyes and a megawatt smile. I can't tell if he's smiling to be polite or to hide an almost laugh.

"No, no, I'm fine, thanks," I say, obviously flustered but totally pretending like this is normal, and secretly praying something embarrassing doesn't come flying out of my bag at him. Nothing like a cute guy approaching you only to get a tampon sling-shot into his eye.

"You sure?" he asks with an amused smile on his face.

"Totally sure, thanks! I have it all under control."

I give the bag one final almighty yank just as he's sitting down across from me. Eureka! The doors slide open wide enough for the bag to wiggle free, but the momentum sends me reeling backwards . . . right into Cute Guy's lap.

"Oh my god, I'm so sorry," I say, leaping out of his lap as if my butt were on fire. My face, I can tell, is turning beet red, and my mind is screaming with a chaos of thoughts, such as: *What is the appropriate apology for lap-sitting?* and *This is why I never take the metro!* and *Is he really wearing Hermès loafers with no socks?* and *WHY DO I FIND THAT HOT?*

This can't be happening. I can execute absolutely

insane footwork in six-inch stilettos – double-tempo hair-flicky shuffle, anyone? – but I can't keep my balance on a train or stop myself from creeping on a guy with attractively bare ankles? What is wrong with me!? I've obviously been deprived of nutrition today – or maybe I've just been deprived of Cute Guys for too long.

A dimple forms in his left cheek as he smiles. "Don't worry about it. Actually, you did me a favour."

"I did?" I say, my curiosity briefly overcoming the huge waves of embarrassment washing over me.

"Yeah. My mom is always saying that the perfect girl isn't going to just fall into my lap," he says with a teasing grin. "Now I can prove her wrong."

My cheeks flush again but this time for a different reason. Is he flirting with me, or am I just totally thirsty in my sad love desert?

I manage a quick smile before racing away as fast as I can to find a seat on the opposite end of the train. I press my hands against my burning cheeks.

By the time I hop off the train a stop later, transfer to a different train line, go one more stop, and finally emerge from Bayfront Station, the flush in my cheeks has gone down, but the memory of me flying into Cute Guy's lap like a Peter Pan stage stunt gone wrong is still burning vividly in my mind. I look grimly down at my tragically pummelled camel bag, the strap now starting to tear from the train escapade. *Jeez.* I've entered the red-level alert for new-bag desperation. This one is clearly bad luck. I check the time on my phone and see that I'm due at the café in five minutes. Not that Alex will care if I'm a few minutes late – if I'm remembering correctly, she's a very laidback, carefree girl. Or, *hella chill* as Juhyun put it in her new wannabe Cali-girl lingo. I rush past rows of waterfront buildings – the sea is visible from here, glittering like a dark jewel under the city lights. In the distance are Singapore's famous Supertrees, spindly branches cutting against the sky, lit a soft purple at their cores. I feel like I'm Alice in Wonderland, so tiny compared to the dazzling, vast wonder here.

Finally, I spot it – Petal. Inside, it's a gorgeous space, the dome top made entirely of glass, an assortment of plants lining the windows and spilling over the interior balcony. I take a seat at the second-floor café and scan for Alex, hoping I'll recognise her without the Twister toga, but the only people here are a young couple sharing an almond croissant and a girl getting a boomerang of herself pouring melted chocolate over her waffle.

I order an espresso and take a seat by the window, shooting Juhyun and Hyeri a quick message to let them know I'm here.

Me: Grabbed a window seat!

The door jingles open, and I look up to see if it's Alex.

My heart nearly flies into my throat.

It's not Alex.

It's Cute Guy from the train.

You've got to be kidding me. I grab a menu and duck behind it, rapidly texting the Cho twins.

Me: Is she almost here? We may need to relocate.

Hyeri: She? Oh ha ha no, Alex is a –

"Rachel?"

I freeze and slowly lower the menu. Cute Guy is standing next to me, holding a coffee. That dimple in his left cheek appears again as he smiles and extends his free hand.

"Hi. I'm Alex."

⋆ Five ⋆

Alexis. That was Juhyun's floormate's name, my brain informs me approximately *way too late.* As for Cute Guy (*Alex,* I correct myself internally), I definitely have no memory of meeting him at Stanford – and trust me, I would have remembered. I gape at him, at a total loss for words. He stands there smiling with that damn dimple, his hand hanging awkwardly in the air. Another second ticks by, and I see his smile growing uncertain.

"Hi, hi! Please sit," I say, remembering my manners. I quickly rise to shake his hand and gesture to the seat across from me, knocking over a napkin rack in the process. "Sorry," I blush. "For earlier, I mean. On the train. And also for right now." *Oh my god, Rachel. Stop. Rambling.* "I swear, I'm not usually this awkward." I take a sip of my espresso, attempting to hide my face in the tiny cup.

He laughs and runs a hand through his well-groomed black hair. "Seriously, don't worry about it. Why don't we start fresh? Pretend we've never shared a metro seat before. Would that help?"

I take a deep breath. Okay, yes. Pretend like it never happened. I can get on board with this. "That would be great."

"Okay. Hi, I'm Alex Jeon. Pleased to meet you for the first time ever and definitely not on a moving train."

"Rachel Kim," I say, smiling. Inwardly my brain has transitioned from screaming about how embarrassed I should feel to screaming about how adorably sweet this very cute Cute Guy is being right now. WHAT. IS. HAPPENING. "Pleased to meet you, too."

"Well, Rachel, now that we've met for the first time without having ever laid eyes on each other before, I have to tell you about something hilarious that happened to me on the metro," he says with a good-humoured grin.

Two espressos and half a chocolate lava cake later, I've learned that Alex is Korean American like me, and grew up in New York but lives in Hong Kong now; that he studied business at Stanford and was a grad student when the twins were at uni; that he loves kalguksu and hates pomegranate soju; that he is the oldest of three brothers; and that he's allergic to cats, but always loads up on Benadryl to visit his grandmother because she has three, all named after her favorite crooners from the '50s: Elvis, Fats Domino, and Little Richie.

Talking to Alex is surprisingly easy. He's charming and funny and attentive, and I almost can't believe that we literally just met. I feel like I've known him for years already. The Cho twins were right when they said we'd get along.

"Wait, do you remember Bubble Day?" Alex asks. In a crazy twist of fate, Alex and I discovered that not only did we both grow up in New York, but before I moved to Korea, we both attended the same elementary school, PS 41 in the West Village.

"Yes!" I say slapping my hand on the table excitedly. "Oh my gosh, best day of school ever."

"Even better than the annual field trip to the Central Park Zoo?" he asks with an eyebrow raised.

"Oh yeah, way better," I say, laughing. "I mean, I loved the seals, don't get me wrong. But come on, Bubble Day was next-level!"

Every year on the day before the whole school started a week of standardised testing, the teachers hosted "Bubble Day" to help us kids learn how to fill out the multiple-choice bubbles on the Scantron forms. We were given bubble gum (which was usually forbidden), and at recess the local firefighters came by and used their hoses to make a huge soap-bubble pile on the basketball court for us to play in. My friend Inez and I used to put a handful of suds on our chins, both of us saying "ho-ho-ho" in our best Santa voice over and over until we were cracking up with real laughter.

I'm so relaxed reminiscing with Alex that I don't even realize the couple from across the café who was sharing an almond croissant is walking towards us until they're right next to our table.

"Excuse me," the girl says with a tentative smile. "Are you Rachel Kim? Sorry, I don't want to intrude, but would you mind taking a photo with me?"

She holds up her phone hopefully. "I don't want to intrude" is one of the most frequent things people say while doing exactly that.

"Oh!" I say, caught off guard. I recover quickly with a smile, sneaking a quick side glance at Alex, who raises his eyebrows in confusion. "Of course. I'd be happy to."

Okay, so maybe I'm not a pushover with just Leah and the Cho twins.

She excitedly hands off her phone to her boyfriend, and we pose for a photo. I can feel Alex staring at us, trying to figure out what he's missing, and suddenly realise that somehow, in our past hour of conversation, we must not have covered what I do for a living. Does he really *not know*?

After the girl thanks me for the photo and leaves, I turn to Alex with a sheepish smile.

"Okay, I feel like a total grandpa asking you this, but . . . are you famous or something?" he says, laughing.

"I mean . . . is it rude if I say yes?"

He laughs again.

"But yeah, people do tend to recognise me. I'm part of a girl group called Girls Forever. We're, um, pretty well-known in the K-pop world."

"Ohh, you're *that* friend of the Cho twins!" Alex says, snapping his fingers. "They've mentioned you before. I can't believe I didn't put two and two together. I'm so sorry." Now he's the one who looks embarrassed. "Between school and work, I've been really out of touch with pop culture, especially in Korea. Seriously, I think the last movie I saw was *Toy Story*."

"Well, that's not that long ago. Didn't *Toy Story 4* just come out a few–"

"Not 4. *Toy Story 3*."

"Ah. Well, in that case, yes, you *are* tragically out of date." I remember going to see it with Akari and the twins one day after school and sobbing our eyes out during the incinerator scene. I think I was about twelve at the time.

"I don't think I'm *that* tragic," he says, straightening his shirt like his pride's been ruffled . . . which also has the effect of drawing my attention to his arm muscles, visible through the blue button-down.

We laugh and I relax again.

"It's no problem," I say. I mean it too. It's been refreshing getting to know someone – and for them to get to know me – without K-pop being in the middle of it all. I can't remember the last time I've met someone new and had it feel so natural so fast.

Alex glances at the time on his phone. "Listen, I'm supposed to meet some friends at a bar nearby," he says. "Do you want to join? They're a cool group, I swear. Not a bunch of grandpas like me."

If you're a grandpa, you're the sexiest grandpa I've ever seen, I conveniently stop myself from blurting out.

For a second, I'm tempted to say yes. I'm really enjoying my time with Alex the Cute Guy/Sexy Ankles/Hot Grandpa, and the past hour has flown by. But meeting that fan was a bit of a reality check. If anyone catches me hanging out one-on-one with a guy, I could get in serious trouble. All it takes is a single post on social media . . . I really shouldn't push my luck.

"I want to, but I probably shouldn't," I tell him, biting my lip.

"Ah." He nods. "Is this like a K-pop magic thing? If you're not back by midnight, you turn into a pumpkin or something?"

I laugh and shake my head, though it's not that far off from the truth. "Not a pumpkin. I look terrible in orange. But . . ." How do I explain this to someone who lives completely outside our bubble? "The rules in my industry are kind of . . . complicated. We're expected to uphold this image of the perfect, innocent girl next door who has no interest in dating. Our loyalty is meant to be for our fans and our fans only. And don't get me wrong, it *is*. We absolutely love our fans. It's just tricky. We don't want to disappoint people, and if we do, then our sponsors are disappointed. And then it's a whole disappointment parade that ends with getting fewer bookings, and of course then there's the media always trying to spin a scandal and . . . Like I said. Complicated. Even being seen alone with a guy can lead to big misunderstandings."

His brow furrows in confusion. "But I mean, we're *not* alone," he says, gesturing around the café. "And . . . it's your life. Wouldn't your label back you up if you wanted to start dating someone? Or you know, spend more time in cafés with your old friend from Bubble Day?"

Back me up. Right. I shake my head, thinking of Kang Jina from Electric Flower who was kicked out for having a boyfriend. That was an extreme case, but I don't want to find out what other punishments DB can dole out. The thing is, when you're on their side, when you're favoured by the company, like I am, your experience can be truly amazing. Challenging, but glorious at the same time. I've been incredibly lucky to have so much support from DB for so many years. And yet . . . they *are* a business. I just don't want to let them down. I don't want to let *anyone* down.

I explain as much to Alex and he nods slowly, some of the brightness in his eyes fading. "Oh wow. Okay. I didn't realise."

"Yeah," I say regretfully. "So, I should just go back. Probably. I mean, it would be the smartest thing to do. I think."

He raises an eyebrow, smiling gently, his dimple just barely appearing in his left cheek. "Okay, Rachel Kim. Let's solve this question Bubble Day style."

I laugh even though I have no idea what he's talking about.

"Here are your choices. Pick wisely, and be sure to shade in the bubble completely with your number two pencil," he says. "A) Come out to the bar with me and my friends, and put us all to shame with some B*Dazzled karaoke." I blush, both embarrassed and thrilled that he remembered my favourite childhood girl-band – one of the many small details I shared with him tonight. "B) Go back to the hotel, forget this night ever happened, and tell Juhyun and Hyeri you tried to meet up with Alex, but you were waylaid by some vicious MRT train doors. Or C) Be responsible and go back to the hotel, but get Alex's number and promise to text him later."

My heart flutters. "I'll take C."

"Good choice," he says, grinning back.

We take the MRT back to Orchard Road after he insists on seeing me back home. As we board the train, he makes a hilarious, exaggerated show of holding the door open for me and making sure my bag is safely inside, which makes me laugh harder than I knew I was capable of laughing at myself. His dorkiness about it suddenly makes me feel way less humiliated than I did at the beginning of the evening.

We sit next to each other on the train, and I keep mentally replaying sitting in his lap. Our legs are touching because the seats are so narrow, and part of me is tempted to take his hand, but that would be ridiculous. When we emerge back on to the street, it's no longer teeming with shoppers. Most of the shops are all closed now, their neon lights and signs glowing softly against the night sky. I take a deep breath, letting myself fall completely in love with Singapore. As we pass by the store with the Balenciaga bag, I pause to look through the window. Even from afar, in the dim lighting, it's so beautiful.

"What's up?" Alex asks, noticing that I stopped walking.

"That's my dream bag right there," I sigh, pointing it out.

He squints through the window. "That blue one? What's so special about it?"

What's so special? Are you kidding me? I whirl on him, shocked. "It's a *Balenciaga*, Alex."

He stares at me. "I'm familiar. But I repeat the question." The look he gives me is like a challenge, and I realise that for a boy who wears Hermès loafers, he's not impressed simply by a designer name.

I draw a breath, as if preparing to teach a seminar. "Okay, see, the craftsmanship on that bag is next-level. The thin-cut leather is lighter than other brands but just as durable, which has totally revolutionised the fashion industry. It's the perfect blend of soft and strong. See the stitching? That's all done by hand." I take a deep breath. I didn't realise how worked up I could get about this. But fashion isn't just about pretty things. It's art that tells a story in meaningful ways, just like this bag.

Alex falls silent, staring thoughtfully at the bag. "All right."

"So you get it?" I ask.

"No, I mean 'All right, you were really having your own little Miranda Priestly moment right then, weren't you?'"

Truthfully, *The Devil Wears Prada* is one of my favourite American movies.

"Okay, Mr. Hasn't-Seen-a-Movie-Since-Y2K," I say, rolling my eyes and reaching out to swat his arm, but Alex grabs a hold of my hand.

"Hey, seriously," he says, looking at me with those warm brown eyes, "I think it's cool that you're so passionate about . . . Balenciaga, was it?" I nod, not trusting myself to speak, the way my heart is hammering. "'The perfect blend of soft and strong.' Well, when you put it like that, it really does sound like a dream girl – I meant bag, bag! Dream bag. Definitely see it now."

He grins again and I swat him playfully, but somehow it's different than when I swatted Leah earlier. Less of an "Oh stop!" moment and more of an "I wish this night was never going to end, but can I at least touch your arm" moment.

For a second, he halts and stares into my eyes. I feel my breath soft and rapid in my throat.

And then, the moment is gone.

Alex walks me nearly all the way up to the hotel. I stop him two blocks away, just in case someone sees us and thinks we're on a date. But . . . would it be wrong to think that? It sure *felt* like a date. A really, really great date.

"So, is this *good night*?" Alex asks.

I look up at him. He smiles with that dimple, and I suddenly feel the urge to kiss him.

I quickly step back. As much as I've missed that falling-in-love feeling, and as incredible as Alex is, K-pop and romance just don't mix, no matter how much I wish they did. I have to remember that.

"Yes," I say. "Good night, Alex."

"Good night, Rachel."

As I turn to leave, I can feel him watching me all the way

until I disappear through the massive sliding-glass doors of the hotel. As a blast of air-conditioning hits me, I feel a wave of regret at our short-lived evening together, but it's quickly replaced by a flutter of excitement. We may have said good night for now, but I *did* choose option C. I wrap my fingers around the phone in my pocket, his number tucked safely inside. I figure there's no harm in texting him as a friend – it'd be just like my group chat with the Cho twins. Totally innocent. Just a chance to build a friendship outside of K-pop. Like they said, I need more friends outside the industry! I can keep my weird obsession with his ankles and sporadic desire to make out with his face and slightly disturbing fantasy of cuddling together while watching *Toy Story* at bay . . . right? Just then my phone buzzes and my heart nearly leaps out of my chest.

Alex: Just wanted to make sure you got inside safely. Thanks again for a great night. Not sure if I should count elementary school, the train, or the café . . . but whichever one counts as our official first encounter, I'm so glad I met you, Rachel Kim.

The grin on my face is unbearably ridiculous, and I can't wipe it off even as the elevator rises to my floor. Something tells me I'm in big trouble.

★ Six ★

The next morning, our flight is delayed. Something about the flight crew exceeding their hours. Normally I'd be anxious to get back home and annoyed at having to hang around a hotel for a few extra hours, but today it feels nice to lie in bed a little longer. I stare at Alex's name on my phone, replaying everything about our time together last night. The way he smiled. How easily he was able to make me laugh. The effortless flow of our conversation. How I wanted to kiss him in the middle of the street.

My phone pings with an incoming message, and I nearly drop it on my face. Oh my god. It's Alex. It's almost like I conjured him up just by thinking of him.

Alex: Guess what I did last night?

Me: Did you try to find your PS 41 school-wide photos? Bc I definitely thought about asking my mom to dig them up for me.

Alex: NO I did not, but that is genius. It's now my mission to find a photo of elementary school Rachel in my archives.

Alex: I did something just as fun, though. I watched Toy Story 4.

Me: LOL

Me: Thoughts, Grandpa?

Alex: The fork (spoon?) character was fun. But I 100% cried more during Toy Story 3. I'm not sure I missed out on much these last ten years, tbh.

I laugh. Before I can reply, there's a frantic knock on my door that makes me sit upright in bed. The knocking gets more urgent, and I quickly roll out of bed, shouting, "Just a second!"

I open the door to find Sunhee standing there, looking breathless, as if she ran to my room. "Rachel, did you see the news?"

"The news?"

She holds up her phone. "We're blowing up on *Reveal*."

Immediately, my stomach sinks. Shit. *Reveal* is one of Korea's most notorious tabloids. If they're writing about Girls Forever, it can't be good.

"Apparently, Ari, Sumin, and Jiyoon were photographed by a fan last night while they were out to dinner," Sunhee says, passing me her phone to look at the article. "The fan posted it online, and the tabloids back home jumped on it. They were with three unknown guys, and *Reveal* is speculating that they're secret boyfriends."

I scroll through Sunhee's phone as she anxiously chews her lower lip. Just like she said, there's a photo of Ari, Sumin, and Jiyoon sitting in a restaurant booth with three guys.

You can't make out the guys' faces in the photo, but the girls are smiling and laughing as they eat and drink. It could be a triple date . . . but it could also just be any other platonic dinner hangout. It's hard to tell.

"This is going to look bad for the whole group. Mina is going to flip out," Sunhee says.

"Forget about Mina. What about the execs?" I ask.

"Ari, Sumin, and Jiyoon are in a meeting with Mr. Han right now," Sunhee says. Voices come from down the hall, and she swivels her head in their direction. "They must be done. Come, on! Let's go find out how it went."

I stick my head out of my room to see Ari, Sumin, and Jiyoon coming down the hall. Ari and Sumin are bickering as always (something about who interrupted who when they were talking to Mr. Han), but Jiyoon looks paler than that time she accidentally choked on a rice cake. She's genuinely distraught.

My gut knots itself up. This is not good.

Before Sunhee and I can say anything, Jiyoon shakes her head. "Not here," she whispers, her voice rougher at the edges than usual. "My room. Everyone's waiting there."

We quickly follow them into Jiyoon's room. Lizzie, Eunji, and Youngeun are sitting cross-legged on the bed while Mina's pacing by the window. As soon as she sees us, Mina storms toward us, arms crossed.

"So?" she says. "How much shit are we in because of you three?"

"Calm down, it's fine," Ari says, holding up her hands.

"Mr. Han said that DB will deny that there's anything romantic going on between us and those boys. He said it should be easy enough since there wasn't anything specifically incriminating. No photos of kissing or anything."

Mina lets out a breath, loosening her arms. "Okay. So our reputation is fine?"

"For now," Sumin chimes in. "Mr. Han said that we can't be photographed with them ever again, though. It'll be harder to deny if there's a second occurrence."

"Who were they anyway?" Lizzie asks.

At this, Ari and Sumin pause, glancing at Jiyoon. It's odd to see Jiyoon so quiet when she's usually the one speaking her mind. She's the kind of person who has zero patience for bullshit, always bubbling with strong opinions. But right now, she just looks empty.

"Jiyoon?" Youngeun says gently.

Jiyoon sighs. "It wasn't a totally baseless rumour," she confesses. "It was actually my boyfriend and his two cousins."

I blink, stunned. Jiyoon? A boyfriend? How could she have a boyfriend that I don't know about? We're roommates!

But then again, would I tell any of the girls if I started dating someone? Honestly, I'm not so sure.

"How long have you two been together?" I ask, trying to keep my voice neutral.

"We've been together long-distance for almost a year. He's an old family friend who lives back in Daegu. We met up when I went home last Christmas, and things just kind of developed from there. One of his cousins lives in Singapore, so we planned a meetup for us all to get together, except now . . ." Her voice catches and she looks away, blinking rapidly. "We have to break up."

"Break up?" Sunhee's eyes widen almost comically. I'm sure she's just trying to be supportive, but something about the way she's sitting on the edge of her seat and soaking in every bit of Jiyoon's story makes me think Sunhee's just seeing this all play out as if it's some tragic heroine from one of her romance novels – instead of a real, actual heartbreak that one of her own groupmates is suffering.

"There's no other choice," Jiyoon says, still not looking at any of us. I can tell she thinks she'll cry if she does. The fact that the girl who usually has no problem staring any one of us down can't even look us in the eye right now is really breaking my heart. "If I get caught with Jin again, my career is over."

It's like I tried to explain to Alex yesterday. For a female K-pop idol, dating isn't ever just dating. It can end up in disaster. It's not fair, but it is what it is, and we all know it.

An unsettling thought creeps into the back of my mind. What about the fan who took a photo with me yesterday? What if Alex was in the background, and the tabloids pick up on it just like they picked up on the photo of Jiyoon and her boyfriend? Not that Alex is my boyfriend. But the tabloids don't know that. I was one-on-one with him, too. It'd be a lot harder to explain that away than a group photo. No. I definitely would have noticed if he was in the frame. That's something

I would pick up on. But I can't help but second-guess myself. I was so caught up in my conversation with Alex that I can't be completely sure.

I shake the thought out of my mind and cross the room, pulling Jiyoon into a hug. She's stiff at first, but then her body slowly sags into mine, her chin resting on my shoulder.

"I'm so sorry," I say. "It's not fair. But at least DB is doing their best to protect you."

Unlike with Kang Jina. I don't need to say it. Everyone knows.

Jiyoon nods against my shoulder. "Yeah. You're right. Thank you, Rachel." She dabs at the corners of her eyes with the sleeve of her sweater. "Oh and by the way, have you brushed your teeth yet this morning? Because your breath stinks." I throw a hand over my mouth and laugh, grateful that the old Jiyoon seems to be coming back.

Everyone starts to head back to their own rooms to pack up before we leave for the airport, but then Mina stops short in the doorway and turns to me.

"By the way, where were *you* last night, Rachel?"

I freeze for a second, pulling away from Jiyoon. "Huh? What do you mean?"

"Jiyoon, Ari, and Sumin were out together with those guys. And the rest of us were at the hotel spa. But no one knows where you were." Mina stares hard at me, her eyes boring holes into my head.

I scowl at the accusation in her tone. "I was shopping with Leah. And then I met a friend for coffee."

It's basically the whole truth. No one needs to know that the friend also happens to be a gorgeous guy who I've been texting since last night.

Mina's eyes narrow, but everyone else seems uninterested.

"You sure you're not hiding anything, Rachel?" Mina says. "Maybe Jiyoon wasn't the only one out with a guy last night."

What the hell? Does she know something? Or does she just know exactly what to say to provoke me?

"God, Mina, why are you so suspicious all the time?" I say, trying to ignore my heart slamming against my chest.

At this, she sighs heavily, crossing her arms. "Someone in this group has to keep tabs on everyone. When one of us messes up, we all look bad. And if I look bad, my dad will–" She breaks off, catching herself. "Anyway, I just want to make sure you weren't sneaking around with a guy last night too."

"Rachel wouldn't hide something like that." Sunhee speaks up before I can, her face going a little red as she confronts Mina. "And she wouldn't risk meeting a guy one-on-one either. She's too smart for that. Right, Rachel?"

I force a smile. "Exactly."

I'm glad that Sunhee's standing up to Mina, and I appreciate that she's doing it on my behalf, but a part of her comment grates on me. It's a reminder that I'm toeing a dangerous line just by continuing to talk with Alex. I always told myself that I wasn't dating because it's so hard to meet people, which was partly true. But now that an amazing guy has, to steal his phrase, fallen right into my lap, I have to face the fact that the real reason I haven't dated is because of all the risks it entails. I can't forget about them, no matter how much I wish I could.

Forget about Alex, I tell myself. It's the mantra running through my head as I choose my airport outfit and finish packing.

I promise myself *not* to think about which movie Alex would choose to watch on the flight home.

I practise *not* thinking about the fact that he had no idea who I was – and how refreshing that felt – as the paparazzi and fans gather to snap photos of us when we step off the plane in Seoul.

In fact, I even spend the night, and the next night, and the next night too, dreaming about how I'm not going to see him again anytime soon, or maybe ever.

All in all, I quickly become a pro at the art of concentrating on not concentrating on Alex. In fact, I become so focused on not thinking about him that I nearly break my shin during choreo the following week at DB.

Even though it's not for another four months, we're already deep in rehearsals for a new number we'll be debuting in the upcoming multigroup concert. It's this televised event where several groups will each perform one solo number, plus a big joint-group number at the end. But even though it's not as significant a performance as our LA concert this fall, the DB trainers push us to perfection no matter what the circumstances are. Tonight's rehearsal is a real nightmare – everyone dancing a half beat out of sync with each other, the choreographer shouting at us for our sloppy form.

I try to focus on the moves: Two steps, hair toss, spin. Shoulder move, clap! But my mind keeps drifting to Alex, and to my upcoming trip to Paris for Nell Kramer's fashion show. I'm dreaming of France in early March, when the air is still brisk enough for thick sweaters and cute scarves, but pleasant enough to enjoy outdoor cafés. But for the next two weeks, it's still freezing-cold February in Korea, and we're in a wake-up-at-the-crack-of-dawn and go-home-past-midnight schedule to prepare.

"Again, girls! From the top!" the choreographer shouts. We groan under our breath and find our way to the opening formation. If we don't want to be here all night, we're going to need to step it up. I clear my mind of everything but me and the song and dancing to the beat.

Finally, once we've flawlessly nailed the choreo more times than I can count, the trainer calls it a night. But before I can even change out of my sweaty clothes, I get called into Mr. Han's office. Confused, I make my way down the halls, retying my hair into a smooth high pony as I go. What could Mr. Han possibly have to see me about? He wouldn't call a meeting just to yell at me for being late on the shimmy move in the second verse, would he?

I knock on the door. "Come in," his voice calls.

As soon as I enter, I see that Leah is there too. We exchange glances and she gives me a quick shrug. She doesn't know why we're here either. Uh-oh. My stomach knots. Are we in trouble for sneaking out on our last day in Singapore? Does he know that I hung out with a friend named Alex who turned out to be a guy? That was nearly a week ago by now, but you never know with DB. They could have been using this time to mull over the perfect punishment. I'm already prepping my defence, blaming the potential for confusion with unisex names, but luckily, Mr. Han doesn't look mad. He looks excited.

"I'm glad I've caught you both. Sit, sit," he says, gesturing to the grey swivel chair next to Leah. I take a seat, tightening my ponytail and folding my hands in my lap.

"I have some good news for you girls!" Mr. Han says, leaning forward on his glass office desk. "The viewers absolutely love you two on *1, 2, 3, Win*. Apparently, the night the episode aired, the hashtag #TeamKimSisters was trending all over the place." I grin at Leah, remembering how MC Yang said the pair of us could be our own little two-woman team. "The network is wondering if you two would be interested in your own reality show," Mr. Han continues. "I don't have too many details yet, but it would be a classic reality TV series with a camera following you around as you live your everyday life and do various activities together. What do you think?"

My mouth drops open. Well, that was totally unexpected. Me and Leah? On a reality show together? Um, *yes please*!

Leah squeals, obviously just as excited. "Are you serious? Oh my god! You're serious? This is real!" she exclaims, then slides down in her chair, clearly embarrassed by her outburst.

She's always so confident around me that sometimes I forget she's barely out of her trainee years and still nervous around the execs.

"That would be an incredible opportunity," I say, stepping in to help Leah out. "We're so pleased you've thought of us."

"Mr. Noh has always wanted to make a duo album with you two," Mr. Han continues. "A sisters album! The timing is perfect. And the reality show will help build momentum for an album release for you. What do you say?"

You know how sometimes if you're crying and someone tickles you, you burst out laughing uncontrollably, because your body has collapsed all of its emotions into one? Yeah, that's exactly how I feel right now.

Leah and I look at each other again and this time, we both squeal.

He laughs. "I take that to mean yes?"

"Yes!" Leah says.

"Of course," I add, crossing my legs as if I'm taking this business opportunity very seriously and not tempted to start jumping up and down on my chair.

"Excellent. I'll keep you ladies updated," Mr. Han says. "Mr. Noh will be very excited when I tell him."

"Thank you, Mr. Han," we both say, bowing.

As we rise to leave, I hesitate. I've been wanting to ask Mr. Han about something since we got back from Singapore but haven't had the chance. This may be as good a time as any. Plus, it's easier to broach the subject with the laidback and approachable Mr. Han than it would be with Mr. Noh.

"Mr. Han, I was wondering if everything is okay with the *Reveal* article about my groupmates?" I ask. "Has it all blown over?"

Mr. Han leans back in his desk chair. "Oh yes. Thankfully, it has. The media's turned their attention over to Jason Lee's new movie, *When I Loved You*, as I'm sure you've noticed."

But of course I haven't, because I have no time between rehearsing until my legs fall off and all my very serious mental work of avoiding Alex-related daydreams. I raise my eyebrows. "Jason's movie? I didn't realise they already started filming."

"Production hasn't started yet. But it's been announced that Song Geonwu is also attached to star in the movie."

Leah's eyes widen. "Wow, Jason is going to be in a movie with Song Geonwu? I loved him in *Tomorrow We Dance*. And basically everything else he's been in. He's so huge. No wonder there's buzz already."

"Yes," Mr. Han says. "And there's some rumour going around that both he and Jason are in love with their female co-star and are battling against each other for her affections. Though, between you and me, I happen to know for a fact that the female lead hasn't even been cast yet."

Ah. Of course. Sounds like classic tabloid garbage to me and exactly the kind of thing Jason would let unfold to get people hyped up for his movie. Still, I'm grateful. Thanks to him and Song Geonwu, the attention has turned away from Girls Forever. Who knows: By the way Mr. Han is smiling slightly, it could be that DB even planted that rumour as a favour to us to take some of the heat off our group. They're always pulling strings behind the scenes. And in this case, I'd be more than happy if they were.

I float home that night on an imaginary cloud of cotton candy and champagne fizz, feeling supported and inspired. The girls are already gathering in the living room when I arrive, cosying up for our monthly movie night, a house tradition. "Rachel, you're just in time! Come join us," Sunhee says, patting the seat next to her.

"Be there in a sec!" I say. "Let me just, um, change real quick."

I disappear into my bedroom, but instead of changing right away, I float on to my bed, where magically my phone floats into my hands as the quiet buzzing commences (obviously I've turned off my notifications – sharing a bedroom and all).

Alex: So I'm looking to get a new outfit . . . What's trendy right now? Male rompers, right?

Me: Oh definitely. Male rompers all day, every day. You should even wear one to work. I hear it's very professional.

Alex: Yeah? I'm sure my boss will love it. What pattern should I get them in? Paisley?

Me: Never mind, I can't take it any more! Someone needs to give you a fashion education!!

Alex: Next time we're both in Singapore, you can help a poor guy out ☺

Me: Love how you throw around "next time" like it's a thing.

Alex: Oh it's a thing.

Me: Agree to disagree.

Alex: I'd never agree to such a thing. We'll have to get together so you can explain to me again why we really can't get together. I'm not sure it's coming through clearly enough over text . . .

Me: You're the absolute worst. Were you on debate team in school or something?

Alex: Actually, yes. It goes with nerd territory, don't judge.

Me: I would never. I judge no one.

Alex: Except men in rompers.

Me: I feel like you are really starting to know me.

I suddenly realise I'm smiling so hard at my phone that my cheeks hurt. Luckily, Jiyoon's watching the movie with the rest of the girls – otherwise she'd for sure demand to know what has me grinning and cackling to myself like a hyena in *The Lion King*. She's been extra sensitive lately anyway, her own breakup still being so fresh.

Ever since the *Reveal* scandal, I had been trying to hold back from texting with Alex, but now that the smoke's cleared and the media has moved on, it seems innocent enough to chat with him again. After all, we're just talking. About how we shouldn't be talking! It's very important to communicate that.

Still . . . I do need to be careful. I open up Instagram and go to my tagged mentions. I already did this last week, that same day I learned about Jiyoon being caught, but you never know if something rolled out after the fact. I take a breath and scroll through my mentions for the zillionth time since then, sifting through all the memes and fan-made edits until I come across the photo from the fan at Petal.

Still no Alex in sight. Thank god. He's safe. *We're* safe.

Even though there is no *We*. There's definitely no *We*.

And I'm going to be more careful than ever to keep it that way.

⭐ Seven ⭐

My morning routine used to be this: Jump out of bed the minute my alarm goes off, slip my feet into the adorable peach-print slippers Umma got me last Christmas, and make a beeline for the bathroom, hoping that no one else is jostling for it. Then I'd get out my caddy of skin-care products, spritz on some facial mist, dab on some eye cream, and about a dozen other steps before finishing with some SPF. Only then, with my full skin-care routine complete, would I worry about any messages I might have got overnight, or about what I'd eat for breakfast.

Now? I stay in bed long after my alarm has gone off, scrolling through my phone and grinning at the screen. Cartoon hyena is my new morning look.

Alex: Hmmm okay. How about favourite vegetable? If you could only choose one to survive the apocalypse. On the count of three.

Alex: 1

Alex: 2

Alex: 3

Me: Cabbage

Alex: Cucumbers

Me: NO!!!! Ugh. Well, this was nice while it lasted, Alex, but we can never speak again . . .

Alex: Cucumbers are fresh, delicious, and great for facials. Besides, what did baechu ever do for anyone?

Me: Baechu = kimchi. You're telling me that if you could only choose one veggie to survive the apocalypse, you WOULDN'T choose cabbage, thus getting rid of kimchi for all eternity?!

Alex: . . .

Alex: Ok. Fine, you win this round. Though I do feel the need to remind you that cucumber kimchi IS a thing and happens to be my favourite.

Me: Lol. Don't make me throw up.

Me: Wait, can we go back to the cucumber facials?

Alex: I know a thing or two about facials. I mean, I do have a face.

Me: Totally didn't notice that before now. lol. But it's great. A guy who is not afraid to self-groom is a good find.

Alex: You might say I'm both soft and strong.

Me: 😋

Oops. Was that too flirty? We've been texting pretty much every day for the past two weeks, usually when I'm alone in my room like I am now, and I've been trying to keep it somewhere between flirty and friendly. Flirty enough to say, *Hey, I think you're really cute and fun to talk to.* But not so flirty as to say, *Hey, how would you feel about making out for an hour or two?*

I'm still wary about getting involved in an actual relationship, especially after what happened to Jiyoon.

Me: That air kiss was for the bag metaphor, obviously. That beauty still haunts my dreams.

Alex: Of course. I'll relay your affections back to the bag.

I sigh with relief. (It is distinctly *not* a swoony sigh, I tell myself, though I would understand if someone passing by thought it was . . .) Mostly my exchanges with Alex have been casual like this. Flirty in a way that could be easily denied. But every now and then, our conversations drift into more serious territory. Like when he shared that his grandmother – the one with all the cats – had a bad fall and was hospitalised last week. Or when I opened up about how I'm worried Appa is overworking himself at his job. As much as I'm trying to keep things casual, I can't help but love those moments when it feels like we're really getting to know each other – beyond just the fansite-survey facts. As silly as some of our banter can be, I feel that pull to know more and more about him. I'm curious about everything, from his opinions on big issues like family and honour, to little things like whether he listens to music in the shower (he listens to the *news hour* during his morning routine! Like a fully-fledged adult and/or total nerd).

I lie on my bed and grin, scrolling through our chat history. He sounds exactly the same through text as he does in person. I can almost hear his voice every time I read his messages. Can almost see that dimple in his left cheek. The thought makes my stomach flip.

I sit up in bed. Wait. This could work great as a song lyric. Truthfully, since coming back from Singapore, my free time has been spent texting Alex and daydreaming about Paris Fashion Week rather than songwriting. But now that I know Leah and I are going to be working on a duo album together, I really do have to push myself to try again. There was one song in particular that I think could be great for a sister duet – sweet and full of heart with potential for some killer harmonies.

I open my bedside drawer and pull out my pale blue notebook. As soon as I flip it open, my fingers freeze on the page.

Or at least, what's left of it.

Someone's ripped dozens of pages right out of the notebook, leaving nothing but a jagged paper edge. All those lyrics I've been working on. Gone. All my outfit sketches. Gone.

I frantically flip through to the remaining pages that are still intact, but find several of them are stuck together. I manage to separate them, only to find that purple nail polish has been spilled all over the paper, so I can't even read my own handwriting.

Who would do this? The tips of my ears begin to burn in anger. Clutching my notebook, I head out to the living room, where the eight girls are spread out, chatting and scrolling through their phones.

"Guys, who did this?" I demand, holding up the notebook.

The girls glance up.

"What is that, your diary?" Eunji asks, looking back down at her phone.

"It's my notebook," I say. "The one I use for sketching and songwriting."

"It looks fine to me," Lizzie says.

She's been making passive-aggressive jabs at me ever since she heard the news about Leah's and my reality show. I know that would have been a dream project for her and her own sister. But if she's salty, I'm not the person to take it out on – it was all DB's decision.

"Really?" I open it up, revealing the ripped and nail polish–stained pages. "This looks fine to you?" I raise an eyebrow at her. Lizzie shrugs and goes back to scrolling through her phone. I'm about to ask the group again – seriously, who would ruin my notebook and what possible reason could they have for doing so? When suddenly, something catches my eye.

On the corner of the couch, Jiyoon is huddled up in her most worn-in sweats, her hair in a greasy topknot, as she eats nurungji off a plate. But it's not the crispy, scorched rice that I notice. It's that the hand holding it features purple nails. The exact same shade of Christian Louboutin *Lilac Dream* that's currently spilled all over my notebook . . .

Jiyoon? Why would Jiyoon do this to me? I open my mouth to say something, only to close it again. Maybe it was just an accident. I can see Jiyoon looking for some paper to place under her hand to catch any stray polish . . . grabbing my notebook . . . maybe the bottle tipped, and she ripped out the stained pages?

"Hey, Jiyoon," I start to ask gently. But Jiyoon just grabs

her plate of nurungji and heads towards our bedroom.

"Sorry, guys," she chokes out. "I don't think I'm up for a movie tonight." The door to our room slams behind her.

The rest of the group looks on, confused and concerned.

"Don't worry, I got it." I tap lightly on our door before following Jiyoon into our room.

She's lying on her bed, curled up, facing the wall. I can tell from the tremble of her shoulders that she's crying. I sit on the bed behind her, reaching over to give her gentle head scratches, like my mom used to do for me whenever I was sick or sad, the tingles running from my scalp down my spine, helping me relax.

"I'm so sorry about Jin, Jiyoon," I say. "But you're one of the strongest girls in this group. If anyone can survive this, you can." I feel Jiyoon sigh a deep breath, her tears starting to slow. She rolls over so she's facing me, a guilty look in her eyes. "Don't worry about the notebook," I say quickly. "I know it was an accident."

Jiyoon's eyes dart down. She swallows, then looks back up at me. "I'm sorry, Rachel," she says weakly. For a second, it looks like she has more she wants to say, but then she averts her eyes again, saying, "I think I just need some sleep now." She rolls again to face towards the wall.

I sit for what feels like hours, rubbing Jiyoon's back. When she's finally snoring softly, I tiptoe out to the living room. I can't sleep. My mind is too busy, whirring with thoughts that I can't seem to quiet. But it looks like I'm not the only one who's been tossing and turning. Mina is sitting on the couch in her pajamas, nursing a mug of hot cocoa.

"What are you doing up?" I say, sitting on the opposite end of the couch and pulling a pillow into my lap.

She barely lifts her eyes from her mug, blowing on the steam. "I'm always up at this time."

"Night owl?"

"Insomnia."

Oh. In all our years of living together, I never realised Mina had trouble sleeping. Now that I think about it, she *is* always the last one to go to bed. Maybe the lack of sleep is why she's so grumpy all the time. Before I can ask more, she looks up at me, raising an eyebrow.

"What about you?" she says. "I thought Princess Rachel needed her beauty rest."

I roll my eyes at the old nickname. "I have a lot on my mind."

"You're not still thinking about your notebook, are you?"

"So what if I am?" I say defensively.

"I thought those songs were just for fun or whatever." She waves an absentminded hand in the air. "It's not like you were actually going to do anything with them. You said so yourself. It's just a creative outlet."

I frown. "That was before I knew about the duo album with Leah. There was one song that I thought could work really well for us, but now it's gone." I sigh. "I just want to do a good job on this."

Mina watches me carefully, taking in my slumped shoulders and the way I'm picking at the tassels on the pillow in my lap. "You're nervous," she says. She doesn't ask it like a question, just a flat-out statement.

"Maybe."

"Why?"

Why? I turn the reasons over in my head. "It's just . . . so personal, you know? A reality show that follows your everyday movements. A duo album with my sister. Don't get me wrong, I'm so excited for all of it and beyond grateful for the opportunities . . . but living my life on camera, for everyone to see? Recording songs without the eight of you? I really want to deliver my best and make DB proud, and I know my performance will reflect on Leah, too, so . . ."

My voice trails off. Did I just confide all that to Choo Mina? What was I thinking? "And . . . that's it," I finish quickly, bracing myself for her inevitable taunting.

But surprisingly, it doesn't come. Instead, she just shrugs, taking a sip of hot cocoa. "I get it. Living up to expectations is hard."

I blink. Is she . . . empathising with me right now?

"You just have to work harder if you want to outrun the disappointment."

"Are you speaking from experience?" I ask carefully. Everyone knows how hard Mina's dad is on her. His word in her life is basically as good as the law.

Her face flickers with something that I can't quite place.

Defensiveness, maybe. Or plain and utter exhaustion. "I'm just smart. Take my advice or leave it."

I think back to the hot tub in Singapore, when we were talking about our bucket-list items. The way her smile lit up when she was talking about Hollywood and how it dimmed again when she thought of her dad. *He would never go for it.*

"You should think about the acting thing again," I say, trying to sound nonchalant. If she can offer me some empathy, I can try to do the same for her. I may be nervous about stepping in front of the camera, but Mina was born for the spotlight. "I think you'd be really good at it. You have the hustle. And you're great on camera."

She smirks. "Where's this coming from?"

"You're not the only smart one. Take it or leave it," I say, smirking back.

She shakes her head, a hint of a real smile on her lips. "I'm going to try to go to bed now."

"Okay." I nod. "And I'm going to . . . sit here and try to remember the song I wrote."

"*You* wrote it. It should be easy to remember your own lyrics."

"You'd think so," I sigh.

She puts her mug down on the coffee table and folds her arms across her chest, nodding at me with a challenge in her eyes. "Try. I dare you."

"What? Out loud?"

Her gaze doesn't waver.

I rack my brain, trying to remember the lyrics. "When the sun sets and the lights fade so fast, don't fear the night or the shadows that may pass," I sing. "We'll be . . . We'll be . . ."

How did the next part go? I trail off. I can't remember.

"Brighter in the dark," Mina says suddenly.

"Huh?"

"Brighter in the dark. That would work well as the next line."

I stare at her, and a chill washes through me at how perfectly I can hear that line in my head. She's right. It's not the original line that I had written, but I have to admit, her suggestion is way better. I nod slowly. "Okay. Yeah. That could work."

"It could even repeat three times with added harmonies in each round," she says, her voice excited now like she's on to something. As if catching herself, she drops her face into a neutral mask and shrugs. "I mean, if you want to. It's your song."

"That could be cool," I say. "Why don't we try it together?"

I sing the first line on my own. "We'll be brighter in the dark."

I sing it again a second time, and Mina jumps in with an effortless harmony. "Brighter in the dark."

Finally, we sing it together a third time, bringing up the harmony. "Brighter in the dark."

Our voices braid together seamlessly, filling up the living room. Damn. We sound good. Not just good, but *great*. We stare at each other. Mina is good at this. And by the way she's looking at me, I know she's thinking the same about me.

"Okay then." She abruptly hops off the couch, breaking the moment. "So you'll stop worrying so much about nothing, then? At least you have one good song for your duo album now."

"Yeah," I say. She's trying to look aloof, but I can see the smile playing on her lips. I give her a full grin. "I guess I do."

"Did you hear about what happened to Hemy from Butterscotch?"

Lizzie twists her body to look back at us from her seat in the van's first row, eager to share whatever gossip she just learned from one of her many sources. It's a few days later, and we're on our way back home after a full day of music-video shooting. Sunhee and Youngeun are fast asleep on either side of me, exhausted from the shoot, but all the other girls lean forward in their seats to listen to Lizzie spill the tea. The van lurches over a bump in the road, and Sunhee's head lolls on to my shoulder. I tuck a strand of loose hair behind her ear.

"Apparently, there's a serial fanboy who's been sending gifts to his favourite idols, and he just sent Hemy something very interesting," Lizzie says, wiggling her eyebrows in a way that suggests that "interesting" really means weird as hell. "Any guesses?"

"Used underwear," Ari says immediately.

"Ari!" Sumin groans. "You're gross."

"What? It happened to Jinny from CandY You, remember?" Ari says.

"That was never proven," I say. Ninety-nine per cent of K-pop fans are amazing, but still, every once in a while, you hear some crazy rumour about a fan who went too far.

"Was it couple rings?" Eunji guesses.

"A condom," Mina says.

"Nope," Lizzie says. "He sent her a portrait of herself. Made entirely from chewed gum."

Everyone screeches.

"Why the hell would anyone want that?" Jiyoon says.

"Better question is, how did that slip through the screening system?" Eunji asks, making a face. "You'd think someone would have caught that before it got to her."

"Well, our managers were going to deliver our fan mail today," Mina says. "If anyone gets a gum portrait, I dare them to take a piece off and eat it."

The girls screech again.

As soon as we get home (and coax a groggy Sunhee and Youngeun out of the van), we find a huge pile of fan mail stacked up in the living room, brought over from DB by our managers. Everything looks safe enough: letters, cards, fan art, small trinkets like key chains and handmade jewellery, and a few flower bouquets for Youngeun, whose birthday was last month.

Most of the gifts are addressed to all of us, but there are individual piles too. No one says anything, but I can see each of us doing a quick scan of the piles to compare sizes. Sunhee's shoulders deflate a bit when she sees that she has the smallest pile this time. She doesn't complain, though. She opens her mail with the rest of us, chorusing along as we take turns reading funny fan mail or gushing over cute gifts.

"Who's that one for?" Lizzie asks, pointing to an extra-large package set aside from the rest of the mail.

Mina looks at the label. "Rachel."

Everyone turns to look at me. It's rare that big mail like this makes it through the screening process. Unless it slipped through by accident, like it did for Hemy from Butterscotch. I gulp. I can tell everyone's thinking the same thing by the way their eyes keep shifting to the package.

"What if it's the serial fanboy?" Eunji says.

"What if he sent you a gum portrait?" Jiyoon says.

"Or his hair?" Sumin adds.

"From which part of his body?" Ari asks.

"Ari!" I say. "Okay okay, I'm just going to open it." I take a deep breath and open the box, bracing myself.

Oh my god.

My hands start trembling before I even finish cutting open the packaging. The signature clean white box with simple black lettering says it all – ten black letters, starting with a *B*.

I hold my breath as I lift the lid.

It's a handbag.

It's *the* bag.

The blue Balenciaga.

"What? What is it?" Mina demands.

I slowly lift the bag, pulling it out of the box with utmost care. Even through the packaging, the leather smells divine.

God. It's even more beautiful than I remember it.

"Whoa, Rachel," Sunhee says, her eyes growing huge. "That's gorgeous."

"I can't believe a fan sent you that," Ari says. "You're so lucky."

"Lucky" doesn't even begin to cut it, but I'm too nervous about betraying my secret to express anything other than shock, like them. In the box is a simple white card that just reads, *The perfect blend of soft and strong. For the woman who is the same.*

Oh. My. God.

"That'll be perfect for your Paris trip," Youngeun remarks.

"Yeah," I say, barely hearing her as I tuck the card away. I need to go text Alex immediately. "I'm going to put it in my room for now."

The girls watch with wistful jealousy as I gather the bag in my arms and shuffle to my room. As soon as I close the door behind me, I grab my phone.

Me: Bag??? THANK YOU!! But really??

Alex: You're welcome! I mean, I couldn't not get it. I had to.

Me: But why?

Alex: I'll let you choose your answer: A) Your outfit needed it.

Alex: B) Your old bag was a safety hazard.

Alex: C) I really really liked meeting you.

Alex: D) All of the above ☺

⭐ *Eight* ⭐

I waffle for days over whether I should take the Balenciaga bag with me to Paris. Honestly, it's so beautiful, I'm terrified of ruining it. What if it gets manhandled by airport security? Besides, I'm not even sure I can accept a gift this extravagant. Especially from Alex. Then again, I really can't bear to be parted from it just yet either.

The morning I leave for Paris, I take it out one more time and decide it's coming. I hold it against me in the mirror.

"Should I leave you two alone?" Jiyoon asks with a smirk as she enters the room with her toothbrush sticking out of her mouth. That night I comforted Jiyoon over Jin, I decided getting to the bottom of what happened to my notebook just wasn't worth it. Our friendship, and being there to support her through her breakup, was more important. And little by little, she's been slowly returning to her regular self. A bit stronger each day. Still, every time she cracks a joke like this, I feel a rush of gratefulness to see the old Jiyoon in full form.

"Ha ha. You're witnessing a very intimate relationship."

I bite my lip, wondering if I should have avoided the sensitive subject of relationships.

But she doesn't seem too bothered by my comment. After all, this is just the reality we all live in. To some degree, we're all used to it.

As she stands around brushing her teeth, I survey our room one more time to make sure I'm ready to go. I smooth out my comforter and fluff my pillows (is there anything worse than coming home from vacation to an unmade bed?), then check to make sure my electronic converters and adapters are tucked into my carry-on. I'm about to unzip my luggage and review my travel wardrobe one last time, when Jiyoon practically lunges to stop me.

"Oh no. No, no, no. I saw you pack and repack that thing forty-seven times over the past week," she says, rezipping the suitcase. "You're going to wear what you have, and you're going to look amazing."

"And you're going to choke on that toothbrush! Don't get spittle on my stuff!"

As soon as she leaves, I reconsider. Honestly, I wouldn't be above repacking for a forty-eighth time (this is a *Nell Kramer fashion show* in *Paris* – my outfits have to be on point), but a quick glance at the time tells me I have to get a move on if I don't want to miss my flight. In the hall I give Jiyoon a quick one-armed hug and hustle out to meet my car. Paris is waiting!

• • •

When I was fifteen and still a trainee at DB, I desperately wanted to go to Nam Hayoon's show at Seoul Fashion Week. She was, and still is, one of my favorite designers in Korea, but her shows are almost never open to the public. That year it was, and I was ready to trade my kidney for a ticket. I begged my mom to let me go (I even made her a PowerPoint presentation listing all the reasons I should be allowed) and miraculously, she relented. At the show, I took so many photos, my phone ran out of storage space. Even though I was standing way in the back, it was one of the best days of my life and hands-down my favourite fashion show experience.

That is, until today.

I'll always hold a soft spot in my heart for Nam Hayoon's show, but going to Nell Kramer's show as an invited guest is on another level. Hordes of paparazzi snap my photo as I make my entrance into the Carousel du Louvre. Inside, the atrium has been turned into a catwalk, with the glimmering inverted pyramid as its crowning jewel. My manager, Jongseok, leads me toward a sign reading RACHEL KIM - RESERVED SEAT tacked to a chair in the front row. No. Freaking. Way. I settle myself into the chair, tucking the reserved sign into my bag as a memento.

Finally, once the room is buzzing with energy, the lights dim and the show begins. It's mesmerising. From the music to the soaring kinetic lights, everything is stunning. You can tell that every last detail has been chosen specifically to set a mood and tell a story – and the show is timed so tightly, it gives me an appreciation for the fact that this, like our performances, is carefully planned and rehearsed down to the second.

And then there's the clothes. The *clothes*. Each piece is unique, and there's a variety of styles – from an enchanting dress made entirely of silk petals to a perfectly tailored animal-print suit with a fitted blazer and cigarette pants – but somehow despite their distinct looks, they all work together, and you get a sense of her voice, her vibe – the delicate and the irreverent mashed together. Nell has styled each of them with glittering hair slides that spell out words like DAMN and WHATEVER, and it gives the show a fun and cheeky tone. I'm entranced.

After the show, Nell herself finds me, gives me a fluttery kiss on each cheek, and says, "So good to see you, darling. You're even more gorgeous in person."

"I loved the zipper necklace with the cape outfit," I say. "It was such a good touch – the mix of industrial and feminine."

She beams. Even though we're inside, she still has a pair of darkly tinted sunglasses on. "I almost took it out right before Amarah went down the runway. I'm glad you liked it."

I feel myself nodding vigorously at Nell, then force myself to calm down so I don't scare her with my bobblehead routine. "It was truly inspiring," I say with minimal head movement.

Just then an assistant arrives at Nell's elbow, whispering something about her after-party.

"Ah well, I guess it's time for me to head out," she says to me. "I'll see you there, Rachel?"

• • •

Nell's voice plays on a loop in my head (she's glad I liked her show! Me! Rachel Kim!) as I hurry back to my hotel room to change into the perfect statement outfit for the after-party. Something that says cool and chic and, obviously, Nell-approved. Luckily, I have just the outfit in mind.

Hanging in my closet is a freshly pressed Nell Kramer menswear suit jacket. I bought it on a whim back in Seoul, and have been waiting for the right moment to try it. I slip it on, wearing it like a minidress and pairing it with a pair of black nylons and stiletto heels. I touch up my matte red lipstick in the mirror and step back to see the whole picture. It's perfect. Except . . .

I take in my side view. The jacket is cut too low for me to wear a regular bra and too oversized to wear no bra. Catch me at the right angle and I might end up with a nip slip. I silently curse myself for not being more prepared as I call Jongseok about getting some fashion tape. It's a little awkward, but our managers have been called upon to procure more embarrassing things than this.

Five minutes later, I throw on a sweatshirt and answer the door, where a concierge presents me with a roll of Scotch tape.

"Oh," I say. "I needed fashion tape? It's double-sided?"

He gives me a perplexed look – he has no idea what I'm talking about. And I'm not sure if it's the language barrier or the fact that he's probably never needed to use the stuff himself. He takes a strip of tape and rolls it back on to itself, making a double-sided loop.

"No, no," I say. "Double-sided fashion tape for clothes.

I need it to stick to . . ." I gesture helplessly at my boobs. He stares at me. I stare at him.

"Oh. *Oh.*" His face goes red. It's awkward. Oh so awkward. He clears his throat. "Oui, mademoiselle. I'll, um, see what we can find."

A few minutes later, a concierge (noticeably not the same one from before) knocks on my door with a cheap stick-on bra from the convenience store down the street.

"This was all I could find," she says. "Will it do?"

It's not ideal, but if I spend any longer fussing over my outfit at the hotel, I'll miss the party altogether.

Well, as they say in France, *c'est la vie.*

The Nell Kramer after-party is at Lapérouse, an old-world eatery a few blocks away in the 6th arrondissement. The party room is filled with well-dressed people who look like they walked straight out of a magazine, sipping cocktails and laughing as a synth-pop playlist blasts.

It's amazing and overwhelming in the best way, and I'm glad that, at least for now, my rigged bra is doing its job. I get several compliments on my jacket/minidress. It's edgy and fresh, but the classic cut makes me feel confident I'm not going overboard.

Nell is surrounded by people clamouring to congratulate her on the show, so I keep my eyes out for the Cho twins, who said they would probably be here. I swear Juhyun can get an invitation from anyone, even the pope.

"Excuse me, Rachel Kim?" a voice says.

A woman in a sparkly white blazer approaches me, smiling broadly. "I thought I recognised you. I'm an editor for *Elle* and a big fan of Girls Forever." She holds out a hand. "I'd love to talk to you about a potential interview."

Oh my god, *Elle*. "So nice to meet you," I say, shaking her hand. "I'd definitely be interested in that."

She beams and starts discussing scheduling and her ideas for the piece. I'm listening intently until I start to feel something shift inside my clothes. I freeze in horror as I realise that the sticky bra on my left boob is slowly sliding down my chest.

No. No no no no. Images of my bra plopping out of my jacket and on to the floor, right in front of this *Elle* editor, race through my mind. I keep my smile plastered on my face, folding my arms tightly around my chest to stop the bra from sliding.

The editor glances down at my chest as she keeps talking, looking confused as to why I'm suddenly showing off my cleavage. Mortified, I quickly lower my arms, awkwardly keeping one hand against my stomach. I don't know what I'm trying to do here – catch the bra inside my clothes before it falls? – but I end up doing a weird half shimmy, half body roll to try to stop the sticky bra from sliding. I'm trying desperately to act natural, but at this point, I'm not listening to a word the editor is saying. I probably look like I've been possessed by the spirit of the inflatable tube man waving his arms in the sky. The bra is nearly at my belly button now. I have to get out of here.

"This all sounds great!" I say, cutting her off midsentence. "I'll call you!"

With that, I race off to the ladies' room, ducking into a stall to restick my bra. I let out a breath. Whew. That was close.

Except . . . I suddenly realise that I never got the editor's name. Or her number. I groan, dropping my head into my hands. God, I probably came off like such an ass. There goes my chance at ever doing a solo interview with *Elle*.

When I emerge from the ladies' room, I see a man, midforties with a stubby ponytail and blue wire-rimmed glasses, heading my way with a wry grin on his face. He's wearing a simple flannel shirt and nondescript black jeans, and yet he looks totally at ease among the fashion elite. Immediately, I'm mortified. Did he just witness that whole sticky-bra fiasco?

But when he arrives at my side, he just pulls something out of his pocket, saying, "Here. My husband is a backstage dresser. He never lets me leave for a gig without this." I look at his outstretched hand and see the most glorious thing in the world: a small roll of double-sided fashion tape. "You never know when you might need to help someone out of a . . . *sticky* situation," he says with an eyebrow raised. I take the tape, profusely thanking my glasses-wearing saviour, and rush back into the ladies' room.

When I emerge a second time, with everything securely held in place, the man is still there. I give him a sheepish smile and thank him again.

"Seriously, you saved my life just now," I say, handing back the roll of tape. "Please also thank your husband for me."

"He'll be thrilled to know he aided one of K-pop's biggest stars." He smiles and extends his hand. "I'm Maxwell Li-Harris. I'm a photographer for *Vogue*. I recognise you from Girls Forever."

"Oh, hi!" I say, shaking his hand. Of course, a photographer. I should have known. The high-fashion ones are always so effortlessly chill. "So nice to meet you."

"I love your outfit," he says, admiring my look. "Nell Kramer Men's Collection from last spring, right?" I nod, secretly thrilled to have my fashion choice validated by someone so established in the biz. "Totally ingenious. Do you have anything like this in your line?"

I blink. My line? "Sorry, I'm not sure what you mean? I don't have a line."

His brow furrows. "You don't? Everyone is always calling you Forever Fashionista . . . I thought that was the name of your label!"

"Oh," I say with a smile, shaking my head. "That's just a nickname my fans call me. They're sweet."

"Please, girl. Don't be so humble," he says with a mock eye roll. "You're a fashion icon, and your fans aren't the only ones who know it."

We laugh and I feel a bubble of joy well up inside me.

"It's too bad you turned down the opportunity for the *Vogue* editorial," Maxwell adds. "I was slated to shoot that project, and

I was really hoping it would work out. I think we could have made something really amazing together." He sighs wistfully. "I had grand plans for a Wes Anderson–inspired photo spread. You were going to be in this fab all-silk-and-leather lineup and holding a trained falcon in each shot. I have a great falcon guy."

Wait, *what*? Now it's my turn to furrow my brow in confusion. I never turned down a *Vogue* editorial. I never even got an offer like that. Unless . . . I flash back to when I overheard the execs talking about an opportunity with *Vogue*. Did DB turn it down for me without even asking me about it? I think back to what Mr. Noh said when I asked him about it: *"There's no opportunity for the group with* Vogue.*"* Which, looking back, kind of sounds like a technicality. Because technically, *Vogue* didn't want the whole group. They just wanted *me*.

Why didn't Mr. Noh tell me about the opportunity? And why did he basically lie to my face when I asked about it? I can feel myself getting worked up – confusion, disappointment, and anger fighting for space in my brain – but before I have time to fully process it all, I spot a familiar face out of the corner of my eye. The sparring in my brain stops on a dime. Oh my god. Is that–? Holy shit. It is.

"Is that Carly Mattsson over there?" I blurt out. I need to make sure my eyes aren't playing tricks on me.

Maxwell gives me an amused look. "It is. Are you a fan?"

"Fan" is an understatement. I *adore* Carly Mattsson – a pop star turned fashion icon and former member of B*Dazzled, my favourite American girl group from my childhood. Carly is a total legend. Who could forget that iconic moment from the VMAs when she cut her hair three separate times for each of her three outfit changes? She went from waist-length hair to a bob to a pixie cut in a single night. And who could forget her peacock-feather look at the Met Gala?

"I had a B*Dazzled concert tee that I wore to sleep every night for years," I confess to Maxwell.

"Didn't we all," he says fondly.

After B*Dazzled disbanded, Carly went on to design her own fashion line and marry a gorgeous Swedish Olympic skier, Oliver Mattsson. I can't believe she's here. In the same room as me. Breathing the same air, dressed in the most chic green jumpsuit, hair swept in an elegant low ponytail and ears adorned with Cartier panther earrings.

"She's even more gorgeous in person," I say in awe. "I never thought I'd be this close to her. Should I introduce myself? Is that weird?"

Maxwell laughs. "Look at you gushing. You know you're an international star too, right?"

"Carly Mattsson and I are definitely *not* on the same star level." As far as I'm concerned, she's in a whole other galaxy.

"Well, I think she'd be pleased to meet you," he says. "But it looks like she's leaving."

Oh no. He's right. My heart sinks as Carly Mattsson disappears through the exit.

"Don't be too disappointed," Maxwell says with sympathy. "Carly always leaves events early."

"How come?"

"She has young kids at home." He shrugs.

"Oh right. Jude, four, and Mabel, two."

Maxwell shoots me another wry grin. Oops. Have I verged into stalker territory?

"Right. Well, you know, work-life balance and all that."

Talk about a dream life – not only is she gorgeous, but she's mega successful *and* still present with her family.

"Carly may be gone, but I see some fans who look like they want to talk to you, superstar," Maxwell says, squinting through the crowd.

I follow his gaze to see Hyeri waving at me from the cocktail bar and Juhyun beside her, blowing me a kiss. I smile and say a quick parting word to Maxwell before rushing over to the twins and launching myself at them for a group hug.

"It's so good to see you!" I cry as they jump up and down, hugging me back. "And in Paris, too!"

"Best," says Hyeri.

Juhyun smiles. "Lives."

"Ever!" I complete. And it really *is* the best. I send up a quick thank-you to the universe for making me lucky enough to experience moments like this with my best friends.

"Girl, it's been too long since we last saw your face." Juhyun looks romantic in her sheer, delicate floral dress with ruffled shoulders. Meanwhile, Hyeri's traded her usual lab-friendly casual look for a chic white blouse tucked into low-slung metallic suit pants. It's clearly not her first time being Juhyun's plus-one for an event like this. She looks just as glamorous as her twin. "Well, since we saw your face in person, I mean," Juhyun continues. "Hyeri always has your music videos playing in the background."

"Nothing wrong with being a proud friend," Hyeri says, grinning. "How are you, Rach? How was the show?"

"Forget the show," Juhyun jumps in, grabbing my arm, her eyes gleaming. "How was meeting Alex? Don't think we haven't noticed you dodging the question every time we bring it up on chat. What's happening between you two?"

"Nothing!" I flush. She's not wrong. I *have* been avoiding the question until now, partly because this felt like an in-person talk, but also partly because I'm still not sure where I stand. How do I explain something that I'm not even sure I know the answer to yet?

"Oh my god, I knew it," Hyeri says, gasping, even though I have confirmed nothing whatsoever. "Look how long she's taking to answer."

I laugh. "No, no, there isn't something. But then again, I guess there isn't nothing . . ."

"Okay, spill," Juhyun says. She grabs her cocktail from the bar. "Tell us everything."

I order a grapefruit Paloma and we squeeze into a corner windowsill, where we can actually vaguely hear each other over the din of the crowd. I start from the beginning, relaying our first encounter on the MRT and then our coffee date at Petal. Juhyun and Hyeri are the perfect audience, gasping and squealing at all the right spots, and I can't help but feel giddy. Even just talking about Alex sends happy flutters through my stomach.

"We've been texting pretty much every day for the past month," I say, squeezing my lime, then taking another sip. "And you'll never believe it, but he sent me *this*." I get out my phone and pull up a photo of the Balenciaga.

Hyeri gives me a playful poke. "He like-likes you!" she says with childlike glee.

"The boy's got good taste," Juhyun says, nodding in approval.

"Are you referring to me or the bag?" I ask with an eyebrow raised, the tequila in this Paloma already making me feel a little bolder and sassier.

"He should have good fashion taste," Hyeri says, ignoring my cheeky aside. "He handles investments for a bunch of fashion houses. I'm sure he's picked up a thing or two over the years."

"He what?" I say, my eyes growing wide. How did I not know that? I mean, I knew from our conversations that he worked in investment, but I had no idea he was involved in the fashion world.

"You don't know?" Juhyun says. "He's kind of a wunderkind. He worked for a big investment bank for like two seconds after school and then immediately launched his own investment fund. He's super successful, Rach! I don't think I've ever met anyone so driven."

"Wow." I'm at a loss for words. I think back to that day in Singapore when we were looking at the Balenciaga bag from outside the shop window. All this time he's been teasingly playing along, pretending to be clueless just to drive me crazy.

"Babes," Juhyun says, a mischievous twinkle in her eye as she sips her Mai Tai. "We have to call him."

"Already on it," Hyeri says, whipping out her phone and dialing Alex on FaceTime.

"Hyeri, no!" Flustered, I grab for her phone.

Alex and I may spend a lot of time texting, but video calls are a whole other territory. What if we're so used to texting now that talking face-to-face ends up being awkward?

"Too late!" Hyeri tosses the phone to me. I fumble for it, nearly dropping my cocktail, but manage to catch it just as Alex's face appears on the screen. He has a five-o'clock shadow on his jaw, but even a rumpled Alex is a very cute Alex.

"Rachel?" he says in surprise. His face splits into a warm grin, his dimple appearing. "Well, hi. I wasn't expecting you through this number. It's so loud! Where the hell are you?"

"Um, hi," I squeak. I clear my throat and try again. "Hello. Hi. I'm – we're at an after-party. I'm so sorry to be calling so late. Isn't it like three a.m. in Hong Kong?"

"Cute, she even has the time zones memorised," Hyeri whispers to Juhyun. "She's got it bad."

I shoot them a pointed look and hope Alex didn't overhear.

"I'm actually travelling for business right now, so don't worry, you're not catching me at an ungodly hour," he says with a laugh. "Hey Juhyun, hey Hyeri," he calls out. I turn the phone around to face them, and they sheepishly wave at the camera before dissolving into a fit of tipsy giggles.

I turn the phone back to my own face. "So anyway," I say, "just thought I'd say hi." Oh my god. This is almost as mortifying as the train incident.

"I'm glad you did," he says. "Definitely the highlight of my day so far."

"Oh yeah?" Pretty sure there are too many lights at this party for him to tell I'm blushing.

"Yeah." He smiles warmly at me, and then his grin grows a little more sly. "Though I did spill wine on myself during dinner, and I had a taxi nabbed from right under my nose earlier today, so don't get too cocky – you're not competing with much."

I giggle, then regret giggling. "Well, I'm glad I could brighten up your day, then."

Juhyun and Hyeri trade looks with their eyebrows raised and I blush, clearing my throat once more. "Anyway, I actually just wanted to say thank you so much again for the bag. It's such an amazing gift, I don't know if I can keep it."

"Oh, please do," he says. "If you send it back, I may end up using it myself and I'm not sure robin's egg is my colour."

I laugh. "Okay. Well. Thank you again. You have no idea how much it means to me."

He smiles back, his eyes crinkling. "It's my pleasure."

We exchange a few more words and then say good night.

As soon as I hang up, Juhyun and Hyeri look at me with knowing grins.

"Yeah, yeah," I say, waving them off, but we all dissolve into giggles.

"C'mon, I know a better after-party," Juhyun says. Leave it to her to try to top this. Of course, whatever she's got planned for us, there's no way I'm going to miss it.

I have a full free day in Paris before heading back to Seoul, but I spend a good few hours of the morning sleeping off the halo of last night. Luckily, my room at the Four Seasons George V overlooks a small courtyard and is blissfully quiet. My head may be aching from that last round at that last party . . . but when I close my eyes, Nell Kramer's gorgeous collection marches through my memory. I am still giddy from it, taking apart each combination in my mind.

Around nine (ish) I roll out of bed and take a long shower, then throw on a giant, cosy, cable-knit cream sweater and black leather trousers before wandering over to the Marais for some of my favourite coffee and a falafel from Chez Marianne. After an hour of wandering the boutiques along the crooked little streets of the Marais, I hop the metro to Montmartre. The cobblestone streets winding up the hill are filled with bursting flowers and colorful cafés, and I can see the Sacré-Cœur basilica in the distance. I post some selfies with the basilica, feeling shamelessly touristy. Normally I'm much more cautious about when and where I post pics, but I feel so relaxed today, and blissfully anonymous. Girls Forever hasn't fully broken into the European music scene yet, so I know I'm less likely to be recognised here.

It's about the hour when Parisians start piling into the outdoor café-brasseries for a cigarette and espresso, and I wander into one of the many that sit on every street corner, and pull out my blue notebook. It's a brisk March day, but with the sun shining and a hot mug in my hands, I feel perfectly at ease. There's a busker across the way, and I'm wondering if his music is going to intrude on my ability to write songs, but I find that it's not lyrics that come out of my pen, it's a design sketch. And then another, and another, pours out of me as a waitress comes and goes, bringing me an espresso and then a little while later, a chocolate croissant.

Away from my normal life, I'm finding it's completely freeing to focus on something else.

I'm so absorbed in trying to get the shape of the puffed sleeves just right on a collection of blouses that I don't even realize how much time has passed. Just as I stop to stretch out my fingers, a shadow falls over me, blocking the afternoon sunlight.

I look up expecting to see the waitress back again. But it's a guy, grinning down at my table and looking a little bit sheepish.

"For someone who is so used to being recognised everywhere she goes, you were ridiculously easy to find just now."

⭐ Nine ⭐

"Alex? What are you doing here?" I try to stand up without knocking over my tiny café table so I can give him a hug but realize I'm still holding my pen awkwardly and, to avoid stabbing him with it, I end up wobbling to the left and looking like I'm a clown on a tightrope. *Smooth*.

He grins wider. "Oh, you know. Just in the neighbourhood. Keeping my eye out for K-pop idols, obviously."

He pulls out a striped wicker-back chair and takes a seat next to me – all the chairs are placed on one side of the tables so that everyone has a view of the street, but sitting side by side suddenly feels bizarrely intimate. I notice he's wearing another one of those impeccable button-downs, this one black instead of pale blue, a leather jacket, and a scarf. His hair has grown out a bit since I saw him in Singapore, and I can see now that he has natural curls. He runs a hand through them now and it's absurdly adorable, so I pick up my espresso cup to distract myself but then remember that it's empty and have to put it back down on the saucer with a noisy clatter. So far my fine motor skills are really abandoning me today. He gives me a self-conscious smile.

"I was in London for a meeting. I just hopped on the Eurostar," he says. "It's super easy."

"Just to stalk the streets looking for me?" I'm teasing, but part of me is wondering – is it possible? Did he really just get as excited as I did by our impromptu FaceTime last night and decide he had to see me?

"Ah well, not *just* that." He flags the waitress and orders himself a coffee. "I thought I'd swing by my favourite tailor at Maison Rambure. Jean-Luc owes me a new suit. And while he was fitting me, I saw this." He holds up his phone to show my selfie from a couple of hours ago. "I figured I'd DM you first, but I needed the walk anyway . . . and then, just as I'm about to text, I look up and there you are. Like fate."

"Mm-hmm. Okay then." I try to hide my smile, and strongly consider getting another espresso just so I have something to hold. I steal a glance under the table. Polished oxfords, probably from Berluti. "That reminds me, I know your secret, by the way."

He looks confused. "My secret?"

"You work in fashion!" I nudge him with my elbow. Okay, it's a pathetic excuse to make physical contact, but I'll take what I can get. "The twins told me."

He laughs easily, stretching out his legs and glancing at the sketchbook on the table. "Well, I don't really work *in* fashion,

I just deal with a lot of brands. Speaking of, you looked pretty absorbed with that. What is it? Are you designing a line or something?"

"What, these?" Now it's my turn to be confused. This is the second time in two days that someone has asked me outright if I'm a fashion designer . . . which is crazy! "No, no. This is just mind-numbing doodling for me."

"May I?"

For a second, I hesitate to let him see it, for that reason precisely. This isn't anything *serious*.

"I've never even studied design formally," I say, sliding the notebook over to him. "I mean, I've always drawn imaginary outfits for fun, like when I'm waiting alone at an airport for a delayed flight . . ." I know I'm rambling, but I find myself weirdly curious about what Alex will think. After all, clearly he's not a stranger to the fashion world. He's part of it, at least on the business end of things. Though, something tells me that even if Alex handled financials for fishing bait and tackle companies, I'd still want to share my fashion sketches with him. I'd want to hear his opinions. I try not to linger too long on what that means. On how good it feels just to hear his voice in person, instead of in my head and over text.

He flips through the pages, his eyes focused and intent. I watch him look at every sketch, trying to read his facial expressions. Does he think they're totally amateur? Is he trying to figure out how to let me down easy? I twist my fingers in my lap, waiting for his verdict. Finally, he closes the sketchbook and looks up at me.

"Rachel, these are good," he says seriously. "*Very* good. I mean, the silhouettes on these two look a little familiar, but then this one is something I've never really seen before and then *this* . . ." He holds up the last one. "This one is just, I don't know how to put it. It's just very *you*. Which is, from my limited understanding, the whole point of design, right? To have a voice."

I flush with surprise. "Really?"

"Of course," he says, nodding, like he's just assessed something as simple as the weather.

His words make my heart race, and now I'm really glad I did not get that extra espresso. "I guess I was inspired after the show last night," I say. "It was incredible. She just has such a clear brand and message. I felt like my brain was a switchboard and all these lights were going off in me at once." Then I tell him about the photographer from *Vogue* asking me if I had my own line. "I mean, I'd never be qualified for something like that, obviously, but it was just so sweet, you know? I guess this is just my imaginary line," I say, taking the sketchbook back. It feels more substantial in my hands now – and also more fragile, like if I lost the notebook, maybe I'd lose this moment, and this sense of conviction washing over me.

"Why imaginary?" Alex cocks his head to the side. "I'm not an expert on design or anything, but it seems like you have the skills to go for it if you wanted to. Plenty of creative directors I work with were not trained at the standard schools or whatever. And these are self-made millionaires I'm talking about. The most common qualities they all have are vision and tenacity."

"But – I can barely even sew," I say, thinking back to the time I tried to stitch up a hole in the sleeve of my Isabel Marant sweater and ended up with a Frankenstein-looking thing from my wrist to my elbow.

"So? Everyone starts from somewhere," Alex says, leaning forward in his seat. "Besides, you wouldn't have to actually sew, or even totally design the clothes all by yourself. You could be more of a creative director – the person who has the unique creative vision." He looks me straight in the eye with his warm brown eyes. "The question is, is designing your own line something you want to do? Would it make you happy?"

Would it? I think on it for a moment. The thought makes me both excited and terrified. It's such unknown territory. An option that I never even knew could be a real possibility for me. And this idea of being a creative director sounds kind of perfect. I can see myself sketching original pieces, picking out the perfect fabrics and materials, communicating the look and feel we want the brand to achieve, and the story that I want the clothes to tell. My heartbeat picks up. My fingers are itching to grab my pencils and start drawing again. But then another thought hits me. Could I actually pull this off with my life? K-pop will always come first; it has to. Music is my first love, and I wouldn't want it any other way. Would I?

"Maybe," I tell him truthfully. "But right now it's kind of just my safe place to play and not worry about perfection."

"Makes sense. If you're just doing it for you, then just do it for you," he says easily, shrugging his shoulders. "Then again, sometimes I find it helpful to think about successful people who are already doing the thing I want to do. That way – "

"Carly Mattsson."

He blinks and then breaks out laughing. "You mean from B*Dazzled?"

I nod, a little embarrassed at my outburst.

"Huh, I would have pegged you as more of a Nikki Casey kind of girl," he teases, referring to Carly's groupmate who always wore crazy-high pigtails and hot-pink platform boots and is famous for dyeing her armpit hair electric blue for the Cannes Film Festival.

"Ha ha. But seriously, I saw Carly at the after-party yesterday and oh my god, Alex," I sigh. "She's perfection. Total goals. If I could do what she does – music and fashion while still making time for my family - that would be a dream."

He thinks for a moment and then nods. "All right. I'll see what I can do."

I raise my eyebrows. "You'll see what you can do?"

A cheeky grin lights up his face as he reaches his hand across the table. For a second, I think he might be trying to hold my hand, and my breath catches in my throat. My fingers twitch on the tabletop, but he passes my hand and picks up my empty mug.

"Well, first I'll see what I can do about getting you a new drink," he says. "And maybe a change of scenery. Shall we wander? Or are you flitting off to Charles de Gaulle tonight?"

"I don't leave until tomorrow morning," I tell him, "so I guess I've got to find *something* to do with myself until then."

"Okay then. We can definitely think of *something*."

I try not to flush at his words as he throws some money for the coffees on the table and offers an elbow. I take it.

From Montmartre, we take the metro down to Rue de Rivoli, popping into a few trendy boutiques. Then we cross the Pont d'Arcole and marvel at Notre Dame, regal against the sky. In Saint Germain we dip into Shakespeare and Company, looking at all the books in a variety of languages, then find a spot in the Luxembourg Gardens to read the ones we bought. Every so often, I find myself looking over my shoulder, gripped by the sudden fear that someone will see us together and recognize me. The stress of being exposed never completely leaves my mind, but it's hard not to get swept up in the romance of the moment. Still, I always keep one eye out, mindful of who's around me at all times.

Whenever I get stuck on what we should do next, Alex breaks it down for me with options. A) Visit a bakery and picnic by the Eiffel Tower. B) Take a sunset boat ride on the Seine. C) Grab drinks in the Bastille. D) All of the above.

The whole day, I have my own multiple choice on loop in my mind.

Should I kiss Alex?

A) Go for it!

B) No way. What if someone sees and takes a photo? Don't be so reckless.

C) Besides, are you really ready to make a romantic connection? Think with your head, not your heart!

D) But what if I just . . . kiss him?

Earlier today while we were walking along the Seine, our hands brushed against each other and I felt tingles all the way up my arm. For a second, he stopped walking. I stopped too. He looked me in the eye and then smiled that smile of his, that dimple in his left cheek making him look simultaneously adorably boyish and sexy as hell.

"You know I really want to hold your hand, right?" he said. He laughed, rubbing the side of his face. "And I wanted to earlier at that café, too. But I'm trying to play it cool." I giggled at his attempt to "play it cool," but then he continued with a more serious tone, "I remember what you told me about how relationships are for K-pop stars. I don't want to pressure you or put you in a situation you don't want to be in. And I don't know if I need to say this, but just to make it really clear, I'm not interested in your fame. I'm interested in you and your ability to make riding the Singapore subway look like an extreme sport."

I burst out laughing at that. I didn't know what else to say. He was so honest. No games, just candid truth. "Thank you," I said, "for saying all those things." And then I reached out and grabbed his hand, threading my fingers through his, and we continued our stroll down the river hand in hand. In that moment, the thrill of his touch overrode the risk of it.

As we continue to explore the city, I can't shake the conversation out of my head. Or how badly I want to kiss him. I haven't felt anything like this since I was with Jason – but at the same time, this is *so* different than when I was with him. I can hardly compare the two. With Jason, everything was intense and explosive, in both good and bad ways. Looking back now, it was puppy love. But with Alex, I feel grounded, and the thought of being with him feels like both safety and freedom and wide-open possibility.

As we near dinnertime, we end up at Hôtel Costes. Its restaurant is small and intimate, with dimly lit, cosy dining nooks. It's definitely the kind of vibe where celebrities can relax and have a drink without worrying about anyone watching them. "Jeon, reservation for two," Alex says to the maître d'.

The waiter comes to lead us to our table, but Alex doesn't move. I glance over my shoulder.

"Are you coming?" I ask.

"No," he says. "I actually won't be joining you for dinner."

"What?" I turn to him, confused. "I thought you made a reservation for two?"

"He did!" a voice says. "So sorry I'm late."

A woman has just stepped into the restaurant, dressed in vintage extra-wide cuffed jeans, paired with a black turtleneck sweater, black ankle boots, black square sunglasses – and a distinctive hot-pink Birkin bag.

Oh my god.

It's Carly Mattsson, in the flesh.

She kisses Alex on the cheek in greeting before turning to me with a warm smile. "You must be Rachel," she says, kissing me on the cheek as well. "It's a pleasure to meet you."

"It's – I – it's so nice to meet you, too," I say, fumbling with my words. I turn to Alex and mouth, *How?!*

"I do the finances for her husband Ollie's sportswear brand," Alex says like it's no big deal. "I called in a favour."

I can't believe this. I'm literally looking back and forth between Alex and Carly like I'm not sure who I'm more amazed by at the moment. Alex gives my arm a quick squeeze.

"Have a good dinner," he says, smiling.

"Shall we, Rachel?" Carly says.

I manage to nod and follow Carly and the waiter to our table without falling over my feet or bursting into tears out of sheer surprise, both of which I feel very close to doing. Carly is completely gracious and doesn't mention how awkward I am. Instead, she leans forward in her seat and gives me a conspiratorial smile.

"Did you know this place has the best chocolate mousse? I'm tempted to skip dinner just to get to dessert."

I laugh, relaxing a little. "I mean, I won't judge if you have dessert before dinner. Exceptions must be made for chocolate mousse."

Carly winks at me. "My kinda girl."

As we start chatting, I find that Carly has this wonderful

gift of making you forget that she's, well, Carly Mattsson. She's totally comfortable in her own skin, jumping into a story about how little Jude's new favourite word is the F-bomb ("honestly, it's better than his last favourite word: 'won't'!") without an ounce of self-consciousness, and I start to feel more comfortable too. As we dig into bowls of truffle risotto with glasses of rich Burgundy, I tell her about my experience at the fashion show yesterday and Alex's comments about my own sketches.

"I don't know if I have it in me to be a real designer, though," I say. "It feels like such a stretch from just me doodling in my sketchbook."

"I get that," Carly says. "But think of it this way. When you were a kid, singing alone in your room, dreaming of one day singing on a stage, did you ever think you'd actually become a K-pop star? I'm sure at the time that dream felt impossible. And yet, here you are."

She's right. I nod slowly. I've never thought of it that way before.

"You're in a good position to start thinking about your own fashion line if that's what you want," she says. "You're passionate and talented and you have fresh ideas, not to mention you have connections in the industry." I cringe, thinking about the missed opportunity to make another fashion-industry contact last night, ruined by my unsticky sticky-boob. Carly doesn't miss a beat. "What's that face?" she laughs.

I blush and hesitantly recount the story from last night. Carly's eyes widen when I get to the part about my weird wardrobe-malfunction-preventing dance moves, and she bursts into laughter. "Don't laugh!" I say, laughing myself. "It was *mortifying*. I feel like there are all these unspoken rules in the fashion world. It's so intimidating. I just don't want to mess up, you know?"

"I know," she says, her laughter fading into an understanding smile. "But the thing is, Rachel, sometimes when you look back on your biggest successes, you realise that they didn't happen because you just sat back and did what you're told. It's okay to break the rules every once in a while. Life's more fun that way." She winks.

I take a sip of my wine, mulling over what Carly just said. It's so counterintuitive to everything I've been taught at DB. In K-pop, I've found success *because* I don't break the rules. I've stuck to the path that's been laid out before me ever since I became a trainee, and it's got me to where I am today. Even this idea of starting my own fashion line feels like it's breaking the rules of K-pop, simply because, well, no one's ever done it before. Am I even allowed to be thinking about this?

"I'm not going to sugarcoat it, Rachel," Carly says. "It's tough as hell to run your own business, especially when you're transitioning over from being in a super girl group. It's a big jump, but if you really want it, you can make it happen."

Big jump? I'm at once flattered by her confidence and overwhelmed by everything she's saying. "Well, not exactly transitioning over," I say. "It's not at all like I want to leave

Girls Forever for fashion. I love what I'm doing with them, and I've always imagined that we would be one of the longest-running girl groups in K-pop history." I smile. "I'm still young. I see myself with them for at least another four or five years. Besides, we're like sisters."

Carly smiles back wistfully. "I remember those days. The B*Dazzled girls and I used to do everything together. I don't think anyone's ever seen me so snotty, not even my husband." She winces. "Or seen me with so little eyebrow, after the Great Overplucking Fiasco of '11. Nikki had to draw them back on for me every day for the next four months."

I laugh. "Really?"

"Oh yeah. Those girls and I are still close as sisters, even though we're all doing different things now. The trick is to make sure you can spot the difference between bickering and bitterness. Everyone bickers. The girls and I used to have misunderstandings over a bunch of silly things. But bitterness is different. It can plant deep roots in your heart and grow into something else altogether. If you can identify what's what, you'll be fine."

God, I wish I could just transcribe our whole conversation. It's like she knows exactly what I'm going through – which, I guess she actually does because she's been there herself. It's so reassuring to talk to someone who really gets it.

Carly reaches across the table and gives my hand a squeeze. "I think you're exactly where you need to be right now, Rachel," she says. "Thinking about your future after K-pop doesn't have to be a contradiction to your commitment to the group. You can be working on your side ideas while still rocking your career with Girls Forever. You got this. Now . . ." She lets go of my hand and picks up the dessert menu instead. "Is it chocolate mousse time yet?"

I love her.

"Yes," I say, beaming. "Way past time."

After dinner, I float back to the Four Seasons, totally on cloud nine. I feel more inspired than ever. That dinner with Carly Mattsson was exactly what I needed and more. And I owe it all to Alex.

As soon as I get to my room, I pull out my phone to text him.

Me: Thank you thank you thank you.

His response comes seconds later.

Alex: I take it you had a good time?

Me: The BEST. I'm back at the Four Seasons. Where are you?

Alex: Walking back from late dinner with some business contacts. Actually, I'm just a couple blocks from your hotel now . . .

I immediately run out of my room and down the hotel stairs. As soon as I burst out the front doors, I see Alex standing under a lamppost. I notice it has started to drizzle. Little flecks of rain land on his face, making his hair look like it's sparkling in the streetlights.

"Hi," he says.

"Hi," I say.

He rubs rain off his face. "Wait, don't come out, you'll get all wet."

"No, no, it's perfect. Much harder for paparazzi to get photos at night, and in the rain." I head towards him, as if drawn by an invisible force.

He laughs. "So you had a good time?"

"Transformative. The chocolate mousse changed my life." I swat at him. "Oh yeah and the company was enjoyable too . . ."

He smiles. "I'm glad."

A taxi pulls up nearby and a couple gets out, giggling, clearly a little drunk, as they stumble into the hotel. We step further into the shadows, out of the way of the hotel doors.

"Seriously, I'm blown away. I don't know how to thank you, honestly."

"No need for thanks. But since you haven't started melting in this rain, how about a walk?"

I don't answer right away. I'm too caught in the moment, in the way the streetlamps are shining on the side of his face, lighting up his eyes, capturing his earnest expression.

"Or . . . option B, you're exhausted from traipsing around with me alllll day, and you want to just say good night now so you can flop into bed . . . " he offers.

I laugh and shake my head. "Option C. None of the above."

He looks confused, but before he can say anything, I step forward and kiss him. For a second, he's too surprised to react, but then his arms find their way around my waist and he's kissing me back, as the rain falls lightly on the cobblestones beneath our feet.

✯ Ten ✯

"I'm back!" I call out as I enter our villa in Cheongdam-dong the next afternoon, slipping off my shoes. I hear a few vague *heys* coming from behind closed bedroom doors, but no one comes to greet me. I guess I shouldn't be surprised. It's nearly nine a.m. on a Sunday when we have no Girls Forever commitments. I'd probably be sound asleep right now too.

I should unpack right away, sort out what's laundry, what needs to be dry-cleaned, and what's clean and can go back in my closet. But between the eleven-hour flight and the eight-hour time difference (it's one a.m. in Paris right now), I'm exhausted. Maybe a quick catnap before I dive into the unpacking ordeal. As I head down the hall, I hear the shower running in the bathroom closest to my room, and smell Jiyoon's signature coconut shampoo wafting through the door.

I open the door to our room, and find that I'm more glad to be home than I would have thought. My hotel room might have had a view overlooking an Italianate courtyard, but it didn't have my Polaroid wall or my nightstand stack of *Vogue* issues dog-eared to my favourite spreads or my little wooden jewellery tree that Lizzie got me for the group's fifth anniversary (despite her prickly moments, she always gives out traditional anniversary presents every year – paper for year one, cotton for year two, and so on). I missed it all, even Jiyoon's messy half of the room, with its unorganised bookshelves and crumpled weighted blanket she claims is too heavy to pick up off the floor. After putting my luggage away in the closet, I curl up on top of my bed, not even bothering to pull the covers back, and close my eyes.

A few moments later, there's a rise of voices in the kitchen. The girls must have been awakened by the smell of shakshuka – ever since Sumin discovered it, she's been asking the managers to have some delivered every weekend. As I breathe in the scent, my stomach growls audibly. I guess the bagel I had on the plane didn't quite tide me over. Well, unpacking and sleep can wait. But food definitely cannot.

I come out to meet them just as they settle around the dining room table. They startle and Sunhee nearly jumps out of her skin.

"Oh my god, Rachel, you scared me," she says, pressing a hand against her heart. "Welcome back!"

"Thanks," I say, flashing her a quick smile.

"Nice hair, Soom," Ari says, pulling out a chair. Sumin's rocking a topknot that's looking a little more bird's-nest than intentionally-messy-but-still-cute. Sumin yawns as she grabs the seat next to Ari, apparently too tired to manage a good comeback.

"Oh, we got this amazing leave-in moisturising and detangling serum in the Nell Kramer show gift bags," I say to Sumin as she pours herself some omija tea. "You can totally borrow it if you want."

"Please, Rachel, we literally just woke up," Lizzie says, flopping down on her chair at the opposite side of the table. "Can you at least give us five minutes before you start bragging about Paris?"

"Seriously," Mina says, opening the fridge and taking out a bottle of sparkling water. "While you were off on your vacation, the rest of us were working, you know."

Um, ouch? I didn't realise offering to let someone borrow a hair care product was bragging. Besides, the only reason DB let me go on the trip in the first place was because we had a gap in our Girls Forever schedule. I know for a fact the girls weren't working on anything major for the group while I was gone.

"What were you all up to while I was away?" I ask, turning the conversation back to neutral ground.

"We grabbed drinks at 902 last night," Sunhee chimes in.

Ah. That explains the dialled-up crankiness. 902's tequila cocktails are lethal. I'm sure everyone's nursing killer headaches this morning.

"Fun," I say with a knowing smile. "Did I miss out on anything else?"

"I shot a supporting role in the new movie *When I Loved*

You," Mina says proudly. "Apparently, it's already predicted to be a box office smash. And they did some last-minute script rewrites to make my character a bigger part, because the female lead they have is such a snooze."

"That's great!" I say. My heart lifts at this news. I'm genuinely happy to hear that she's beginning to pursue her dream in acting. "And your dad's on board?"

"I don't need his permission," she snaps, but the proud look on her face falters slightly. "Besides," she says, her expression regaining its confident smirk, "once he heard who was going to be costarring in the movie with me, he basically *had* to let me do it."

"Oh right, isn't that the movie Jason's in?" I ask.

"And Song Geonwu," Mina adds. "You know anything he's in is going to be a big deal. The day I was on set, he arranged for an ice cream and coffee truck so all the cast and crew could stay energised. It was so cute. He's so different in person than what you see on TV. Really down to earth. But of course still gorgeous."

Eunji looks enviously at Mina. "And *I'm* going to be doing a shoot for *Vogue*," she says, sitting down next to Lizzie.

"Yes, we know, Eunji," Lizzie says curtly. Eunji ignores her, reaching for a bottle of Yakult with a smug smile on her face. It's strange to see this little trio sniping at each other, when usually they're the queen bees, united in their efforts to rag on the rest of us.

Wait a minute.

It just hit me.

Eunji got the *Vogue* shoot?

So DB didn't just turn down the offer for me, they *reassigned it*. I can't believe it.

"DB told me about the shoot last week," Eunji continues, as if Lizzie hadn't spoken. "It's the first time a K-pop idol has had a feature spread. I can't believe they wanted me," she says in a tone that has to be the world's weakest attempt at modesty. Behind Eunji, Mina rolls her eyes. Eunji may not have great style, but everyone knows that the media and netizens agree that Eunji is probably the most classically beautiful girl in the group. "I'm going in for a wardrobe fitting on Tuesday," she adds.

Mina comes over to the table with her sparkling water, and there's a particular set of her jaw, a glint in her eye. "Speaking of wardrobes – I noticed your favourite manager, Hajoon, has a new Montblanc watch. What, your family couldn't afford a Rolex?"

Parents do this sometimes – bribe managers, or even lower-level DB execs, to get special perks for their daughters. But no one usually brings it up as boldly as Mina just did. Then again, no one is usually as bold as Mina, period.

"Sunhee's been doing cool things too," Youngeun cuts in smoothly.

Jiyoon, who has emerged from the bathroom with her hair wrapped in a towel, nudges Sunhee in the side with a grin. "Yeah! Sunhee here landed a hosting gig for SOAR Drama and Entertainment's new radio show. Tell her, Sun."

Sunhee blushes and smiles. "I'm going to host their new talk show. It's really cool. They're trying to make a more intimate space for artists to talk about what drives them creatively."

"I always said you have a face for radio, Sun," Lizzie says, snickering.

Sunhee's smile falters, and Youngeun reaches over to squeeze her arm. "You'll be fantastic," she says.

When it comes to Sunhee, most of the girls fall into one of two camps: picking on her more because she's the youngest, or being extra protective of her because she's the youngest. Youngeun may be levelheaded, but she's a mama bear when it comes to protecting our maknae.

"Definitely," I agree. "What a perfect opportunity for you!"

And I mean it. Sunhee will be great at that. She might not be the most drop-dead gorgeous member of the group, but she's totally lovable, largely thanks to her fun TV personality. I wish she could see that instead of letting the other girls get to her so much.

But I can't help but remember why the radio show sounds so familiar. It's the same show that Mr. Park, the SOAR exec at the party in Shanghai, approached me about. He said he'd be in touch with DB, but I never heard anything after that. Apparently, the DB execs decided to give the opportunity to Sunhee instead.

I'm genuinely happy for her, but I can't help but feel a flicker of annoyance at DB. This is the second time now that I've realized they've prevented opportunities from reaching me.

First *Vogue*, now the SOAR radio show. They're obviously taking all the offers coming in for specific girls and distributing them as they see fit. On one hand, I can appreciate that they want to keep things equal for all of us – I think about the fan-mail piles, each of us sizing up to see who got more and who got less. You definitely don't want to breed that sense of inequality in a group if you can avoid it. But on the other hand, it's a jolting reminder that I owe everything to DB – anything I want to pursue, it needs to have their stamp of approval first, or it will never happen.

I think of what Carly Mattson told me – but more than our conversation, I think of the air of confidence she has about her life, finding balance, and doing the things that make her happy. *Would it make you happy?* Alex asked me about dipping into the fashion world.

Yes, I realise. It would.

But there's no point in spending any further thought on it until I talk to the people who matter most.

DB.

"Thank you for meeting with me, Mr. Noh. I know you have a very busy schedule."

Mr. Noh leans back in his brown leather office chair and crosses his legs. "Not a problem, Rachel. You know you're always welcome here."

Hard to believe him when he's peering at me through his glasses like he's trying to dissect my brain. I haven't had a private meeting with Mr. Noh in years, and I'm finding myself a little out of practice. There's always a delicate dance to these conversations – me, trying to give the appropriate respect, while also standing my ground and requesting what I think is fair; him, trying to be a reasonable and generous employer, but also making sure I know who's boss.

"What's on your mind?" he asks.

"I'd like to start my own fashion line," I say, cutting straight to the chase. That's another rule of private Mr. Noh meetings – don't waste his time. My legs keep threatening to shake under the table, but I force myself to stay still and continue on, keeping my voice measured and calm. "As you know, I've always been interested in fashion, and my recent trip to Paris made me realise that I have the potential to get more involved in the industry. I want to assure you that this wouldn't change anything about my commitment to Girls Forever. It would simply be a side thing, not a replacement for the group. You know, like Mina's acting, or Sunhee's radio hosting," I rattle off, tactically slipping in those references so that Mr. Noh can't brush my request aside too easily. After all, if he's letting the rest of the girls pursue side gigs, why shouldn't he allow this?

"Well–" Mr. Noh starts to say. And I can tell that he's about to argue that a fashion line is different. After all, movies and radio shows are par for the course in our industry, but no other K-pop idol has ever tried to launch a fashion brand. At least, not to my knowledge. I see my dream slipping away, so it's time to pull out the big guns.

"Or Eunji's *Vogue* shoot . . ." I say, letting it sit there.

Mr. Noh's face betrays no acknowledgment, but I know he's thinking back to our earlier conversation before Singapore. When he blatantly denied there was any opportunity with *Vogue*. I can practically hear his mind whirring as he calculates the pluses and minuses of granting my request. Okay, no more chess game. I need to make him see that this really is a dream for me, and that it won't pose any drawback for him.

"And I'd like to offer the company a royalty from my fashion brand," I say, unclasping my bag to pull out a draft of a royalty agreement that Alex and I had discussed. "For the length of my contract with DB, a portion of my fashion sales would go to you. Mr. Noh, Girls Forever is my top priority, and nothing will change that," I continue earnestly. "If anything, if my brand were ever to become successful, it may even help boost our popularity and help us reach a wider audience."

Mr. Noh steeples his fingers under his chin, considering. I hold my breath.

I made my case. I appealed to his business sense. The company has a clear financial incentive. Our goals are aligned, not in opposition.

Now all I can do is wait.

And hope.

And–

"All right," he says finally. "We appreciate the offer of royalties. It suits you, having your own fashion line – I don't see why not."

I let out a breath, the terror lifting from my chest. I bow my head. "Thank you so much."

"In fact, we could even make this a DB official company if you'd like," he says eagerly. "Keep it all in-house."

I hesitate. I think back to how insecure I felt when Alex was looking through my notebook. I sold Mr. Noh on the idea just now because if it *worked*, we would all benefit . . . but what if it doesn't? What if I fail spectacularly? I still want fashion and design to be my safe space to play, like I told Alex. The pressure of doing it for DB would mean having to do it perfectly right out the gate. I try not to falter as I answer him.

"I'm so grateful for your offer, Mr. Noh," I say, keeping my voice level, "but I'd like to see what I'm capable of on my own. I'm really still in the, ah, exploratory stage." More like *no idea what I'm doing* stage, but he doesn't need to know that! Not to mention, I don't know if I feel right about putting my fresh new idea under DB's control. I was happy to offer them royalties as a goodwill gesture, but I still want this to feel like my thing, not DB's thing. "Would it be all right if I did this outside the company?"

He looks sceptical – and we both know why. How the hell would I actually pull something like this off? Most likely, it's going to be a fun little side project that never sees the light of day. But he blinks, betraying no emotion, and says, "I suppose I don't see why not. I'll reach out to Mr. Han to sort out the details. But I want to see you do your best. Your line may not be under DB, but you're still a star within the label, and whatever you do reflects on us. Understood?" *Aka: don't embarrass yourself – or us.*

"Of course," I say, brimming with equal parts excitement and terror. He said yes. He said yes! "You know that I always give my best and I promise, this will be no different."

That night, the girls and I are settled in the living room eating Choco Pies and watching a singing competition show. During a commercial break, I tell them all about my meeting with Mr. Noh. They gasp, Youngeun grabbing the remote to turn the TV on mute. For a moment, everyone sits in silence.

"Your own fashion line," Youngeun says finally. "That's . . . wow."

I flush. I didn't want to make a big deal out of it since it's still so early in the process, but the girls know how much it means to get Mr. Noh's approval for something like this.

"I'm really, really excited for it. I have so many ideas," I say. "But also kind of terrified? Like I can't believe he actually said yes."

Mina nods slowly. "Yeah, this is definitely . . . unexpected," she says coolly. "I guess it makes sense, though. You do put together cute little outfits sometimes."

"Yes! You're so good with clothes!" Sunhee gushes. "You're going to be awesome."

"Thanks, Sun," I say, grateful for her genuine enthusiasm.

"Sunhee's right," Jiyoon agrees. "This is right up your alley."

"I just hope I can do a good job," I say, taking a deep breath.

Younguen nods reassuringly, then reaches for the remote to turn the volume back on. But before she can, Lizzie speaks. "Wow, Rachel. A reality show, duo album, and a fashion line? That's a lot. I sure hope you can handle it all," she says, but the sarcastic tone in her voice suggests otherwise.

"This won't impact your involvement in the group, will it?" Mina adds, pressing her lips together.

I suspected that of all the girls, Mina would be the most worried about what this would mean for the rest of the group. Like she once said, *"When one of us messes up, we all look bad."* I can't blame her for being worried. I'm going into uncharted territory, and whatever I do will inevitably reflect on the rest of the group – and on her.

"Don't worry," I say firmly. "Girls Forever is still my number-one priority. I may not be sure of everything, but that I'm a hundred per cent certain of."

Another silence falls over the group, this one a little tenser than before. After a beat, Sumin clears her throat and says, "By the way, Rachel? Can I still borrow that hair-moisturising serum thing you said you got in Paris?"

"Yeah, sure," I say. Then suddenly, struck with the cosiness of the moment and gratitude for all the girls' support, I add, "You can have it, even."

"Really?" She grins. "Thanks!"

"So, how was Paris?" Ari pipes up.

"Yeah, did you eat any weird foods?" Sumin asks. "Like escargoats?"

Ari frowns. "It's escargots."

"That's what I said."

"No, you didn't. You said 'goats,' dummy."

And then they're bickering like an old married couple, Mina is complaining about not being able to hear the TV, Eunji is rolling her eyes, but in a fond way, and I'm smiling. New things lie ahead, but some things never change.

⭐ *Eleven* ⭐

On the first day of seventh grade, my pre-algebra teacher, Ms. Pan, had us go around the room and share one interesting fact about ourselves. I'd been in Korea for three years at that point, and my old standby fun-facts – *I just moved here from New York. I'm a K-pop trainee. I have a little sister* – were no longer new or unknown to most of my classmates. Besides, at thirteen, there was pressure to share something that would set you apart as cooler and more adult than your peers. Like Mindy Koo, who shared that she got her cartilage pierced over the summer, or Ara Choi, who celebrated her birthday with floor seats to a Beyoncé concert. As I sat there, waiting anxiously for the moment when I'd have to speak, I suddenly felt every single thing I'd ever done – interesting or not – completely fly out of my head. And sitting on set now, recording an episode of Dal TV, I'm feeling the exact same way.

The interview has gone great so far. Ryu Daehyun is one of my favourite hosts. He's funny and warm, and always gets us comfortable and laughing. But he also sometimes likes to throw out more serious questions, like "How can K-pop change the world?" or "What's a charity or social cause that's meaningful to you?" So when he said, "Okay, girls. Now I have one last question," I sat up a little straighter on my stool, wondering if he was about to go somewhere deep.

But instead, Daehyun says, "If you had to describe yourself in one word – yes, Sunhee, just one word!" he says, laughing as the camera pans to Sunhee, who is already opening her mouth to protest. It's become a recurring bit on today's episode of the show that Sunhee loves to talk. Daehyun even timed her to see how long she could ramble without drawing breath. She went sixty-seven seconds. After the laughter dies down, he continues. "Okay, one word to describe yourself. Go."

"Passionate," Mina says.

"Honest," Jiyoon adds – it's true, but also a calculated move. She's *still* living down the bad press from Singapore.

"Cute!" Sunhee says, pressing her hands against her cheeks and making Daehyun laugh.

The microphone goes down the line, with each girl sharing her word. I don't realise I've tuned them out, until suddenly I feel a nudge at my side and turn to see Sumin elbowing me, offering the mic.

"Okay, Rachel Kim. What word would you use to describe yourself?"

I open my mouth, then close it again. Oops. I'd been daydreaming about my FaceTime date last night with Alex, where we watched a Bob Ross tutorial on YouTube and each followed along on MS Paint to hilariously terrible results, and I completely forgot to be thinking of my own one-word description.

Come on, Rachel.

Just pick a word – any word. It's just a silly talk show, not some actual, life-defining moment. Besides, what kind of question is this? No one can describe herself in just one word. Actually, that's a good point . . .

"Doesn't follow silly rules," I say, counting off each of the *four* words on my fingers. It's ironic because, of all the girls in the group, I'm actually probably one of the biggest sticklers for the rules – never wanting to ruffle feathers or risk getting on DB's bad side. But then I think of Carly's advice in Paris, how it's okay to break the rules every once in a while. It's what makes the journey fun.

"Ohhh," Daehyun says, wagging his finger at me. "Looks like we've got a rebel on our hands!"

I shrug my shoulders and smile innocently, as if to say *Who, me?* as Daehyun closes out the show.

Once the recording is done, the girls and I all walk back to the greenroom to grab our stuff before heading home to the villa. Everyone makes a beeline for her own bag: Youngeun fishes a simple herbal lip balm from her crossbody and reapplies, complaining that the studio lights always dry her out. Lizzie immediately pulls out her monogrammed compact mirror from her Chanel quilted bag to check how her makeup held up. Across the room, Jiyoon is gathering the contents of her overstuffed canvas tote, scooping up crumpled tissues and allergy pills that had spilled across the table. I think wryly to myself, someone should tell Ryu Daehyun that if he really wants to get to know the members of Girls Forever, he should just ask us what's inside our bags. That'd certainly give him a more accurate picture than the "one word."

And with that thought, I suddenly have an amazing idea.

For weeks, I've been trying to think of a hook, an angle, or a theme for my first fashion collection, but everything I've come up with so far – the seasons! The rainbow! Animals! – has felt unoriginal and played out. Then there's the bigger question of what types of pieces the collection will be comprised of. Based on my conversations with Carly, I've determined that starting small with a limited accessory line would be the best way to ease my way into the industry. But that still leaves a big choice about what kind of accessory to focus on. Shoes? Sunglasses? Watches?

But of course. Why didn't I think of it before? I should do a line of bags. A woman's bag is one of the most personal accessories, because it contains the things she can't do without. I think of my Balenciaga. Part of what makes it so special is what it represents – my love for fashion and meeting Alex. I want to design bags that can be meaningful to others. I want them to have that experience of finding the perfect bag for the exact moment of life they're in.

And suddenly, I can see it – a line of bags, each inspired by a key moment in my life. My childhood in New York.

Being scouted and moving to Korea. The trainee years. Girls Forever's first tour . . . Of course, the designs can't be too literal – I need my line to appeal to everyone, not just me! But I hope anchoring the collection with these personal memories will help me bring the full force of my creative passion to the project. And then, maybe someday, a girl will walk by a window and see one of my bags on display, and have her own transformative experience. And the bag will take on *her* memories and experiences.

I immediately rush to my current bag (an old Chloé Faye bag I decided to bring to the shoot today, not wanting to risk leaving the Balenciaga unattended), where it's resting on a makeup chair in the corner. I grab my phone and text Alex, asking if he'd be willing to pass along the contact info for some of his connections in the fashion accessory space.

Alex: Sure, I can set you up with some names. So did you land on a direction for your line?

Me: YES! I finally have the idea. THE IDEA.

Alex: Awesome!! Is it snow boots for cats? Please tell me it's snow boots for cats 😉

Me: lol. I'll FaceTime you when I get home. Thank you again for the contacts!!

Alex: Happy to help xx

"Hello, girls," Mr. Han says, stepping into the greenroom just as I stash my phone away. We all call out hellos back. His eyes find me. "Ah, Rachel – just the person I was looking for." He strides over to me and pats me on the back. "I wanted to let you know that we finished drawing up your contract in regards to your fashion line. It should be in your inbox by the end of the day today."

"Thank you!" I say. "As soon as I see it, I'll get on reviewing and signing it."

"Perfect – oh, Youngeun, I wanted to talk to you too," he says, beckoning her over.

"Yes, Mr. Han?" she says, sounding hopeful.

"You need to pull the cake pops out of your parents' bakery," he says. "The ones that you designed to look like light sticks. We haven't authorised you to use the Girls Forever light sticks copyright, so this is confusing to fans. We need you to stop selling them by the end of today, or there could be legal trouble."

"Legal trouble? But they're just cake pops!" she blurts, and then her eyes widen at having talked back.

"So they shouldn't be hard to get rid of, right?"

"Yeah, I guess . . ." She shuffles her weight from foot to foot. "Have you thought about my YouTube baking channel idea? I already wrote up some scripts of some videos I could do . . ."

He smiles apologetically. "I'm sorry, but DB has decided that won't work. We just don't have a precedent of any of our idols doing YouTube channels."

Youngeun shoots a glance at me, then in a tentative voice says, "But there's no precedent of anyone doing a fashion line before . . ."

Now all the girls are looking at me. I feel like I've just been shoved under the bus.

"That is slightly different," Mr. Han says. "DB has let idol groups sell clothes as merch before. But Youngeun, please don't let this stop you from baking for fun in your free time. Cake pops aside, that is completely okay with us."

It's a bit condescending, but before Youngeun can open her mouth, he waves at us and heads towards the door. "I've got to go, but I'll see you girls later."

Silence settles around us, until Jiyoon glances at her watch. "The cars should be here now."

Youngeun sighs. "You'll all have to go without me. I'll meet you at the villa later. There's some cake pops I have to go and eat now."

✦ Twelve ✦

"Ooh, Unni, I love that colour!"

Leah looks over from her plush salon armchair as the pedicurist paints peach-sparkle polish on my toes.

"I was just thinking I should have gone for something bright, like yours," I say, nodding to her lime-green toes.

"Nah, that colour is way more your style. Classy and elega–"

"Sorry to interrupt, girls." I jump, startled to see the director standing over us, headphones slung around his neck. "Just wanted to let you know that once your pedicures are done, we're going to start moving over to the next filming location."

Right. This isn't just a sister date.

We're filming our reality show.

Even with the cameras fixed on our faces, it's easy to forget that we're on set when I'm absorbed in conversation with Leah. Honestly, it's a little strange to think that people are going to tune in and watch these regular, everyday moments between the two of us. As much as I wanted to give my fans an up-close-and-personal experience through this show, I can't help but feel like I'm not quite delivering, what with me feeling like a zombie half the time.

April has been crazy, between shooting the reality show, and work I've been putting in to start a fashion line – which I've decided to name RACHEL K. – from scratch. I've had meetings with production partners and pitch calls with potential retailers, and spent hours sketching. It's been exciting to stretch these new creative muscles, but also extremely nerve-racking.

Meanwhile, Mina's been doing press for *When I Loved You*, which they're rushing to get out by the end of next month; Sunhee had her first recording session for her radio show; Eunji's booked two more modelling gigs after *Vogue*; Ari's in the midst of previews for Seoul's upcoming production of *Wicked*; and even Youngeun has been busy putting in extra time at her parents' café, developing new (DB-approved) recipes and helping to draw in crowds.

It's great to see all my groupmates living out their dreams, but it's also strange to realise that we're at the point in our careers where we can dedicate time to pursuing our own specific interests. And now that Girls Forever is at the top of our game, we can take longer breaks between performances and albums – actually, the longer we break between tours, the more rabid the fan response is when we do come back. I know that by the time we take the stage in LA this fall, our +EVERs are going to be more supportive and enthusiastic than ever!

Leah and I waddle in our toe separators over to the dryers. Once we're seated, my phone pings with an incoming message. I glance at the screen and grin.

"What are you smiling at?" Leah asks.

"It's–" I pause, remembering that the cameras are still rolling. "Appa."

She gives me an amused look. "Right. Got it."

I glance over at where the cameras are set up. There's only one camera operator today, with a handheld on his shoulder. I can tell from where he's standing that he won't actually be able to see my phone screen, so I tilt it towards Leah and let her read.

Alex: I'm currently passing by a pet store and I just thought of the perfect name for a tuxedo cat . . . Armani. Or Ar-meow-ni?

Me: Stopppp. What's the deal with your family and cats? Aren't you allergic??

Alex: Wait. You mean everyone doesn't get itching eyes and a scratchy throat when snuggling a ball of fluff? I think I may have a problem.

Me: It's a clinical obsession. That and the bad puns!

Alex: So what are you doing rn? I'm back in London, it's 3am, I'm currently scrolling through a bunch of boring reports, eating some Hot Cheetos, and wishing I had someone to share them with.

Alex: Like a cat, I mean.

Me: Gasp! Hot Cheetos are my fave!

Me: It's morning here. I'm getting my toenails done – basically they are the colour of Hot Cheetos.

I giggle and Leah rolls her eyes at the texts, but in a loving way. "You guys are absurd. In the best way, of course."

Another text pings in from him:

Alex: PS I miss you.

Me: Me too . . . Any chance you have a favourite shoemaker in Seoul that you're thinking of visiting soon?

Alex: I'll find a way. I love having you in my pocket wherever I go, but I want to see you in 3D, not 2D ☺

Leah looks up at me with puppy dog eyes. "Awww," she says, "he *so* loves you." I nudge her gently, careful not to jostle either of us too much and risk smudging our toes. "Appa, I mean!" she recovers. "Appa loves you so much."

We both try and fail to stifle our giggles.

The director calls cut, telling the camera operator they've gotten enough B-roll. As soon as the camera operator starts to pack away his equipment, I turn to Leah and speak a little more freely.

"Hey by the way, look at these late-night texts I keep getting from Appa." I start scrolling through my messages to show her.

"Ew, Rachel! TMI!" Leah says in a fake-scandalised voice, covering her eyes.

"*Real* Appa." I swat her shoulder.

"Oh yeah. He's pulling late hours at work again." Leah rolls her eyes. "You know Appa. Once he gets into a project, he doesn't know how to stop. And with the grand opening next week–"

"Grand opening?"

"Apex," Leah replies. I blink. "The athletic complex? Appa's new job?" she adds, seeing my confused face. "I thought he told you about it."

Wait, what? Appa has a new job? Last I knew, he was working as a lawyer at Choo Corporation, Mina's dad's company. As Leah fills me in – Appa was approached to run legal for Apex, a new state-of-the-art gym-meets-spa-meets–sports complex here in Seoul, and jumped on the chance to combine his law experience with his first love, sports – I rack my brain trying to think of how I could have missed this huge development.

We spoke briefly a couple weeks ago, but I had to jump off to take a call on the other line from the handbag production team. Did he mention his new job then? The late-night texts I've received from him have just been normal Appa stuff, like – Glow is on the radio! Thinking of my talented daughter!! Followed by a heart emoji, a thumbs-up emoji, and, inexplicably, a unicorn emoji. No mention of Apex or his new role. But maybe that's just because I never gave him a chance. I feel a stab of guilt thinking about how I usually just ignored the messages, or sent a cursory tap-back "like" in acknowledgment.

"Don't worry," Leah says, sensing my concern. "He knows how busy you are."

But Leah is busy too. Her life as a debut idol is just as crazy as mine, and yet she seems totally in the loop – one of the benefits of living at home, I guess. My stomach clenches, thinking how if I didn't have Leah as my go-between, I'd feel even more disconnected from my family than I already do.

"Well, keep an eye on him for me, will you?" I ask her. Then I snap another selfie of the two of us and send it off to Appa, along with about a hundred hearts, and make myself a promise to see him and Umma in person as soon as I can.

Twenty minutes later, our toes sufficiently dry, we're getting ready to head to lunch when suddenly Leah says, "Hey, Unni . . ." She's glancing at her phone as we clip off our mic packs and hand them back to the sound engineer. "Are you supposed to be at a rehearsal right now?"

"Huh? No. Why?"

She shows me her screen. All eight of my groupmates are clustered together for a selfie, posing with peace signs and finger hearts, Ari at the front. *Quick selfie before practice! Now shall we start singing?* her caption says.

Wait, what? I grab the phone out of Leah's hand and zoom in on the photo. Yep, they're definitely in one of DB's practice rooms, and this was definitely taken today. I know that Ari was wearing that same striped T-shirt with the rose-gold heart locket when I left the house this morning. I've never missed a rehearsal before. At this point in our career, we're expected to know our numbers after just one or two times running through them, so we don't even have that many rehearsals any more. They're only scheduled for something big, or for when we need to learn a whole new song. Is that what I'm missing out on right now? How could this have happened? DB wouldn't have scheduled a reality-show shoot day if I also had practice.

"I'm calling my manager," I say, reaching for my own phone.

"Hello?" Jongseok answers.

"Hi, Jongseok," I say. "I see that the girls are at practice right now. Was there one scheduled for today?"

"No," he answers, "not officially. They must have scheduled the extra practice on their own. Is there anything else I can help you with?"

"Can you hold on a second?" I ask, muting myself. To Leah, I say, "It's just an unofficial practice."

She reads my expression. "Do you want to go?"

I don't have to, but something feels off about the girls scheduling a practice without me. Maybe they didn't loop me in because they knew I was busy filming, but my gut is telling me it's more than that. My gut is telling me to go.

"I feel like I should," I say. But what about the rest of our shoot? The crew is going to kill me.

"I'll take care of it," Leah says, as if reading my mind. "I'll tell the director I have cramps and need to lie down for a while. You can totally tell he's the type to get stupidly squeamish over any sort of 'women's issues,'" she says, rolling her eyes. "How much time do you think you need? An hour? Two?"

"I can't be sure. I have no idea what's going on."

"Just keep me posted," she says.

I give her a quick hug. "Thank you so much, Leah."

"Love you!" she says with a huge smile, then suddenly her face contorts with pain and she grabs her middle. "I'm not feeling so well . . . " she says, heading towards the director's chair. Oh she's good. Guess all those years watching K-dramas have given her some acting tips.

I shove my feet back into my boots – so much for not ruining my pedicure – and get back on the line with Jongseok. "Can you pick me up and take me to headquarters?"

As soon as Jongseok drops me off, I head for the practice rooms. The girls turn in surprise when I burst in.

"Rachel," Mina says, hands on her hips. "We thought you forgot about us."

Forgot? I can't have forgotten about something they never told me about – unless, did they?

"I didn't," I say carefully. "How much did I miss?"

"We just started," Youngeun says.

"It's nice for you to grace us with your presence," Lizzie says, narrowing her eyes. "I hope you don't make a habit of being late now that you have other more important things on your schedule."

I shake my head, ignoring the bite in Lizzie's comment. "You know there's nothing more important to me than the group. But come on, let's start rehearsal and not waste any more time!"

The girls mumble in agreement and we begin to practice, focusing on our vocals. I'm still catching my breath for the first few verses, but soon I'm singing seamlessly with the rest of them, filling in the new harmonies with ease. I'm so relieved I didn't miss the whole practice, but when we finish, I decide to stay behind for a few extra minutes to make up for the time that I did miss. The rest of the girls leave the practice room to hit the vending machines, but Sunhee lingers.

"Don't stay behind too long, Rachel," she says. "We'll probably head back to the villa soon. Come with us, yeah?"

"I have to get back to my shoot with Leah." I shake my head, exhausted. "It's a packed schedule."

"Yeah, I didn't expect us to have practice today," Sunhee admits with a shrug. "Lizzie asked for a room this morning because she was feeling shaky on the harmonies. I think she sounds great now, though."

I blink. It was Lizzie? She's one of our top vocalists and has never been insecure about her harmonies before . . .

"But you guys knew I had the reality show today – it was on the schedule," I say, fishing for more info on why Lizzie set up the rehearsal when she *knew* I wouldn't be free.

"She's had a lot going on lately." Sunhee shrugs again. "Maybe she just forgot about your show."

Yeah right. I think about all the snide remarks she's made since Leah and I started filming. It's clear she's still upset that she hasn't been able to bring her own sister into the DB family.

I wave goodbye to Sunhee and sigh as I start packing up my sheet music. I'm not going to stop the reality show just because Lizzie's little sister, Esther, isn't a K-pop idol. Just like I'm not going to stop developing my fashion line because Youngeun can't make her light-stick cake pops. Just like I don't expect Sunhee to give up her radio show just because I didn't get to have one. Our individual projects are, well, individual. We shouldn't be trying to sabotage each other when one of us succeeds any more than we should be making fun of each other when one of us fails.

As I reach the DB lobby and grab a car back to set, I think about texting Lizzie. But this seems like a conversation better had in person. There has to be a way for us to get past this. But in the meantime, one thing is clear: if I'm going to make all of this work, I'm going to have to be more focused than ever. If that means calling my managers every single morning to confirm nothing "last-minute" has been added to the schedule by one of my groupmates, then that's what I'll do.

As soon as I get home that night, I'm ready to burrow under the covers and not come out until summer. Leah was a champ and managed to buy me a couple of hours to take care of my Girls Forever rehearsal. Then, after we wrapped filming, DB called us over to the studio to do some more work on the album. They've been having us try out different duets, though I haven't got up the courage to share my own song – the one Mina helped me recreate – with DB yet. Tonight, they had us record some classics. To be completely honest, it wasn't a great session. I was still worked up about the drama surrounding the earlier rehearsal, and the execs kept giving us contradictory instructions – yelling at us one minute for diverting too much from the original song arrangement, then criticising us for being boring and expected the next.

The only thought on my mind now, as I tiptoe into the villa, is thank *god* I did laundry yesterday. It's definitely a fresh, cosy pyjamas kind of night.

Jiyoon is already asleep when I enter the room and click on my bedside lamp.

"Rachel, is that you?" Jiyoon opens a bleary eye. "Ugh. What time is it? What are you doing?"

"It's late," I say gently. "Go back to sleep."

I change into my pyjamas, then gingerly open the closet door, trying to avoid the hinges squeaking, to hang up my checkered blazer, when suddenly I freeze.

My Balenciaga bag is missing.

I always leave it right there, on the upper shelf. I should be seeing a pop of beautiful blue leather right now, but instead I'm staring at a crumpled-up Moschino T-shirt I never wear, and a half-empty box of tampons. I drop down on my knees, my hands scrambling frantically over my closet floor, turning over my box of scarves and extra shoes. Where is it? I know I left it here.

I look over at Jiyoon. Her eyes are closed, but I can't tell whether or not she's fallen asleep again.

"Jiyoon," I whisper. "Do you know where my bag–"

"What the fuck, Rachel?" She blinks slowly and scowls. "If you're going to come home so late, at least have the decency to not wake me up too." She rolls over so her back is to me and puts a pillow over her head. "And can you please turn off the lights?"

For a second, I feel bad. Though it's been a couple of months, I know Jiyoon is still really down about her forced breakup with Jin, and the humiliation of the scandal. I've seen her crying and sniffling into her pillow when she thinks I'm asleep. Lord knows when I'm going through something like that, a good night's rest is the only thing that makes me feel even *slightly* better.

But at the same time, I want to grab her shoulders and shake her awake again and demand if she knows anything about my missing Balenciaga. I want to race through the villa, banging on doors, turning on lights, until I find out who took my bag and why. To demand answers about why they tried to sneak in a rehearsal without me.

But I'm just too exhausted – physically and mentally – to stir up drama in the middle of the night.

I flip off the light and slip out of the room, pulling out my phone to call Alex. Texts won't cut it right now.

He answers on the second ring. "Hello?"

"Hi," I whisper, stepping out into the hallway and sliding down onto the floor with my back against the wall.

"What's wrong?" he asks immediately.

"How do you know something's wrong?"

"I can tell by the way you said hi. You sound like Eeyore."

That gets a weak laugh out of me. I fill him in on the "last-minute" rehearsal fiasco, before admitting that the Balenciaga is gone. To my embarrassment, a lump rises in my throat as I talk and my eyes start misting.

"Sorry," I sniff. "I just feel like all these things are getting to me, you know? I'm starting to feel overwhelmed with work and the reality show and all the fashion stuff I want to do, and I feel so whiny for complaining about all these amazing things, but I can tell I'm starting to lose control. At the end of the day, I just want to rest and recharge, but when I live in a house with eight girls, that's not even a guaranteed thing. I miss living at home and I miss my parents. I can't even remember the last time I saw them, even though we live in the same city." I take a deep breath, wiping my eyes. "Sorry," I say again. "That was a lot."

"First of all, don't apologise for how you feel," Alex says. "And secondly, you're right. That is a lot. And can I just say something? Taking your bag isn't a small thing. And trying to make it look like you're slacking on your Girls Forever responsibilities is *definitely* not. That's crossing a line, Rachel."

It sounds so obvious when he says it. It *is* wrong. I think again of Carly Mattsson's words. Is this still bickering? Or has it now become a result of bitterness? Are the girls really just being thoughtless or are they purposely trying to hurt me?

"It'll be okay," I say finally. "This is probably all just one person," I add, my mind drifting towards Lizzie. She's always been cutthroat – maybe even more than Mina. At least with Mina, I actually believe that she's ruthless because she genuinely has such high expectations for herself and everyone around her. With Lizzie, it's just a petty streak a mile wide. "It's not the whole group," I tell Alex. "Once I figure out who it is and have a talk with her, things will be better."

"You sure?" he says.

"Yes," I say. But I can hear the doubt in my own voice.

"What are you going to do tonight?" he asks.

That's a good question. What am I going to do tonight? My brain is so fried, I don't think I have the capacity to make a coherent decision right now. "Could you give me some choices?" I say meekly.

"Of course," he says, his voice gentle. "A) Go all Hurricane Rachel and wake those girls up and get some answers." That gets another watery laugh from me. "B) Crawl back into bed, and try to tune out Jiyoon's snoring. C) Check into a hotel for the evening, and get some actual rest to clear your head."

"Thank you," I say softly. "Option C sounds perfect."

"Good, 'cause I just reserved you a room at the Park Hyatt," he says with the hint of a smile in his voice.

"You think you know me so well," I say, amazed to find that even after this awful night, I'm smiling too. He really *does* know me that well.

Maybe better than anyone.

It's scary to think about. That we could be so close, so fast. Honestly, maybe the fact that our relationship has mostly grown through texts and phone calls has helped get us to this intimate place so soon. Texting with Alex, I'm not worrying about how my hair came out that morning, or whether I'm hogging the shared popcorn at the movies. I can just be utterly myself, without any of that self-consciousness that you usually have to deal with. It's like the shield of the phone screen makes it easier to be vulnerable. Even now, sitting in the dark living room with my mascara melting and snot dripping, I feel totally safe. *I love him.*

Wait. WHAT?

Where did *that* thought come from? But it's like my brain is completely separate from the rest of me – chanting, *I love him, I love him,* over and over. But I don't really mean it. I can't. Can I? I've only known the guy for two months. I've had relationships with gel manicures longer than that.

I need to get off this phone before those three words – that I definitely *don't* mean – slip out. I thank him again and hang up, trying to steady the heavy thumping in my chest. Then I tiptoe back into my room, slip on some sweats and sneakers, throw my pyjama shorts into a tote bag along with my toiletries kit, and head out the front door.

By the time I check into my hotel room, wash up, and lie down in bed, I feel totally drained. Exhausted. Dead. Zapped. I'm about to turn off my lights when my phone pings.

Alex: All set?

Me: Cosy and comfy and ready for sleep. Wish I could thank you in person. Remind me again why you live in Hong Kong?

Alex: I could tell you it's because it's the financial hub of Asia, but really it's OX Café. Their oxtail soup would be worth living on Mars for.

Me: If you say so . . .

Alex: Don't take my word for it. Come try for yourself. Lane Crawford wants to have a meeting about your line. Can you make a trip over the second week in May?

I leap out of the bed and start silently screaming and jumping. This is huge. Up until now, I've only had success getting one department store here in Korea to agree to take the line. I never even considered that my bags could be in stores *internationally*.

And perhaps even more exciting than the business opportunity is the chance to be with Alex in person, to visit him where he lives, maybe even meet some of his friends. Up until now, we've only spent time together in neutral sites – Singapore and Paris – where we were both travellers. Spending time with Alex on his home turf feels like a big step. I'm equally excited and terrified.

Deep breaths, Rachel. In. Out.

I sit back down. I remind myself it'll be super risky there. Hong Kong has notoriously ruthless paparazzi. But if I'm travelling for a legitimate business reason, that should help explain any photos they might snap of the two of us together . . .

Playing it cool, I finally type back:

Me: I'll check my schedule and see if I can fit it in.

Me: PS, have Hot Cheetos waiting.

Thirteen

There are sequins everywhere. And I mean *everywhere*.

We're in the middle of a costume fitting for the multigroup concert in June where we'll be performing our newest single, "Midnight Prism." The costume concept is actually pretty cool. We'll come out in these sleek, slinky black gowns. Then, when we hit the chorus, we just unclip a hook on the side, and the dresses transition into these glowing, holographic-rainbow sequined minidresses, representing that color and joy can emerge from even the darkest night. I look myself up and down in the full-length mirror as a stylist fits me in a strapless violet minidress. The sequins are a little loose and keep sprinkling down on to my feet whenever I move. I suspect that for several days I'll still be finding hidden violet sequins in places sequins should never be.

I glance to my right, where another seamstress has a tape measure around Lizzie's waist, making adjustments to her aqua-blue sequinned dress. I've been mulling over how to handle the "impromptu" rehearsal situation since yesterday. I know I need to broach the subject with her, but I'm just not sure the best way to go about it.

As for the *other* thing occupying every last one of my brain cells since last night – the one about certain feelings I may or may not have for Alex – I've pushed that completely out of my head. It's too huge to contemplate while I've got a seventy-five-year-old woman pinning sparkly fabric under my boobs.

The seamstress finishes jotting down my measurements, then tells me I'm free to change back into my real clothes. But before I do, I decide to take a chance connecting with Lizzie.

"Hey, Lizzie?"

She turns to look at me, wincing as the movement jabs pins into her side.

"Um, hey," I continue awkwardly. "I was just wondering how Esther is. You guys are really close, right? I know how hard it can be to be away from your sister." I've decided not to bring up the rehearsal directly. Maybe Lizzie really *was* concerned about the new harmonies. And besides, if she did try to catch me missing rehearsal on purpose, better to get to the root of the problem, rather than focus on what's already been done.

Lizzie blinks at me. "You know what it's like?" I nod slowly. "Funny," she says, "I thought you got to spend fourteen hours a day with your sister every week filming a reality show." Shit. She's right. I start to double back, to agree with her and acknowledge how lucky Leah and I are, when Lizzie continues, "Or go back even further. I thought *you* were the one who got to live at home with your sister, instead of moving into the trainee house and hardly ever getting to see her."

She's right again, although I can't believe she'd hold a grudge from way back in our trainee days. I feel my cheeks redden, ashamed that I've taken for granted what precious time I do get to spend with Leah on a regular basis lately. I thought Lizzie and I had common ground here, but in reality, I'm in a much more fortunate position than she is.

I open my mouth to apologise, to better articulate the sympathy I feel for Lizzie's situation, but Lizzie just snaps "Are we done?" at the seamstress, who nods and lets her walk away.

"Her parents are splitting up," Sumin says, coming to stand beside me in an orange sequinned dress. "Apparently, it's been really rough on her sister."

My head whips around to where Lizzie is now sitting on the couch with Eunji. I had no idea. Why didn't she just *tell* me? I think back to all the times over the past month when I've come home chattering on obliviously about the shoot with Leah, about how excited my parents are for the show to start airing. I feel like a total jerk.

"Just give her some space, she'll be fine," Sumin says.

I'm dying to go over to Lizzie and apologise, but I try to heed Sumin's advice. Maybe she does just need some space.

Just then, Youngeun calls out from one of the makeup chairs, where she's been flipping through a magazine. "Hey, look at this." She flips the magazine around to show the rest of us. "*Entertainment Daily* did a fan poll, and Girls Forever got eighty-six percent of the vote." We all gather around the magazine to take a look for ourselves.

"Eighty-six?" Sunhee says with a frown. "That's not even a B+."

"It's not like a test score, baboya," Mina says, rolling her eyes and grabbing the magazine from Youngeun. "There were over twenty girl groups to choose from. The second-place group only got nine percent of the vote – "

"Ha! Sucks to suck, Butterscotch," Jiyoon interjects, looking over Mina's shoulder.

"–and everyone else got less than one per cent. We dominated," Mina finishes smugly, before handing the magazine off to me.

I scan quickly and farther down, *way* further down, I see Akari's group, TeenValentine, with a measly .03 per cent. I toss the magazine to Sumin. It may seem like just a silly fan poll, but the agencies take these things seriously. Besides Girls Forever's runaway win, DB also represents eight of the other groups in the top ten. JVC, Akari's agency, has only four, and they're all in the lower half of the rankings. I'm sure things are going to be tense over there for a few days. I wish I could send a text of support to Akari now, but our friendship has dissolved so completely over the past five years that I don't even have her current number.

"'I love Girls Forever because Lizzie's dance breaks are always next-level, says Clare of Melbourne,'" Sumin reads aloud from the article. "'She's totally my bias wrecker. Sorry, Eunji!'"

Lizzie grins as Eunji elbows her in the ribs. "Don't worry, Eunj, everyone's still saying how hot you look," she says, patting Eunji playfully on the butt.

"It's the new silver hair," Youngeun says as Eunji smiles softly. "You look so sexy, Khaleesi."

Eunji came back from her *Vogue* photo shoot with gorgeous silvery platinum waves. I'll admit, seeing her striking new look did give me a pang of jealousy over the shoot that should have been mine, but this morning's interaction with Lizzie has reminded me that I need to be grateful for the opportunities I *have* been given – not feel sorry for myself for the ones I have not.

And while I'm still frustrated about my missing Balenciaga, this little dose of perspective (and a good night's sleep in the Park Hyatt's amazing body-temperature-regulating bamboo sheets) has me feeling a little better than I was when I first discovered it missing from my closet. I've realised that the girls don't know how much the bag means to me. How could they? They think it's just some freebie from a random fan, and it's not like I ever told them anything different. Someone probably just borrowed it without asking. Wouldn't be the first time. Still . . . I *would* like to know where it is . . . I clear my throat, trying to keep my voice level. "Hey guys? Have any of you seen my Balenciaga bag? It's missing from my room."

"You mean the blue one the fan sent you?" Ari says, fussing with the cap sleeves of her yellow minidress as she slips on a pair of sky-high Prada platforms. "I haven't seen it."

For a second, I consider telling the girls the truth – that the bag wasn't just from a random fan, but from someone important to me. But this thing with Alex still feels so precious and new – we haven't even officially "defined the relationship" yet – that I'm hesitant to let them in. It's almost like if I tell them about Alex, if I let myself get too comfortable with the idea of us being together, then the universe might conspire to take it away from me. It's the same fear that sends my heart pounding every time I picture myself arriving in Hong Kong a few weeks from now. The *realness* of it all is so much scarier to contemplate.

The rest of the girls shrug and shake their heads. "Didn't you take it with you to Paris?" Eunji asks. "Maybe the airport lost it."

Frustration rises in my throat. I've worn that bag at least three times since Paris, and I know the girls have seen me using it – Eunji herself was complimenting the tasselled zipper pulls not two days ago. One of them has to have taken it. It's not like my bag grew a pair of legs and walked out of my closet on its own. But . . . Carly's words from our dinner in Paris roll through my mind. *Make sure you can spot the difference between bickering and bitterness.* Last night, I was certain that we'd moved into bitterness territory, but now it seems more likely that whoever took my bag probably just borrowed it and doesn't want to fess up in front of everyone else now that I've made it such a big thing.

Alex told me I have to put my mental health first.

And I know he's right. But I don't freak out when Leah takes my stuff without asking. So why am I treating my groupmates any differently? We may not be blood, but they're my sisters too, in a way. I know Leah and I are unique – we almost never fight. I think part of it is having such a big age gap between us. It's meant that we've never really been in each other's spaces – fighting over friends, or boys. But if we were as close in age as my groupmates and I are, I'm sure we'd have done a lot more squabbling growing up. This is normal sister stuff. Just bickering, not bitterness.

"Okay," I say with another deep breath. "Well, if everyone could keep an eye out for it around the house, I'd appreciate it."

"Kay," Lizzie says, hanging up her aqua-blue dress and sliding her Balmain jeans back on.

"Will do," Youngeun adds.

Well, I guess that's as good as I'm going to get for now. I slip out of my pinned violet minidress, a handful of sequins sprinkling into a pool at my feet as I redress into my white cashmere sweater and black miniskirt. I woke up super early at the hotel this morning and got back home before any of the girls were awake. I was already dressed and ready to go to the fitting when they all shuffled into the kitchen to grab Mason jars of overnight oats on our way out.

Then, just as we're about to leave the fitting room, one of our managers enters and approaches me.

"Rachel?" she says. "Mr. Noh would like to see you in his office when you're finished here."

"Oooooh," Jiyoon says dramatically, like I've just been called to see the principal. "Somebody's in trouble," she singsongs.

I roll my eyes, but feel a clench in my gut. *Am* I in trouble? Has he changed his mind about my fashion line already? Maybe I'm overthinking. After all, last time I was called into a private exec meeting, they offered me and Leah a reality show. I guess this could really go either way.

"I'll be right there," I say, and the manager nods and scurries back towards Mr. Noh's office. I quickly finish getting dressed and slip out of the fitting room. I guess there's only one way to find out.

As soon as I walk into Mr. Noh's office, I know right away.

It's bad.

I can tell by Mr. Noh's steely expression and the fact that Mr. Han is there, pacing the room, hands clasped tight behind his back. He stops pacing when I walk in.

I bow. "Ahnyounghasaeyo, Mr. Noh, Mr. Han."

"Sit," Mr. Noh says, his tone matching the expression on his face.

I do, folding my hands on my lap. For a few excruciating seconds, everyone is silent. The atmosphere in the room is so tense, I can practically feel the knots forming in my shoulders from how tightly I'm holding them. And then Mr. Han speaks.

"Did you stay at a hotel last night?" he asks.

I blink. I don't know what I expected, but it sure wasn't that. "I did," I say slowly.

"The front desk clerk at the Park Hyatt leaked it to *Reveal*," Mr. Han says. "Rumours are flying that you were there to meet your secret boyfriend."

My heart nearly flies into my throat, but I keep the shock on my face toned down. Hearing this admonishment from Mr. Han, who can sometimes feel almost more like a peer than an exec, is somehow even worse than hearing it from Mr. Noh. All traces of geniality are wiped clean from Mr. Han's young face – his mouth a grim line, his eyes cold. For his part, Mr. Noh is silent, watching me like a hawk, his expression giving little away about what's going through his mind. I instantly feel like I'm back in one of our chess matches. I carefully school my face, hoping my expression reads *They said what!?* and not *Oh shit, do they know about Alex?* Still, I *can* deny this allegation – I can say unequivocally that I did *not* go to that hotel to meet a boyfriend. After all, Alex was not there, and Alex is *not* my boyfriend. We've never used those terms with each other. It's like DB refusing to acknowledge Jiyoon's relationship with Jin because there was no photographic evidence of them actually doing anything romantic. Still, it feels like I'm avoiding an execution based on a technicality.

"That's ridiculous," I say with more confidence than I feel. "I was completely alone at the hotel. I only stayed there because our recording session ended late and I didn't want to disturb anyone by going home." Maybe it's not the *whole* truth, but it's most of the truth. It *was* late when I left here. They should know – they were both in that recording studio with me until almost two a.m. They don't need to know that when I got home, I was melting down over a lost bag.

I can still feel Mr. Noh's eyes on me, appraising. I swallow hard. Finally, he speaks.

"What you're saying may be true, but you still should have known how this would appear to the public," he says coldly. "You've been in this business long enough to know how things work. What you did was both selfish and thoughtless on your part."

I look down at my lap. He's not wrong. I *do* know how things work in this industry. My mind flashes to Alex. If the paparazzi are already sniffing around for details about a possible secret boyfriend, with only the flimsy evidence of my one-night solo hotel stay, what am I going to do when I'm in the same city as him again? The media is going to be all over us in Hong Kong. I couldn't bear to have what happened to Jiyoon and Jin happen to me and Alex. Even an innocent, platonic-looking picture of the two of us together could spell the end of our relationship. And getting caught wouldn't just be a disaster for me personally, it'd look bad on our entire group, not to mention DB. I think about our fan-poll ranking. It's clear that Girls Forever is truly the most beloved girl group on the K-pop scene right now. Our fans hold us to a high standard, and we've always met it. I can't let any of them – my groupmates, the company, or the fans – down. "I'm so sorry, Mr. Noh," I say, looking up at his face, my cheeks burning in shame. "I won't let it happen again."

He nods once with finality. "We expect more from you, Rachel. We're letting you off with a warning today, but this kind of behaviour is unacceptable. Understood?"

"Yes, Mr. Noh."

"You're free to go now."

I rise to leave and then pause, remembering something else from last night. "By the way, I should tell you. Lane Crawford in Hong Kong is interested in carrying my fashion line, so I'll need to travel there for a meeting in a few weeks. Do you think we could have that worked into my schedule?"

Mr. Noh raises his eyebrows and I can tell he's impressed. I feel the slightest hint of relief that I'm living up to my promise to make sure my fashion brand reflects well on DB.

"I don't see that being a problem," he says. "I'm glad to see you taking this fashion enterprise seriously."

I grin with pride. "Thank you, Mr. Noh," I say, bowing.

"Oh and Rachel, don't forget," Mr. Noh says just as I'm about to exit his office. I pause and turn back to him. "Everyone is counting on you. Don't let us down."

⭐ *Fourteen* ⭐

Don't let us down.

The words repeat themselves over and over in my mind throughout the next few weeks, even as April in Korea – full of crisp breezes and jacket weather – morphs into early May, when the many trees throughout the city begin to blossom. May is one of the prettiest months in Seoul, and I'm finding the spring is filling me with design inspiration – florals! Pastels! Seersucker!

But through all of the excitement and the anticipation of my Hong Kong visit, there's this quiet current of worry. This meeting with Lane Crawford is a big deal, and I need it to go perfectly. I spend the whole three and a half hour flight writing out flashcards to prep for my presentation.

When I touch down at Hong Kong International Airport, Alex is waiting for me in his car for a quick escape. Since he's not really a target of media attention, we figure he won't be followed or recognised. But he told me he's "prepared for anything," whatever that means. Meanwhile, I'm wearing big sunglasses with an inconspicuous baseball cap pulled low over my face. So far so good. But just to be safe, he parks in the long-term lot and texts me where to go to find his car. I slip into the front seat and lower my sunglasses, glancing into the rearview mirror.

"Are we in the clear?"

"I think we are." He turns to look at me with a grin. "Hi."

"Hi." I grin back. He leans across the console and then we are kissing, and I can feel the energy between us.

"Got something for you," he says as we pull apart, reaching across my body to open the glove box.

He pulls out a snack bag of Hot Cheetos, adorned with a stick-on bow.

I burst out laughing and lean in for another kiss.

"Wow, what service. This is definitely boosting up your Uber rating, sir."

I can't wipe the smile off my face, even as I realise my baseball cap has fallen off the back of my head. Who cares? Part of me wishes we could just spend the rest of the weekend right here, in the darkness of the parking lot.

We drive out of the lot and into traffic.

Suddenly, a flash of movement in the rearview mirror catches both of our attention. To get out of long-term parking, we still had to pass by one of the pickup areas outside the arrival terminals. Several people who were hanging out by the airport doors, waiting for their rides, have started running toward the van parked behind us. I see one of them reach into his duffel bag and pull out a camera.

Oh my god. How is that even possible? Are they freakin' *magic*? "Alex, it's undercover paparazzi!" I say, panicked. "It must be for someone else, right?"

"Oh shit," Alex says. "Not worth any chances. Buckle up, Rachel. It might get a little bumpy."

I fumble for my seat belt as he peels through the traffic.

And much to my shock . . . the van immediately follows us, swerving around cars to stay right on our tail.

"Shit, shit, shit," I say. "They're following us!"

Alex presses harder on the gas pedal, picking up speed. Cars honk furiously at us as we weave through the lanes. My heart thumps wildly in my chest.

"Don't worry, I'm an excellent driver," he says.

I twist in my seat to see the van still hot on our heels. "They're gaining on us!"

Alex presses a button on the car's touch screen to make a call. The phone rings, and whoever he's calling picks up immediately.

"Alex?" the voice says.

"Hey, Daniel. You see the situation?"

"Yep, I see it," Daniel says.

"Who is that?" I ask.

"My buddy. He drove with me to the airport in his separate car in case something like this happened. See the red Honda behind us?"

I was so fixated on the van that I didn't even notice the red car speeding through the lanes behind us. It has the slightest lead against the paparazzi van, but they're pretty neck and neck.

"Time for the plan, A?" Daniel asks.

"Time for the plan," Alex says. "Rachel, hold on tight."

The phone goes dead as Alex zooms off the highway and on to the city roads, followed closely by Daniel and the paparazzi with hardly any regard for traffic light signals. I cling on to the car handles for dear life, my heart racing, sweat starting to form at my forehead. As terrifying as this all is, I can't help but feel slightly thrilled by the adrenaline pumping through my veins. Wait until I tell Leah that I was in a high-speed car chase! If I make it out alive, that is.

Alex makes a sharp left, swerving into a narrow alley. Daniel is right behind us and the paparazzi van right behind him. The alley is getting more and more narrow, nearly scraping the sides of our car. Oh my god, oh my god. We're not going to make it.

Suddenly, Daniel slams on his brakes, the red Honda skidding to a stop in the middle of the alleyway. The paparazzi van nearly crashes right into him, but they stop just in time. With Daniel's car blocking them, and the alley too narrow for the van to go around, the paparazzi are stuck, forced to back out of the alley and find another route. I see them in the rearview mirror, the photographer stepping out of the passenger door and slamming his hand on the hood of the van, just as we squeeze out of the alley and make our escape.

Alex and I both let out a victory scream.

"I can't believe that just happened!" I cry. So this was what he meant by being *prepared for anything*.

"I told you I'm a good driver," he says, laughing and slapping his hands against the steering wheel. "Whew. That was fun."

As we get further and further away from the alleyway, my heart rate starts to go back down to normal. I place my hand against my chest, feeling my heartbeat, and turn to look at Alex. "When you said we can get through anything together, you really meant it, huh?"

Alex grins. "Yep. It's you and me against the world, Rachel. You, me, and our good friends like Daniel, that is."

I laugh. Me and Alex against the world. With him by my side, I really do feel like we could take on anything.

High-speed car chase and all.

Even though Alex offered to host me, I booked a room at the Four Seasons – it's just safer that way, with the possibility of paparazzi still lurking. The chase scene at the airport hammered home the fact that we'll have to lie low this trip. As much as I'd love to stroll through the street markets hand in hand with Alex, I'm just as happy to spend the weekend hanging in his apartment, flipping through the books on his shelf and making fun of his colour-coordinated cereal boxes. His buddy Daniel has been amazing helping us get between the hotel and Alex's apartment without being spotted, going ahead as a lookout and scoping out any potential photographers who might be hiding nearby, even offering to create a diversion if we need one.

It's sweet how willing he is to help his best friend, though when Daniel starts to describe how he'd use leftover sparklers from New Year's as a distraction technique, Alex eventually has to say, "Okay, 007, I think we've got it from here." From the way Alex says this, I get the sense this isn't his first time having to temper Daniel's plans, and eventually, I learn that Alex and Daniel were bonded for life during a college-prank-gone-wrong, which somehow involved an evil bunny, a priceless violin, and an LSAT tutor.

Sunday night, we're hanging at Alex's place, trying to make our own oxtail soup, since going to OX Café would be too risky, when all of a sudden Alex lets out a swear and runs out of the kitchen.

"What? Did I ruin it?" I say, instantly jumping back from the stove. I warned him I wasn't exactly a pro in the kitchen, but he insisted I could handle stirring the beef and vegetables.

"No, it's not that. I'm supposed to be on a video call with my family for my grandma's birthday today!" Alex yells from the next room. I turn down the stove's heat and join him in the living room just in time to see him pull out his laptop and settle on to the couch, glancing at the time on the screen.

"Oh good," he says. "We're only five minutes late."

"We?" I say hesitantly, taking a seat next to him. "You want me to meet your family?"

"Of course!" he says, still focused on logging in. Then his fingers pause over the keyboard and he turns to look at me. "But you don't have to if you don't feel comfortable. I understand."

I smile and give Alex a kiss on the cheek. "If you trust them, I do too."

The butterflies kick in as Alex logs on to his family video call. I've never met the family of the guy I'm dating before, except for that one time in Canada when I wound up having dinner with Jason's three exuberant aunts, but that wasn't really anything official. I tuck my hair behind my ears and smooth out my white T-shirt, stained with tomato paste, wishing I had time to put together a more proper "meet the family" outfit. Alex's grandma, parents, and brothers pop up on the screen.

Along with what appear to be a dozen of his aunts and uncles and cousins.

I freeze. When he said he had a video call with his family, I didn't realize he meant his *whole* family. I do trust Alex, and I want to trust his family, but my K-pop survival instincts are ringing all kinds of alarms. What if someone takes a screengrab and sells it to *Reveal*? What if someone posts a group shot on Insta, and the netizens find it? What if? What if? What if?

"Halmoni!" Alex says. "Happy birthday!"

Alex's grandma has the exact same smile as Alex, her eyes crinkling and dimple flashing as she waves joyfully at the camera. "Alex! Good to see you!" I spot two of her three cats weaving their way across her lap. Judging by the size of the grey one, I'm guessing that's Fats Domino.

"Sorry I'm late," Alex says. He clears his throat and grins, glancing at me. "Everyone, this is my girlfriend, Rachel."

Girlfriend?

The room suddenly feels too hot, like I'm still standing in front of Alex's gas range, steam from the pot blasting into my face. He's never used that word to describe me before. At least not in my presence. As close as we've become over the last few months, and as strong as my feelings are for him, putting such a definitive label on our relationship seems like a step too far, too fast. Like I'm going from doing something I *probably* shouldn't do, to something I *definitely* shouldn't do. K-pop idols can't be *girlfriends*.

I feel Alex's eyes on me and realise everyone is waiting for me to respond.

"Ahnyounghaseyo," I say quickly, bowing my head. "So nice to meet you all. Halmoni, happy birthday." My heart is thudding in my chest. I glance at the tiny boxes of various Jeons who have dialled into the call, noting a few of the younger family members whispering to each other and nudging each other in the ribs. I hear "Girls Forever!" whisper-shouted from a box in the corner where a girl with a ponytail who looks about ten is sitting on her mom's lap. Then they realize their mic is on, and immediately switch themselves to mute. Well, guess the cat's out of the bag.

"Hello, Rachel!" Alex's mother says, pulling the focus away from the apparent fan. I recognise her right away from the family photos he's shown me. She has a calm, reassuring vibe, and even through video chat, I feel instantly safer in her presence. "Alex has told us so much about you. Congratulations on the fashion line!"

I bow my head again. "Thank you so much. Alex has been an incredible support."

"Hello! Hello! Sorry, I'm late. Happy Birthday, Umma." A bigger man with messy hair and an untucked dress shirt blows into the frame, his webcam jostling as he gets himself situated. Based on the scattered vibe he's giving off, and the eye rolls I spot from some other Jeons, I get the impression that this is somebody who is often late to family gatherings.

"My uncle Hugh," Alex whispers to me.

"Work's been a nightmare. Everyone's merging and acquiring like it's going out of style," Hugh rambles in a blustery rush. "Anyway, what'd I miss?"

There's a pause, and then eventually Alex's mother chimes in with, "We were just being introduced to Alex's girlfriend, Rachel."

"Oh excellent, where are you, Rachel? How do I get this thing to show everyone at once?"

"Put it on gallery mode, Uncle Hugh!" the ponytailed girl says.

Beside me, Alex starts silently chuckling, and I can't help but giggle too. "Hi, I'm over here!" I say. "It's nice to meet you, Mr. Jeon."

"Ah, there you are. Great to meet you. So Rachel, what do you do? In the finance biz like my nephew here?"

Again, there's a pause. Incredulous faces fill each frame, and the ponytailed girl looks personally offended.

"Um, I'm a singer," I say hesitantly.

"Oh, good for you! Best of luck with that – the entertainment industry can be so hard to break into. I know a guy from school – forty-five and still singing in cafés. Pretty sad, really. Oh Nora, I heard you had a monster soccer game last weekend!"

And with that, the conversation shifts to Nora and Jeremy, Alex's ten-year-old twin cousins from Seattle, who take turns showing Halmoni their soccer trophies and new cleats. Over the next thirty minutes, I try to let myself relax into the conversation, but the word *girlfriend* keeps ringing in my ears.

Eventually, when Halmoni informs us all that it's time for Elvis's diabetes shot, the call ends. Alex closes the laptop screen and turns to face me, taking my hands in his.

"How was that? I hope it wasn't too overwhelming," he says. "I promise, no one was recording or anything. My mom warned them all ahead of time – they get it. Well, I mean, except Uncle Hugh, obviously. But I think you're safe there."

I shake my head and smile. "I'm not worried about that." And it's true. I may have spent most of the video call worrying about the official status of my relationship with Alex, but even through my nervous state I could tell that his family was genuinely kind and respectful. There's no way Alex's mom or Halmoni or even little cousin Nora would sell us out. "Your family's pretty great," I say to Alex.

He grins back. "Yeah. They are." For a moment, I get lost in Alex's eyes, picturing us at future Jeon family gatherings, imagining how Alex's mom and Umma would get along, how Nora would die at the chance to spend time with Leah . . . Would it be so wrong to let myself be his girlfriend? To call him my boyfriend and bring him home to meet Appa?

Buzz! Buzz!

The timer on Alex's stove buzzes, alerting us that the oxtail soup is done. And with it, I feel all my happy fantasies zapping away. *Don't let us down,* Mr. Noh said. I think of Kang Jina and Jiyoon, who chose to follow their hearts and paid the ultimate price: Jina losing her career as an idol, and Jiyoon losing her boyfriend.

I need to get out of here. My brain is a scrambled mess. I should be focusing on how to best position my bags for Lane Crawford, not getting lost in fantasies of things that will never happen so long as I'm a DB idol.

I hop off the couch, grab my jacket from the back of the dining room chair, and look around for where I left my bag.

"Hey, where are you going?" Alex says, standing in the living room doorway, his brow furrowing in confusion. "Don't you want to taste the fruits of your labour?"

"I just realised how late it is," I say, avoiding his eye. I feel bad about abandoning our plans for the evening, but I know it's for the best. I can't let myself get distracted. My work has to come first. "I have a lot of prep work to do for tomorrow's meeting. I should probably just grab some room service from the hotel." Finally, I spot my bag hanging on the knob of his apartment door, and sling it over my shoulder. "But I'll see you tomorrow, right?"

"Sure," he says, still looking at a loss.

"Great, see you then!"

I throw open his door and am halfway down the hallway when I hear Alex say, "Bye?"

Fifteen

My first year as a trainee, I had a meeting with the DB executives. Eleven-year-old Rachel was so racked with nerves that when I was dismissed and could finally unclench my fists, I found both palms marked by deep crescent-moon imprints. They didn't fade for the rest of the day. Even now meetings with DB execs can still be slightly terrifying. But at least with the execs, I know what to expect. Mr. Han is the most easygoing, but that doesn't mean you should push his buttons. Ms. Shim might give you some intense eye contact, but she's usually fair. Mr. Lim can be highly opinionated but also gives out compliments more freely than the rest.

Fashion industry meetings, though? That I have no road map for.

The secretary peers over her computer screen at me. "Let me know if you change your mind about coffee or tea."

"Thank you, but I'm good," I say. I already consumed too much caffeine back at the café in the hotel lobby where Alex and I met up earlier this morning.

I still felt bad about bailing so suddenly last night, even though Alex didn't bring it up. But when I asked how the oxtail soup turned out, he just gave a small, tight smile and said, "It was delicious. Wish you could have tasted it."

We ordered iced coffees (I figured a straw meant less opportunity for spillage on my carefully selected outfit), and Alex quizzed me with my flash cards until it was time to head to Lane Crawford.

"You'll be great," he said as we approached the gleaming glass office building. "I'll meet you back at Four Seasons after."

"You're not coming?" I asked, alarmed. I assumed Alex would be by my side at the meeting, offering moral support.

"Nah, I'm just the facilitator. I get you guys in a room together. You take it from there," he said with a confident smile. "Remember, Rachel, this is your vision. No one knows this line better than you. You're going to nail it." And with a quick kiss, he was gone.

In the Lane Crawford reception area, I glance at my watch. The meeting was supposed to have started twenty minutes ago.

Finally, the secretary leads me into a sleek conference room with floor-to-ceiling windows that give us a view of the bay. A woman dressed in a chic pantsuit, her dark hair pulled into a low ponytail, rises from the mahogany table to shake my hand. "You must be Rachel Kim. I'm Celeste Nguyen, senior buyer for Lane Crawford Hong Kong. It's nice to meet you."

I smile and shake Celeste's hand, but on the inside I'm panicking. I was expecting to speak with assistant buyer Richard Chang, a more junior executive. He was the one I did all my research on, the highlight reel of his career meticulously printed on flash cards I spent the whole night reviewing. I know that Richard has a soft spot for quilted bags and that he thinks the colour chartreuse is the worst thing to have ever happened to fashion; I know nothing about Celeste.

"Richard had a last-minute emergency, so I'll have to take today's meeting," Celeste explains.

"That's great!" I say brightly. "I mean, not great about the emergency, but . . ." I trail off and paste a small smile on my face. *Calm down, Rachel.*

"So," Celeste says, taking a seat and gesturing for me to do the same. "Rachel Kim. You have an impressive resume as part of Girls Forever."

She keeps her face neutral and I can't quite read her tone – is she a secret fan? Does she hate our music? Did she only look me up five minutes before the meeting?

"We've carried a celebrity fashion line before," Celeste continues. "Do you know the Ong sisters?"

I nod – Christine Ong has starred in some of the most popular films in Asia, and Michelle Ong, while not an actor herself, married a famous one. Well, actually, they never got officially married. I remember an interview where Michelle said while she loved her partner, she didn't want to confine herself to a specific label, because terms like "husband" and "wife" are steeped in meaning and complicated connotations. Kind of exactly how I feel about being called Alex's girlfriend yesterday. I love the sentiment behind it, but the term itself is so loaded for me as a K-pop idol.

"Anyway, it was definitely quite the experience working with the Ongs," Celeste wraps up, and I realise I've tuned out her whole story.

"That's so great," I say.

She raises an eyebrow at me. "You think it's great that Christine had a massive fight with Michelle and tried to pull their line hours before it was set to launch in our stores?"

My stomach drops. "Of course that's not what I meant," I say quickly. "I only meant – it's great to hear how experienced you are and how you're able to handle anything. I feel like I can trust my designs to you."

It's only after the words are out of my mouth that I hear how I made it sound like she has something to prove to me, and not that I have something to sell to her.

Celeste waves my words away. "It was fine. They only had nine pieces in their collection – I've never seen someone try to launch a brand with so few items. Even if Christine had succeeded in cancelling it – I don't think anyone was taking the line that seriously anyway, with it being so small."

I swallow the lump in my throat. I have even fewer than nine pieces – I have *six*. Is that going to be a problem? I'm suddenly realising that I have no idea what's standard for an accessories brand launch. Six felt like a good number, especially for big statement pieces like my bags, but maybe I should have researched this more.

Celeste laces her fingers together. "So, what inspired you to get into fashion?" she asks.

"I've loved fashion since I was a little kid," I say, delving into my story. My nerves begin to calm as I explain my journey into fashion. This is the one part of today's presentation that I didn't need any notecards for. "While I ended up pursuing a music career, I'm not just a singer and dancer. I'm a performer, and part of performance is what you wear. There is so much power in what clothes and accessories you choose."

Celeste nods, then says, "Let's see your line sheet and your samples."

I bring over my handbag prototypes and walk her through the construction and my choice of colours, each bold and distinct yet complementary to each other. I've talked about these bags so many times, the words flow naturally.

"And with the detachable strap," I say when I get to my trainee years-inspired bag, "you can fit in anywhere."

Celeste pauses, running her hand over the bag's leather strap. "This is lovely. Can I see the rest of the bags?"

"There are only six," I say hesitantly.

A crease forms between her brows. "Ah, I see."

Definitely should have researched more.

"I plan on having hundreds of new handbag designs for the next season," I find myself saying even as I think, *Hundreds?!* What am I thinking? Hopefully Celeste will understand I'm speaking in hyperbole – unless one hundred bags really is par for the course? My head is swimming. Designing the bags was so much fun that I didn't realise how out of my depth I am when it comes to the *business* of fashion.

"Let's talk about this season, though," Celeste says, brushing past my possibly ridiculous, possibly totally normal promise to have hundreds of new bags next season. "What's your delivery?" She's glancing over my one-sheet of business specs.

"I want to deliver something that is practical and suited to everyday use, but is still a statement piece," I say confidently. But Celeste looks confused.

"What about your delivery *time*?" she asks. "How fast can you get your handbags to us should we end up wanting to have them in our stores?"

"I can have them delivered as quickly as you need them," I say, embarrassed to have misunderstood the fashion business shorthand.

"You don't need to check with your production team?" Celeste raises her eyebrows.

Shit. Of course I do. What am I doing making promises about delivery time without checking on the logistics? "Um yes," I say sheepishly. "I'll have to get back to you with the specifics."

Celeste smiles – but is it a real smile, or is she just being nice? "Why don't you leave these prototype bags with me, and my team will review them further. We can reconnect in a few weeks. Maybe you'll have a better sense of your logistics and plans for next season then?"

I nod and summon a small smile as she leads me back to reception. I'm grateful that she's even offering to review the bags further, but I can't help but feel like all this meeting did was expose how much of an amateur I really am.

On the flight home, I make a plan. I might have flubbed the Lane Crawford meeting, but I can't let myself dwell on it. Going forward, I'm just going to have to make sure I'm nothing less than 100 per cent prepared, 100 per cent professional. And as for whether or not I'm technically Alex's girlfriend, and what it all means . . . well, I can't dwell on that either. I can't. There's too much on the line for me to let myself get distracted.

Back in Seoul, I throw myself into all my commitments. With our performance for the multigroup concert now just a month away, Girls Forever rehearsals have kicked back into high gear. It turns out Sunhee is going to miss the event because it conflicts with a radio awards show she's attending, so we have to rework all the dance formations for eight girls instead of nine. Choreo combinations play on a loop in my brain. Hip pop. Hair toss. Shoulder shimmy. Hip pop, other side. During reality-show shooting with Leah, I try to just relax and enjoy myself, knowing that our authentic sister relationship is what they're trying to capture on film, but even then I have a constant stream of thoughts running through my mind: ignore the camera, but make sure you're in frame. Don't order risotto for lunch again; last time you had the garnish stuck in your teeth, and the netizens had a field day. Don't look tired. Don't look stressed. Don't, don't, DON'T mention Alex on camera.

I have alarms set on my phone to make sure I get to everything five minutes early. I don't miss a single practice. I'm not late for a single phone call with Lotte, the Korean retailer carrying my line. I throw back three espresso shots before each twelve-hour-shoot day with Leah. I can't let anything slip. I need to be on my game 24/7. I have to reassure DB that I'm keeping all my commitments on track, that I can do it all. And maybe, more than anything, I have to reassure myself.

"Unni, are you doing okay?" Leah asks me when we meet at the studio to record for our album. "You look really tired."

"I'm fine, I'm fine," I say.

She frowns like she doesn't believe me, but she doesn't push it. Instead, she holds up a tray of iced coffees, passing one to me. "Here. I got this for you."

I could weep on the spot. "You're a lifesaver," I say, ripping the wrapper off the straw and downing half the coffee in one sip. The brain freeze kills, but I don't have the option of drinking cold liquids at a normal pace. No time for luxuries like that.

Finally, we wrap our recording session and I race back to the villa to prep for tonight. We've been invited to the premiere of *When I Loved You*, and the hair and makeup team DB arranged for us has already been at the villa for two hours. We usually only go all-out like this for awards shows, but I guess for Mina's cinema debut, an exception will be made.

When I get home, I find the living room has been turned into glam central, with lighted mirrors and pop-up salon chairs everywhere. Most of the girls are already dolled up – Sumin's putting on a pair of delicate chandeliered earrings while Ari slips on a pair of Manolos. Eunji is staring at herself in the mirror, looking a little pale, applying and reapplying her lipstick. It's been a while since we had a red carpet event – and we've never attended one with *the* Song Geonwu. Everyone is anxious to look their best.

I change into my Fleur du Mal silk robe and try to scarf down some red bean doughnuts from Noe Bakery while a stylist loads my hair up with curlers.

"If you eat that too fast, you're gonna bloat up," Mina says with an eyebrow raised. She looks stunning in her sleek high ponytail, dramatic eye shadow, and off-the-shoulder jumpsuit, but I can sense a bit of nervous energy behind her placid expression. Her dad's going to be at the premiere tonight, and though she'd never admit it, I know she wants to impress him with her acting performance. You can always tell when Mina's nervous about something because she starts projecting total confidence about whatever she's uncertain about. It's actually kind of impressive. All week she's been haughtily reminding us that while the whole group was invited to the premiere, *she'll* be getting VIP treatment as a member of the cast. And now she's all glammed up and ready for the spotlight. Honestly, I'm relieved. Going to an event where I can just *be* there and not have to worry about being centre stage is the closest thing I'm going to get to rest right now and I'm all for it. "I'll leave some Spanx on your bed," Mina says as she heads down the hall toward her own room – and I honestly can't tell if she's being nasty or genuinely trying to be helpful.

A makeup artist swoops in to start my face, and I can tell by the way she keeps going back and gently dabbing more concealer under my eyes that I must have some seriously dark circles going. Once my makeup is complete, the hair stylist comes back and tells me my rollers need to set for another ten minutes, so I head to my room to change into my dress. I'm reaching into my closet to grab the garment bag – and trying not to sigh as I see the still-empty spot where my Balenciaga should be – when suddenly my phone starts trilling out the FaceTime ring. I lay the gown on my bed, lock the bedroom door (sorry, Jiyoon), and answer the call.

"Wow, great look! Very Lisa Simpson," Alex says, grinning at my curlers.

After the Lane Crawford meeting, Alex drove me to the airport to catch my flight back to Seoul. I was quiet and crabby the whole ride, and Alex could tell that the best thing was to just let me stew. I hate to admit it, but in that moment, I was actually kind of annoyed at him. Why didn't he tell me he wasn't coming to the meeting? His last-minute absence totally threw me off. And why did he call me his girlfriend to his family without even talking to me about it first? If I'm being honest, *that* was what really had me distracted during the meeting.

But as soon as I left him at security, with a quick kiss on the cheek and terse "Bye," I knew my frustrations were misdirected. I was pissed at myself for screwing up that meeting. I had no one to blame but myself for how it went. Before the plane took off, I sent him a string of texts, thanking him for setting up the opportunity and apologising for being such a grouch.

So now when Alex's face pops up on my phone screen, easily cracking a joke, I feel like I can let go of the awkwardness of Hong Kong. I may not have broached the whole boyfriend/girlfriend conversation yet, but we're back to being Alex and Rachel – and for now, that's the only definition I care about.

"Thanks, Lisa Simpson's my biggest style icon, didn't you know?" I say with a straight face.

He laughs, but then his expression grows serious – mock serious, though; I can always read him. "Hey, listen, I have something kind of bad to tell you."

"Yeah, what is it?" I ask, smiling.

"I know I'm Korean, and this is kind of blasphemous to say, but I've never actually had soondubu before."

I make a gasp of exaggerated horror.

"I know, I know," he says. "Do you know a good place? I was thinking you could take me next week when I'm in Seoul."

This time, I gasp for real.

"When you're *what*?"

"Last-minute business trip just came up," he says, grinning ear to ear.

I know just the place I'd want to take him to – I have a million places I want to take him, people I want him to meet. Leah spilled the beans about Alex to my parents as soon as she and I got back from Singapore. Umma's been hounding me ever since to send her a recent photo, his school transcripts, a list of his favourite foods . . . If she knew Alex was coming into town, I'm pretty sure she'd be standing at the arrivals gate at Incheon with a sign bearing his name. And honestly, I'd love for him to get to know my family, to learn more about my life before K-pop. I want to take him to my old school, where I first met the twins. To the Dongdaemun Night Market, strolling Mukja Golmok looking for the best dumplings. Live music at Owl's Rooftop.

But how much of that can we actually do? There are eyes everywhere here. If being with Alex on his home turf felt like a big step, being with him here in Korea would be *huge*.

"If you're worried about the paparazzi getting pictures," Alex says, reading my expression, "I have a friend who lives in Seoul. She can come out with us – that way if the paparazzi get photos, it'll be photos of two girls and a guy. It's less suspicious."

I shake my head. "No, I want to see you one-on-one."

"We'll figure it out," he says encouragingly.

"Any word from Lane Crawford?" I ask. Celeste had said we'd reconnect in a few weeks, but it's been radio silence ever since.

Alex's face grows serious again. But this time, I can tell it's for real. "Not yet," he says gently. "But that doesn't necessarily mean it's a pass. Maybe they just haven't had a chance to review the designs again yet."

My heart sinks. Or maybe they *have* reviewed them and they decided I'm too amateur to even bother responding to. Given the awkwardness of the meeting, I wouldn't be surprised, but it's still a blow. I hate that I let myself get my hopes up. An international presence for my first-ever fashion line? What was I thinking?

Just then, the doorknob wiggles. "Rachel!" Jiyoon calls out. "Why is this locked?"

"Oops, that was by accident!" I yell. To Alex, I whisper, "I gotta go," and then I hang up the phone.

When we arrive at the premiere, the girls and I pose for a group photo. I quickly smooth out my dress – a cream-coloured fitted strapless maxi with a ruffle trim and thigh-high slit – and sweep my waves over one shoulder, smiling for the camera. After nearly six years of this, I've learned how to give the world a radiant beam, even when inside, I want to curl up and cry. After we get the group shot, Mina rushes up to greet Park Yuhwa, who plays her mother in the movie, even though they're only ten years apart. As Mina poses for a few more shots with Yuhwa, the rest of us start heading towards the event hall. I can feel the cool of the air-conditioning as Sumin holds the door open for me, and I'm dying to step inside, out of the warm late-May evening air, when suddenly I hear my name being called.

"Rachel, hi!"

I turn at the familiar voice and see Maxwell Li-Harris waving at me from behind a camera. The *Vogue* photographer from Paris! I wave back as he approaches me.

"So good to see you again!" I say. "What are you doing in Seoul?"

He gestures to his camera. "Working, of course." He laughs. "It's for that feature we're doing on Korean entertainment's crossover to the West. I begged Anna to let me come grab some shots here in Seoul – it's been too long since I've had a good triangle kimbap from a 7-Eleven here."

I laugh. "Surely there are better kimbaps out there?"

He shrugs. "It hits different when you buy one from 7-Eleven." He leans back to admire my outfit. "You look fabulous as always. That colour looks great on you. And those hair clips!"

I touch the gold-bar statement clips pinned to the side of my hair. I'd thrown them in after the stylist took my curlers out and I was feeling a little too poodle-y. The clips help tone down the volume.

"Why thank you."

"That cream-and-gold combo . . . You're totally matching with the main male leads!" he says excitedly. "I have to take your photo together."

"Oh," I say in surprise as he ushers me over to where Jason

and Song Geonwu are posing for the cameras. I'm not really up for more photos, but duty calls.

"Rachel!" Jason says when he sees me. He's wearing a cream suit with a muted gold shirt. We really are coincidentally matching. "So glad you could make it! Did you see Sena yet?" He gestures across the red carpet, and I see Sena wrapping up an interview with the *Star*, her bright red hair glowing against the sheeny pearl of her gown. She winks at us, and I give her a quick wave back.

"Rachel Kim from Girls Forever?" Song Geonwu smiles and bows in greeting. Wow. He looks exactly like he does on-screen. Tall and built with a lopsided grin and a distinctive beauty mark just below his right eye. He smells like citrus cologne. He's wearing a sleek black suit with a cream-coloured shirt underneath. "Great to finally meet you," he says while keeping his teeth together in a megawatt smile. I realise Maxwell is already snapping away, and quickly turn my lips up into a smile as well. When Maxwell takes a break to check his camera's digital screen, Geonwu continues more naturally, "I've heard great things."

He has? From who? I'm sure Mina wasn't talking me up. Could it have been Jason?

"You all look perfect!" Maxwell calls out. "Can you get a little closer for these next shots?"

Jason and Geonwu both take a step in, and Geonwu puts his arm around my waist while Jason slings his arm over my shoulder. Out of the corner of my eye, I see my groupmates waiting for me so we can all go into the party together. Not just waiting. Watching, Mina's eyes narrowing the longer I spend between the two male leads of her movie.

As soon as Maxwell finishes up with his photo spree, I wave goodbye to Jason and Geonwu and rush to go join the girls. "Thanks for waiting," I say.

There's an obvious shift in energy. Mina, who couldn't stop chattering and beaming the whole way here, is fuming now. Even Lizzie and Eunji are shooting me dirty looks.

"Really, Rachel, you have to steal my thunder tonight of all nights?" Mina mutters under her breath as we head towards the screening room. Her glance darts off to the side, and I follow her gaze to find Mr. Choo waiting in line for the men's room, arms crossed, a severe expression on his face. Oh no. Did he catch my spontaneous photo op just now? I know how much tonight means to Mina. And how important it is that *she* be the one the media reports on tomorrow – not just for her own pride, but also so that her father will take her acting dream seriously.

"No, Mina, I'm sorry," I say earnestly. "You're totally the star tonight. It's just Maxwell is a photographer I met in Paris, and– "

"Paris, again?" Lizzie rolls her eyes. "We get it, Rachel. You went to Paris. You met cool people. You don't have to bring it up every chance you get."

"Honestly," Eunji says, looking even more annoyed than both Mina and Lizzie. In fact, she doesn't just seem annoyed.

She looks legitimately upset. "What gives you the right to just take whatever you want?" she practically spits. Then her brows are knitted together for a moment, as if that's not quite what she meant to say. Mina gives her an odd look, then Eunji mumbles, "I mean, Mina's spotlight. You can't just take it."

Before I can open my mouth to say something to fix this, my eight groupmates walk into the event hall without me.

⭐ Sixteen ⭐

I spend the whole premiere screening half watching Mina cry over Song Geonwu after a car accident leaves him with amnesia, and half watching real-life Mina three seats down from me out of the corner of my eye. When we first sat down, she was still fuming. But luckily for me, once the film got underway, she seemed to calm down. Probably distracted by watching herself on the big screen. Actually, even I have to admit that Mina's pretty good. I'm glad she took the chance and pursued this, even though she knew her father wouldn't like it.

Farther down the row I hear stifled sobs. Eunji has tears streaming down her face. I mean, sure, this moment when Geonwu tells his father he'll never forget him is moving, but not *that* moving. Between her tears now and her weird outburst earlier, something more has to be going on. She's definitely been acting a little off lately. Since our trainee days, she's always followed in Mina's wake, but I never got that same cutting edge from her that I did from Lizzie. I actually always felt a little sorry for her. She's kind of like Sunhee – she doesn't know her own worth. She really is one of the most strikingly beautiful girls in the group, but she still feels like she has to latch herself on to Mina and Lizzie in order to hold power over the rest of us.

I may not be able to fix the situation with Lane Crawford tonight, or sort through my feelings about Alex and our relationship, but I can try to connect with Eunji.

I'm so lost in my thoughts that I don't even realise that the movie is over until I'm startled by the whooping and cheering from our row when Mina's name flashes on-screen in the credits.

At the after-party, I decide to seek Eunji out.

"Can we talk?" I say, gently touching her shoulder.

At first I think she's going to shrug me off, but after a beat of hesitation, she concedes with a sigh. I lead her to a plush navy-blue velvet banquette in a quiet corner of the event space.

"Is . . . is there something going on, Eunji?" I ask. She fiddles with the chain of her music-note necklace and avoids my eye. Her elegant collarbone seems even more pronounced than I remember. Has she lost weight? "Look," I say leaning back in my seat, "I know we haven't always been the best of friends, but I'm asking because I feel like you've been kind of off lately, and . . . well, I'm worried about you."

She glances at me, then looks away again, this time blinking back rapid tears.

"Eunji?" I say, softer now.

She presses her lips together, tears filling her eyes despite her efforts to stop them. She glances around to make sure no one's listening and lowers her voice. I lean in to hear her. "It's Song Geonwu," she says. "We're . . . dating."

Oh. Didn't see that coming. I think back to all those times Mina bragged about her role on *When I Loved You* and Eunji would grow tense. She wasn't jealous about the acting opportunity – she was jealous about the time spent with her boyfriend. I'm not sure the best way to comfort her . . . not sure how much I want to reveal about my *own* dating life.

"Oh wow, Eunji," I say, patting her back lightly, "that has to be really hard. When did you guys start dating?" I ask, trying to think of when their paths might have crossed before. "And how do you ever get to see each other?" I add. She and Geonwu might have the benefit of living in the same city, but he's way more recognisable than Alex. If I can't even figure out a safe way for Alex and I to meet up when he's here, I have no idea how they've managed to stay under the radar so far.

"Oh, who cares," Eunji says, dabbing the corners of her eyes with the heel of her hand. "It's pointless now anyway. I'm ending it."

"Why?" I ask.

"Come on," she says, her voice thick. "Did you *see* the way he was looking at you? And how he kept putting his hand on your back? He's obviously into you." She presses the heels of her hands against her eyes, her shoulders slumping. "I should've known he was a player."

Oh Eunji. I pull her into a hug, squeezing tight. "Hey, hey. You've got it wrong. He is *not* into me. It was literally just a photo op because we were wearing matching outfits. And besides . . ."

I let go of Eunji, my hands still on her shoulders. She was honest with me. The least I can do is be honest with her, too, especially if it will help clear up this misunderstanding and reaffirm her faith in her relationship. I hate seeing her so broken.

"There's another guy I've been seeing lately," I confess. "His name is Alex. And I'm not interested in dating anyone else."

Eunji's eyes widen. "What? Really?"

"Yep." I swallow down a sip of my champagne and wait. For what, I'm not exactly sure. I half expect Mr. Noh to jump out from behind the bar and yell, "Gotcha!" It seems like acknowledging the existence of my love life to someone other than Leah should result in a lightning bolt from the blue or *something*.

But Eunji just breaks into a brilliant grin and says, "*Rachel!* I had *no* idea!"

I smile back weakly. "Well, you know how it is . . ."

And in that moment I realise that Eunji actually *does* know how it is. I've been so concerned about keeping things with Alex private, worried that bringing in too many outside forces could ruin this fragile thing we have, that I never considered how opening up to one of my groupmates might actually ease the weight I've been carrying.

"Oh my gosh," Eunji says, looking more alive than I've seen her in weeks. "We should totally go on a double date!"

I nearly choke on my sip of champagne, sending bubbles up my nose. How on *earth* would we get away with that? But Eunji looks so happy, and I feel more connected to her now than I have in all my years of knowing her, and I don't want to let this moment go.

"Okay, yeah. That would be fun. I've never gone on a double date before."

We finish our drinks and head back to the party, but before we reach the rest of our group, Eunji puts a hand on my arm to stop me. She takes a deep breath, then says, "Rachel, I'm sorry about before. I just got really in my head about things, you know? Relationships are hard sometimes, especially when you're famous."

I nod. "I get it." Oh, do I ever.

Hesitant at first, she holds out her arms for a hug. I grin and wrap my arms around her.

Now I just need to come up with a top secret plan for a double date featuring Korea's biggest star of film and television, and two-ninths of the biggest K-pop girl group on the planet.

No problem.

DOUBLE-DATE ITINERARY

6:00 – Rachel arrives at restaurant; heads to private room C.

6:03 – Alex arrives at restaurant; pretends to take phone call. Hovers near hostess stand until Eunji arrives.

6:05 – Eunji arrives at restaurant; immediately goes to ladies' room. Rachel will text Eunji when coast is clear.

6:08 – Geonwu arrives at restaurant; heads to private room F.

6:10 – Alex meets Rachel in private room C.

6:13 – Geonwu moves from private room F to private room C.

6:15 – Rachel texts Eunji to meet at private room C.

Note for all: Reservation is made under the name Kim Yumi. A private room for four has been booked at the back of the restaurant. When your time comes, head straight there, no pit stops!

Eunji and I plan our double date to a tee. And I mean to a *tee*. As anxious as I am about putting all four of us in a room together, I'll admit, secretly planning it all with Eunji is actually really fun. It feels like we're trying to figure out how to execute an *Ocean's*-level scheme. We spend hours looking up different restaurants with private rooms in inconspicuous neighbourhoods, before ultimately settling on Marigold House. It's nice, but out of the main flow of things, tucked away in Gangbuk. It's still a risk, no doubt about it, but I feel pretty good about Marigold House – after all, the staff there has kept bigger secrets than this – rumour has it the prime minister held top secret meetings here when he needed to negotiate a major piece of legislation without it being leaked. Plus, Eunji knows the hostess from elementary school and swears she'll be cool. I'm still a little nervous about the whole situation, but Eunji and I have done our best to make this double date as covert as possible. And I take comfort in the fact that if Alex and I can manage to evade road-raging paparazzi in Hong Kong, we should be safe grabbing a quiet dinner here in Seoul.

It's a whole ordeal coordinating schedules so the four of us arrive at different times and are not spotted together. Alex is a saint for going along with all of it, and keeps insisting that he doesn't mind all the cloak-and-dagger stuff. He's actually really excited about meeting Eunji. I know it's because I've specifically kept my relationship with Alex private, but it's still strange to realise none of my groupmates have met Alex, or vice versa – that two huge parts of my life don't overlap at all.

Finally, the night arrives. I spend way too long on my outfit, finally deciding on a simple white T-shirt, black leather leggings, and cropped moto jacket – sadly, it's far more important to look inconspicuous than to dress up.

Part A of Mission Double Date goes without a hitch. We arrive at staggered times, exactly as planned, and within twenty minutes (okay, so not *exactly* as planned) of stepping out of my nondescript black car, I find myself sitting around the dinner table with Alex, Eunji, and Geonwu, amazed that we're actually pulling this off.

I feel like I've entered some kind of parallel universe as we laugh and talk over plates of black cod, charcoal-grilled chicken drizzled with house-made chili pepper sauce, wild mushrooms nestled over sticky barley rice, and bluefin tuna layered with thin slices of Korean pear.

"Wow, this is amazing," Alex says, taking a forkful of tuna. "I'd come back to Korea just for this."

"You said you live in Hong Kong, right?" Geonwu says. "I've been there once for a fan meeting. Great place."

"Look me up next time you're there," Alex says, and I'm amazed at how guys can know each other for five seconds and already act like best pals – even when one of said guys is Korea's biggest heartthrob. But maybe that isn't a guy thing. Maybe it's an Alex thing. He's so comfortable with himself that he has this incredible ability to make everyone around him also feel at ease.

Just as I'm having this thought, he reaches out and grabs my hand, his fingers softly running over the back of mine. He looks at me with those deep brown eyes.

"Wow," Eunji says softly from across the table, looking at us like we're everything she wants in the world. "How long have you two been together?"

I pause, a forkful of grilled chicken halfway to my mouth. *Together.* Do I count the first time we met in Singapore? Paris, where we first kissed? Hong Kong, just a few weeks ago when he referred to me as his girlfriend for the first time?

But while my brain is turning over all these possibilities, Alex easily answers, "Three months."

Eunji raises her eyebrows. "Three months. That's like, forever by K-pop standards."

"Really?" Alex asks. "Well, I don't know about you, Rach, but I'm planning on this thing lasting a lot longer than three months. We're just getting started," he says, looking into my eyes. And it's like I can really see forever staring back at me. It's equal parts amazing and massively overwhelming. I break our eye contact and shove the bite of chicken into my mouth. My cheeks redden and my eyes water, but I don't think it's from the heat of the chili sauce. Alex speaks of our relationship with such easy confidence, but for me, it's like there's a nine-hundred-pound gorilla skulking in the corner of the room with the word "GIRLFRIEND" tattooed on its forehead. Half of me wants to just ignore it and focus on how much I enjoy being with Alex, but the other half knows I can't.

I swallow down my grilled chicken and turn back to Eunji and Geonwu. "So how did you two meet?"

Eunji smiles slyly. "Apparently, he's been trying to get my number for months. He kept asking his friend who knows me to set him up on a date."

"It wasn't months," Geonwu says defensively. "It was several weeks. And then a few more weeks after that."

"I'm pretty sure several weeks plus a few weeks equals months," Eunji teases.

We all laugh as Geonwu blushes with a bashful shrug.

Throughout the dinner, Geonwu keeps reaching for Eunji's hand under the table, lacing his fingers with hers as he chats. It's so natural the way he does it, like he's been doing it all his life, and I can tell how happy it makes Eunji. She looks so alive, and the two of them seem really in love. Though, I guess looking like he's really in love is literally how Geonwu makes his living. I shake the thought out of my head. Not now, Rachel. Don't ruin the mood.

"Tell them about your latest sponsorship opportunity, babe," Geonwu says excitedly.

Eunji smiles shyly. "I just found out I'll be doing a photo shoot for SK Amore's new line of scents. It's going to be so much fun."

"That's great news!" I say. "You'll be amazing at that."

When it's time to leave, we go the same way we came: one by one. Getting out of here without drawing attention is Part B of tonight's mission, and I'm praying that it will go just as smoothly as Part A. First Geonwu leaves. Then fourteen minutes later, Eunji. Alex and I sit side by side, looking at the time on our phones and counting down fifteen more minutes.

"So, you sure we can't take that nighttime stroll by the Han?" Alex asks with his eyebrow quirked, but I know he's just kidding. We already agreed that we have to keep things majorly low-key and covert for this visit. Still, he is going to give me a lift back to the villa, so we still have at least twenty minutes or so left to be together.

"Tempting," I sigh. "But we've probably risked too much as it is tonight. Any more, and I'll just turn completely paranoid. And trust me, Paranoid Rachel is not very good company."

"You're always lovely company, paranoid or not." He glances at his phone. "Time for my exit. See you soon."

He gives me a grin and a kiss on the cheek before turning

to the door – but before he can slip out, I grab his arm, spin him back around, and press my lips to his.

"So much for the tightly coordinated schedule," he says when we break apart, laughing softly.

"I needed a proper goodbye," I say.

"We're not saying goodbye here," he says. "We still have the car ride."

And then he kisses me again, slowly, sweetly, reminding me of all the small moments we miss with the distance between us.

"We're really messing with the schedule," I say.

"I'll see you in the car," he says, letting go of me.

Then he's out the door.

When it's time for me to go, I pull the collar of my moto jacket up around my chin, throw on a baseball cap (I really am trying to look as un-Rachel as possible), and walk out of the restaurant and directly into the waiting car outside. Alex got a rental with extra-dark tinted windows, just to be safe. As I slide into the front seat next to him, I chance a quick look around. No paparazzi in sight. The car pulls away. I can't believe it was really that easy. Part B of the mission, success.

I sink back in my seat, relieved.

"Happy?" Alex asks, glancing at me from behind the steering wheel.

"Very."

"You were really anxious about tonight, huh?"

I turn to look at him. He's smiling, but there's worry in his eyes. I gently smooth the crease between his eyebrows.

"It's all right," I say. "It went well. Much better than I expected. I'm hoping this means we can see more of each other whenever you're in Seoul without having to look over our shoulders all the time."

He smiles, catching my hand with his. "That would be nice. But you know I don't mind all the sneaking around." I beam at him, grateful as always that he's so willing to put up with all the drama that dating someone with my life entails. "It's actually kind of hot," he adds.

I playfully slap him on the arm and he laughs.

"Hey," he says, growing a bit more serious, rubbing his thumb across the back of my hand. "I got an email right before I got to the restaurant, but I didn't want to tell you during dinner. Celeste says that they want to see your next-season designs by launch day. If you can promise that, then they will agree to stock your first six bags."

I'm so distracted by the feel of Alex's soft hand in mine that it takes my brain a minute to catch up to what he's saying. Lane Crawford *is* going to take my line? I squeal and do a little happy dance in the passenger seat. Alex laughs and dances along with me as best he can from behind the wheel, but then his brow creases. "Listen, this is amazing, and you should be psyched, but for next year's designs they're expecting a lot – three times what you presented them at the first meeting."

I take a deep breath, not wanting to let anxiety cloud this happy evening, but my chest suddenly feels tight. Three times more? That's eighteen bags. It took me the better part of two months to come up with the six bags I have. Can I design *eighteen* original bags in the same amount of time? On top of everything else I have going on in my life?

"Hey, you got this," Alex says, seeing me on the verge of hyperventilating. "The designs don't have to be nearly as polished as the ones you first presented to Celeste." He reaches over again, to once again hold my hand in his. "I'll be there for you the whole way. And you can just hand in sketches and still blow them away. I've seen everything you've been able to come up with in your sketchbook. You're brilliant, you're creative, you're talented."

It feels good to get a pep talk from him, and it feels good to be holding his hand.

The car pulls up to the villa all too soon. I look regretfully out the window and sigh again. "I wish you were staying longer. This was so short."

"Same," Alex says, putting the car in park.

I smile and lean forward to kiss him. His lips are warm and soft, and as his hands gently trail down my waist, I fall deeper into the kiss. I press my palm against the back of his neck and he pulls me closer, more urgent now. We're kissing and kissing and kissing and I can't imagine ever wanting to stop. But eventually, I start to feel the presence of that nine-hundred-pound Reality-Check Gorilla again, and I force myself to lightly pull away.

"I should go in," I say quietly, our foreheads pressed together.

"Mm-hmm, right," he says back, his voice hoarse.

We sit that way for a few seconds, just listening to each other breathe. Finally, he takes my hands and kisses my knuckles.

"Good night, Rachel," he says.

"Good night, Alex," I whisper back.

I step out of the car and into the warm June breeze before turning back to blow him a kiss. And then I run inside, before the magic of this pretty near-perfect night can slip away.

The next morning, after I hop out of the shower, I find the girls sitting around the kitchen, eating breakfast. Everyone, that is, but Eunji.

"Is Eunji still sleeping?" I ask Lizzie, who shares a room with her.

"She went out not too long ago," Lizzie says. "Why?"

"Just wondering," I say. I wanted to ask her how the rest of her night with Geonwu went. Just as I'm thinking about texting her, my phone pings with an incoming message.

It's Mr. Noh.

Mr. Noh: Rachel, please come to DB headquarters IMMEDIATELY.

My stomach lurches.

Mr. Noh hardly ever texts me directly, and he's never told me to come into headquarters "IMMEDIATELY" in all caps before. This must be serious. I rush to my bedroom to get ready, twisting my still-wet hair into a bun and throwing on a pair of jeans with a loose striped tee. The whole way to headquarters, I reread Mr. Noh's message, looking for clues on what this might be about.

But as soon as I step into his office, it instantly becomes clear.

Eunji is already there, sitting on the couch, her face streaked with tears.

We lock eyes.

They know, she mouths.

⋆ Seventeen ⋆

Photos. So many photos.

Mr. Noh pulls them up on his computer, swivelling the screen to face us. There's Geonwu leaving the restaurant. Giving a tip to the valet. Getting into his white Bentley. Then, with the time stamp only minutes later, Eunji leaves the restaurant. She's made an attempt to hide her identity, with her oversized black square sunglasses, but then, in the next set of photos, you can see that as soon as she opens the door to Geonwu's car, she lifts the sunglasses atop her head before sliding into the passenger seat. It's undeniably her. But still, there's nothing romantic about these photos – it's just two people sharing a car ride, totally innocent . . .

Then, Mr. Noh clicks ahead.

There's Eunji and Geonwu at Waffle Scoops. Him stealing a lick of her ice-cream cone, the photo such a tight shot that I can even make out the Oreo bits in it . . . And then, the nail in the coffin: a photo of the two of them kissing. Several photos, actually.

A shudder goes down my spine. As bad as I feel for Eunji, the main thought pulsing through my brain is: this could have been us.

But it's not. I hold my breath as Mr. Noh finishes clicking through the photos emailed to him by *Reveal*, but there are no photos of me and Alex at all. I might hate that nine-hundred-pound gorilla most of the time, but right now I'm grateful for its constant presence. Without it lurking in my brain 24/7, Alex and I could have easily got carried away and ended up caught too.

I suddenly realise – this is why it was so easy for us to leave the restaurant last night. Not because we lucked out and there were no paparazzi at all. But because the paparazzi had already left to tailgate Eunji and Geonwu to the ice-cream shop by the time we came out.

I glance at Eunji. I've never seen her so distraught before. Her face is completely pale, and she's hunched over in her seat like she's trying to make herself as small as possible. She keeps wiping at the tears on her face, but as soon as she does, fresh ones take their place. My heart physically aches for her. Shit. I can't even imagine how awful this must be for her. Well, that's not true. I *can* imagine. I *do* imagine, every time Alex and I are together. Worst-case scenarios running through my head all the time. And now Eunji is living my worst nightmare.

"*Reveal* says that if you admit to dating Geonwu, they won't release all the photos," Mr. Noh says, his mouth set in a severe line. "They'll only release the ones of you getting in the car with him." Eunji seems to brighten the tiniest bit, but then Mr. Noh continues, "*If* you sign an agreement allowing *Reveal* to formally report on your relationship." Eunji slumps back down in her seat. "Of course, if you decide to go with this plan, DB will also release a statement confirming your relationship with Song Geonwu," Mr. Noh finishes.

Eunji bites her lip. Formal reporting means going public and going public is a big deal, especially when you're not ready.

"I suggest you consider this decision carefully, Shin Eunji," Mr. Noh says. "This is the only way to protect your image from further damage. SK Amore has already got wind of this. They called me this morning to drop your sponsorship."

Eunji looks up, stricken. I can't believe SK Amore could have learned about this so quickly, but I guess bad news – or, at least, scandalous news – travels fast in this industry. Eunji points to me, her voice shaking. "What about Rachel? She was there too. Does she also have to confess?"

"There are no photos of Rachel," Mr. Noh says. "No photos, no confession."

Eunji's mouth drops open in disbelief.

"But if what Eunji says is true," Mr. Noh adds, shifting his stern gaze to me, "you'd better watch what you're doing, Rachel. I called you in here this morning to give you a warning, and so you could see for yourself the consequences of this kind of behaviour. You don't want to end up like your friend here."

I swallow hard and bow my head. "Yes, Mr. Noh.

I understand." I feel so guilty, I can't even look at Eunji as she signs the agreement to let *Reveal* report on her. This is unfair and I know it.

As soon as we leave Mr. Noh's office, I reach for her hand. "Eunji . . ."

She snatches her hand away, face blotchy with tears. "This is so fucked up! We were *both* out with our boyfriends. How come you get to get away with it and I don't? Why does nothing bad ever happen to you?"

Her voice rises in frustration with each word.

"I'm sorry, Eunji," I say, my hand falling limply by my side. Is that what she thinks? That nothing bad ever happens to me? It's true, I've been very fortunate and I'm grateful for all the opportunities I've been given, but it's not like I'm just waltzing through some picture-perfect life. I open my mouth to try to connect with Eunji again, but before I can say another word, she turns on her heel and strides away.

What if it's me next?

It's the question on everyone's mind. First Jiyoon. Now Eunji. Who will be the next one to have her secret boyfriend exposed? No one says it outright, but I can tell we're all thinking it from the tense atmosphere in the villa. From the nervous glances that are constantly thrown in Eunji's direction. From the urgent, whispered phone calls I hear when walking by Sumin's door on my way to the bathroom late at night. From the look on Lizzie's face as she scrolls through *Reveal*, reading the article published about Eunji and Geonwu for the thousandth time. Her expression clearly saying, *What if this was me?*

And I feel it more than anyone. Alex and I have almost been caught together twice now. Three times, if you include that fan photo way back in Singapore when we first met. This double date was totally reckless, and it's only by sheer luck that I'm not in the position Eunji's in now.

When the news broke, Alex FaceTimed me right away, but I let it go to voicemail, shooting him a quick Can't talk now text. I have to put some distance between us, rebuild the boundaries that my heart charges past every time we're together. I've been playing with fire, and it's only a matter of time before I get burned.

For three days, I try to talk with Eunji, but she refuses to be alone with me, fleeing every room I walk into, shooting daggers at me as she goes. Actually, Eunji is hardly speaking to anyone – not even Mina and Lizzie. The only person she'll talk to lately is Jiyoon. The two of them have never been particularly close, but it's clear that Eunji knows that Jiyoon understands what she's going through better than any of us. I try to support them both, but lately it seems like every little thing I do is unwelcome. I try to stay out of everybody's way, hiding in my room to focus on the eighteen new designs I have to come up with, but even so, I feel like I'm tiptoeing around the villa, constantly trying to avoid land mines that could blow up without warning.

When we arrive at the multigroup concert, the tension is still thick in the air.

"You better not screw up the choreo today, Sumin," Ari says as she pulls her long black dress over her yellow sequinned minidress. But unlike their usual harmless squabbling, there's real bite behind Ari's words. "You always miss the beat on the last step in the chorus. It's literally the easiest part of the whole dance, and you still manage to do it wrong."

"*Excuse* me?" Sumin says, shooting Ari a glare. "How about you worry about yourself. Every time you're sharp on the high note in verse two, I feel like my eardrums are bleeding."

Ari opens her mouth to snap back when Mina interrupts, glowering at both of them. "Can you two shut up already? You're giving me a headache."

For once, I agree with Mina.

I've got to get out of here for a bit. Done with my hair, makeup, and outfit, I slip out of the dressing room into the wings backstage just as SayGO starts their set. Perfect timing.

Leah and her groupmates look way too cute in their black-and-white varsity jackets and combat boots. I grin and snap a photo as Leah dances to the centre for her part.

"Enjoying the show?" a voice behind me says.

I turn to see Jason approaching, dressed in a red leather jacket with distressed black jeans. I smile, tucking my phone away.

"Hey! You look great," I say. "Are you up next?"

"Yep. I'm nervous, though." He nods towards the stage. "Your little sis is a tough act to follow!"

I smile thinking how eleven-year-old Leah would have

died to hear Jason say those words. Oh, who am I kidding? Sixteen-year-old Leah would probably feel the same.

"Good luck out there," I say. "You'll be great."

He winks. "Aren't I always?"

Same old confident Jason. I watch as he makes his way to the stage, grabbing his guitar from a stand as he goes.

"Rekindling something, are we?"

I jump about a foot in the air at the sound of Mina's voice.

"What?" I say. "No, of course not. That's ancient history."

"Good," Mina says, her eyes boring into mine, "because getting involved with another idol right now would be monumentally stupid, you know that, right?" I nod, but don't say anything else. Eunji's been so inside her shell the last three days, I'm pretty sure she hasn't told any of the other girls about my involvement in her and Geonwu's outing. About how I, too, was nearly caught with a boy of my own. *Monumentally stupid?* Mina, you have no idea. "Come on," she says. "The stylists want to do a once-over on all of us together before we go on."

We head back to the dressing room, but as we approach the door, we stop. Mr. Noh is standing there, having an animated conversation with one of the executives from Mnet, the TV network that's airing the concert. Mina and I exchange a glance, then inch closer to try to hear what's being said without being obvious.

"Absolutely not," Mr. Noh is whisper-shouting. "I told you that would be unacceptable."

"Well, they're already here. And they're slated to go on

in ten minutes," the executive says, consulting a clipboard in front of him. "What do you want me to do? Tell them not to go on?"

Mina and I exchange another glance. Who are they talking about?

"Yes," Mr. Noh says. "That's exactly what I want."

"Be reasonable, Youngchul," the executive says, rolling his eyes.

"Cancel N&G, or I'm sorry but I'll have to withdraw my artists."

"Which artists?" the executive asks, glancing nervously toward the Girls Forever dressing room.

"All of them," Mr. Noh says with an air of finality that I've heard many times before.

The network executive gapes at him for a moment, then mutters, "Fine," as he rushes off towards another dressing room, where I imagine N&G is about to get some bad news.

I stand, frozen, processing the jarring scene that just played out before me. It's clear that DB has essentially blacklisted N&G. And because the company is so powerful and represents so many other successful groups, they can basically leverage the rest of us to prevent groups like N&G from getting any kind of fair shot after they leave DB. It makes a lot more sense to me now why we've barely heard from them in the past year. They didn't hide themselves away to work on a new sound – the company has been preventing them from getting any exposure. It's a stark reminder of what you stand to lose if you ever find yourself outside DB's protective bubble.

"Come on," Mina says again as we slip back into the dressing room for our final costume check. I can see the concern on her face, but she quickly buries it away in favour of a smooth, unbothered expression.

The stage lights dim as we make our way out and take formation. "Midnight Prism" has a lot of high-energy dance steps, and the signature slide move in the chorus is always a fan favourite. It's easy enough for even non-dancers to imitate, and I love scrolling through my phone, watching fans show off their moves. I assume my opening pose, back to the audience, one arm stretched high above my head, hand delicately draped downward. Adrenaline pumps through my veins like it does every time we get ready to perform.

The spotlight turns on, the music begins, and the crowd goes wild.

Here we go.

As tense as things have been for the group these days, onstage we're totally synchronised. Even Ari and Sumin are flawless in their choreo, smiling like pros and making it look easy.

I'm having a blast, really getting into the performance and realising just how much I've missed this over the past five months. As we approach the chorus, I mentally prepare to unclip my long black dress and toss it behind me right as we go into the slide. We've practised the move a million times, making sure we all do the costume change at the exact same moment, and that we toss our black dresses away with enough clearance so that nobody slips on the fabric (Jiyoon almost completely wiped out during practice once, Youngeun's discarded dress playing the part of a banana peel under her feet). But by now, we're pros. We could do it in our sleep. We've nailed it a thousand times in rehearsal, and now we'll get to show off our hard work for the fans.

The moment comes, and I easily slip the hook out of the eye to reveal my dazzling violet sequinned minidress underneath. I hear the audience gasp and cheer at the unexpected reveal. I easily toss my black dress behind me and slide, my right foot leading and my left foot trailing behind. I throw in a wink to the audience, just for fun, when suddenly–

Pain.

Blinding pain in my left foot.

I look down to see Eunji, on my left, slamming the spiky heel of her stiletto directly down on my left big toe. I let out a gasp of pain as I stumble, nearly crashing into Youngeun on my other side. Luckily, I right myself just in time, quickly falling back into formation, turning my gasp of pain into what hopefully looks to the audience like one of those *Ooh!* faces. As the rest of the dance goes on, my stage smile is frozen on my face, but my toe is hot and throbbing, and I have to blink fast to stop my eyes from watering with pain.

What the hell was that? Did Eunji do that on purpose?

I shoot a quick glance in her direction, but she's smiling

and dancing like nothing happened. Does she even know what she just did? She must. How could she not feel my foot under hers?

We finish the rest of our performance without any more accidents, striking our final pose to hoots and cheers from the audience. I look out at the sea of smiling faces, spotting the glowing Girls Forever light-up headbands that our +EVERs love to wear to our shows. For a moment, all the pain in my toe disappears, and I'm riding high on the joy of performing and making our fans so happy. But as we head backstage, the pain comes rushing back. And when I see Mr. Noh waiting for us, the pain doubles.

"Rachel, what was that?" he demands. "You missed your step and nearly fell flat on your face!"

"I'm sorry, Mr. Noh," I say, biting my lip. I can already feel my toe swelling.

"You better get your act together before your big concert in LA," he says, narrowing his eyes. He shoots a look at the other girls. "And I mean that for all of you. You're a group. If one of you looks bad, all of you look bad."

"Yes, Mr. Noh," everyone says, chagrined.

What a disaster. I keep trying to catch Eunji's eye in the dressing room, but like the last three days, she won't look my way. My toe throbs. There's already some dried blood around the nail, which looks purple and bruised. I hope it doesn't fall off.

As we finish getting changed and head backstage, Jason jogs over to me, comfortably out of his stage clothes and dressed in an oversized white hoodie. "See you at the after-party?"

Right. The after-party. I hesitate. Leah is going, and so are the rest of the Girls Forever members. It probably wouldn't look great if I didn't go. But honestly, all I want to do right now is go home, lie on the couch with a hot cup of tea, and nurse my foot while brainstorming new bag designs for Lane Crawford. Over by the SUVs that will take us to the party, I see Eunji snickering with Mina and Lizzie. As they board their SUV, Lizzie overdramatically trips over her own feet, in what I imagine must be an imitation of how I looked stumbling onstage. Eunji and Mina dissolve into another round of giggles.

"Actually, Jason, I may just head home for today," I say.

"Sure thing," he says, holding up his hand in a casual wave goodbye.

I wave back, then make my way to where the managers are waiting, hoping Jongseok can drive me back to the villa instead.

I slump in the car, mulling over what Mr. Noh said. He's not wrong. We do have to get our act together before our concert in LA. It's coming up in just a few months now, and it'll be our first big show since our Glow Asia Tour. If we can't even pull off a single song in a local performance like tonight, how are we going to get through a whole international concert together?

I sigh, reaching for my phone. As I go to unlock the screen,

I see that I have five missed calls from Appa. My heart starts racing. Why has he been so desperate to reach me? He hasn't phoned me in ages, and suddenly I have five missed calls?

I call back right away.

"Rachel?" he says, picking up on the first ring.

"Appa, hi. Is everything okay?"

"More than okay, actually," he says. I can hear the smile in his voice. My heart rate returns to normal, and my brain stops picturing hospitals, fires, and other disasters.

"Is that Rachel? Are you telling her the news?" Umma's voice says in the background. "Put her on speaker so I can talk too!"

A second later, I hear both their voices on the phone.

"Rachel, can you hear me?" Umma says.

"Hi, Umma, I'm here," I say. "What's going on?"

"You tell her," Appa says.

"No, no, you," Umma says.

I tap my fingers on my knee, my leg jiggling nervously up and down. "Can *someone* please tell me? I'm dying over here."

"All right, we'll do it together," Appa says. "Three, two, one . . ."

"We moved to Cheongdam-dong!" they both chorus into the phone.

"What!" I cry. "What do you mean you moved to Cheongdam-dong? Cheongdam-dong as in the neighbourhood where I live?"

"Five minutes away from where you live, to be exact," Appa says gleefully. "We really wanted to move closer to you, so I've been working extra hard to save up enough to buy this place."

Wow. Real estate in Cheongdam-dong is not cheap. I think back to all those three a.m. texts from Appa. He must have still been in the office when he sent them. I can't believe he worked so hard just so they could be nearer to me.

"It was quite the challenge to keep it a secret from you, especially for Leah," Umma laughs. "She was always asking when she could tell you," she continues. "But we wanted it to be a surprise."

Happy tears fill my eyes. "Oh my god. I can't believe you're so close to me now! This is amazing news. When did you move?"

"Last week. We just settled in," Appa says. "We wanted to get it ready before we told you. When can you come see the place?"

"Text me the address," I say. "I can head over right now!"

As soon as we hang up the phone, I lean forward in my seat to speak to Jongseok. "Could you actually drop me off somewhere else?" I smile.

"No problem. Where to?" he asks.

"Home."

⭐ Eighteen ⭐

The first thing that greets me as I walk through the door of Umma and Appa's new apartment is the smell of warm kimchi fried rice, hot off the stove, with a sunny-side-up egg on top.

"Eat, eat," Umma says, ushering me over to the walnut farmer's table in the eat-in kitchen. "If I knew you were coming today, I would have prepared something more!"

"No, no, this is perfect," I say. The smell of Umma's cooking alone is so comforting that I want to wrap myself up in it like a duvet cover. "But wait, I want to see the rest of the place!"

"We'll give you the full tour later," Umma says firmly, sitting me down in a kitchen chair. "But first, eat."

There's no arguing with Umma when she tells you to eat. I pick up a spoon and dig into the fried rice. Oh, heaven. When's the last time I had a home-cooked meal like this? Not that I don't eat well as an idol. In the past five months alone, I've had mouthwatering, steaming xiaolongbao in Shanghai, chili crab so fresh it could have walked off my plate in Singapore, and decadent chocolate mousse in Paris. But none of those foods – and none of those places – can compare to a simple, delicious meal, lovingly prepared at home. Even a "home" that's brand-new to me.

I look around the apartment from my seat, drinking in as many details as I can. It's both bigger and newer than our old place, with huge windows and an amazing view of the nighttime city lights in the distance, but I'm glad my family decided to bring most of our old furniture over. There's the area rug with its edges frayed from time; the white couch that Umma bought after Leah turned twelve, saying we were responsible enough now not to get it dirty. Ten minutes later, I promptly spilled banana milk all over it. The living room is full of Appa's potted plants, green leaves arching up toward the family photos hanging on the walls. I trace a curling vine of a hoya plant with my eyes, following as it loops along the frame of one of my favourite photos of Leah – the one with her missing both front teeth. Even though it's a new home, it feels so familiar, it makes my heart ache.

"What happened to your foot?" Appa asks, his eyes landing on my red toe.

"One of the girls accidentally stepped on me during the performance," I say, tucking my left foot behind my right calf. I don't want Appa to worry. "It's okay. It feels better now."

He makes a tsking sound. "Still. Let me get you some ice," he says, already halfway to the freezer.

I used to hate it when Umma and Appa would fuss over

me, but today I soak it all in, letting Umma refill my water glass and Appa tend to my toe. I watch them the whole time, rememorising their faces. It really has been so long since I've last seen them. Christmas, I guess? But no, wait, we were still on tour over the holidays. I remember FaceTiming them and Leah from my hotel room in Taipei, trying not to cry as I watched them open presents from our old apartment. Looking at them now, I feel like they've got older. Umma's face is lined with more wrinkles than I remember, and Appa's hair is definitely getting greyer. I guess I never stopped to think about how when time was flying for me, it was also passing for them. It hits me how much time I've missed with them.

"Ready for the full tour now?" Appa says as I finish my last bite. He's bouncing with energy and suddenly looks so much like the young pro-boxer Appa of my youth that I almost laugh out loud.

"So ready," I say.

They show me the living room, the master bedroom, Leah's room. I see she hasn't got any neater than she was when she was a kid, but her bedroom is no little girl's room any more – no NEXT BOYZ posters pasted everywhere, no galaxy pattern on her duvet cover, no stuffed animals lining her bed. Okay, actually, I still spot one rabbit plushie nestled into her pillows.

The hallways are lined with art pieces that Umma and Appa collected throughout their marriage. Vintage *New Yorker* covers, charcoal sketches of Seoul, and a caricature of the two of them that they had done on the Coney Island boardwalk on their first date – with Umma's forehead twice as big as the rest of her face. Everything in this house has a story. I can't imagine my family in a more perfect home.

"This is the guest room," Appa says, leading me to the final room in the apartment. "But we hope you think of it as *your* room whenever you come and visit."

He opens the door and steps back to let me enter first, and I stare in awe. A fresh jar of lilacs – my favourite flower – has been placed on the nightstand. I inhale the fresh scent of my favourite Baies candle from Diptyque, and picture Umma rushing to light it as soon as she and Appa hung up the phone with me earlier tonight. There's a spacious bamboo-top desk under the window and a coffee mug filled with sharpened pencils.

"We thought you could use this desk for when you're sketching your designs," Umma says, guiding me towards it. She opens one of the drawers and pulls out a small, flat drawing-board light box and turns it on, causing it to glow softly. "And there's this – if you ever need to trace anything. I read about it online."

"Oh!" Appa interjects. "And I have to tell you about this great little diner I found, just a couple of blocks away from Cheongdam Park!"

I feel tears well up in my eyes as Appa goes on about how they can cook your eggs into special shapes, like a whale or a star, at the diner. I know that they don't actually love Cheongdam-dong as much as they love other parts of Seoul. I remember in my early trainee days, when my dad would bring me to DB for practice, he'd always comment on the luxury cars that lined every street we passed. Mercedes. Maserati. BMW. He'd rattle them off with ease, but I could tell even then that the everyday opulence of the city's ritziest neighbourhood made him uncomfortable. When I first debuted, I took the whole family out to dinner at the Class. I was so proud to be able to treat them, and I know they were grateful, but the whole time, Appa joked nervously about not knowing which fork to use, while Umma kept muttering under her breath about how ridiculous the prices were. For my mom especially, this move is a big deal. She's all practicality and simplicity, and Cheongdam-dong is definitely . . . not. I can't believe they went through all this trouble just to be closer to me. Though, I suppose I shouldn't be surprised. After all, they sacrificed a whole life in New York to move to Korea just so that I could pursue my dreams. So I guess a move across the city is really just par for the course for the best parents in the world.

The front door slams open and I hear Leah's voice calling out from down the hall, "Unni, are you here? I'm hooome!"

I run out to meet her. We scream when we see each other and she races over, throwing her arms around my neck.

"How was the after-party?" I ask.

"Fine, fine – Heaven drank too much champagne and then made us look for her missing phone when it was just in her clutch the whole time. The usual. But come on!" she says. She spreads her arms out and twirls around. "What do you think of the place?"

"Um, it's completely perfect," I say. "I can't believe you didn't tell me!"

Leah beams as Umma and Appa come out to join us. "I'm good at surprises. So are you going to sleep over tonight?"

I look back over my shoulder at the room with the lilacs and the mug full of pencils. Already, this place feels more like home than the villa ever could. And it's so close by . . .

"Actually," I say. "How would you all feel if I moved in instead?"

That night, I stay up late sketching at my new desk, then fall asleep in a pair of pyjamas borrowed from Umma. It's the best sleep I've had in a while. The next morning, Appa and I sit at the kitchen table with bowls of kongnamul guk. Umma made it for us before heading out to her morning class at Ewha. I try not to feel guilty for how long her commute is now, and make a mental note to cook breakfast tomorrow – at least I can save her time that way. Leah's already out for the day too, but the new apartment is close enough to his office that Appa can enjoy breakfast with me before heading in.

"Are you okay, Daughter?" he asks as I look down at my soup, swirling the soybean sprouts around with my chopsticks. "You look like you have a lot on your mind. You're not regretting your decision, are you?"

"Not regretting, no," I say. "I just wonder what the girls will think."

"Your members," Appa says sympathetically.

I nod. "And the media." Last night, everything felt so right, but as soon as I woke up this morning, I was filled with the impending dread of telling everyone the news. It's true that the little annoyances of living with eight girls had begun to grate on me, and clearly things have been tense around the villa for the past few days in the wake of what happened to Eunji, but truly I'm not moving out because of what I'm leaving behind – but because of what I'm moving *to*. "I don't know," I say to Appa. "I guess a part of me feels like I should have stuck it out at the villa, even though I already feel so much better living here. I don't want to disappoint anyone, or look like I'm giving up."

He holds my gaze across the table. "If there's one thing I know about you, it's that you're *not* a quitter. You're just doing things your way, like you've always done."

I swallow the lump forming in my throat and nod. "Thanks, Appa."

He smiles. "Now eat your soup."

Somehow my dad saying that in his simple way is exactly what I needed to hear. After breakfast, I gather up the courage to make my way to the villa. I have to face the girls sooner or later and I have to pick up my things. The whole walk there (all five minutes of it), I practise what I'm going to say over and over in my mind. But no matter how much I try to get the words right, I still can't picture how the girls will react. I guess there's only one way to find out.

. . .

As soon as I enter the villa, I can hear them chatting in the living room, dishes clattering, TV on in the background. I take a deep breath. Here goes nothing.

I step into the living room with a wave. "Hi, girls. Good morning."

Everyone stops what they're doing to look at me. The girls are all in their lazy-day-off morning looks, all rumpled pyjamas and messy hair buns. Lizzie nudges her glasses up, raising her eyebrows.

"Looks like someone had a late night," she says. "Are you just getting home now?"

"Yeah, Rachel, where were you?" Mina says, eyeing me over her coffee mug. She smirks. "Did you get drunk at the after-party and hook up with someone at the hotel?"

Before I can tell her that I wasn't even *at* the after-party, Eunji interjects.

"Come on, Mina," she says. "Give Rachel some credit. She would never do that to her boyfriend."

Silence falls over the room.

Spoons drop into bowls. Eyes widen in surprise.

The only sound to be heard is a Bacchus energy-drink commercial blaring in the background.

"Boyfriend?" Sumin finally says.

Shit.

It may sound to the others like Eunji is defending me, but I can tell from the particular arch of her brow that she knows exactly what she's doing. That she knows I'd prefer to keep my relationship with Alex private, but is spilling it to the rest of the group anyway.

"Yes, boyfriend," I answer, though the word still feels awkward in my mouth. "His name is Alex. We met in Singapore and we've been talking ever since."

"Wow," Sunhee says, eyes bright. "I can't believe you met him in Singapore. That's where Jiyoon . . ."

Her voice trails off and she casts an apologetic glance at Jiyoon, who stiffens. She doesn't have to finish her sentence. We all know she means that's where Jiyoon got caught.

"So you *were* with a guy that night in Singapore," Mina says with a hand on her hip. I think back to how I explained it away – getting coffee with a friend of a friend. Well, at the time, that's all it was. But now I can see how bad it looks. Especially given what happened to Jiyoon that night.

"Yes," I say slowly. "Our mutual friends connected us. But we were just friends at that point. Our relationship didn't turn romantic until later." I'm not quite sure why I feel the need to clarify this, especially since the look on Jiyoon's face clearly indicates that it doesn't make a difference. "But anyway, I wasn't with him last night," I say quickly, changing the topic. "I was with my family. Actually, I have something important to share with you all." Here we go. "I'm moving out of the villa and back home with my family. I know this might seem sudden, but my parents recently got a place really close to here, and they had a room prepared for me and everything. It won't affect my commitment to the group or to any DB activities at all. In fact, I think it will help! It'll be like a fresh reset." I'm so nervous, I'm rambling. I clamp my lips together and smile meekly. "So what do you think?"

There's a moment of stunned, awkward silence.

Finally Jiyoon clears her throat. "Wow. You're lucky your family's so close," she says with a hint of envy. "That must be nice to have the option to live with them."

"I wouldn't mind living with my family too, to be honest," Youngeun adds. "That'll be a nice change for you, Rachel."

I nod, grateful for Youngeun's levelheadedness. I start to head to my room, but before I can take even one step—

"Can we go back to the boyfriend, though?" Sunhee says. "What's he like? Do you have a photo?"

So close.

"He's really sweet and kind," I say hesitantly. It feels weird talking about Alex right on the heels of Eunji and Geonwu's scandal. From the pinched expression on Eunji's face, I can tell it's still a sore spot for her. I deflect the rest of the conversation. "I don't have many photos, though. We are long distance, after all."

"Well, congratulations, Rachel," Mina says with a smile. "On the relationship and the move. That's a lot of big life things happening for you."

"Thanks, Mina," I say slowly. She doesn't say anything more, but I can't help but feel uneasy. All things considered, they took my news about the move really well. But the unexpected reveal about Alex has me on edge. The girls wouldn't out my relationship, would they? I suspect that more than one of the girls has a secret boyfriend of her own. Lizzie and Sumin were looking particularly worried when Eunji and Geonwu were exposed. They wouldn't want more members of Girls Forever under the media spotlight for secretly dating, would they? That would only draw unwanted attention to themselves.

"Okay, well, I'm going to go pack." I make a beeline for my room before they can ask any more questions about Alex.

I go into my room and empty the contents of my dresser drawers. My parents offered me a bunch of empty moving boxes, but I figured I'd see what I could squeeze into my various suitcases first. I'm rolling up T-shirts, socks, and pyjamas to line the bottom of my Away suitcase when suddenly I sense a presence in the doorway. I look up, expecting to see Jiyoon, but it's Eunji.

Her face is blank, impassive. She hovers there silently for a moment, then says, "So. You're really moving out?"

"Yep," I say, rolling up a pair of woolly socks.

"You're shattering the snow globe," Eunji pouts. But rather than sounding accusatory, she seems almost wistful. I look up and see a hint of emotion starting to show in her eyes.

"Eunji," I say, and her bottom lip starts to tremble. I reach for her hand and bring her to come sit beside me on Jiyoon's bed (mine is covered in clothes). "I'm so sorry for what happened. It was totally unfair. It could have easily been me and Alex, and honestly, it's just really bad luck that you and Geonwu happened to go out first and get caught." I feel a shiver down my spine again, realising just how true this is. "Probably one of the waiters recognised Geonwu and tipped off *Reveal*. How could any of us have known?" I tentatively put my arm around her shoulder, and though she stiffens, she doesn't pull away. "I'm so sorry it happened that way. So, so sorry. I can't believe how messed up this whole thing is."

"Yeah." She looks away, her voice breaking. "It is."

"But please don't be angry with me. We need each other to get through this. The real people to be angry at is the media," I say. "For forcing us to go public with relationships before we're ready. And," I say, instinctively lowering my voice as if Mr. Noh could somehow hear us here in the villa, "DB for going along with it. How hard is it for them just to say 'no comment'?" I know DB has our best interests at heart and is just trying to protect us within the framework of the industry, but sometimes I wish they'd stand up for us and our right to privacy more than they do. "And – at least they aren't forcing you to break up like with Jiyoon and Jin."

"I guess so," she sighs. Her shoulders deflate, the anger seeping out of her and turning into defeat. "Ugh. This is what I get for dating someone as famous as me. *More* famous, actually. I should have gone for a nobody like you did. It would have been so much easier to go under the radar."

I know on some level she's right, but still, does she not realize how rude it is to refer to Alex as a "nobody"? Oh well. Not the time.

"What does he do again?" Eunji asks. "Finance, right?"

I nod. "He does investments for fashion companies. He's actually been really amazing in helping me launch my handbag line." As I say this, my eyes automatically drift towards my open closet, to the blank space where my Balenciaga should be.

But wait.

Not *should* be.

Is.

The blue Balenciaga bag is back.

It's sitting on the top shelf, right where I last left it.

But it sure doesn't look the same as when I last saw it.

The leather is cracked and there's what appears to be a pen-ink stain on the front side. It's definitely been used and not gently. I jump up from the bed and run my fingers over the ruined leather, my chest pinching.

"Oh baby," I mutter. "Who did this to you?"

I'm torn between feeling intense relief that the bag has been returned, and renewed annoyance that it was taken in the first place. Leaving a bewildered Eunji, I go out to the living room, bag in hand. I know it's a stupid thing to get hung up on, but it's my last day living with the girls. If I'm going to get answers about who borrowed the bag without asking, it has to be now.

"Guys, seriously, who borrowed this?" I say, trying not to sound too annoyed. "Come on, it's not a big deal, just please, someone fess up."

"Really, Rachel?" Lizzie says. "You're going to spend your last day here accusing us of theft?"

"I wasn't accusing–" I start.

"I can't believe you're really moving out, Rachel." Sunhee looks at me with sad eyes.

I swallow my frustration, my irritation shrivelling to a crisp. Right. Bigger picture. I have to focus on the fact that I'm moving and what a big change that is for everyone. I'm the one basically bringing about the end of an era, so I have to be the bigger person here.

"It'll be okay, Sunhee," I say. "If anything, I bet we'll be closer than ever. One fewer girl to fight over the bathroom will do wonders for everyone. I promise."

"I guess so," Sunhee says.

"Oh, and Lizzie," I say, turning to her. She raises an eyebrow warily, waiting to see why she's being called out. "I know how important your sister is to you. If you wanted to move back home too, I would totally support you with DB." Lizzie casts her eyes downward, looking the slightest bit chastened.

"And hey," Jiyoon says cheerfully, "look on the bright side – now I get my own room!"

"We should rotate the single rooms," Sumin says quickly, bringing up an age-old point of contention. The villa has five bedrooms, and there's nine of us. Which means everyone has a roommate except Mina, who got the one solo room. Until now, that is.

"I call dibs after Jiyoon," Ari says, throwing her hand up in the air.

"No fair, I was going to call it!" Sumin says.

As they bicker, I look down at the cracked leather of my bag. They say distance makes the heart grow fonder. I hope that that will really be the case for us.

☆ Nineteen ☆

GIRLS FOREVER, FOREVER NO MORE: RACHEL KIM PREPARES TO GO SOLO!

We fell in love with Girls Forever when they exploded on to the K-pop scene nearly six years ago, but as the saying goes, all good things must come to an end. Has half a decade been long enough for Rachel Kim to fall out *of love with the group? A source close to them tells us, "Rachel's been unhappy with the other eight girls for a long time – she actually never got over the Jason/Mina love triangle, and has spent years forcing the rest of the girls to choose sides." Another witness says they overheard an epic showdown happen at the girls' villa last weekend, causing Rachel to storm out with her suitcases . . .*

This is only one ridiculous story out of dozens that the tabloids have been churning out since I moved back home.

In order to do damage control, DB doubles down on booking group photo shoots and advertisements for the nine of us, making sure the world still sees us as one big happy family.

"Hang in there, girls," Mr. Han says during our latest shoot. "Your schedules will go back to normal soon, but right now, it's important that you stick together. The public's confidence in Girls Forever's sisterhood has already been shaken enough these days."

I frown, grated by his comment. I know the company has more power to influence the media narrative than Mr. Han is letting on.

"And remember, ladies," Mr. Noh warns, joining Mr. Han on set. "You don't want to give your fans any reason to be worried about you when they should be celebrating your comeback." Well, that's at least a sentiment I can get behind. It's late June now, but I know September, and our LA concert, will be here before we know it. We have to pull it together for +EVER. Our fans have supported us through everything, and we don't want to disappoint them now.

The good news is, things within the group really *have* improved since I moved out. As exhausting as our schedule has been lately, I find that I'm excited to see the girls when I arrive at whatever set we're shooting at; anxious to catch up with everyone and hear what went down at the house the night before.

"Oh my gosh, you should have seen it," Ari gushes as we pull on black-and-white racing suits for a car commercial. "Strawberry milk *everywhere*. I've never seen Lizzie laugh so hard."

"They were totally cuddling!" Sunhee whispers as a makeup

artist on the Coca-Cola shoot touches up our bold red lips. "Seriously, it was adorable. Jiyoon was the little spoon. But don't tell Mina I told you."

When I come home late from a long day of Girls Forever commitments, Umma is right there to greet me with a cup of barley tea and a warmed-up plate. I eat star-shaped omelettes with Appa on the weekends, and help Leah memorise the Mandarin lyrics for SayGO's first Chinese album. And when I'm not promoting with Girls Forever or spending time with my family, I'm glued to the bamboo desk in my new room, working on design sketches for my line of bags.

When I first learned about Lane Crawford's stipulation that I needed to have a second season's worth of designs ready to go by launch, I honestly thought there was no freaking way. But amazingly, as June comes to a close, I find that I'm already halfway through designing the required eighteen bags. I don't know if it's the distance from the tension at the villa, the comfort of being surrounded by family, or this perfect setup Umma created for me with the bamboo desk and light box, but it's like moving home has opened up a floodgate of creativity. Ideas are pouring out of me so fast, my pencil struggles to keep up. The brand launch is fast approaching, and it's probably still going to come down to the wire, but for the first time, I feel like I might actually pull this off.

"Ooh, that looks cool," Leah says, peering over my shoulder one evening in early July. "Which one is that?"

I'm working on a series of bags inspired by our move to

Korea after I was recruited by DB, and the trainee years that followed. They're sleek, rectangular mini bags with removable straps, allowing them to function as both a crossbody and a clutch. They'll come in different colours with different strap styles, so you can mix and match. I changed so much in those seven trainee years, I wanted these bags to reflect that sense of growth, of evolution.

"Oh, I get it," Leah says after I explain the inspiration behind the crossbody-to-clutch concept. "It transitions from day to night, just like you transformed from normal girl into K-pop superstar."

"Yeah, exactly," I laugh.

"This one is gorgeous," Leah says, grabbing a handful of photo samples from a recent shoot with Lotte Department Store. They're doing a big ad campaign for the launch here in Korea. I lean over Leah's shoulder to see the picture she's referring to – it's a shot of me against a bright white background, with a huge smile on my face, trying to balance a triangular-shaped bag on my head. "That's the New York one, right?" Leah asks. I nod. This was one of the hardest bags to design. I agonised over the specific charms for the zipper pulls, wanting them to be evocative of New York City without feeling too cheesy. "You have to put one on hold for me," Leah says. "It's got such a cool vibe."

I grin. "Celeste called it 'nostalgic yet fresh.'" Since Alex told me that Lane Crawford was going to carry the bags, I've been in close contact with Celeste and her team. Even though he's technically an investor in the brand, I didn't want Alex to have to be the go-between for me and Lane Crawford. Especially now . . .

Just then, my phone buzzes, and my heartbeat accelerates by several degrees. Each time Alex texts me, I feel like there's a radar beam pulsing out from my phone: *Hey, look over here! Rachel Kim is texting with a boy! She's kissed him too! And he calls her his girlfriend!* With all the increased media speculation since Eunji's scandal and my move out of the villa, spending time with Alex in person is increasingly feeling like an impossibility. But every time I text or FaceTime with him, it just makes me want to see him more, so I've tried to rein in the frequency of our chats to spare myself the temptation. I know I should be honest with Alex about my hesitancy to make things officially official between us, but my own mind is so conflicted, I wouldn't even know how to begin to explain to *him* what I'm feeling. So for now, it's just easier to keep him at a distance.

My fingers are poised to type back Sorry, been slammed lately, but when I look at my screen, it's not a message from Alex I see.

Yujin: Hey you – Coffee at DB HQ next Tues.?

It's been a long time since I last caught up with my mentor from my trainee days, but Chung Yujin is the same as ever. Brisk and no-nonsense, but at once warm and inviting, her eyes bright with curiosity, her hair electric blue. We're sitting at the DB headquarters rooftop café, sipping iced coffee under big white umbrellas propped up over gleaming glass tables.

"It sounds like you're doing great," Yujin says when I've finished catching her up on all the things I have going on.

"Definitely great, and definitely busy," I laugh. "And the brand launches in early August, so things will only get busier from here," I say, thinking of the marketing materials I have to approve, and the launch-day interviews I have to prep for over the next month. "Not to mention all the group promos DB has us shooting."

"Ah yes, you all have been going nonstop lately," Yujin says with an eyebrow raised. "And I heard you moved back home with your family?" she adds, clearly noting the connection between my recent relocation and the sudden influx of group promos.

"Heard from DB, or heard from *Reveal*?" I cringe. "They've been running tons of bogus stories about me."

Yujin sets down her coffee cup and leans forward, her face thoughtful. "Listen, Rachel, the world has its eyes on you. You know that, right? You know that's why *Reveal* and all the other media outlets cover you so closely. Especially now with all the exciting things you have going on."

I blush a little, feeling both pleased and embarrassed.

"And it's great, you totally deserve all the success," Yujin continues. "But if I've learned anything through my years of training, it's that the internal competition within groups can breed some serious resentment. Especially once a group reaches a certain level. First you're all working together, trying to reach the top. But once you do, it's not uncommon for members to try to reach the top *within* the group. You've been together now, what? Five years?" Yujin asks.

"Six," I say. "As of next month. But honestly, Yujin, things between the girls have been fine. Better even, since I moved out. You know how the media likes to spin things. They're not happy unless there's some big conspiracy to report on."

Yujin looks unconvinced. "Speaking of which . . ." Her eyes narrow, pinning me under her gaze, like a trainee who's been caught with a forbidden cell phone at rehearsal. "I understand you were with Eunji at a certain dinner?" she asks pointedly.

Her words hang in the air for a moment, and it suddenly dawns on me that maybe this isn't just a friendly catch-up. Maybe Yujin's been sent here by DB to deliver a warning. I take a long sip of my iced coffee before answering. "Yes," I say slowly, "I was, but–" I pause, trying to choose my words carefully. As close as I've always felt to Yujin, the fact is, she's still DB management. "You have nothing to worry about there, Yujin. I'm . . . handling things."

Sure. If *handling things* means avoiding Alex altogether so I don't have to actually deal with the enormity of this situation.

I take a deep breath and look Yujin in the eye. "I understand what my responsibilities are as a member of this group, and a DB idol." It's true, and I also know that's what Yujin needs to hear in order to give a positive report back to Mr. Noh.

"Well, that's good," she says, her face softening somewhat.

"But you know as well as anyone that how things *are* and how things *look* are not always the same. And in our business, the latter is just as important – if not more so."

She leans back in her chair, her eyes scanning the rooftop café. Trainees, idols, and management mingle over lattes and pastries. On the surface, everyone seems to be enjoying a casual coffee break, but I'm sure most are engaged in serious conversations like the one Yujin and I are having. Like she said: appearances don't always reflect reality.

"I've got it!" she says suddenly, slamming her hand on the glass table. "You should host a party for the group's anniversary next month. I'm sure DB is planning something, but if you can take the reins on that, it could go a long way towards showing the girls that no matter where you're living or what *side projects*" – she raises an eyebrow at me again, and I feel my cheeks redden at the implied double meaning – "you might have going on, Girls Forever will always be your first priority."

I sip the last drops of my iced coffee, taking in her suggestion. Yujin's right. Being with her has brought back so many memories of my trainee days, and nearly all of them feature Akari. It hurts knowing how I ruined that friendship. I can't let the same thing happen with my groupmates. For now, it's just the media speculating that there's a rift between the Girls Forever girls, but I know just how powerful the media can be. Read a story enough times, you start thinking it might be true. I don't want the girls to start doubting my commitment to the group. Throwing an anniversary party for the group will solidify how much I care about them, and hopefully give the media something new to write about.

I smile at Yujin. "I'm all in."

"You look lovely tonight, Rachel," Jongseok says as I climb into the back seat wearing a simple but classic white pantsuit with gold hoop earrings, a big shopping bag slung over my shoulder.

Just as Yujin suspected, DB was happy to let me assume the role of hostess for the Girls Forever anniversary event – and made sure all the media outlets knew I'd be doing so. Over the past three weeks, I've logged countless hours arranging menus (Sumin is allergic to strawberries; Jiyoon hates artichokes) and consulting schedules (must not conflict with Sunhee's radio show, Ari's musical, or Mina's acting gigs; all nine of us *must* be present per DB mandate). And of course, all the while I've been finalising plans for my brand launch, which is somehow now only a week away. Before heading to the restaurant tonight, I sent off the last of my eighteen sketches for the Lane Crawford second season. It took more than one honey-butter-chip-fuelled all-nighter to get it done, but I managed to pull it off. Pressing "send" on my email to Celeste this afternoon felt like an immense weight had been lifted. I know tonight's dinner is just as much for the media coverage as it is for us, but still, I can't wait to enjoy a relaxing evening celebrating with the girls.

As we pull up to the restaurant, my phone pings with an incoming message.

Alex: Happy anniversary!!

My heart flutters seeing those words typed out from Alex. I know he's referring to Girls Forever, but still – I'm instantly transported to some future day when we're celebrating an anniversary of our own. I feel the now-familiar tugs of guilt and longing. There's so much I want to say to him – about us, our future, my fears, my hopes. But it never seems like the right time, with so many other commitments vying for my attention, and with the paparazzi ready to expose us at every turn. For now, I send him a string of heart emojis before tucking my phone away into my pocket.

The press is already out front at OASIS411 by the time I arrive. I wait in my car until all the girls arrive so we can enter the posh, palatial restaurant together. OASIS411 is the total opposite of Marigold House, where Eunji and I had our double date. It's ostentatious and high-end and all about the opportunity to see and be seen. The group arrives shortly after I do and the cameras go wild, snapping photos of us as we hug in greeting and linger in the warm July breeze, giddy and excited for our celebration. We even take one official posed shot in honour of our sixth anniversary, arms looped around each other, before waving at the paparazzi and disappearing into the restaurant.

We're whisked away to a private dining room, but unlike my double date with Eunji, this one has floor-to-ceiling windows, and I would not be surprised if there are more photographers in the shrubbery outside, hoping to score some pics through the glass. But as soon as the doors close, the hyped-up atmosphere from ten seconds ago dies down, leaving us in a tepid silence instead. It's like the past several weeks we've spent performing our group camaraderie for the promo shoots has left us drained of any authentic sense of friendship.

After a few awkward beats, Mina asks, "Did you go on a shopping spree before coming here or something?" She nods at the shopping bag on the floor next to my chair.

"Must be nice to have time to go shopping," Lizzie says coolly. "I've barely had time to sleep these days, but Rachel can raid the Galleria." I start to protest, but just then a waitress comes in and reads off the preset meal I've arranged for tonight's dinner.

When she reads off the grilled halibut entrée, Jiyoon snorts. My heart drops a little. I took the time to pick out this menu specifically for the girls, keeping in mind everyone's favourites. But maybe I missed the mark?

"Sorry," I say once the waitress has left. "If you guys don't want the halibut, I'm sure the kitchen can prepare something else . . ." I want this night to go perfectly – not for the media, but for us. Six years is a major accomplishment for a girl group, and we should be celebrating that.

"No, no," Jiyoon laughs. "I love halibut – great call, Rachel. I was just thinking about that seafood commercial we did back in year three. Do you remember that?"

"Oh my god!" Lizzie says. "I think I blocked it out of my memory."

"With the live lobsters?" Youngeun says. "Sunhee wanted

to take one home as a pet." She pokes Sun in the arm.

"I did not . . . " Sunhee starts to say, but Jiyoon overlaps her–

"Like excuse me, how the fuck did anyone think that was a good idea?"

Ari bursts out laughing, holding her stomach, just as a waitress comes in and begins passing round an amuse-bouche of heirloom-tomato-and-eggplant chutney on crostini.

"Okay, the lobsters were bad, but I'll take that over the time we had to roll around in melted chocolate for Pepero Day," Sumin says. "That was seriously unhygienic."

"Oh my god, I blocked that out of my memory too," Lizzie groans. "*That* was actually the worst."

Leah and I used to love exchanging boxes of the chocolate-dipped cookie sticks on Pepero Day, but after being dressed up as a literal human Pepero stick, I've distinctly lost my taste for the holiday.

"I still puke in my mouth a little every time I see Pepero now," Mina admits. This time we all burst out laughing, and Ari grips her stomach tighter, waving her hand in the air for us to stop.

"Seriously, it hurts!" she says.

That only makes us laugh harder. As the first course comes out – gorgeously plated mini-servings of cuttlefish-stuffed saffron risotto, beef-and-pumpkin consommé with ravioli, and oysters with tuna crudo – we keep sharing memories from the past six years, reminiscing from our worst moments to our funniest and scariest ones.

"One of my scariest moments was when we thought we lost Sunhee at the airport in Taiwan," I say, inelegantly slurping an oyster. "And the flight was about to take off. Do you remember how much we panicked? We thought you got kidnapped, Sun."

"I'm sorry," Sunhee laughs, her face turning red. "Breakfast didn't sit well with me."

"You could have *told* us you were going to the bathroom!" I say, laughing. "Mina nearly called for the air marshal!" Mina rolls her eyes, but a small smile peeks out and she looks fondly at Sunhee.

"My scariest moment was when a fan fainted because she was so excited to meet us," Sumin says. "Youngeun was about to climb over the table and do CPR on her."

"That's what first aid training is for," Youngeun says seriously.

"I remember that fan," Ari says. "She woke up on her own after ten seconds and was so embarrassed, but after we all gave her a hug and took a photo with her, she said it turned into the best day of her life."

"That was sweet," Mina admits. "Our fans are the best."

"Hold up, is Choo Mina getting sentimental?" Eunji says, grinning.

Mina shrugs, spearing a piece of ravioli with her fork and popping it into her mouth. "You didn't hear it from me."

The night slips away hour by hour as we keep eating and

chatting and swapping stories. I wish the media could see us like this – loose and punchy, our guards down as we reminisce about the times we've shared, all of us genuinely enjoying each other's company. But then again, maybe that's what makes moments like this so special. They're ours alone. These girls may get on my nerves like no other, but at the end of the day, they're the only ones who have gone through everything with me in the past six years. We really are family, whether we like it or not. And tonight, I think to myself looking around the table, I like it a lot.

"By the way, I thought I should tell everyone," Lizzie says, "DB has given me permission to move back in with my family. I'll be leaving the villa next week." Her eyes dart to mine in the briefest acknowledgment before she looks away, reaching for a sip of her drink.

"Me too," Youngeun says. She turns to me with an appreciative smile. "My mom's thrilled. And she wants all of you to come to the café soon – I think she's already called Mr. Noh fourteen times about setting something up, so look forward to that being added to your schedules." She gives a half smile and rolls her eyes. "Anyway, we really have you to thank, Rachel. I've thought about moving home before, but I never would have brought it up with the execs if you hadn't first. Thanks for the inspiration."

I feel a wave of relief. After hearing over and over again how much grief my moving out was giving DB with all the bad press, I feel so glad to hear that something positive has come out of it for the group. "That's great news," I say. "Really great news. And speaking of inspiration . . ." I reach for my big shopping bag, feeling butterflies in my stomach. I've been waiting for this moment all night, but I suddenly feel nervous. "I have a gift for each of you."

One by one, I pull out eight handbags from inside the shopping bag. "These are the bags from my fashion line. They're all inspired by important moments or phases in my life. And for the past six years, you guys have been there for every single big moment. So I wanted you all to be the first to have one." I lay out the bags on the table, flushing with nerves, and maybe a little bit of pride. I hand out the NYC bag, the Trainee bag, the First Tour bag, and my favourite, the one I call the Rachel Now bag. It's buttery smooth and spherical shaped, and meant to represent my current life as a globe-trotting K-pop star.

I can't stop smiling as they fight over which bag will be each of theirs. I'm so glad they like them. My groupmates are so unpredictable sometimes that I was keeping my expectations low, but I didn't realise how much their support would mean to me until now. I watch as Eunji tries on the Trainee bag, the one that transitions from a crossbody to a clutch. I thought I changed a lot during my seven trainee years, but I see now that these past six years – the ones since we debuted – have been just as formative, if not more. I've grown into a well-rounded person who can love K-pop with all her heart but still pursue other passions.

Well-rounded. The perfect description of the Rachel Now

bag. I make a mental note to put that in one of the promotional posts, then remind myself to stay focused on the moment. Our anniversary. I can't believe it's been six years already. As I look around the room again, my eyes get a little watery. We've been through so much together, these eight girls and I.

I raise my glass. "To six years of Girls Forever."

We cheers. "And many more to come!"

Twenty

"Shh, don't wake her up yet."

"Scootch over."

"Okay ready, count of three?"

"HAPPY LAUNCH DAY!"

My eyes fly open to the blast of party horns, and I shoot up in bed. "Oh my god, I think I'm having a heart attack!? You guys scared the crap out of me!"

Everyone bursts out laughing as I fully wake up and take in what's going on around me. Gold-and-pink confetti is raining down on my head. Umma leans against the doorframe while Appa sits on the chair at the bamboo desk. At the foot of my bed, Leah, Hyeri, and Juhyun are all squished together, perching on the edge of the mattress, wearing birthday hats.

"What is all this?" I laugh as Leah plops a pink birthday hat with golden trim on top of my head.

"We're celebrating RACHEL K.'s birthday, obviously," Leah says. "Only *you* would sleep in on a day like this!"

"Leah, it's eight a.m.!"

"I know, but still! We've been up for two hours prepping!"

"Juhyun and I can't stay," Hyeri says, and I notice she's dressed for the lab in a simple pair of fitted grey pants, long-sleeved blouse, and name tag, "but we had to swing by to tell you good luck."

"You're going to absolutely kill it, babe," Juhyun says, reaching over to give me a one-arm hug. "I'm meeting my brand manager for coffee, and then I'm dragging her straight to Apgujeong Rodeo Street so I can pick up one of your bags for myself. I already have a whole vlog planned for it."

"Aw, you don't have to do that," I say with a small smile, a little embarrassed by all the to-do.

"Are you kidding me? Of course we do!" Juhyun says, looking at me like I'm crazy.

"And," Hyeri adds, "even if we didn't have to – you know, due to the rules of best friendship – we would anyway because those bags are fierce!"

"Well, if you insist," I say, smiling brighter. For the millionth time since we met back in fourth grade, I'm struck by how lucky I am to have such amazing friends. Just then, Hyeri's Apple Watch starts beeping out an alarm.

"Okay, now we really have to go before I'm officially late," she says, hopping off my bed.

"Celebratory drinks later?" Juhyun asks as she follows Hyeri towards the door.

Truthfully, I can't even let myself think ahead all the way

to tonight – I'm too nervous about what the day holds. But I nod anyway and jump out of bed to give the twins each a big hug, then wave goodbye as they hustle out of my room.

"Thank you," I say to Leah and my parents when it's just the four of us. "This was so sweet of you."

"You worked so hard for this," Umma says, squeezing my shoulder. "We couldn't just let it go by like an ordinary day."

"Wow! Our daughter, a designer," Appa says proudly.

My heart swells. I can't believe we made it to launch day. That *I* made it to launch day. Last night, I lay in bed for hours thinking about today. What will it feel like to see someone walking down the street wearing one of my designs? Or what if nobody buys them? I tossed and turned, picturing the bags sitting there on department store shelves, collecting dust. While it's true that I'm doing this on my own, I know everything I do reflects on DB and Girls Forever as a whole. And seeing the pride in my father's face right now, I know it reflects on my family, too. They'll, of course, love me no matter what – whether I succeed at this new venture, or fall completely on my face. But even so, I'm terrified of letting everyone down.

Leah blows her party horn, breaking me from my nervous thoughts. "We brought a special breakfast for you, too, Unni!" she says. "Egg-and-cheese breakfast croissants from that new brunch place across the street." She says *croissants* in an exaggerated French accent. "They're soft and flaky and amazing – you have to come try one while they're still warm."

"I can already taste the butter," I say, grinning. "I just have to do one thing first. I'll meet you out there."

I reach for my phone as Umma, Appa, and Leah leave my room. I already have an Instagram post scheduled for today. One last time I check over the photo of me posing with all six of my bags slung over my shoulders. I stare at the photo, pleased with the final result. The bags are cohesive – they make a statement about colour and whimsy and living your best life – but they are still all very distinct from one another, so I had to think carefully about what kind of backdrop and outfit would complement them all. In the end, we shot the pics in front of a plain white backdrop, with flowers of every colour scattered on the floor. I wore a sleek pale-wash denim pantsuit.

Meet your new favourites at: RACHEL K., the caption says, encouraging people to follow us at @rachel.k.shop.

I take a deep breath.

Here we go.

I click "post."

Okay. Oh my god. It's done. As soon as I'm sure it posted, I turn off my phone and stick it under my pillow to make sure I'm not tempted to recheck it a thousand more times. I'll be constantly refreshing my feed if I don't. I can already feel my fingers itching to grab my phone and see how people are responding, so I quickly leave my room to wash up and join the others for breakfast.

There's nothing like croissants to start the day. They're buttery and flaky just like Leah said, and I inhale half of

mine before I even take my first sip of hot tea – an Earl
Grey with extra whole milk, which is my go-to on those rare
cosy mornings in. For the better part of breakfast, I'm able to
ignore the anxious butterflies in my stomach and just enjoy
celebrating the launch with my family. But the pastries are
gone all too soon, and even though I have a stylist coming
over at ten to help me get ready for an interview, I'm too
nervous to focus, so instead I offer to help Leah pick out an
outfit for SayGO's upcoming fan meeting. Then I flop down
on the living room couch and flip through the channels,
barely registering what's on the screen, until Appa comes
in and asks why I'm watching the animal channel, and I
suddenly realise I've been tuned into the mating rituals of
meerkats for who knows how long.

Just as I'm dying to check my phone, the stylist, Missy,
arrives, and we move into a frenzy of outfits and hair and
makeup. I can hear my phone dinging from inside my room.

"Do you want me to take a peek first?" Missy asks as
we wrap up, seeing me visibly twitching to grab my phone.
Jongseok will be here in about five minutes. I'm meeting the
interviewer at a cute café nearby.

"It's okay," I say. "I got this."

If there's anything I learned from being in the entertainment
industry for the past six years, it's that you have to brave the
public eye sooner or later. No one can do it for you, no matter
how much you might want them to.

At the last second, I grab my phone as I head out the door,

and take a look as I step into the car waiting for me out on the street. My lock screen is *flooded* with texts.

Suddenly, the breakfast sandwich threatens to come back up, and all the nerves I've been trying to hold back take over.

I quickly tap in my pin and start scrolling through the messages.

Carly Mattsson: Rachel, LOVE your bags! Congratulations!! I'm so proud and excited for you xoxo.

Juhyun: Umm Rachel, your line is amazing!! I'm literally bragging to everyone at Lotte right now that I'm friends with the designer.

Hyeri: Seriously! I just stepped out during my lunch break. I can't choose one bag . . . I need all of them in my life!

My Instagram post is getting so many likes and comments per second that I can barely keep up. An article praises my bags for being "fresh and functional" while another celebrates "the unique point of view." I start reading one of the articles posted by *NYLON*:

RACHEL K. is the first fashion line launched by a K-pop idol. As expected, the Girls Forever (Korea's number-one girl group – read our feature on their meteoric rise here) star's line is drawing in fans from all around the globe, but it's clear already that the appeal of RACHEL K. stretches far beyond lovers of K-pop. At this rate, Ms. Kim should expect an influx of new fans, not just for her music, but for her dynamic debut as an up-and-coming fashion designer.

I feel like I'm dreaming. I was hoping the line would not be a complete flop, but this is beyond anything I could have ever expected. Still, just because critics are praising the bags, it doesn't mean that customers are buying them.

If it was surreal seeing the press coverage of my bags, it's even more surreal seeing them for sale in actual stores. Inside Lotte Department Store, I watch from the swimwear section as a handful of shoppers pick up my bags and try them on in front of a full-length mirror. Once they're gone, I walk over to check things out myself. Seeing my designs lit up under store lights, alongside designers like Prada and Fendi, I feel a flutter of excitement and adrenaline. I can't believe this is really happening.

They've created this gorgeous hot-air balloon display, except instead of wicker baskets, each balloon holds a handbag at its base. The balloons themselves are crafted out of shimmering crystal, suspended in the air against a gold-sequinned backdrop. I quickly snap a picture of it to send to Alex.

"Oh my god, it's Rachel!"

At the sound of my name, I turn to find a small crowd has gathered here in the accessories department.

My bodyguard steps forward to keep the crowds back as more and more fans start screaming and waving in my direction. "Hi, Rachel! Hi! We love your bags!"

I wave back with both hands, smiling so big that my cheeks hurt. "Thank you so much for the support, everyone!"

I walk down the line, shaking everyone's hand and thanking them individually. There is the young woman who tells me that she's buying herself a RACHEL K. bag to celebrate her recent graduation from law school – and she only pursued a career in law because I inspired her to chase her dreams. There is the high school girl who tells me she got a job – her first ever – at a frozen yogurt shop and pulled double shifts every opportunity she could just to afford one of my bags. Her mother, who's standing in line with her, jokes to me that I'm the one who finally gave her daughter a work ethic. Everyone is so lovely and excited, it's actually kind of overwhelming.

By the time I get back into the car, all I want is to slip on my comfy knit joggers and eat a nice bowl of patbingsu in bed . . .

My phone buzzes, jolting me out of my sweet-shaved-ice dreams.

A notification reminds me that I've missed three calls from Alex. I immediately dial him up on FaceTime. He answers on the first ring.

"Rachel?" he says, his face appearing on the screen. "There you are. I've been trying to reach you!"

"Um . . . can you believe this?" I say, putting my hand over my mouth. I'm at a total loss for words.

"Yes, I can!" he says, laughing with the biggest grin on his face. "I can definitely believe it. Your line is incredible and you worked so hard for this. God, I wish I could be there with you in person to celebrate."

"Me too," I say wistfully. Alex has been stuck at home in Hong Kong for the past several weeks working on a tricky business negotiation, the timing of which feels like both a blessing and a curse. As much as I'd love to share this moment with him, I've been so dogged by the press today, there's no way we'd have been able to spend time together without being caught.

"So listen, I have great news," Alex says on my screen. "The early numbers from Lotte are really strong."

"They are?" I ask. "How strong?"

"With numbers like this, you could even think about opening your own boutique a couple years from now."

My own boutique? I can't even imagine it. Adrenaline shoots through me – a mix of excitement and fear. This thing is *growing*, and it's all happening so quickly. Don't get me wrong, I'm ecstatic. But it's scary, too. There's certainly no going back now. And what started as a little experiment is now out in the world. It's got its own momentum, and good or bad, I won't always get to control what comes next.

Twenty-One

If I thought I was busy *before* launch, I don't know what I was thinking. Days pass marked by Girls Forever commitments, calls for interviews about RACHEL K., designing and planning orders for new bags, and shooting social media promotions.

Is this what having it all looks like?

The craziest part about success that most people don't know: No matter how huge the moment is, it doesn't actually change your day-to-day life as much as you would think. You're still hurrying to get out of your shower in the morning and make it to group appearances on time. You're still cranky when you get stuck in a long line trying to grab an iced mocha to go. You're still worried about making the right impressions. You still miss your family. You still don't know how to wrestle the fear in your chest when you think about the future – including the amazing guy who called you his girlfriend in front of his whole family even though you weren't quite ready for him to.

I know I should talk to Alex about our relationship. About how that term sends twin jolts of joy and anxiety through me each time he uses it. But at the same time, things feel so good right now, that I don't want to risk it. My brand is being received better than I could have hoped. I just celebrated my six-year anniversary with the girls and feel closer to them than ever. I'm back at home with my family. And, even if we don't get to see each other as often as we'd like, I have an amazing guy in my life. I don't want to ruin all that with difficult conversations. At least for the moment, it's like I've achieved some perfect but fragile equilibrium. Like I'm balancing a dozen plates, but one wrong move will send them all shattering down.

There's no heat on earth like Shanghai in August. As soon as I exit Pudong Airport, I can feel the humidity, my skin prickling with sweat. I'm dying for a shower, but we won't be checking into the Peninsula Hotel this trip. In just under eight hours, we'll be right back here to catch our return flight home to Seoul.

My schedule this week was packed with DB commitments, but there was no way I was going to miss the chance to present my line at the grand opening of Lane Crawford's new Shanghai flagship store. It's normal to miss things because of personal projects sometimes – like when Sunhee missed the multigroup concert because of the radio awards show, or another time when Mina had to do some reshoots for *When I Loved You* and missed the seven appearances we had booked for that day. But with the LA concert coming up, I didn't want to miss any of the group promotional events we have planned. So, I told DB I could make the trip to Shanghai and back in a single day. Now I just have to try to survive it.

When we arrive at Lane Crawford, Jongseok leads me to a greenroom to get prepped. There, Celeste runs me through the event schedule while my hair stylist tries to wrestle my hair into a sleek, complicated twist. Then, I'm whisked out on to a stage they've constructed in the middle of the store, under a sparkling glass atrium. Cameras flash in a sea of fans sporting Girls Forever T-shirts and glowing headbands. I present my six bags to the crowd, explaining the inspiration behind them, and sending extra love to my groupmates back home. After the presentation, I get half a minute to down an espresso shot and some fried pork dumplings before I'm back in the greenroom to do some one-on-one interviews with a handful of news outlets, effortlessly switching to greet each one in either Mandarin, English, or Korean. And then, in a blink of an eye, I'm back at Pudong Airport, boarding my flight home.

I wake up just as we're pulling up to Umma and Appa's apartment.

"Good night, Rachel," Jongseok says as he drops me off. "See you tomorrow."

But his words barely register. I'm already half-asleep again as I trudge up to the door and board the elevator. My bed is calling me like a siren song, but before crawling into it,

I sit down at my bamboo desk to compose a thank-you email to Celeste for organising today's event. But before I can even open my laptop, sleep finally overtakes me.

Once, when we were in our debut year, Girls Forever had to take a five-hour overnight bus ride from Seoul to Jeonnam on the southern coast. Normally we would have flown, but there was a pilot strike grounding all planes, and there was no way DB was going to let us miss our fansign. When we finally arrived, every picture I took featured my head tilted at an awkward angle – my neck totally bent out of shape from trying to sleep against the bus window all night.

This morning, the crick in my neck is ten times worse.

I wake hunched over my desk, a piece of notebook paper stuck to my face with drool.

God, what time is it?

I groggily tap my cell phone, only to find that it's dead. Of course. I never plugged it in last night. I fish out my charger from my carry-on bag and anxiously wait for my phone to reboot. I want to call Alex and tell him about yesterday. Besides talking business on launch day, we haven't really connected in what feels like weeks. I just want to hear the sound of his voice. To see his smiling face, even if only through FaceTime. Finally, my phone springs to life. I'm about to dial Alex's number when a notification pops up on my screen:

Today 9 a.m. – GF @ Youngeun's café

For a moment I'm totally confused. Then it comes back to me.

Youngeun at the anniversary dinner, telling us all her mom wanted us to come to the café.

DB putting it on our schedule for this week.

Jongseok saying "See you tomorrow" as he dropped me off.

As my phone continues to wake up, a series of missed calls from my manager pop up on the screen, the time stamps at 8:45; 8:50; 8:55.

It's currently 8:57.

"Shit. Shit. Shit," I chant, racing through our apartment, shoving my feet into my Nikes while hastily running a brush through my tangled mess of bedhead. Or deskhead, as the case may be.

"Language, Daughter!" Umma calls as I run out the door.

Jongseok's car is idling outside our building when I burst through the lobby doors. "Sorry! Sorry!" I say, slamming the car door behind me. Jongseok says nothing, but flashes me a look in the rearview mirror. I take a deep breath and sit back in my seat, and will Jongseok to break a few speeding laws.

When I finally arrive at Youngeun's café, I race inside, bracing myself for the crap the girls will undoubtedly give me for my late arrival. But when I enter, all the girls seem happy to see me. Like, genuinely glad. It's more than a little unnerving to see their big smiles and friendly waves as they beckon me over.

I slide into the large booth by the window, feeling like the girl in the horror movie who has no idea she's about to get murdered by a chainsaw-wielding maniac.

"Hi, everyone. Youngeun, the place looks great," I say, nodding to the little Mason jars of wildflowers that adorn each table.

"Thanks, my mom went all out after DB said they'd do the photo shoot here."

Just then, I notice a couple of DB photographers flanking inconspicuously around us, snapping some supposedly candid photos of our hangout. Suddenly I realise that's why the girls are in such a good mood.

They're putting on smiles for the camera.

A small group of fans have clustered themselves up by the coffee bar – far enough away from our window booth that they can't hear what we're saying, but definitely close enough to keep looking at us out of the corners of their eyes as they take longer than any human needs to stir sugar into their lattes. One whispers behind her hand to her friend, who glances furtively in my direction, then looks at her watch. They totally saw my late arrival.

Finally, after ten minutes of excruciatingly chipper small talk between the Girls Forever girls, the DB photographers say they've got what they needed.

The moment they're gone, Youngeun wheels on me.

"What the hell, Rachel? Where were you?"

Her harsh tone has me totally taken aback. Youngeun is normally so measured and thoughtful. I've never seen her show her temper like this.

"I'm – I'm so sorry," I stammer. "I got home late from

Shanghai last night and totally forgot to set an alarm. I'm so sorry I was late."

"You know this café is important to me," she says, folding her arms across her chest. "We all supported you when you started doing your line, but the one time I'm looking for support back, you can't be bothered?"

"No, Younguen," I start. "It was an honest mistake, I'm so sorr–"

"Here." She tosses a small cellophane bag tied with a ribbon in my direction. "My mom made these for everyone. We all took pictures with them. At least, those of us who were here did."

I look down and see a cookie, intricately decorated with icing. It's me. Me in cookie form. I glance around the table. The rest of the girls all have cookie versions of themselves too – Lizzie's with pale yellow icing for her blond hair, Sunhee's with full rosy cheeks. I can't believe Mrs. Yoon went through all this trouble for us. I look up at Youngeun at a loss for what to say, how to apologise. But before I can even try, she storms off towards the kitchens.

I slump in the booth and sip my cappuccino. It's gone cold, the espresso leaving a bitter taste in my mouth. Mina leans over and unwraps my Rachel cookie, and I don't even try to stop her. "So," she whispers. "Your fashion line won't affect your commitment to the group at all, huh? I can totally tell."

Then she takes a huge bite right out of my head.

• • •

I hide out in the ladies' room at Youngeun's café for exactly thirteen minutes, weighing the pros and cons of having to face the girls again, versus having the +EVERs at the café speculate about what digestive issue I must have that's causing me to disappear to the bathroom for such a long stretch of time. Eventually, I decide it's time to face the music. Oversleeping was a complete accident, but I did hurt Youngeun and I have to own that. As I make my way down the hall back toward the dining area, I hear voices coming from the booth by the window.

"I'm like shocked, though. A few little bags?" Lizzie says. "I didn't think it would do this well."

I freeze in my steps, and lean against the wall, hidden from view.

"Ugh, I know," Eunji sighs. "Like, sure, they're cute and all, but why is the world going bananas over these?"

My skin grows cold.

"It's bullshit is what it is," Mina says. I can almost imagine her rolling her eyes. "My dad is so pissed that DB let her do this. It's totally different from appearing in a movie or musical. This is a whole second career."

"Or a career *change*," Jiyoon adds with a trace of bitterness.

"I mean, if she wants to do fashion, fine," Youngeun says. "But it seems like she's getting special treatment. DB wouldn't even let me do a measly YouTube channel, but Rachel can create an international company? Did you hear they're selling the bags in Hong Kong, too?"

"I know. Honestly, I didn't think Rachel would put her

fashion line ahead of the group, but it really does feel that way, doesn't it?" Sunhee says sadly.

"I saw it coming," Ari says with an air of self-satisfaction.

Sumin lets out a heavy sigh. "This is just between us – but sometimes I just wish everything she did didn't go so *perfectly* for her. Doesn't it seem like she hardly has to try, and good things just fall into her lap?" The girls murmur in agreement.

"And did you see that interview that ran this morning? She's all *Girls Forever* this and *Girls Forever* that. Like, are you really that loyal or are you just using the group to support yourself?" says Lizzie.

Still hidden around the corner, I feel my face flush with hurt, and I'm shocked to discover a few tears gathering in the corners of my eyes. I expect it from Mina and Lizzie, but I thought Eunji and I were closer now. And the others . . . I can't believe they think my saying the group was part of my inspiration is just me capitalising on the group's fame for my own gain, when it couldn't be further from the truth! That's especially low.

I'm about to head back into the café, feeling like I've been punched in the gut, when I hear Lizzie say, "Don't worry. We have a plan."

As she starts to describe this "plan," she lowers her voice, so I can't hear her any more. I lean further around the corner, trying to catch what she's saying, but at that exact moment, Mina glances up and we make eye contact. Shit.

Mina nudges Lizzie to stop talking. I swallow hard. No

point hiding now. I hastily wipe the tears away and step out from behind the corner.

"Hey, Rachel," Mina says, quirking an eyebrow, "the managers are going to be here in ten minutes to pick us up. Think you can manage to be on time for that?"

I stare at her for a beat, willing her to back off. But she just stares back at me.

Finally, I break eye contact and head for the door. "I'll be waiting outside."

I may have blinked first, but that doesn't mean I have to let them see me cry.

Twenty-Two

Hey, it's me. Guess we've been playing a little phone tag lately. Let's see, updates: Looks like we're finally going to contract on the Shearson deal, so I might be able to have something resembling a life again. Um . . . Halmoni loved the cat sweater you picked out. Unfortunately, Elvis may have to lose a few pounds to fit into it, but don't worry, she's got him on some diet kibble, so . . . Anyway, I guess the only other thing to report is how much I miss you. Call me back when you can.

I replay Alex's message again while I wait for Leah to meet me in the DB lobby. Even through a voicemail his voice brings me a sense of calm – which I'm desperately seeking these days. Luckily, yesterday's disastrous café visit was the last thing on my schedule for this week, so I'll have some time to calm down before I have to see the girls again. I still can't get over the whiplash of what happened – one second I'm feeling like a jerk for missing Youngeun's special cookie moment; the next, I'm feeling like I've been stabbed in the back with a chef's knife.

For so long, I was worried about my fashion line not being successful enough – Mina's constant reminders ringing in my ears: *When one of us looks bad, we all look bad.* But I never expected that the girls would think my brand was *too* successful. I think back to what Yujin said at our coffee date – that eventually, even the closest groups can be torn apart by internal competition. Is that what's happening to us?

I hear a group of people making their way down the main staircase, and look up expecting to see Leah and her SayGO groupmates. They had an early-morning recording session, and I promised Leah I'd be waiting with red bean doughnuts as soon as they let out. But instead, I see a crowd of angry-looking adults.

"–*better* take it seriously. Do you know how much money I've given that man over the years? I practically paid for his second vacation home!" a man in a blue suit says.

"Yah! Not to mention the eyelid surgery I did for his wife at *half price*," a woman with a bob and severe bangs adds. Something about her seems familiar, but I can't quite place what.

"Unni!" At the sound of Leah's voice, I turn to see her and her groupmates arriving in the lobby from another staircase. "Please tell me you have the goods."

I smile and wave the box of doughnuts. "Gotcha covered."

We're about to leave the lobby when my cell starts buzzing. I shove the doughnut box into Leah's hands, frantic to finally catch Alex on the phone. But the call is coming from an unknown international number. Normally I'd just let it go to voicemail, but part of me hopes it might be Alex calling from another number for some reason. I duck out of the DB building and sit on a nearby bench to take the call.

"Hello?"

"Hi, is this Rachel Kim?" a woman with a British accent says.

"Speaking," I say.

"So glad to have reached you. My name is Cynthia Barnes," she says. "I'm an executive at Discipline."

I sit upright on the bench. *Discipline Sportswear.* That's Ollie Mattsson's – Carly's husband's – activewear brand. "Yes, hi. How can I help you?"

"We're putting together a shoot in the Swiss Alps to promote the new skiwear line, and we'd absolutely love to have you model for us."

A photo shoot in the Swiss Alps? For Ollie Mattsson's brand? I hardly think twice. "Yes! I'm absolutely interested."

"Wonderful," Cynthia says. "We're also hoping that if things go well, we could plan an event with you and Ollie to meet some fans, and we'd have you sing, of course!"

A photo shoot *and* a solo fan meeting? Is she about to offer me a lifetime supply of Choco Pies next? Because I'm pretty sure that's the only way this could get better.

"I'm sorry to be reaching out to you directly like this," Cynthia continues, pulling me back from my chocolate dreams. "I tried to connect with your management team earlier today, but they told us everyone was in a meeting, and well,

I didn't want to wait. You see, things for the photo shoot are coming together quite quickly – we'd need you in Switzerland by September fifteenth. I know it's a bit last-minute."

"Um yeah, a bit," I say, chewing on my lip. "I'll just need to run it by management and make sure I'm available."

"Please do and have them get back to us soonest."

I hang up with Cynthia and stare at my phone in a daze. I can't believe it. Did that really just happen?

I quickly fill in Leah, then race back into DB headquarters. The Discipline shoot is just over a month away. I can't waste a minute getting DB's permission.

"Excuse me, Mr. Noh?" I tap on his open door lightly. "Sorry, I didn't see your assistant out there, and I know Jongseok is at the vet with his dogs this morning–"

"Ah . . . yes." Mr. Noh looks up from his desk. He seems distracted, but ushers me into his office. "Come in, Rachel."

"I've just been given an opportunity to do a photo shoot for Discipline Sportswear," I say as soon as I'm seated. "They're offering to fly me to Switzerland for the shoot in mid-September. Do you think there's any way we could have that worked into my schedule?"

Mr. Noh stiffens. "I didn't get a request from Discipline to work with you," he says.

"They reached out to me directly," I say carefully. "They said you were all in a meeting this morning?"

There's an awkwardness in the air as Mr. Noh glances down at the papers on his desk, then hastily turns them facedown.

"Yes, well," Mr. Noh says, "you'll need to get me the exact dates. You leave for the LA concert on September thirtieth – obviously we can't have this trip brushing up against that." I nod. "But," Mr. Noh continues, "I suppose if the timing works, and you've already said yes . . . then we can't turn them down, can we?"

I let out an inward sigh of relief and bow in thanks. "Thank you so much, Mr. Noh."

As I turn to leave, Mr. Noh holds up a hand, stopping me.

"Just a reminder, Rachel" – his eyes flash behind his glasses – "to keep your priorities in order. I certainly hope you're not forgetting what they are."

Priorities. The word replays in my mind over the next several weeks.

Am I prioritising the right things? Am I giving all my commitments the attention they deserve? The only thing that's given me an ounce or two of peace is the fact that the girls have been unusually quiet. Their nasty comments about my fashion line still sting, but I've tried to push them to the back of my mind. And thankfully, I've been too busy with RACHEL K. to let myself wallow. Even so, ever since overhearing them whisper behind my back about some mysterious "plan," I've been feeling nervous, waiting for the other shoe to drop. But now I'm starting to wonder if it was just another instance of petty drama that has blown over while I've been focused on other things.

Even when they found out about my upcoming Discipline photo shoot, they were surprisingly chill.

"Discipline? That's that sportswear line by Oliver Mattsson, right? Cool," Jiyoon said, giving me a half smile I couldn't quite read. The rest of the girls seemed to be consumed with staring at their own schedules and trying to reconcile how they were going to accomplish it all. For once, maybe they are just as busy as I am, and they don't have the energy for drama.

Maybe I have been worrying for nothing.

Maybe they were just letting off steam that day in the café.

And yet, something squirms in my gut . . . the knowledge that it's never, *ever* that simple, when it comes to Girls Forever.

"Hey, Jongseok," I say to him as he drives me to DB for a vocal rehearsal.

"Yes, Rachel?"

"Have you noticed the girls acting a little . . . different lately?" Maybe if there really is some sort of sinister plan afoot, Jongseok would have heard of it.

"Different?"

"You know, like, they've been leaving me alone. Not as much drama as I'm used to," I add with a knowing smile. I catch Jongseok's eye in the rearview mirror. He smiles at me. Jongseok has probably borne witness to more of the house drama than any of the other managers, though you would never know it, because he's also the least likely to snap at any of us. He keeps his cool in every situation, which is why over the years I've come to make sure he's the one managing my personal schedule and travel rather than any of the other managers on the team.

"Well, of course, that would be because their parents are keeping them so busy recently. Hard to compete with what *you've* accomplished, though!"

"Their parents? What do you mean?"

Jongseok chuckles. "The girls – and all their parents – met with DB a couple of days after your launch. You could almost see the smoke coming out of their ears."

At Jongseok's words, I instantly think back to that day I was waiting for Leah in the DB lobby. Those angry adults stomping down the stairs. That woman with the bob haircut and blunt bangs who looked familiar. Envisioning her furious expression now, I suddenly realise why. That piercing look in her eye. It's the spitting image of Lizzie when she's pissed.

"Everyone was very upset that you had got the chance to do a fashion line. They claimed they had no idea about it," Jongseok explains.

"Oh my god." I can't believe they'd say that. My groupmates knew all about my fashion line. I've kept them in the loop every step of the way, and I have plenty of texts with them to prove it! Then I remember. The "plan" the girls were gossiping about at the café . . . *this* must what they were talking about. "What did DB do?" I ask Jongseok.

"Well, the company explained that you had DB's total

permission and approval for your line. And then they said everyone was free to try and start their own companies, if that's what they really want," he says with a shrug.

"Oh! I . . . Oh," I mumble, genuinely surprised. "Well, good. I'm glad to hear it." As I process this, it occurs to me that this is quite possibly the best-case scenario. Everyone is free and empowered to pursue whatever they want. If I can have it all, the rest of the girls should be allowed to have it all too.

After all, when one of us wins, we all win. Right?

"All right, ladies. Let's call it a night," our vocal coach says after we finish running through the new songs in the set list for the LA concert. "You sound beautiful."

It's true, we did sound great. Harmonising with the girls tonight felt like the perfect metaphor for things finally starting to heal between us. But even so, the intel I got from Jongseok is weighing on my mind. It's clear that we still have some things to sort out. Luckily, it seems like maybe the girls are feeling the same way.

Sunhee stops me after practice, inching towards me, almost shyly. "Hey. It's been a while. We feel like we never see you any more. Why don't you come by the villa tonight? Lizzie's coming, and Youngeun too – she's going to make tteokbokki. You should come, it'll be like old times."

"Okay," I say, giving Sunhee a small smile. I'm glad we're going to get the chance to address what happened with their parents. Maybe it was just a misunderstanding, or maybe

Jongseok got the story wrong. Hopefully, going over to the villa tonight will help clear the air. "That sounds great, actually. I'll just run home and shower and then meet you guys there."

"Great." She glances back towards the rest of the girls, now fully on board their SUVs and waiting for her to join them. "Can't wait."

A few hours later, I let myself in through the front door, carrying doughnut twists that Umma sent with me. I told her there'd be plenty to eat with Youngeun making tteokbokki, but moms – or at least mine, anyway – can never send you out the door empty-handed. "Girls, I'm here!" I call.

It's dead silent inside. Weird. Did they go out? I texted Sunhee from the car to give her my ETA . . .

I walk into the living room and nearly jump out of my skin in surprise. The girls are all standing in the middle of the room, waiting for me with their arms crossed, like they're about to stage an intervention. I feel like I've walked on to the set of some strange dystopian movie. Or maybe horror. Their eyes lock on mine, but when I glance at Sunhee, she looks away guiltily.

This isn't a hangout. It's an ambush.

"Rachel, take a seat," Mina says briskly. "We need to talk."

She gestures to the couch. I slowly sit down, lowering my box of doughnut twists.

"What's going on?" I say, looking up at the girls. My heart

is thumping in my chest. Standing together like that, they look like an impenetrable wall. I've never felt so alienated from the group.

"We've been discussing it," Lizzie says. "And all of us feel like you're no longer committed to the group."

"That's not true," I say. "I mean, I know I've been busy these days, but Girls Forever is my number-one priority. It always has been and always will be."

"Well, it sure hasn't felt that way. So maybe you need to prove it," Mina says. She glances at the other girls and then looks back at me. "We're going to need you to put your brand on hold."

I must have heard her wrong.

"Put it on hold?" I echo.

"Yes," Mina says firmly. "At least until the end of our contract with DB."

My stomach recoils. That's four years away. My brand is just starting out. I can't afford to put it on hold now, while it's still so new. If I did, it would basically mean ending RACHEL K. altogether. Are they seriously giving me an ultimatum? Asking me to choose between fashion and Girls Forever?

"I – you – this is a little dramatic, isn't it?" I say.

"We're thinking about what's best for the group while all you've been thinking about is what's best for you," Lizzie accuses.

"That's not fair," I say, stung. "You all have side things

going on too. Mina's movie. Ari's musical. And besides," I say, hurt turning to annoyance the more I think about what they're asking of me, "as you *and your parents* know, DB gave me permission to launch my line."

Lizzie glances at Mina. I don't think they knew I was in the loop about how they met with DB a few weeks ago. "That's not the point," Lizzie mumbles.

"And besides," Sumin jumps in, "we're not constantly jet-setting around the world for fashion shows and photo shoots. Aren't you leaving for Switzerland in a few days? Right before our big concert?"

"You were late to events all summer," Ari says with a hand on her hip. "It was totally rude, right, Youngeun?"

I want to argue the point – besides what happened at the café, I really have not been late to anything. At least, not by more than a minute or two. And there have been girls who have actually *missed* events and performances altogether because of personal projects. Why am I getting singled out? But at the same time, I do have to admit that with all I've had on my plate since the launch, the fashion brand has been taking up a pretty big chunk of real estate in my brain these days. Not to mention the whole Defining-the-Relationship thing with Alex that I've been spending all my brainpower trying to *avoid* thinking about. Of course, I'm still totally committed to Girls Forever, but maybe I haven't been as good at juggling things as I thought. Maybe there's some truth to what they're saying.

"You're always exhausted these days," Youngeun adds coolly. "You clearly have too much on your plate. You're going to have to let something go sooner or later."

"I'm sorry, Rachel, but they're not wrong," Jiyoon says with a shrug. "Try not to take it personally. But we really think you need to make a decision."

Sunhee bites her lip. I wonder if she's going to defend me, but she says nothing.

"So," Mina says, raising her eyebrows. "What's it going to be?"

I stare at them in disbelief.

They're posing this to me like it's a choice, but obviously I'm not going to choose to leave the group. I've been doing K-pop since I was recruited at eleven. I would be nothing without this, without them. Besides, it's like I said: Girl groups are like a Jenga puzzle. If I left, it would spell bad news for the rest of them, and I don't want that, either. Mina's always saying that if one of us messes up, it reflects badly on the whole group. Well, my quitting the group *or* quitting my fashion line a month after it launched – would definitely make the group look bad. We may be the agency's shining star right now, but if Girls Forever started to slip in popularity, or became too marred with drama, DB wouldn't hesitate to shut the group down. Are the girls really willing to take that risk by making me choose?

"Look, I need some time to think about this," I say.

Lizzie starts to retort, but Mina cuts her off. "Fine.

Get back to us once you've had a chance to figure out your priorities," Mina says.

Priorities.

There's that word again.

Twenty-Three

"Holy crap, Rachel."

"Leah!" I scream, dropping my highlighter brush as I swivel around. "You scared me!" She's leaning on the doorframe to the bathroom. It's six a.m. and I thought I'd be out of the house before she even woke up. My flight to Switzerland leaves early.

"No, *you're* scaring *me*. I just wanted to say goodbye and wish you luck before the big shoot, but you're acting so jumpy these days. What's going on?"

I shrug, going back to my makeup. "It's nothing. We've just been working nonstop. We're in the doghouse with DB because of this new dance number we keep botching," I remind her. "They basically threatened to pull the LA show if we don't shape up. We have to be on top of our game – now more than ever, with, you know, everything that's gone on."

She nods sympathetically, then comes to sit on the closed lid of the toilet. "Yeah, that's rough. But Unni, no offence, you look like you've been hit by a double-decker tourist bus. Are you even sleeping?"

I snort at her alarming specificity. "Gee thanks, Leah."

She laughs. "I just mean I'm worried about you. Be honest. Are you really okay? Are you sure there's not anything else you're not telling me?"

Damn it, why are sister spidey-senses so powerful? Of *course* there's something I'm not telling her. It's been four days since the girls gave me their friendly little intervention . . . aka The Ultimatum. My stomach has been twisted and wrenched into such a tight knot since then that I'm seriously shocked I've been able to get down any food. And she's right – I haven't been sleeping.

I sigh and turn to face her. "Okay, maybe a little."

"Knew it!" She leaps up to sit on the edge of the sink, looking a little smug.

I swat her knee. "The reason I haven't said anything is that I'm still processing it."

"Are you going to keep me in suspense forever? Processing what exactly?"

And so I spill. Everything. About the "plan" I overheard at Youngeun's café. About the horde of angry parents at DB. And last but not least, The Ultimatum. Are they just pissed that I was the first one to start a company? Or are they actually genuinely worried about my mental health and how much I'm juggling?

And worst of all – does it even matter, so long as they might be *right*?

"Whoa, whoa, Rachel, slow down," Leah says when I get to this part of my confession. "I'm sorry, but you are giving the other girls wayyyy too much credit. The only person who knows how much is too much is *you*. They are your groupmates, of course, and you care about what they think, but you don't work for them. You don't answer to them. You work for DB. And you work for *you*. Do *you* think you're in over your head with everything you're juggling?"

"I don't know," I tell her truthfully, and feel my throat get tight. *Shit. Do not cry right now.* I don't have time to fix my eye makeup before it's even dried. "And the hardest part is I'm not sure how I'm *supposed* to know. The past few days have been hell. The past couple of weeks, really. I'm sorry I haven't said anything. I just don't want to mess up. I don't want to disappoint everyone."

It hits me for the first time that for the past decade, I've always known one thing: that I wanted to be a K-pop star. But once I knew that, I was simply on a track where other people decided my success, and my fate, for me. As long as I played by their rules, I kept moving one step ahead. But now there's no road map for the next steps. I'm drawing the map myself . . . *while* trying to navigate it. And now . . .

"Leah," I say, feeling both the weight of it all and the relief of finally sharing how I'm feeling. "I'm terrified at all times these days – terrified of ruining everything I have, of letting others down, of not being the best. It's so much pressure. How can I possibly know if what I'm launching into next is right or wrong?"

"Well, what does Alex think? He always seems to have good advice."

"I . . ." My voice breaks and there's no way to hide it, especially not from Leah.

"Rachel," she says gently, grabbing my shoulders. "Are you and Alex . . . over?"

"No, no," I rush to assure her. "It's not that. It's just – I haven't told him about all this either."

"But why?" Leah asks. "I don't get it. Why wouldn't you just talk to him about–"

"Because!" I say with more force than I mean to. I set down my eyebrow pencil and lean against the sink so I'm parallel with Leah. "Because," I continue more softly, "I've known these girls for half my life, and Alex hasn't. I feel like I owe it to the group to figure this out on my own." Alex has always been supportive of my goals. And he wholeheartedly supports the group, too. But I have a feeling the girls won't see it that way. If Alex is the one who helps me come to a decision – whatever that decision ends up being – will the girls hold that against me too?

"So you're, what, just avoiding him because you don't already magically have all the answers?" Leah says with an air of unsentimental practicality that sounds a lot like Umma.

"Kind of." Truth is, I've been responding to his texts with Super busy rn let's discuss it soon though! And Ha ha totally and Gotta run. He must suspect something is up, but so far he hasn't called me out on it. I just miss him so much and trying to talk about these weighty things over text feels so insufficient.

"Doesn't he deserve to know how you're feeling? He's your boyfriend, isn't he?"

And that's the million-dollar question right there, isn't it? It's clear Alex wants to be my boyfriend – already considers himself to be so. And I want that too. But in the real world – my real world – the label "boyfriend" is precarious territory. Juhyun used to say, in high school, you can pick two: friends, good grades, or sleep. Well, apparently, in the world of K-pop, you have to choose between your group, your passion, and your love life. Choosing between the three feels like being forced to pick which finger you could do without. But at the end of the day, you have to figure out what your priorities are.

"I–" I stop myself from answering her. "I'm gonna be late for my ride. Thanks for listening. I love you."

"I love you too, Rach," she whispers. "You'll figure it out. You always do." And then I'm out of the bathroom, grabbing my suitcase, and racing out the door.

"We will now begin our initial boarding for flight 872 to Geneva."

I can hear the announcement just as we're approaching the gate. Jongseok and I scan our boarding passes, then hurry down the gangway.

When we arrived at the airport today, there were double – no, triple – the paparazzi I'm used to. They've been on me even more since the RACHEL K. launch. I stopped by Nature Alley to grab my usual preflight almond-butter-and-chia smoothie, and nearly dropped the whole thing down my white silk blouse when a photographer jumped out from behind the espresso machine to snap a pic. Usually when I'm travelling solo (as opposed to with the group, when DB has us on a tight schedule), I love taking my time in the airport, stopping to pick up a fresh stack of magazines for the flight, stocking up on gum. But today I was glad we were running late. I just wanted to get through the airport as quickly as possible.

Finally, I'm on the plane, with my earbuds and my favourite pillow all ready to go, but when I go to cue up my relaxing flight music on my phone, I notice a media alert with my name in it. I'm tempted to just switch to airplane mode and forget about it until we land, but . . . that's obviously impossible. I click on it right away.

RACHEL KIM MYSTERY MAN EXPOSED?

Oh. God.

Now I *have* to read on.

For months, netizens have been speculating about the existence of a possible secret boyfriend for Girls Forever lead singer, Rachel Kim. Between her sudden and unexplained Seoul hotel stay this spring, to rumours that she was also in attendance at the dinner date that exposed groupmate Shin Eunji and boyfriend Song Geonwu, there have been several clues pointing towards Rachel Kim having someone special in her life. But Rachel has yet to be photographed with any male suitors. So, if there is a mystery man, who is he? Well, after receiving an anonymous tip from a close source, we believe that Rachel's secret beau just might be Korean American business mogul Alex Jeon. Rachel stans have placed Ms. Kim and Mr. Jeon in the same cities, at the same time, on several occasions: Singapore, during Rachel's filming of 1, 2, 3, Win; Paris, during her Nell Kramer fashion show appearance; and Hong Kong, during her Lane Crawford fashion-line meetings. It's worth noting that Mr. Jeon's company is a known investor in Ms. Kim's RACHEL K. fashion line. But while no photo evidence exists to confirm whether their business relationship has turned romantic, our anonymous tip assures us that is indeed the case. What do you think, netizens? Could this Alex Jeon be the mystery man of Rachel's dreams?

If my stomach was knotted before, now it's hardened into a solid rock of chia smoothie and dread.

This "close source" . . . There are only two groups of people in my life who know about Alex: our families and close friends, and my group. And our families would never go to the tabloids about me.

But could one of the girls really have done that to me? Maybe they didn't mean to. Maybe they slipped up and said the wrong thing to the wrong person . . .

Or, maybe the girls don't just think it's fashion that has to go.

Maybe they think Alex has to go too.

The thought of ending things with him makes me want to throw up. Whatever I decide to do about The Ultimatum, I'm going to have to do it soon, before things get even crazier.

Which, inevitably, they will. Because this is the life I've been given, for better or worse. And no one else is going to make the next choice for me.

By the time we make it to the hotel in Zermatt, it's already past ten p.m. My body is still on Korean time, aka six a.m. the next day, and my brain is on a whole other planet's orbit. From the airport, we took a train four hours into the carless village of Zermatt, before switching to a cable car to take us up to the mountainside hotel near the chalet where we'll be shooting. Discipline had offered to arrange for a car transfer directly from the airport, but back when we made the travel arrangements, I was so excited by the idea of arriving by train, seeing all the twinkling lights of the village as we pulled in, that I turned down the offer. Needless to say, I'm now regretting that choice. I'm physically and mentally exhausted, and cranky as all get-out. I'm so ready to submerge in a hot bath and then collapse into bed, that I barely take in the breathtaking view from the window – the mountains, snow-capped even in September, all aglow in dying sunlight, casting peach and lavender streaks through the sky.

Once the bellhop leaves me alone, I open my suitcase and start digging for my matching cashmere sweats and hoodie. They're calling my name from somewhere in here. As I rummage, I'm already whipping off my sweater and starting to unbutton my top.

Knock, knock, knock.

What the? I look up from my suitcase. I thought about calling down for some room service, but I didn't think I'd actually done it . . . Then again, I'm so beat, I'm not willing to rule out the possibility that I zombie-ordered some late-night French fries to eat in the tub.

I walk over to the door and open it a crack, but no one is there. Either there's a ghost haunting the Zermatterhof, or I'm imagining things in my sleep deprivation.

Knock, knock, knock.

Hold on. It's not coming from the door. It's coming from . . . the closet?

I walk over to the closet door, grabbing the flower vase full of asters on the nightstand on the way, thinking if there's someone hiding in my closet – more paparazzi? – I'll smash this over their head and run for help. Then I realise that's insane – I would never use such extreme measures, no matter how much I secretly hate the paparazzi.

Besides, it's just as likely the sound is an actual ghost, and I'm pretty sure blunt force has little impact on noncorporeal creatures.

I take a deep breath and swing the closet door open.

"Are you going to bludgeon me with that?"

"God!" I say, my hand momentarily leaving my chest and letting my shirt fly open, before quickly clamping it closed again.

"No, the name's Alex Jeon – we've met. But I do get that a lot." He grins cheekily, sticking out his hand for me to shake as he leans casually against the doorframe of what I now see is not a closet at all, but an adjoining hotel room.

"I thought you were a ghos–paparazzo," I say, putting down the flower vase and rubbing my eyes, trying to process what's happening.

At least he has the decency not to mention whether I just flashed him with my bra.

His eyebrows quirk up. "Were you about to say *ghost*?"

I blush a bit and roll my eyes before throwing my arms around him. "Oh my god, I'm so glad you're here!" I'm surprised to feel myself welling up with happy tears. It's been so long since we've been together, and the stress of the past few weeks has been brutal. Seeing him here, smelling his familiar cologne, is like a soothing balm for my frayed nerves.

"I thought I would surprise you," he says, laughing as I practically squeeze him to death. "It's been months. Is it okay that I came?"

"What? Of course!" I look at him like he's grown three heads. How on earth could this *not* be okay? But then, I remember. The *Reveal* piece. *RACHEL KIM MYSTERY MAN EXPOSED*. Someone in my own inner circle supposedly leaking details about me and Alex to the press. "I'm so happy you're here," I say, giving him one last squeeze. "But, um – no one saw you, did they? There was an article . . . Apparently people have been catching on to our shared travels."

I flop down on to my bed, rebuttoning my shirt the rest of the way up. The cashmere jogger set will have to wait.

"Yeah," he says, following me and coming to sit on the end of the bed. "I saw it. Not until I landed in Geneva this afternoon, though."

Geneva. Yet another city that the tabloids can connect the both of us to.

"Alex . . . " I groan, turning my face into the pillow.

"I immediately deleted my social media," Alex quickly assures me, placing a hand on my shoulder. "I only had seven Instagram followers to begin with, and they were all family, so there's nothing on it." I can't help it, I roll over and laugh. He has this ability to cheer me up even when the world is only getting crazier around us.

I look up and meet his eyes and see nothing but sincerity and concern there. Alex *is* careful. I know he is. The paparazzi and tabloid outlets simply will stop at nothing to ferret out any details of my personal life and expose them for all the world to see.

And ever since the girls' ultimatum, I've felt so weak and overwhelmed. I'm balancing so much. It's like an unexpected gift that he's here right now. "Thank you," I whisper.

He says softly, "It's you and me against the world, right?"

Alex looks at me expectantly, waiting for me to confirm what he just said. My heart knows it's true, but it's like my brain can't make the words come out. Back in Hong Kong, flying through the streets after we evaded the paparazzi, it felt so easy to believe those words – *you and me against the world*. But lately, it feels like the world has the upper hand.

"Okay . . . " he says finally. "So, do you want me to skip the photo shoot tomorrow so we can stay more discreet? The 'mystery man' can just hang around the hotel." He's giving me a wry smile and proving once again how much he cares about me – he's willing to navigate anything just to be here.

"No, come," I say impulsively. "I'm sure Ollie and Carly are looking forward to seeing you. We'll take separate cars and–"

"Meet at the chalet," he finishes, reading my mind.

"Exactly."

"Okay. Good night, Rachel."

He lingers for a moment, like he wants to kiss me good night but isn't sure if he should.

"Don't worry," I say, leaning in. "I think we're clear of ghosts and paparazzi."

Alex grins back and meets me halfway, our lips connecting in an all-too-brief kiss. I'm still revelling in the moment, eyes closed, when I hear him slip back into his hotel room and close the adjoining door.

I sigh. "Good night," I say to no one.

I get ready for bed, finally digging out the cashmere sleep set from my suitcase and washing my face, skipping the luxurious bath altogether. I've been tired all day, but when I finally lie down to sleep, my brain won't cooperate. I lie awake, tossing and turning and thinking about Alex. His being here was the best surprise. For the first time in days, I felt like I could finally breathe again. But now that he's on the other side of the hotel wall, I feel all my anxieties begin to creep back in.

I wish I had told him about the girls' ultimatum, which still feels like a dumbbell on my chest and makes all of this even more complicated. I wish he was here next to me instead of in the opposite room, so we could fall asleep in each other's arms. *I wish I wish I wish.*

I've never felt like this before. This all-consuming, ironclad sense that Alex is my person. That he's the one. It's thrilling and terrifying all at once. Yes, there's still a small voice in the back of my head warning – *Don't let the media catch you. Don't ruin everything you've worked for* – but at least for now, I'm not letting that fear overpower me. It's just one of the many emotions swirling through my brain as I roll over and mush my pillow into a more comfortable shape. Beyond the nervousness, there's joy, confusion, excitement, and most of all, utter, utter exhaustion. I snuggle further into the blankets, thinking of Alex's dimple, and chic sportswear, and soft snow, and before I know it, I'm drifting off to sleep.

☆ Twenty-Four ☆

After I moved back home, Leah thought it would be hilarious to sneak into my phone and change my alarm to her voice, so I wake up at the crack of dawn in Switzerland to the sound of her voice saying, "Unni, time to wake up! Unni, time to wake up! Unni, time to wake up!" on an endless loop.

I groan, fumbling for my phone to turn off my alarm. As soon as Leah's voice is quieted, I go to check my notifications – then realise what I'm doing. I was about to check my messages from Alex, like I do every morning. But there are none, because he's in the room next to mine and could just knock instead. I'm exhilarated at his proximity, but things still feel . . . unsettled. Once you think you know for sure that someone is your person, what do you do next? I feel the enormity of it start to sink in again, but I don't have time to linger on what it all means. I've got a photoshoot to get to.

I roll out of bed to get ready. We need to be on the mountain super early, before the mild September air turns the snow to slush. In the mirror I see heavy, dark bags under my eyes. Damn it. The makeup artist is going to have a field day trying to cover those.

On my way to the shoot in the car that Discipline arranged for me, my phone lights up with a text.

Sunhee: Rachel, I saw that story in REVEAL about Alex . . . Are you okay?

I sigh at the mention of The Article, as I've started to think of it in my head. But I'm pleasantly surprised about Sunhee's support. After all, someone who callously sold me out to a tabloid probably wouldn't bother to check in on me, right? I start to type back, but I'm interrupted by a flurry of incoming texts.

Sunhee: Are you going to come forward with the relationship?

Sunhee: Does DB know?

Sunhee: Do you think you're going to have to break up with him?

Sunhee: Have you seen this?

With the last text comes a link to some website, but the preview of it is slow to load.

Of course. I should have known Sunhee wasn't reaching out with genuine support. She's just living for the drama. And now I'm back to worrying if one of my groupmates really *was* the anonymous tip. Still, I want to know what the "this" is that she's referring to. I'm terrified the link will bring me to photos of me and Alex together, or some other bit of undeniable proof of our relationship, but instead it just brings me to a forum page where netizens are speculating and theorising.

Some are saying everyone should respect my privacy; some think we'd make a cute couple. There's also someone who, for some reason, is convinced I'm engaged to an American pop star. It's all actually pretty tame and nice, and I'm struck with gratitude once again that I have the best fans in the world. But then my eyes zero in on the comments that Sunhee must be referring to – there's a thread of comments badmouthing Alex, saying he's just with me because he wants to become famous.

I'm about to write back to Sunhee to assure her that it's all just gossip, but my fingers pause over the screen. It doesn't feel right to just let the internet run wild with hurtful gossip about Alex. He didn't sign up to be a public figure, like I did. But at the same time, if I try to set the record straight, I'll just be confirming the existence of our relationship – a step I don't think either one of us is ready for. I sigh and put my phone away. I'm old enough now to know that communication is key. When I see Alex today, we'll sit down and talk through everything.

But as soon as I get to the shoot location – a gorgeous ski chalet near the Matterhorn peak – I'm whisked away to hair and makeup. From the hair and makeup trailer, I enter the main lounge, dressed in Discipline's soon-to-be-released metallic olive-green winter parka, a high-fashion-meets-high-function look. The stylist on set paired it with simple black leggings and almost tactical-looking boots. I can tell Discipline's winter line is meant to make me feel powerful. Adventurous. But still fashion-forward. Like I could ski a black diamond, then pop into a five-star slope-side restaurant for drinks. I try to channel that energy as I make my way toward set.

"Rachel, you're here!" Carly Mattsson enters the lounge in a black parka of her own. We'll be modelling together today, and I feel myself perk up a little at the thought of being dressed in matching outfits with *the* Carly Mattsson.

She kisses both my cheeks in greeting and then gestures to the bearded man coming up behind her. "This is my husband, Ollie. Ollie, this is Rachel Kim."

"So thrilled to be working with you, Rachel," Ollie says with a slight Swedish accent, shaking my hand warmly. "I've heard such great things about you."

"Nice to meet you, too," I say. I wonder what he's heard about me. Has Alex mentioned anything? Where is he anyway? I glance around the chalet just as he enters through the doors.

"Good morning, everyone," he says. If I have black bags under my eyes, Alex looks like a literal raccoon. I guess he didn't sleep too well either. He smiles at me briefly, but it doesn't quite reach his eyes, and there's definitely no dimple poking through. Before I can cross the room to talk to him, he walks away to greet Jongseok and some of the Discipline staff who are here for the shoot. I feel a knot of anxiety in my stomach. Did something happen? Another *Reveal* article?

I walk towards Alex, rolling the hem of my parka nervously between my fingers. He's finished his conversation with the staff, but now he seems engrossed in his phone. I linger back, not wanting to interrupt in case he's reading something important for work, but then he pockets his phone and slips out of the chalet. Before I can chase after him, the photographer calls out to me. "Ready to go, Rachel?"

"Totally!" my voice says, as if it came from a robot programmed to sound like me.

But as much as Robot Rachel tries to focus on finding her light and showing off her cute cropped parka and thermal leggings, Actual-Disaster Me keeps getting distracted. Carly, I can't help but notice with jealous admiration, is all dynamic motion, lunging and kicking up snow with her boots, but I'm stiff as a, well, *robot*, next to her.

"Ladies, let's get a little more action. Can we try the skis on now?" the photographer says. He takes a quick break while we gear up, leaving Alex and a couple of the execs somewhere back inside the hotel, and soon, we're all on the slopes, posing at the top of what is in actuality a small practice hill covered in fake snow, but it's steep enough to look like we're on the actual ski trail down the mountain.

"Rachel, give me a little more effortless. We're on winter vacation, not competing in the Olympics. Why the fierce brow?" the photographer shouts over at me. I try to laugh at his joke and loosen up, but my Robot Rachel smile has also turned my legs into two tons of metal. I've been trying to balance while facing Carly, keeping all of my weight on the inner part of my right ski so I don't go sliding out of place . . . trying to hold everything so it's perfectly still, so he can capture the best shot. Only "still" is apparently looking more like "miserably stiff." This is all starting to feel like some sort of really bad metaphor about balance.

"Let's feel the fresh mountain air. This is relax time, this is – Rachel?"

In the middle of the word "relax," my right ski has given out. I try frantically to straighten myself – I'm actually a pretty decent skier, usually, so that shouldn't be tough – but I'm so caught off guard that instead my legs start speeding away from me in two directions and I go down hard, wrenching my right boot out of the ski.

When I try to collect myself, burning from the mortification, I realise I twisted the ankle harder than I thought – it twinges when I stand back up. It's not bad enough to need medical attention, but all of a sudden, the entire crew is surrounding me, making sure I'm okay. "It's fine, it's no big deal," I repeat to them all – in several different languages – but everyone's treating me like I'm made of glass, and two of the men actually pick me up to carry me indoors, with Carly following behind and Jongseok offering to get an ice pack from the concierge.

I am half-tempted to ask for a second one to hide my beet-red face in for the rest of my entire lifetime. *If things go well, we could plan an event with you!* Cynthia had said. Well, I think I can kiss that solo fan meeting goodbye, because things are clearly *not* going well. Carly, who I so wanted to impress, is being extremely patient, but we all know I've basically ruined the shoot, and it's all I can do to keep from crumpling into a ball and weeping. I'm so tired – the weeks of not sleeping must have got to my legs. Maybe this really is burnout. Maybe, I think again, the girls were right, and if I keep trying to have it all, I am just going to fail at everything.

Maybe that's already starting to happen.

Carly must be able to tell how much of an emotional wreck I am, because she begs for us to get a few minutes off and then suggests we do some casual shots, still in our outfits, inside the lounge. "So the whole day is not lost, yes?" she says. "I'm pretty good with a camera. What do you say?"

During the crew's break, it's just us sitting on the leather couches in the sunroom, which has been cleared out for our use, and I've got my legs up on a glass coffee table – now in a pair of Discipline snow boots.

"You sure you're all right?" Carly asks me. The sun is glowing in a halo around her hair, and I realise this room really does have perfect light for a shoot. I hope we can at least get a couple of decent shots out of this.

"Yeah. I've never had my dignity been beaten so hard by a bunny slope, but otherwise I'm fine." I give her a soft laugh. "Honestly, I'm just so mortified. I hope I haven't ruined everything." My voice wobbles.

"Ruined everything? Oh please." Carly gives a casual hair flick. "I should tell you about the time we tried *waterskiing* on a shoot."

"Hah. I appreciate it, but you don't have to make me feel better about screwing up."

"Oh honey, I'm not trying to make you feel better, but this story is too good. In fact, I don't even have to tell it to you – YouTube can." She calls up a video from seven years ago – one that involves an insane-looking wobble, tangled legs, a bikini that did not stay put, and an epic wipeout, all within about seventeen seconds. Someone has turned it into a GIF, so the wipeout just repeats over and over again in slow motion. It's . . . awful.

And also hilarious.

"You can laugh," she says, and as she catches my eye – this mature, accomplished icon who is everything I wish I could be – we both start hysterically giggling.

By the time the crew and photographer return, we're wiping tears of laughter away from our cheeks and getting our makeup frantically retouched for the final session of the day.

"You were such a trooper," Carly says when we wrap, giving me a hug. "How's the ankle?"

"Already much better. Thanks," I say, grinning. At the very least, I finally feel more at ease. No more Robot Rachel, trying to be the damn best. It's just real Rachel left now, take her or leave her. I glance around. "You didn't see where Alex went, did you?"

"Alex?" Ollie says, appearing by his wife's side. "He had to go back to the hotel to deal with a work thing, but he asked me to tell you to meet him at Cloud Nine at eight p.m."

"Cloud Nine?" Carly says, her eyes sparkling. "That place

is beautiful. And the food is to die for. Rachel, you have to dress up! Just maybe choose a low pair of heels. We don't want any more accidents while you're here. Ollie, please make sure she signed the litigation waiver," she jokes.

I laugh, though there's still a cold swirl of worry in my stomach. *Don't get caught.* "I will," I tell her. "Thanks for passing the message on, Ollie. And thanks to all of you for being so patient with me. I've really appreciated the experience of working with you and your team. It's been incredible." And it's true – even with my momentous fail, getting to spend this much time with Carly and absorbing everything I possibly can from her has been worth it, even if I never get called to another modelling gig again.

Cloud Nine at eight p.m. Finally.

Time to clear the air with Alex, and let him know everything I've been thinking.

It's time to tell the truth.

Now I just have to decide *which* truth.

You'll figure it out, Leah said right before I left. *You always do.*

Let's hope she's right.

★ Twenty-Five ★

There are about 5,071 discarded outfit choices on the floor of my hotel room, and it's 7:56. Dinner with Alex is in four minutes, and I'm curled up in my underwear in a complete ball of indecision, when my phone pings.

It's probably Alex wondering if I'm bailing on dinner, or if I've completely lost my mind. Maybe he heard about the fiasco on the slopes today and is disappointed. I felt better after the second half of the shoot indoors, but now I'm wondering if I just let Carly's good spirits distract me from the awful truth of the situation. I still have to make up my mind about my fashion line and about Alex, and I can't do it. I feel totally paralysed.

With a groan, I roll over and look at my screen. It's now 7:57. But the ping was not a text from Alex – it was from my mom.

How are you doing, daughter? I'm thinking of you up in the mountains. I know you love the snow. Hope you were careful on the slopes. Love you.

Tears start to come to my eyes and before I can stop myself,

I'm calling her. "Umma," I say as soon as she picks up.

"Rachel, is everything okay?"

I let out a sniffly breath that's half tears, half laughter. "I think so? I can't believe you're awake!"

"It's only three," she says dismissively, like it's no big deal that she's stayed up all hours of the night just to check on me. I guess I shouldn't be surprised. My mother has always been there when I need her most. "Now, what's wrong?"

Umma waits patiently on the other end of the line. I can almost see her knitted brow, her hands folded in her lap, as she waits for me to be ready to speak.

"He's the one," I blurt out.

She's silent for a moment, and then lets out a soft sound, something between a tsk and a chuckle. "Daughter. I'm happy for you."

"Is this how it felt? With Appa, I mean?"

Before she can reply, I'm already barrelling on. "Alex is everything to me, but I'm freaking out. It's just that sometimes it seems like the world doesn't want us to be together. And with everything else going on, I'm just so overwhelmed, and I don't know how to *tell* him, and . . ."

I stop talking because my mom is *laughing*.

"Umma! Are you laughing at me? I'm serious!"

"I know you are, my daughter. But the answer is, there's no such thing as absolute certainty."

"What?" I sit up and pound the bed. "Have you just been lying to me my entire life, then?"

She tsks. "No, Rachel, not lying. I *knew*, in my heart, that I loved your father. But that doesn't always mean the world will back you. You have to trust yourself and your own feelings. Stop listening to anyone else. You don't know with your head. You know with your heart."

I sit there feeling petulant and silly, like a little kid who has just learned there's no dessert unless you finish your dinner first. It's 8:02 and Alex, wonderful Alex, Alex who has totally changed my life for the better in a million and one ways, but who, if we're caught, also poses the biggest risk to my world falling apart – that Alex is waiting for me downstairs at the restaurant.

"Umma, I'm late for a dinner with Alex, and I don't know what to do or say or even what to wear." I'm being a baby, I realise, but I just don't want to let my mother go just yet.

She gives a soft laugh. "I can't tell you what to do or say. And you're the fashion icon, not me. But when in doubt, wear a little black dress. Now go get ready. You should not leave a handsome man waiting like that."

And then my mother, queen of the outro, hangs up on me.

As a member of one of the biggest K-pop groups out there, I've been to the best restaurants the world has to offer, but nothing can beat Cloud Nine's views of the Swiss countryside. As soon as I arrive, the hostess leads me to a secluded outdoor patio at the back of the restaurant, where I can watch the sun setting over the mountains and the rolling green hills. String lights are hung up along the rafters, setting a romantic glow over the heated patio. The outdoor seating section is small, with only three other tables, all of which are empty. It occurs to me as the hostess leads me to the table that I didn't pass by any patrons in the inside dining room either . . .

Alex is already seated, waiting for me at a table in the corner. He looks suave in a crisp white dress shirt and silver-and-blue skinny tie. He rises when he sees me, his eyes widening as I approach. I'm wearing a fun little black Miu Miu dress with crystal buttons, a ruffled neckline, and a heart-shaped rhinestone belt. I twisted my hair into a high braided bun and put on dangly pearl drop earrings and heels.

Alex doesn't speak for so long that I start to second-guess myself, fussing with the sleeves of my dress.

"You look great," he finally says at the same time I say, "That tie looks nice on you."

We both laugh awkwardly, taking a seat. There's silence for a moment, neither of us knowing exactly where to start.

"So I heard the food here is really good," he says.

"The view is great too," I add. "Really pretty."

"Mm-hmm."

We fall silent again. Oh god, it's awkward. My stomach is doing somersaults. I fiddle with my napkin, about to launch into a discussion on how the weather is really quite lovely tonight, when Alex rescues me by saying, "I ordered us a bottle of Bordeaux. I hope you don't mind."

"Not at all," I say, relieved. "I love red wine." *Oh my god, get it together, Rachel.* It's go time. I have to tell him about how I feel. That I've fallen in love. That he's *The One*! But first, I have to tell him about The Ultimatum. And everything I'm weighing. I have a decision to make.

I wish the wine would hurry up and get here so I would at least have something to do with my hands. I can tell by the look in Alex's eyes that there are things he wants to talk about too, but neither of us knows how to break the ice.

"I heard the rest of the shoot went great," Alex says after the waitress comes to uncork our bottle and pour our glasses. He takes a sip. "How's your ankle? I can't believe I wasn't there. Are you okay?"

Thank *god* he wasn't there. Doing the mid-slope splits that nearly stretched a hole in the butt of my trousers, while the designer of said trousers was watching, was probably one of my top ten embarrassing moments of all time, and that's coming from the same girl who vomited on Jason Lee's shoes during an audition.

"I've had worse falls during dance practice." I smile, waving off his concern. I scan the menu. There are a million meat options – everything's a loin of something. I finally spot a gnocchi starter that sounds sort of light. With my nerves racing like they are, I'm not sure I could handle a full entrée. *Hey waitress, can I get a side of "I might be freaking out mashed potatoes" to go with the "or maybe I should just quit fashion while I'm ahead salad?"*

Our orders placed, we spend the next few minutes making

small talk, sharing stories about learning to ski growing up – me in the Catskills, him at Killington, though the whole time I'm trying to keep my body from shaking. I tell him about how Leah and I used to mix up Sweden and Switzerland, until our family started calling them "Meatball" and "Cheese." Alex laughs politely, but I know I'm scraping the bottom of the barrel for conversation topics. I go for another sip of wine and am surprised to find my glass is already three-quarters gone. Well, I guess it's time to get down to it. Maybe there's no polite or natural or not-awkward way to do this, but it has to be done.

"Hey, so where did you go during the shoot today?" I ask, chickening out. I reach over and top off my wineglass, adding a splash to Alex's as well. I am starting to feel it go to my head. I need to be careful. This night is not about "Cheese" or "Meatball"; it's about the biggest choice I've ever had to make – one I still haven't decided on, even as I take just one more small sip of the wine . . .

"Um, actually, I was dealing with this," he answers, pulling out his phone. He taps something on his screen, and slides it over to me. I blink in surprise. It's a series of email chains, all to Alex, from various news outlets. I scan a few subject lines, and quickly realise they've been bombarding him with questions about our relationship, and his involvement in my fashion line. There's also about a million social media notifications – netizens accusing him of shattering the Girls Forever snow globe, assuming I left the villa to go live with him.

"Oh no. Alex . . ." As an idol I'm used to this level of scrutiny, but Alex is just a normal person. A "civilian" as Mina likes to call them. He's never had to deal with this kind of stuff, and he shouldn't have to. "I'm so sorry."

Alex gently tilts my chin up so I'm looking right at him. "Seriously, don't feel bad. I know all that internet stuff is just bullshit. But still, I understand that we have to be careful. I got Ollie to help me reserve the entire restaurant so that we could dine in peace tonight without the possibility of any paparazzi. And today during the shoot I called a few of my contacts at various media outlets to see if they thought I should put a statement out or something. I just wanted to do what was best for you, for your reputation. I didn't want to say something wrong and screw up. I guess I probably should have just asked you." He smiles sheepishly, but then his face grows serious again. "It made me realise, though, that we need to be totally honest with each other. Not just right now, but all the time. If we're not, there's way too much room for misunderstandings to get between us."

Right. Misunderstandings. Like when one person flies halfway across the world to be with someone, and the other person almost smashes a vase over their head.

"Even with the *Reveal* story, I'm glad you're here, that you were at the shoot today. Our relationship has been life-changing for me, Alex. I just–"

"Rachel, I need to tell you something."

"Your dinner has arrived!" The waitress sweeps in at that

exact moment with plates of gnocchi and lobster drizzled in champagne sauce.

"Thank you," Alex says with a pained smile.

As soon as she leaves, Alex and I look at each other from across the table.

"You were saying?" I ask.

But Alex looks a little pale and gestures at me. "No, no, I interrupted you. What were you going to say?"

I came here hoping to truly communicate with Alex about all the things I'm thinking and feeling, but in this moment I'm suddenly at a complete loss for what to say. Do I tell him about the girls' ultimatum? That I'm thinking of stepping back from fashion? Do I tell him that this – us – is yet another thing the girls think is getting in the way of our group? How do I even start? Is all this uncertainty a sign that I've stretched myself too thin? Or am I uncertain because I'm overthinking it?

When I look at Alex, I don't *feel* uncertainty about him. As a person, he's everything I want. The uncertainty is about me, not him. I think about what Umma told me. You can't know with your head, only with your heart.

"No," I say, trying to give myself a few more seconds to listen to what my heart is saying. "I, um, I lost my train of thought. You go ahead, please."

"Okay." His face grows serious, and he extends his hand across the table for me to take. I do. "What I was saying was . . . I'm falling in love with you, Rachel," he says, his eyes never leaving mine.

In that moment, my breath stops.

He loves me.

He squeezes my hand, the most beautiful smile lighting up his eyes. All of the *Maybe I should*s and *We'd better just*s fly from my mind. When he looks at me like this, I suddenly stop thinking about *should*s. I stop thinking altogether. Is this what Umma meant?

I realize that I'm smiling – huge. A smile that hasn't felt this good in a very long time. The complete opposite of Robot Rachel smile. I can't help it. *His* smile is contagious. I love the crinkles on the side of his eyes. I love that dimple in his left cheek. I love how his voice is a perfect mix of husky and warm. I love everything about him.

I love him.

It's as simple as that. And now the moment is here. The moment when I say it back. When I tell him everything I've been holding in, that I've been feeling. Oh my god. This is huge. Okay, take a deep breath. Just let it out.

"Alex, I . . . I . . ." *I love you. I'm sorry dating me can be so complicated. I don't know what I'm doing, but I know this one thing to be true – you're perfect for me. You and me against the world.* "Alex, I love . . . this wine!"

I can't say it. As much as I know in my heart that it's true, saying the words out loud would mean destroying my plausible deniability forever. I'm just not ready for that. Luckily, he plays off the awkwardness, and doesn't act like he just let the words *I love you* hang in the air without hearing it back. If he's hurt or upset, he's hiding it well – his dimple still out in full force as he offers me a bite of his lobster. Still, I search his eyes for any sign of disappointment, and try to convey through my own that even though I'm not ready to *say* that yet, I do feel it. It's beyond clear to me now that I can't let the girls and the rumours get in the way of us. You don't walk away from someone you love.

But I *am* ready to fess up about some other things.

After we get a round of waters to clear our heads, I finally let loose about The Ultimatum and my doubts about pursuing RACHEL K. any further.

Alex practically drops his fork. "The Ultimatum? Are you kidding me? That sounds like an Arnold Schwarzenegger film. Jesus, Rachel, these girls are supposed to be your *sisters* and they're asking you to choose between the two things you love most?"

Well, three things I love most, I want to interject, but I don't.

"Well, yeah, when you say it like that, it does sound kinda bad."

He stares me right in the eye and gets serious. "Look. If you want to quit the line because it's too hard, or it's not making you happy, then fine. But if you're just afraid of taking the risk – or worse, afraid of what your group thinks, let me just say we never get where we want in life if we follow our fear. It's one thing my mom always taught me."

"I think your mom and my mom would like each other," I say with a smile.

"Let me ask you one thing." He sits back. "Does fashion make you happy?"

"You know the answer to that," I tell him. "Completely. It's just . . ."

"I know, I know. You're used to playing by the rules everyone else has set for you."

Nailed it. "Playing by the rules has got me where I am today, Alex. I can't just dismiss that."

"I would never ask you to, Rachel. Only to follow your happiness. Stop listening to other people and listen to yourself. What's your heart saying?"

Jeez. First my mom and now Alex. Did everyone get some How to Listen to Your Heart handbook except me?

My heart is saying I want to make out with his entire face.

My heart is saying I love him.

My heart is saying why limit myself when I *can* have it all.

"I want to play by my own rules too," I tell him. "I should get to do what makes me happy. I *am* going to do what makes me happy."

"Whoo!" He pumps his fist like he's watching a ball game and his team scored. It would be slightly embarrassing . . . if there were anyone else at this restaurant to notice. Instead, I just laugh, relief flooding through me.

"I want to toast to us," he says, grinning as he pulls himself together. "Because I believe we can get through anything together. Paparazzi. Online trolls. Hotel ghosts. Life-threatening incidents on the subway and the slopes. All of it. It's you and me, Rachel Kim. Against the world."

I laugh. "You're a dork."

"Don't make me stand up and start clinking my glass," he warns. "I wouldn't want to embarrass you in front of . . ." He looks out over the empty patio. "Marta," he finishes, nodding to our waitress.

"Okay, okay." I laugh, raising my glass. When I look into his eyes, I feel powerful. I feel like nothing else matters. Because with him, I know I'm always going to be okay, even if I don't always have the answers. Maybe I don't have to know everything to be certain, at least, of this. "To us."

Back at the hotel, we say good night before disappearing into our respective rooms. Barely two minutes have passed before I walk over to the adjoining door and knock three times.

"That better not be a ghost," he calls. "I hear this hotel has one."

"Ha ha," I say.

He opens the door and grins, pulling his tie loose from his neck. I bite my lip. Why does it look so sexy when he does that? I lean against the doorway, putting one hand on my hip.

"I have a question for you," I say.

"All right, shoot."

"Could you help me unzip this?" I ask innocently, turning my back to him and sweeping my hair, recently freed from its bun, across my shoulders.

I can almost see him visibly gulp.

"Sure," he says, reaching for the zipper. I feel his fingers warm against my skin, goose bumps forming along the path of the zipper.

"How come it took you so long to respond to my outfit when I got to the restaurant today?" I say, knowing exactly what I'm doing. "I did put in some extra effort, you know. Did you not like it?" I look at him over my shoulder again with innocent eyes.

A smile quirks up the corner of his lip and he steps closer, putting one hand on my waist. "No. I liked it. Too much, actually. You knocked all the words out of my head."

"Smooth talker."

"I mean it." He leans in closer, his lips inches from mine now. He closes his eyes and presses his mouth against my neck instead, sending shivers down my spine. "But you look beautiful no matter what you wear."

I sigh as he kisses my neck, wrapping my arms around his shoulders, my dress left halfway unzipped. He brings his mouth to mine and I kiss him back, gently at first and then more passionately, my lips growing soft and tender at his touch.

He pulls back to look at me, his eyes heavy with desire. I tug on his loosened tie, pulling him deeper into my room. He softly closes the adjoining door behind him and we tumble on to my bed, our lips finding each other once more.

Last night, I was up all night missing him, wondering if all my decisions have been a mistake.

But not tonight.

Not tonight.

✦ Twenty-Six ✦

On the way back from the airport, I don't even bother going home first – I ask Jongseok to take me straight to the Girls Forever villa.

As I had hoped, most of the girls are gathered in the dining room enjoying a weekend breakfast of banana pancakes when I arrive, so I quickly round up the rest of the group – luckily, both Youngeun and Lizzie have swung by for pancakes too, so everyone's together.

"Have you decided?" Mina asks as soon as we're all seated.

"Yeah," I tell her, and feel how all the girls immediately snap their heads to attention.

"I've been thinking about it a lot over the last couple of days," I go on. "And I've made my decision."

There is total silence.

"I'm not going to stop my fashion line and I'm not going to quit the group."

Immediately, I can see the domino effect of reactions across the room as a collective breath is released. Some of the girls seem relieved, others sympathetic, and others – like Lizzie and Mina – annoyed.

Lizzie rolls her eyes. "Seems like our concerns really got through to you, then."

"I took your concerns very seriously, trust me," I deliver back. "But I love both of these things way too much to let either of them go. I've never been anything but dedicated to the group, and I've always tried my best to not let you down."

I'm met with silence. Eventually, Ari can't take it any longer.

"So you're ignoring what we said? You're just going to keep doing what you're doing?" she says. "And you just want us to, what, be okay with it?"

I almost laugh, thinking about how I made the same defiant decision back on that silly TV interview.

"I mean, yes?" I say. "That's exactly what I'm saying."

I think of what Leah said. *You don't answer to them. You don't work for them.*

"Why can't we all just be supportive of each other?" I press on. "Honestly, I really hope we can move past this because it's not worth the drama." I clear my throat. "Also, I appreciate everyone's concern about how much I've got going on." I pause, not quite sure how to word it. I don't want to outright accuse them of leaking the story about me and Alex to *Reveal*, but I want to make clear that I won't put up with that sort of thing. "But please . . ." *Stay the hell out of my personal life.* Ugh.

I can't say that. "Please know that my relationship with Alex is not up for debate. And we'll go public when *we're* ready to do so." I scan the group, looking for any sign of recognition that might reveal who the anonymous tip was, but the girls keep their faces schooled.

A sigh escapes my lips. I want to fall into the open dining room chair, but I don't – this isn't my home any more. I want to grab a plate of pancakes and smother it in syrup, and chat with them about K-dramas. I want things to go back to normal.

I just want us all to be happy.

It's as simple as that.

"I just want us all to be happy," I say out loud to the girls. "Really. I'm just trying to do what makes *me* happy, and I want that for all of you as well." Even though a big part of me is still frustrated with them, I do mean this. "We only release one album a year now. We have more time and luxury to pursue our own passions, and you all are free to start whatever ventures you want, including fashion lines. I would have your backs a thousand per cent on that. I just ask that you have mine, too."

The girls say nothing, though I notice Sunhee has tears in her eyes. So maybe I really have got through to them. Some of them, anyway.

But then Mina pipes in, "Well, you already made things harder for us. It's only ever the first person who does something who can be successful at it. You should have thought about that."

I sigh. Maybe that's true, but we've all been the first to do something: Mina was the first to break into acting, Sunhee was the first to do radio. Besides, I never actively did anything to bring them down, and I'm tired of arguing this.

"Honestly, it's pretty selfish of you, Rachel," Eunji says with an air of superiority. "Starting a fashion line. Now other handbag designers might not work with us for shoots or endorsements – they'll see it as conflict of interest. I bet you didn't think of that either."

"Right." Lizzie nods. "If we had known what you were doing, we never would have agreed to it."

"But you *did* know!" I shout, surprising myself. I've been trying to keep a cool head during this conversation, but I can't let the girls keep denying that they knew about RACHEL K. This has to stop. "I don't know why you keep saying you weren't aware of my plans for the fashion line. I've kept you in the loop from the start." I can feel my whole body buzzing.

I take a deep breath, trying to calm down. The girls stare at me, shock and tension still reflected on everyone's faces. I wait a beat to see if anyone will speak, but no one does. "Well, I have a bag to unpack, so I'd better go."

I turn and walk out, trembling slightly. I can't believe I just said all that. But I'm also proud of myself – for standing up for the truth. It's like the feeling I get when I'm onstage, all the lights pouring down on me, and I'm all nerves and anticipation. But then the music starts, my brain stops thinking, my heart takes over, and I feel a rush of confidence. But with the girls, it's like someone has forgotten to press play and I'm forever waiting for the music.

. . .

The girls don't confront me again – for the next ten days, I stay out of their way and they stay out of mine. I use the gap in the group's schedule to escape to Jeju Island with Alex for a quick visit, which helps clear my head. But of course, the girls and I can't avoid each other forever. We leave for the big LA concert in *two days*, and we're now cramming.

Our final rehearsal starts at six a.m., and I get to the studio at exactly 6:02. The rest of the girls are already there, along with our dance instructor. They turn their heads to look at me as I race through the doors.

"You're late," Mina says, her voice sharp.

"I'm so sorry," I say, trying to catch my breath from racing down the halls.

"Were you out last night or something?" Lizzie asks.

For a second, I consider lying – something tells me they won't take too well to the truth – but I decide to just be honest. "I was reviewing some new ad campaigns for RACHEL K.," I admit. "But you haven't started yet, right?"

I look over to where Eunji is still lacing up her Puma sneakers. Ari and Sumin are sitting on the floor half stretching, half Insta-scrolling.

"It doesn't matter if we started yet or not," Mina says, scowling. "It's the principle of it. We all know how important the LA concert is. We all showed up exactly on time, and you just waltz in whenever you want."

Normally I would play nice, but this hypocrisy is getting

to me. "What about the time you missed seven appearances because you were filming for your movie? All of us have been late or absent before, Mina." I look to the rest of the girls for backup, but they're all silent, looking down at their feet or exchanging glances with one another. Even though they're not saying it, I can tell – they all either agree with Mina or are once again afraid to speak up against her.

"Whatever," Mina says. "Let's just start. We can't waste any more time waiting for Princess Rachel."

The old nickname stings. But some things, it seems, really do never change. I mentally flash to our anniversary dinner – to Mina toasting our group, and all the girls clinking glasses. Will we ever get back to that place? I let out a breath and prepare to dive in. After all, I have to prove my commitment now more than ever. Can't let everyone think I'm getting distracted by RACHEL K.

"I'm ready," I say quickly as the instructor turns on the music. "Let's do this."

For the next two hours, we practise the newest dance number. It was only added to the roster a week before the concert, and no lie, this may be one of the worst rehearsals I've had in years. We're all so painfully out of sync, bumping into one another during formation changes, landing our moves on different beats. Our instructor keeps stopping the song and making us start from the top, over and over. The more we mess up, the less patience she has.

"Are you even trying?" she cries out over the music.

I am. We are. But there's a weird energy in the group, and it feels like everyone is distracted. After so many years performing at the top of our game, it's not like us to be this off right before a concert.

"Not good enough! Am I looking at the world's leading K-pop group, or a bunch of baby trainees, hmmm? Again! Rachel, try to *count* this time."

At one point, Mr. Han comes into the studio to observe our progress. We start the song from the beginning and try extra hard to nail the routine, but when we get to the part where we have to split our formation into four lines that cross each other like a hashtag, I end up in the wrong line. Again. Lizzie has to put her hands on my shoulders and practically shove me back into place. This part has been frustrating me all day, and clearly, it's irking everyone else too. The instructor stops the song and Mina whips her head towards me.

"Rachel, what the hell!" she cries. "Why is it so hard for you to remember what line you're supposed to be in?"

Excuse her. I'm not the only one who's been making mistakes today. Three times during the opening verse, Ari has used her left foot for the stomp when she's supposed to use her right. The third time, she elbowed Youngeun so hard, I saw tears spring to her eyes. I open my mouth to snap back at Mina, but I bite my tongue instead. *Just let it go, Rachel.*

"What? Say it," Mina says, taunting me. "I know you want to say something."

"I don't," I lie, trying to keep the tensions down.

"You obviously do."

"I *don't*."

"Come on, Princess Rachel. Maybe if you got it out of your system, you could focus on the actual practice for once!"

"Okay, girls," Mr. Han says, stepping in between us. His face is a mixture of disappointment and concern. "Let's take ten. Grab some water and cool down. It looks like it's going to be a long one."

Mina glares at me before grabbing her Hydro Flask and stomping out of the studio. The rest of the girls scatter to get water and snacks, and I head to the bathroom to splash my face with cold water. Mr. Han is right. I need to cool down. I dry my face and look at myself in the mirror, then run through the dance moves by myself. Here, alone in the bathroom, I nail every single one. I can do this. I just have to focus on the routine and not let Mina get under my skin. I have to stay focused. For the sake of the LA concert. For the sake of *us*.

I head out of the bathroom and down the hallway, hoping I have time to grab a protein bar from the vending machines too, when I nearly run into Mina and her father. I quickly pull myself back around the corner and press myself against the wall, and they're so engrossed in their conversation that they don't notice me.

"The investors want to pull their support from your line," Mr. Choo growls at her. "They saw an eyewear line just drop – with designs that look identical to the ones you've been developing. Don't tell me you've been stealing them. Choos are above that."

"I didn't! It's just a coincidence, I swear – how unique can you make eyewear look anyway?" Mina rolls her eyes, but then she shrinks under her father's withering stare.

Mr. Choo scoffs. "This never would have happened to Rachel Kim."

"Please, Appa, can't we just forget the eyewear line? I want to do acting. I'm *good* at it."

"No," Mr. Choo says curtly. "You need to fix this, Mina. Choos don't lose."

And with that, Mr. Choo spins on his heel and walks away, leaving an utterly defeated-looking Mina behind him.

I back away before Mina can spot me, giving up on the idea of having a protein bar to boost my energy before practice restarts. There's an awkward tension in the air as the girls file back into the studio. Mina's the last one to rejoin the group, an expression of fierce determination on her face. And then, we're focused on the dance and only the dance. The hours pass by and we slowly get better. I don't mess up the formation change for the rest of the day, and I feel myself getting sharper and sharper as we go along.

"Let's call it a day," Mr. Han sighs finally. "But you all better be practising in your sleep for the next two nights. Sweet dreams and I'll see you on the flight."

That night, I lie in bed, scrolling through my phone. Usually Alex and I FaceTime before I go to sleep, but he's out having drinks with another potential Hong Kong buyer for RACHEL K. I shoot him a quick text.

Me: Hope you're having fun! Don't do anything I wouldn't do! xoxo

I sigh as I climb under the covers. With the stress of the day, and knowing I'm going to be in the States on a totally different time zone for the next week, missing him feels like a physical ache in my chest that just won't go away.

But there are little things that help. I pull up the Snap Map on my phone. I know it's kind of silly, but sometimes zooming out and seeing our location icons on my screen makes it feel like we're not so far apart. As soon as I open the app, though, it's not Alex's avatar that catches my eye. It's the girls'. All eight of them, clustered together in one location.

I sit up in bed, frowning. I thought everyone went home after rehearsal. Only a handful of them still live in the villa, so it wouldn't make sense that they'd all be there – unless they decided to keep hanging out without me.

I zoom in closer and see that they're not at the villa at all. They're at DB headquarters.

My mind immediately flashes over our rehearsal schedule. Mr. Han clearly said we were dismissed. Everyone got ready to leave together, and that was a couple of hours ago. Did everyone stay late except me?

I quickly dial up Jongseok, already climbing out of bed and trying to find my socks in case there *is* a surprise add-on to today's rehearsal that I need to rush back for.

"Jongseok, hi, it's Rachel. Does Girls Forever have a rehearsal space reserved for tonight?"

"Tonight? No, we're totally empty except for the trainees and a couple of first-year debuts – Crown Jewel, and F/MK."

I thank Jongseok, hang up, and roll back into bed, relieved that I'm not missing another practice. But now I'm totally confused. What would the girls be doing at DB headquarters this late at night if they're not rehearsing? I pull up the map again. Sure enough, there they all are – eight little avatars all clustered on Samseong-ro. Then again, Snap Map isn't always accurate – half the time Alex's avatar looks like it's floating in Victoria Bay. The villa is pretty close to headquarters, close enough that the app might glitch and show the wrong location. They could be at the villa or even at Bar Nine-Nine right next door, where we'd sometimes go for drinks after a tough rehearsal.

It stings a bit to be left out of their hangout, but I take a breath and let it go. Sometimes you're just not included. It's happened to all of us at one time or another. I guess it's just my turn. And besides, being left out isn't the worst thing in the world, as long as we can keep the peace.

I switch off the lights, letting go of all my thoughts and drifting off to sleep. I need it more than ever.

But it turns out, my sleep is doomed to be cut short, because early the next morning, before I can even think about starting to pack for our trip tomorrow, I wake up to a text. And when I look at my phone, my stomach sinks.

It's from Mr. Noh.

Mr. Noh: URGENT. Report to the boardroom at DB headquarters immediately. Please bring your mother.

This is the second time now that he's texted me something like this, the first being when the news broke out about Eunji and Geonwu. I haven't even had breakfast yet and I already feel like throwing up. *They found out about me and Alex.*

They must have. There can be no other reason for a text like this.

A million forms of panic and regret swoop through me, and I'm suddenly so dizzy, I worry I am going to pass out.

I take a few deep breaths. I scoured the internet for photos after Switzerland and found nothing. So I thought we got away without a trace . . .

I must have been wrong.

I cringe as I quickly check my news feed and Google alerts. But there's no mention of me and Alex in the press. I breathe a sigh of relief, though that doesn't mean there *won't* be a piece coming. I will probably enter Mr. Noh's office to see photos from another tabloid and threats to break it off if I don't want to risk the photos being printed . . .

But I'm not going to be blackmailed into a breakup. I'm just not. It's me and Alex against the world. We will figure it out.

I tell myself this, and desperately try to believe it, but inside, I am twisted in a knot. There's another detail that feels off – why are they asking my mother to come? Unlike other parents, mine are pretty hands-off about my career. I can't even remember the last time they had a meeting with DB.

I try not to spiral as I text Umma at work and quickly get dressed. I put on a pair of leather pants with a pale pink blazer

– an outfit I always feel powerful in no matter how many times I wear it. I need the extra boost of confidence to face whatever is waiting for me at headquarters.

I arrive at DB and Umma's waiting there out front; she squeezes my hand but looks just as confused as I feel. As we make our way to the boardroom, my phone rings with an incoming call from Sunhee. I turn it on silent. Whatever she wants will have to wait.

I knock on the boardroom door and enter.

Mr. Noh is there along with Mr. Han and a few other DB execs. By now, my heart is basically up inside my throat, making it hard to swallow. Why are so many execs here? I'm instantly reminded of the time when I was a trainee and I had to convince the execs to give me a second chance in this very boardroom. Only that time, I had Yujin there to back me up. This time, I have my mother, which only gives me a greater sense of foreboding.

"Ahnyounghasaeyo," I say, bowing.

"Rachel, Mrs. Kim," Mr. Noh says. "Take a seat. We ask that you please don't record this meeting."

My joints are stiff as I lower myself into a chair. I've never been asked not to record a meeting before – it's not something that would have ever occurred to me anyway. What is going on? I look to my mom, but again, she's equally lost.

Mr. Noh's face is drawn and serious and, surprisingly, a little shell-shocked as if he himself isn't ready to say whatever it is he called me in for. He clears his throat, folding his hands on top of the table. The other execs stay perfectly silent, looking at me with sombre expressions. I glance at his desk, expecting to see a photo of me and Alex kissing at the train station in Zermatt. But the desk is startlingly clear.

"Thank you for being here," Mr. Noh says. His eyes meet mine, then dart away. I've never seen him look so uncomfortable. "We called you in here today to talk about something important." His voice sounds strange, almost strangled. "Starting tomorrow, you won't need to participate in any of the group activities. I'm sorry to say it, but there's just no other way around it . . ." He looks at me expectantly, like he's hoping I understand what he's trying to say. But I don't. At all. No other way around *what*? Then Mr. Noh takes a deep breath and says, "I'm so sorry, Rachel, but it's no longer possible for you to be a member of Girls Forever."

Twenty-Seven

My mind goes completely blank.

My brain cannot compute the string of words that just came out of Mr. Noh's mouth.

I stare at him like he's speaking a foreign language I'm not fluent in – grasping for meaning from the few words I recognise.

No longer a member.

"I–what–" I start to say, but I can't find any more words to make sense of this moment.

"What do you mean?" Umma asks for me, steel in her voice. "Are you saying she's terminated?" I am so grateful to have her on my side – but horrified she has to witness this. She's the one who had to sacrifice so much for my career, which is – what? *Over?*

Mr. Noh meets Umma's unflinching gaze. He won't say the words, but it's clear from the look on his face that Umma is right. I have been terminated from my group.

"We're sorry it's come to this, but unfortunately, there was no other way," Mr. Noh continues. "Of course, we'll keep you on the company roster. Your DB contract doesn't expire for another four years, so . . ." He trails off.

It's one of those things that's so ridiculous and so unbelievable that even though I'm sitting right here, feeling the leather swivel chair under my arms, seeing the glint of the boardroom lights on the shiny mahogany table, it still feels like a strange dream. Or nightmare. I don't know whether to laugh or to cry, and I think I'm doing a little bit of both. Ms. Shim averts her eyes as a strange, snotty noise escapes me.

So this is really happening. I am no longer a member of Girls Forever. With my brain finally coming to grips with the *what* of it all, I finally find myself questioning the *why*.

Suddenly, Kang Jina's face flashes across my mind. She and Electric Flower were at the absolute peak of their success as a group, and they forced her out anyway. I think of her that day, after the news came out – drunk on soju, eyes wild, telling me, *They'll fucking ruin you.*

She was right.

Is this happening because of Alex? Kang Jina said she was let go because of her secret boyfriend. And yet, Eunji, who was caught dating in secret, was only given a slap on the wrist and forced to go public with her relationship. DB seemed to figure that the loss of her sponsorships and the media scrutiny of her romantic life would be punishment enough. Why are some of us given the chance to recover from our transgressions, while others are terminated? For six years, I've given DB everything I have – missed holidays and birthdays, performed sold-out concerts on one hour of sleep, and once with a 101-degree fever. And they've given me so much in return – the chance to live my dream, to travel across the globe, to meet people I never would have met, including our amazing fans. For six years, even through all the hard work and difficult choices, DB and I have stuck by each other. How can they throw all that away now, just because I fell in love?

A box of tissues is slid across the conference table, and I look up to see Mr. Han looking at me with a mix of regret and revulsion, like I'm a mangled bird his cat brought in. There's something about the pity in his eyes that gives me the strength to finally ask, "Can you at least tell me why this is happening?"

"It's your groupmates," Mr. Noh says, bringing my thoughts to a screeching halt.

I had been bracing myself for photos of me and Alex together. An exposé in *Reveal*. A terse reminder about DB's strict no-dating policy. Once again, it's like my brain is half a step behind my ears. My *groupmates*?

"What do they have to do with any of this?" Umma asks, voicing the question looping in my own head.

Mr. Noh nods at Mr. Han, presumably wanting him to take over and be the bearer of bad news, or at least the worst part of it. Mr. Han grimaces, like picking up the mantle of this conversation is the absolute *last* thing he wants to do. But like all of us in this room, when Mr. Noh makes a decision, we have no choice but to comply.

Mr. Han sighs. "Last night, the eight other Girls Forever members came to us. They said they were blindsided by your fashion line, and well . . . they said they wouldn't go to the LA concert so long as you were going too." He looks at me apologetically, his shoulders sagging. "We're sorry, Rachel, but if the girls won't share a stage with you, we just can't see a place for you in the group any more."

I feel like someone sucker-punched me right in the stomach, leaving me completely bruised and breathless. Tears prick my eyes and I hate myself for it. I don't want to cry in front of the execs. Not now. Not like this. But I don't know how else to react.

An ultimatum. The exact same move they tried to pull with me. And when that didn't work? They went behind my back to strike a deal with DB. Leveraging themselves just like Mr. Noh leveraged all the DB groups against N&G. I suddenly remember the Snap Map. The girls *were* all together at DB headquarters last night. I can't believe while I was lying in bed, they were here, putting an end to my career. Destroying our sisterhood.

I thought the impossible choice they posed to me was just a power play to make me give up my fashion line. I never thought they were *actually* trying to force me out of the group. I think of all the times I explained away the girls' actions – to Alex, to Leah, and to myself. I tried to give them the benefit of the doubt. To see things from their point of view. And now I'm not sure if that was just incredibly naive, or if deep down, I saw the writing on the wall and just couldn't admit it.

But no, I don't accept that. There was no writing on the wall – not for something as bad as this. There's no way I could ever have expected it. It's unprecedented. Unheard of. And profoundly cruel.

My fists tighten, nails digging into my palms. I push down my emotions – the hurt, the sadness, the rage – and instead morph into survival mode. I adjust the sleeves of my pink power blazer and look to Umma, and let her presence give me strength. I need to channel her. I need to be practical about this.

"Just to be clear, Rachel," Mr. Noh says with the slightest hint of apprehension in his voice. "We still want the best for you. We can take care of this situation and help you control your public image. You're still part of the DB family."

Family. The word hits a nerve in me. I called Girls Forever my sisters. Even with all the petty jealousies and bickering, I never, ever thought they would turn on me like this. It hurts in a way I can't fully process yet, a way that I know will crush me completely if I allow myself to wade through the shock and feel the full force of its devastation.

It's been clear from Mr. Noh's facial expressions from the moment I walked into this room that he doesn't want to be doing this, but he feels like he has to. He's trying to reassure me with his words, but they feel like empty promises.

Mr. Noh closes his leather folder – the well-known signal that this meeting is over. The other execs start to awkwardly rise from their seats, but then Mr. Noh opens his mouth to speak again and they all plunk back down. "In the meantime, Rachel, you – I mean, Girls Forever – has the LA concert. They're leaving tomorrow . . ." *They*. Not we. "You will stay home and say that you're sick. We'll take care of the rest." And with that, he rises from his chair at the head of the table and strides from the boardroom, the other execs following in his wake.

This is it.

No LA concert.

No Girls Forever.

My career as a K-pop star is over.

September 30th.

The day I was supposed to leave for LA with the girls.

Instead, it marks the day after I was cut from the group.

As the first rays of sun start to peek over the Han River, Umma, Appa, Leah, and I all sit around the living room, staring at the phone in my hands. Umma and I have told them everything, and it's hard to say who is in deeper shock, them or me.

"Should I do it?" I say. "Should I post that I'm sick?"

Mr. Noh told me to pretend that I'm sick as an excuse for missing the LA concert. Of course, I know why they want to me lie. DB owes the concert promoters nine girls. If I'm not there, they'll be in hot water unless they have a good reason. But can I really make a public statement that's so far from the truth?

I look around at my assembled family, genuinely seeking their advice. We've been here all night, and I still don't know what I should do. But the clock is ticking. The girls leave for LA this morning. I need to make a decision.

"I think it's okay to say that you're sick for now," Appa says gently. "You need rest, Rachel. It'll be the simplest excuse that won't get you too much media attention. And you certainly are not *well*." If I look half as dead as how I feel inside, I can only imagine they must be alarmed. Of course, typical Appa, worried about my well-being above all else.

"I don't know, Appa," Leah says doubtfully. "It might get Unni even *more* unwanted media attention. They might try to spin it in a way where Unni is too burnt out from RACHEL K. to make time for K-pop any more."

As someone inside the system herself, Leah clearly understands better than Appa how the world of K-pop works. I note how she subtly corrects him, sharing her insight while still being respectful, and am struck again by just how much she's grown up.

"I still can't believe they caved to that ultimatum," Alex says from my laptop. I video-called him last night so he could be a part of this family conversation too. He's been up with us all night, railing against DB's weakness and saying how a good businessman should have known how to handle a threat like that. "If it were me," he continues now, "I would have said, 'Fine. The plane is leaving for LA tomorrow. If you show up, great. You've done your jobs. If you don't show up, well, then *you* explain to your fans why you missed the concert.' You *know* if he had just said something like that, the girls would have fallen in line."

I'm used to Alex supporting me and standing up for me in his quiet way, but it's strange to see my normally laid-back boyfriend (no point in avoiding the forbidden term now) so agitated. I now see clearly how he's managed to become so successful at such a young age – his business instincts are on point, and he has the strength to stand by them.

I look outside. The sun continues to rise, and soon enough the girls will be arriving at Incheon Airport for the trip to LA. It'll only take a matter of minutes for our +EVERs and the media to spot that I'm not there. If I don't post something before then, DB will make their own statement to the media, and I'll be forced to accept whatever narrative they choose.

My stomach churns at the thought. What will my fans think if they read that I was "too overworked" or "too overwhelmed" to bother with Girls Forever? That I'm too busy for K-pop and, by extension, too busy for them? The thought of disappointing the +EVERs makes me feel even worse than the betrayal from my groupmates does. I just can't do that to them. I can't.

But then what's the alternative?

"You need to speak your truth, Rachel," Umma says over

my shoulder. I look over to the armchair where she's been sitting silently. My mom is often reluctant to wade into any discussion of my career. We came to an understanding years ago, and I know that she supports me, but she's made it clear since I was a trainee that she's wary of the K-pop industry. And even though I know she's proud of me for following my dream, I also know that she sometimes wishes I had chosen an easier path for myself. Since our meeting at DB, part of me has been waiting for Umma to say *I told you so*. But of course she never would. I lean forward to look at her now, trying once again to draw some of her strength into myself. "You need to speak your truth," she says again. "Don't let anyone put words in your mouth. Say what you want to say."

"I just don't want to cause any more drama," I say, folding back in on myself on the couch. And it's true. Even after everything DB and the girls have done to me, vengeance is the last thing I want. "Maybe it's better if I'm just quiet and do what they want me to." My voice sounds small. Like a tiny ant, easy to squish underfoot without a second thought. I press the heels of my hands to my eyes. I'm so tired, and not just because I didn't get any sleep last night. This exhaustion is bone deep. Maybe I really *should* just stay silent and let this all end.

"Oh no, no, no," Appa says, sensing my defeat. "It's fine if you want to say you're sick, but only if *you* want to say that. Not because you feel like you have to roll over and do whatever DB tells you to do. What do I always say? We roll with the punches, but we don't stop fighting."

"But if I tell the truth about what happened, there's no way DB will let me off the hook for exposing them like that," I say, swallowing hard. "They offered to play nice and deal with the fallout themselves. I'm basically publicly rejecting that offer. And if that happens . . ."

My voice trails off. I don't need to finish my thought. Everyone knows.

If that happens, then what?

Will I be able to strike out on my own, without DB?

I think about N&G, the spinoff group who hasn't been able to perform on TV ever since they left the company because of DB's blacklisting.

Am I willing to risk any chance I have of future success just to tell my truth right now?

"Whatever you decide, Rachel, we're behind you," Alex says. "Just know that you can get through this, and you will. You're going to keep going, and you're going to make a path for yourself that's even better than anything you could have imagined."

"What he said," Leah says, nodding, and I'm surprised to find a small chuckle escape me.

"Alex is right," Umma adds. "Your best years aren't behind you. They're waiting for you. You are my brilliant, strong daughter, and you can meet whatever challenges life throws your way."

I take a deep breath, letting their words sink in. I needed to be reminded to not give up on myself just because DB and the girls did. "Thank you. All of you. What would I do without you?"

"Do you need some multiple-choice options to help you make your decision?" Alex asks gently.

I shake my head. "I know what I need to do."

This is going against every peacemaking bone in my body, but I know in my heart it's the right thing to do.

After I say goodbye to Alex, I open my phone and begin typing up a post for Instagram.

And just like Umma said, I speak my truth. At least, as much of it as I feel safe enough to say. "My Dearest +Evers, I am devastated. Serving as a member of Girls Forever has always been my priority and the true love of my life. But now, for no justifiable reason, I am being forced out . . ."

I type out a few more sentences, trying to keep myself together as the tears start to fall. *I'm doing this for the fans,* I remind myself. *They deserve to know the truth.* Then I put down my phone and brace for the rest of the world to blow up, the way mine already has.

Twenty-Eight

It's been seventy-two hours, but it may as well have been seventy-two weeks. Time has lost all meaning. The hours bleed into days as I mope around the apartment, wearing my slouchiest sweatpants and foregoing showers for messy ponytails, ignoring the crazy tabloids and rumours eating up the story and spitting out wild theories. Umma and Appa were understanding at first, but after a while, they have started begging me to at least consider a shower.

After posting about leaving the group on Instagram, I've been living in, for lack of better words, a media shitstorm. At first, fans thought I was joking, that my account had been hacked, that DB would never in a million years kick me out of Girls Forever. But when I didn't show up at the airport to go to LA with the rest of the girls, they knew it was for real.

The aftermath was wild. DB released a statement saying that I chose to leave to pursue fashion instead of K-pop. So much for family. It hurt to read such blatant dishonesty, but

I can't say I was surprised. I rebutted their statement, but the media continues to swirl with rumours. Even Alex's name got dragged into the mess, and people are citing him as the reason that I left the group – calling him the Yoko Ono of Girls Forever. In an effort to avoid any further media backlash, I asked him to stay in Hong Kong and be discreet. It's no time for him to swoop in and try to be a hero, much as I wish he were here with me right this second.

"Stop reading those articles," he says when I start another rant about the awful, untrue things being said about him online. "You know they're not doing you any good."

He's right. I should definitely stop.

But I can't seem to help myself.

I spend countless hours every day reading the news. I scour everything from business articles about how DB's stock value has dropped millions (this gives me some minor satisfaction at least) to netizen commentaries on fan boards. Some of my most loyal fans are sticking by my side and supporting my truth with heartfelt posts that make me cry, but others blame me for this entire mess.

I don't know why I think I'll feel better reading these comments. The deeper I dig, the worse I feel, but I can't seem to stop.

I hit a new low when DB announces a new subgroup: LM. Lizzie and Mina. This must have been in the works for a few months. The track list for their album is already out . . . and the title single is "Brighter in the Dark" – the song I rewrote with Mina. The rest of the track listing is just as familiar.

"Sparkle You."

"Today I Will."

"Rocketship."

Every single song on this list is from my blue songwriting notebook.

Every. Single. One.

I thought Jiyoon ruined my notebook by accident that night I held her while she cried about Jin. But now I think she must have ripped out the pages and given them to Mina and Lizzie. I guess I'll never know for sure. Just like I'll never know who took my Balenciaga or who tipped off *Reveal* about me and Alex. And does it really matter? In the end, I still wound up here.

And besides, I know how this works. Technically, DB owns all the rights to anything music-related created by an artist while under contract. So even though I'm the original author of these songs, DB is free to make use of them any way they choose.

Including giving them to LM.

Once again, DB is distributing opportunities as they see fit, but this time, it's on a whole other level.

What can I even do? Go to social media again, tell my side of the story? Would anyone even believe me?

"I would put down that phone. For at least the next two weeks, or possibly forever," says a voice from my bedroom doorway. One I haven't heard in a very, very long time. I look up, dropping my phone in shock.

• • •

Of all the people I could have expected to see right now, the very last one is Akari Masuda. My old friend from the training days. She was my closest friend at DB. But she was traded to another company, and when she needed me the most, I wasn't there for her. And yet, somehow, in *my* hour of need, she has appeared like a vision.

"Akari?"

"Leah DMed me your new address. And your mom let me in. She even gave me a taste of the soondubu jjigae she's brewing on the stove. News flash: it's delicious." Akari walks right into my room and sits on my bed, as if we've done this a thousand times before, even though this is her first time at my parents' new place, and the first time she's spoken to me or even been this close to me in over six years, other than our brief eye contact at *1,2,3 Win*. Up close, she is a startling combination of exactly the same as I always remembered, and totally different. In addition to the changes to her face, her hair is cropped at a new angle. She looks older and more sure of herself. But the spirit and attitude of Akari are still everywhere, even in her familiar smell of passion-fruit body spray.

A wave of nostalgia washes over me as I recall the countless times we *did* used to do just this: flop down together on my bed back at my old apartment, and scroll through YouTube together or vent and laugh about our latest training debacles.

"That's good," I say vaguely. Umma's been cooking more in the last few weeks than in my entire childhood, but I haven't been able to bring myself to eat much. My mind, sluggish from hours of lying around in my sweats, scrolling through the dark bowels of the internet, is now trying to pick up the pace and understand what Akari is doing here.

But she answers for me. "So. I had to come when I saw the scandal. It's pretty ugly. I'm sure you're feeling shattered."

Ouch. Please don't tell me she came to throw it in my face when I'm already down . . . I don't think I could take that.

"Akari, I know things didn't end all that well between us, but–"

She turns to face me, her head cocked a little. Her eyelids sparkle with makeup. "Don't worry, Rachel. I'm not here to rub it in. Though, yes, you *were* kind of a shitty friend," she says ruefully. I cringe as she's talking. But before I can try to apologise again, she continues. "The reason I had to come to talk to you is because I *get it*."

Oh. This is definitely not what I expected, but then nothing about her presence right now, in my bedroom, casually fiddling with the tassels on one of my pillows, is expected.

"Thank you."

"Some crazy shit can go down in this industry, huh," she offers.

"Tell me about it," I mutter.

"I would know," she adds. The moment feels fragile, like it could shatter at the slightest touch. But I'm surprised when she sighs, her shoulders sagging, and begins to open up, as if I've genuinely asked her to *tell me about it*. "Things were always tough, even when I was training at DB. But after I got traded, it just got a lot worse. I was set to debut with TeenValentine, but at the last second, they decided to kick me out. My mom had to beg the label to take me back. She said she'd pay for every single plastic surgery they wanted me to do."

"Wow. I had no idea."

"Not many people do. So that's what happened. I did it all. They took me back and put me in the group. All it took was my mom forcing me to get new eyes, a new nose, and a new forehead. But there's a piece of it I haven't told anyone, not even my mom."

She looks at me with so much sadness and depth, it almost takes my breath away.

"And you want to tell me? Why?" I ask, genuinely curious. My stomach has tied itself in knots. I know this sort of thing happens in our industry all the time, but the vulnerable, broken way she has just admitted it – it hits home with renewed power. It's one thing to have surgery to alter your appearance by choice. And another thing to have it virtually forced on you, a condition if you want to continue to pursue your greatest love.

"I don't know why. Maybe because, after all these years, I have regrets too. I don't know. Maybe I needed you a long time ago and I was too afraid to admit it. And then we'd grown apart and it felt like it was too late."

I have the urge to wrap my arm around her, but I don't. "I'm listening now," I tell her.

"So the thing I've never said before is that after I recovered from surgery, I had the strangest trauma from it. No one talks about that, but it's not as uncommon as you might think, even for a relatively standard procedure. For months I didn't recognise myself in the mirror, and I felt . . . I felt like I had had a piece of myself cut out. Like, my *self*. Like I genuinely wasn't a whole person. Like everything I used to know about who I was had gone away. Debuting with TeenValentine kept me busy, but that didn't help either, because that was all part of the New Akari's life. And I didn't have anything left of my old life to anchor me or remind me of *me*. I didn't have you."

"Oh Akari." I'm trying not to cry at her story. As fragile as I've been feeling lately, this is Akari's moment, not mine. I need to be strong for her, not make it about me. "I'm so sorry. I wish I had known. I wish I had been there for you. I *should* have. That's what friends do, and I failed you on that." It's hard for me to say those words, let alone to admit they're true. I'm not used to failing at anything, not truly, and especially not something important and meaningful and deep like this. "I'm sorry about everything," I add. "But especially for the ways I hurt you. If I could go back and do things differently, I would." I hang my head, feeling the full brunt of my regret. It hurts to acknowledge it, but it also feels good to finally say it out loud. "I wish I had been by your side through all of it."

She clears her throat. "It's okay, though. Really, it is. I didn't come here just to try and get an apology out of you. I really have moved on." She tucks her cropped hair behind her ear and looks me in the eye. "I had some help getting through it all – professional help."

In the world of K-pop, talking about mental health is still somewhat taboo – another one of the infuriatingly archaic elements of the industry. I feel a fierce swell of pride for Akari having the strength to get the help she needed.

"Anyway," she continues, "we have a new album coming out that's already getting amazing early press, so honestly, I'm doing better than ever." Her eyes are still a little watery, but she sits up straighter and gives me a half smile that is the most Akari smile ever. "In fact, *that's* why I came over. To tell you I'm a badass bitch and I'm flying high!" she says with a jokey snap of her fingers.

I give a surprised laugh. "Well, that's amazing. I'm happy for you! I'm sorry I'm in such a sad state to celebrate you, though . . ."

"Oh Rach. You don't get it." She takes my hands. "That's my point. I know what rock bottom is. Been there, seen that, hated it with a vengeance. I was angry at the industry; I felt betrayed. I felt unsure of what came next, or what any of it meant about me. I worried I'd never be able to trust anyone again, because it felt like no one really loved me for *me*. But I'm living proof that after rock bottom, life gets better again. Not just better, though. Like, *way* better."

I smile wider, so proud of my friend for the way she was able to bounce back. I just wish I felt more certain that I could do the same. "I don't know, Akari. Maybe that's just because you're a super-badass bitch. I'm not sure it works out like that for everyone."

"Well, yes, I do possess exceptional levels of badassery," she says with mock bravado, prompting another grin from me. "But I guarantee that life will get better, even for a mere mortal like you. Because here's the deal: When you face the worst thing – when you face what you fear most – then you're suddenly free of it. You realise if you survive that, nothing can break you. Does that make sense? I'm at a place now where I love New Me, and I feel a kind of freedom I didn't used to have when we were younger. I was always in your shadow when we were trainees, and I would never let that happen now, LOL."

We both laugh, and for the first time in weeks, I feel a tiny crack of sunlight pouring into the darkness inside me. I feel like there's hope. Akari *does* look different to me, changed, but it's not physical, I realise. It's the maturity. The confidence. The *ease*.

"Thank you," I whisper. "Thank you for telling me."

Just then, my phone rings, making us both startle. I haven't been taking a lot of calls these days, but I glance at the caller ID and raise my eyebrows in surprise.

"It's Carly Mattsson," I say.

"Oh my god! What does she want?" Akari asks.

"I have no idea," I answer truthfully. Then my stomach drops. This must be the call I've been dreading. The one telling me that my solo event with Discipline is off. There's no way they'll still want to work with me after everything that's happened.

"Well, go ahead and take it. I have to run now anyway. But I'm glad I got to see you." She gives me a quick hug – not a long, cosy, meaningful friend hug. Just a sweet, passing gesture. A hug that feels a lot like moving on.

"Hello? Hello? Hi! Carly! Are you still there?" I'm a little breathless as I pick up the phone before I miss the call, still reeling from the unexpected conversation with Akari.

She laughs. "Still here."

"So nice to hear from you," I say, definitely sounding a little too cheerful. I force myself to take a deep breath, and brace for the bad news.

"I heard about what happened, and I wanted to check in. How are you making out?"

"It's been . . . hard," I admit, my voice shaky. I take a breath. "But I'm all right. Starting to feel hopeful again," I add, because it's true. Because I'm seeing now that maybe life will go on and maybe I will pick up the pieces and maybe I'm lucky, at least, to know that I *am* surrounded by people who know me and love me.

"Really?" Carly says. "That's fantastic. Because you've got a solo performance to prep for."

"What?" I squeak. It's, quite frankly, the very last thing I thought I would be hearing. "I figured that was cancelled, considering . . ." I trail off. *Considering the general implosion of my life and reputation since Discipline first offered me the event.*

"Absolutely not. That's why I'm calling. I wanted to make sure you knew we are one hundred percent still on board. Rachel, we liked working with you because of who *you* are, not because of what you were a part of," Carly assures me. "Believe me, I've been through tabloid hellstorms. More than once. Careers go on. Yours already has. RACHEL K. has been doing so well! That's got to feel good. Especially while you're dealing with all this crap."

And even though it sounds crazy, she's not wrong. Against all odds, my brand has been thriving. I was worried that the scandal of me getting kicked out of Girls Forever would erase all of RACHEL K.'s early success, but as it turns out, my name being all over the media has only added to its recognition, and people are flocking to my bags. It's helping me reach a demographic way beyond my core audience. More department stores are requesting to carry my bags every day, and design partners have already reached out to me about adding an eyewear line as my next release.

"Yes," I say. "The line has been a light in this fog for sure."

"The fog will clear," Carly says. "The misery won't last forever. I'm promising you."

It sounds a lot like what Akari said, and I feel a wash of admiration and awe for women who have gone through so much worse than I have. But Akari forgot to mention something else I'm learning about what it means to hit rock bottom – it shows you who really matters in your life. People who actually see you for *you*. It gives other strong women a chance to come forward, reach out a hand, and say *I've been there*.

"I believe you," I tell her with a small smile.

"That's all I ask. Well, no, that's a lie. There's one more thing," Carly goes on, her voice as perky and fast-paced as ever.

"The main reason I called. Like I said, Discipline still wants to do a brand partnership with RACHEL K. in Asia. So what do you think?"

What do I think? I thought the shoot with them was a disaster – my awkward splits–slash–face-plant in the snow may not have been turned into a GIF on the internet, thankfully, but it still replays in my memory on a not-infrequent basis. That catastrophe, plus all that's happened since I was cut from Girls Forever . . . Even after all Carly's kind words, I honestly don't understand why they'd still want to be associated with me.

"But how – *why*?" I blurt out, fearing I'm sounding about as awkward on the phone as I was in person on the slopes.

"Well, for starters, people are obsessing over the winter campaign."

"They are?" I've been so narrowly focused on the cascade of press around my splitting from Girls Forever – and trying, when I have a spare brain cell, to answer queries about bag delivery times and fabrication specs – that I hadn't even realised the Discipline campaign had gone live, let alone that it was doing well.

While we're talking, I race over to my laptop and start googling for the images, scrolling through with my eyes rapidly widening. I see that they barely used any shots from the slopes – but picked up quite a few from inside the lodge. I see how natural we both look in the sunlight pouring through the windows – me and Carly laughing like old friends. It hits me that maybe it was through failure that the best shots actually came.

When I wasn't scared of screwing up any more because I already had. When there was nothing left to do but relax and shine.

Still . . .

I've never sung a solo before.

Sometimes as part of a Girls Forever show, yes, but never at an event when I appear all by myself from beginning to end. My head is spinning.

It's one thing for some of my fans to stand up for me on the internet but quite another thing to expect them to come out for an event – it would be a huge statement, and some might see it as a betrayal of Girls Forever. Would they think it disloyal of me? Would it seem like proof of my desire to leave the group even though I never wanted that? And what would DB think?

"I . . . will have to consider all of this carefully," I say honestly.

"Of course. Take as much time as you need," Carly says. "But Rachel?"

"Yes?"

"Don't overthink it."

"What do you mean?"

"Have you ever heard the phrase *What got you here won't get you there*?"

"Um, I think so?"

"You've led an amazing career so far as part of Girls Forever, but sometimes the universe needs to kick you in the butt to show you that there's more out there beyond what you've already achieved. If you keep doing what you were always doing, you'll keep seeing the same results. If you're forced to break out in a new way, you'll see *new* results. Follow what I'm saying?"

It kind of *seems* like what she's saying is that my getting kicked out of the group was somehow meant to be. That's a tough one to swallow, but I think about what my mother told me when I was curled up in a stress ball in Switzerland. That I need to start thinking more with my heart and not just my head. The old Rachel planned everything to a tee. She did what she had to do to please everyone.

And this is where it has landed me.

"Rachel?"

"Still here. And yes, I think I see what you mean. What got me here won't get me there."

"Exactly. Call me when you've decided."

And with that, I'm left with a dial tone . . . and the realisation that everything that lies ahead of me is in my own hands. Maybe I've been asking all the wrong questions – *How will everyone else feel? What will DB say?* Maybe the real question is, *How will I feel?*

I get to decide whether to let this scandal swallow me whole and bring me down, or get up, wash my hair, put on a power outfit, and forge my own way.

Twenty-Nine

The look on Alex's face when he arrives at baggage claim at Incheon and sees me standing there waiting for him in the airport is absolutely priceless. The shocked expression only gets more extreme when cameras start flashing all around us, as I race toward him and wrap my arms around him.

"Rachel!" he gasps in surprise. Then he whispers in my ear, "They're everywhere, babe. Paparazzi on all sides. We're surrounded."

I whisper back. "I know. And I don't care. You and me against the world, right?"

He pulls away, staring at my face for a second . . . and then lets out a startled laugh, which in turn makes me start giggling.

"Let's give them a show," I say. "May as well." And right there, in the midst of all these flashes and hollers from the crowd, I reach up and kiss him. "Oh, and by the way," I whisper, pulling my lips from his, "I love you, Alex Jeon."

Alex freezes for a beat, his eyes growing wide, and then he does the dorkiest fist pump I've ever seen.

And then, because how can I not, I kiss him again.

The crowd that has now gathered to watch goes wild. In the back of my mind, I know there are some folks out there who will be livid as soon as the pictures are out, which will be within the hour. There are some brands that would have sponsored me and now they'll refuse to. There are even some fans who will disown me.

There are risks – and I'm embracing them all now.

Because for every person who doesn't like the real me, there will be a new one who gets it. For every door in my old life that closes, I'm going to find another one to open.

Besides, it's like Akari said. Once you've had to face your worst fears, you can finally be free of them. And it's true: How can I be afraid of more bad press when I'm already swamped in it? I've seen the worst they can do. And my brand is thriving anyway. DB is the one hemorrhaging stocks, not RACHEL K.

Let them say whatever they will say. I refuse to live in fear any more.

What got me here won't get me there.

I take Alex's hand, and he swings his duffel over his shoulder with the other hand. "Come on," I tell him. "Let's go home." And together, we part the crowd, smiling and waving like we're a freaking royal couple.

I may not know what the future holds, but with all these

cameras flashing around us, their light filling my peripheral vision like fireworks, I know it is going to be bright.

The next morning, the first thing I do is pick up the phone.

"Hi, Carly? It's Rachel." I take a deep breath. Leap of faith, here we go. "You know the event you were talking about? Let's do it."

Who am I without Girls Forever?

Can I succeed on my own after being kicked out?

Will my fans still show up for me?

These questions have been circulating in my mind for the past four months. And honestly? I have no answers. Not yet. But I'm here to try to get one step closer to finding out.

It's the day of my partnership event with Discipline Sportswear, and I'm sitting in the greenroom, waiting to be called out to the stage for my first-ever solo performance. The plan is for me to sing covers of a selection of my favorite classic Chung Yuna ballads, then do a fan signing, followed by a photo shoot. For the shoot, we're pairing Discipline sneakers with my bags for a campaign about fashion on the go. Ollie's even talking about working together to design a sporty belt bag, but that's for down the line. Today, I'll be rocking smudged multicoloured sneakers, and for the bag? Well, as much as I love all the purse designs I created, I followed my heart and had to create a new one especially for Discipline. It's the New Rachel bag: a playful mini top-handle bag, with a tiny infinity symbol on the seal. Because, as Carly herself said, the show must go on. And as my dad always says, we roll with the punches, but we don't give up the fight.

My heart is hammering in my chest, and my palms are clammy. I check to make sure my mascara isn't smudging, that my lipstick is still in place. For the solo performance and fan meeting, I'm wearing a simple glittery black headband with a matching dress. Classic, but with a little bit of sparkle. Sometimes a little bit is all you need.

There's a knock on the door, and a security guard pokes his head in. "Ms. Kim, we're ready for you."

I take a deep breath and rise.

Here's the pact I made with myself ever since I said yes to Carly's invitation. No matter what the crowd is like today, I'm going to give them my all. Even if there's only one fan out there, I'm going to make sure that one fan has the best K-pop experience they've ever had in their life. I've learned the value of loyalty, and if anyone is willing to stick with me through everything that's happened, well, I'm going to pay them back tenfold. Today and for all the days to come.

I follow the security guard as he leads me towards the stage. I pause, pressing a hand against my heart. It's racing with anticipation. But it's not just nerves any more. It's excitement.

I've missed this.

I walk on to the platform beneath the stage that will carry me up through a trap door. I take one more deep breath as the man operating the lift begins to count down.

3, 2, 1.

Above me, the stage floor parts, lights flooding down through the opening.

And then: the lift begins to rise.

Immediately, the thunderous roar of a cheering crowd overtakes me. I squint in the spotlight, certain I'm imagining things, but no. It's real.

The crowd stretches for what seems like miles. There are thousands and thousands of fans, screaming their support, waving signs, wearing homemade T-shirts and glowing LED headbands.

They aren't just any glowing headbands, though. My heart squeezes as I realise it. They spell out *RACHEL*.

"Rachel, we love you! We missed you so much!" a fan shouts above the sounds of cheering and stamping feet and clapping hands. I'm so overwhelmed with gratitude that tears fill my eyes. In that moment, my heart is so full, it overflows.

I think back to that day, years ago, back when I was first starting out, when a fan told me that I changed her life and made me cry. I guess some things never change.

And maybe, maybe, some things *can* be forever.

My fans still make me cry and they're still the best.

They've changed *my* life.

I blink back my tears and step up to the mic, giving them the smile I know they love. A smile from deep inside my heart. A smile that's real.

Epilogue

"Where do you think this would look good?"

Alex holds up a framed illustration of what looks like two fairies in crowns playing soccer and somehow breathing fire at the same time.

Um, nowhere? I want to answer, but hold my tongue.

"My cousins mailed it to me all the way from Seattle," Alex says proudly. *Ah, that makes more sense.* "A Nora and Jeremy original. I bought the frame myself. I still need to authenticate the signatures, though," he says, pointing to the scrawled names in the corner.

"Oh yes, art fraud is so rampant in elementary school these days," I say with mock seriousness, and Alex grins. "Definitely belongs on the bookshelf," I add. "Front and centre."

"Got it."

It's early spring and I'm helping Alex move into his new apartment in Seoul. After working remotely in our den for a while and realising that it is possible for him to do his job from Korea, he decided to officially relocate. Lately, I've been busy helping him move and settling into a new routine of my own.

RACHEL K. has been flourishing internationally, and I've started writing songs for a possible future solo album, though I've been struggling with writer's block these days, with images of my torn-up song diary emerging in my memory when I try to focus. It's okay, though. I'm trying not to put too much pressure on myself. Right now, it's just about learning to love music again, and finding my own creative voice. Besides the beginnings of an album and my work with RACHEL K., the only other creative pursuit I've been working on these days is this scrapbook I've been putting together as a gift for Leah. SayGO just earned their third number-one hit single, and I wanted to congratulate her somehow. I know that she is close with her groupmates and that they'll probably celebrate together. DB might even throw them some sort of party – three number ones in your debut year is a huge accomplishment. But I never want Leah to feel like she has to rely on her groupmates or DB for support. After all, we've both learned that that support could disappear in an instant. But family is forever.

I scroll through old photos on my laptop as Alex arranges his bookshelf, whistling "Let It Go" to himself while he works – after many virtual movie nights with the twins in which they refuse to vary the film selection, he's got it stuck in his head. The apartment is still new, but it's already starting to feel like home. I've been spending a lot of time here, bouncing back and forth between Alex's place and my family's apartment.

I pause as I come across a series of photos from Girls Forever concerts throughout the years. There are so many. I think I have more photos of myself with Mina, Lizzie, Eunji, Ari, Sumin, Jiyoon, Youngeun, and Sunhee than I do with literally anyone else in my life. It's strange to think that there won't ever be a photo with the nine of us in it ever again. My heart tightens at the thought, and I have to swallow the lump in my throat.

Since the day DB kicked me out, I haven't had any contact with my former groupmates. It still stings to think about them, but the pain gets a little less every day. I've finally started to believe what Carly said about the fog clearing and the misery not lasting forever. It's like what Umma said too. My best days aren't behind me. They're waiting for me. Some days it's easier to hold on to that than others, but I'm still here and that's enough for me to keep on going.

I click through a few concert photos, feeling nostalgic. My favourite pictures are the ones that show the crowd. Even in a still shot, there's an energy in the fans that shines through. I can even spot a few glowing *RACHEL* headbands in the pictures. I grin.

I've always appreciated my fans, but after everything that's happened this year, my gratitude for them has only grown deeper. They're the ones who literally got me through my darkest moments. They inspire me, and I hope that I can inspire them, too.

My phone buzzes with an incoming text. I startle and close my laptop, somehow thinking that if it's Leah texting me, she'll be able to see my scrapbook-in-progress through the phone. But when I glance down at the screen, I see an unknown number.

Don't think this is over. There are still scores to be settled. I'd watch my back if I were you. PS: Doesn't your little sister still work with DB? She better watch her back too . . .

I roll my eyes and immediately delete the message, though I can't help but shudder. It's hard not to feel a rise of anxiety at these messages. I've been getting texts like this every so often. I have no idea who's sending them, but every time my phone pings with another threat, it's a harsh reminder that things aren't going to be easy moving forward.

I open my computer and look again at the photo of my fans. For every hater, I try to look instead to the beacons of light that guide me back to myself. I let my gaze drift over to the large window in Alex's living room where beams of daylight are streaming through. For a second, they remind me of my fans, lighting up the darkness, reminding me why I'm onstage in the first place, and giving me the strength to keep going. I just need to look to them, and I know there will be a path forward.

Suddenly, inspiration hits me like a lightning bolt zapping right through my writer's block. I quickly grab a pen and one of Alex's spare pads of legal paper littering the table, flipping it over to a clean page.

The title comes to me first. "Golden Sky."

A tribute for my fans, who shine brighter than any star.

This one's for you.

ACKNOWLEDGMENTS

As always, my gratitude goes first and foremost to my Golden Stars. Your constant support, excitement, and love for this series have kept me going through the writing process. Thank you for being my inspiration.

My endless thanks also go to the entire team at Simon & Schuster. To my editors, Jennifer Ung and Alexa Pastor – Jen, thank you for all your incisive notes, and for guiding this story through such a long journey; Alexa, thank you for stepping in and seeing my vision through to the end. To those on my marketing and publicity teams – Chrissy Noh, Karen Masnica, Anna Jarzab, Emily Ritter, Lisa Moraleda, and Milena Giunco – I appreciate everything you've done and continue to do to get my books out to readers. To Paul Oakley, thank you for the stunning new artwork that perfectly captures Rachel's inner and outer journey in these novels.

I'm so grateful for my team at United Talent Agency too – many thanks to Max Michael, Albert Lee, and Meredith Miller for making sure these books reach my fans all over the world. Thanks as well to those at Inkwell Management – Stephen Barbara, you have championed this project since the beginning, and I am so grateful.

To the incomparable women at Glasstown Entertainment – I couldn't have done this without you all. To Lexa Hillyer, for bringing all my ideas to life with such imagination and depth. To Jenna Brickley, for your plotting brilliance and keen insights. To Olivia Liu, for your hard work and care to detail. Thanks as well to Laura Parker and Lynley Bird, for working tirelessly to get this story to screens. And, of course, special thanks to Sarah Suk – in your hands, these words shine bright!

To my family – I love you so much. I am only where I am because of you. To my parents – thank you for the unconditional love and support. To Krystal – you are the best sister and my favourite cheerleader.

Last but never least, I want to thank Tyler. This book, and so many other dreams, would not have been possible without you. Thank you for being beside me always on this journey – I wouldn't have wanted it any other way.

A GUIDE TO THE KOREAN WORDS AND PHRASES IN *BRIGHT*

ahnyounghasaeyo: formal greeting

appa: father

baboya: silly person

baechu: cabbage

halmoni: grandmother

kalguksu: knife-cut noodle soup

kimbap: rice and seaweed roll

kimchi: salted and fermented vegetables

kongnamul guk: soybean sprout soup

maknae: youngest person

nurungji: scorched rice

oppa: used by a younger female to address an older brother; can also be used for older male friend

patbingsu: shaved ice with red beans and toppings

soju: distilled rice-based alcoholic beverage

soondubu jjigae: soft tofu stew

sunbae: someone with more experience than you

tteokbokki: spicy stir-fried rice cakes

umma: mother

unni: used by a younger female to address an older sister; can also be used for older female friend

Read on for an
exclusive extract of
Jessica Jung's first book,

Shine

✫ One ✫

Head up, legs crossed. Tummy tucked, shoulders back. Smile like the whole world is your best friend. I repeat the mantra in my head as the camera pans across my face. The corners of my lips turn up in a perfectly sweet "don't you want to tell me all your secrets" pink-glossed smile.

But you probably shouldn't. You know how they say three can keep a secret if two are dead? Well, that couldn't be truer for my world, where everyone is always watching and your secrets can actually kill you. Or, at least, they can kill your chance to shine.

"You girls must be thrilled!" The interviewer is a middle-aged man with oily, slicked back hair and fair skin. He might have been handsome if his garish hot-pink satin tie and red shirt combo weren't so distracting. He leans forward eagerly, his eyes gleaming at the nine girls seated before him, a sea of perfectly tousled beach waves and unblemished faces glowing from years of skin-brightening face masks, choreographed down to the angle of our sleekly crossed legs and the descending order of our pastel rainbow-hued stilettos. "Hitting number one at all the music shows, and with your debut music video no less! You're one chart away from an All-Kill! How do you feel?"

"We couldn't be more excited." Mina jumps in eagerly, flashing her perfect teeth in a beaming smile. My face muscles ache as I stretch to match her.

"It's a dream come true," Eunji agrees before loudly popping her gum and blowing a huge strawberry-scented bubble.

"We're so grateful for the opportunity to do this together," Lizzie chimes in, her eyes practically glowing under layers of silvery eye shadow.

The interviewer's eyes light up, and he leans in conspiratorially. "So you all get along? I mean, nine incredibly beautiful girls in one group. That can't always be easy."

Sumin gives a soft, effortless laugh, pursing her perfectly lined bright-red lips. "Nothing is ever 'always easy'," she says. "But we're family. And family comes first." She links arms with Lizzie sitting next to her. "We belong together."

The interviewer flutters a hand over his heart. "Just precious. And what do you love about working together?" His eyes travel slowly over the group, finally landing on me. "Rachel?"

My eyes immediately shift to the huge camera sitting behind the interviewer. I can feel the lens zooming in on me. *Head up, legs crossed. Tummy tucked, shoulders back.* I've been preparing for this moment for years. I smile wide, turning the interviewer into my best friend. And my mind goes completely blank.

Say something, Rachel. Say anything. This is the moment you've been waiting for. My hands have gone clammy, and I can sense the other girls start to shift uncomfortably in their seats as my silence fills the room. The camera feels like a spotlight – hot and prickly on my skin – as my mouth dries up, making it almost impossible to speak.

Finally, the interviewer sighs and takes pity on me. "You've all been through so much together – training for seven years before making it big! Has the experience been everything you hoped it would be?" He smiles, lobbing me an easy question.

"Yes," I manage to croak out, a smile still plastered on my face.

He continues. "And tell me a little more about what life was like as a trainee before your big girl-group debut. What was your favourite part of living in the trainee house?"

My mind spins around for an answer as I discreetly wipe the sweat off my hands and on to the leather seat beneath me. An idea pops into my head. "What else?" I say, lifting a hand, awkwardly wiggling my perfectly manicured fingers, all white and lavender stripes, towards the camera. "Eight girls to do your nails for you. It's like living in a 24/7 nail salon!"

Omg. What is wrong with me? Did I really just say my favourite part of training was having eight girls to give me free manicures?

Luckily, the interviewer's laughter booms loudly throughout the room, and I feel relief coursing through my body. *Okay, I can do this.* I giggle along with him, and the other girls quickly join in. He flashes his greasy smile at me. *Uh-oh . . .*

⭐ *About the Author* ⭐

JESSICA JUNG is a Korean American singer, actress, fashion designer, and international influencer. Born in San Francisco, Jessica grew up in South Korea, where she trained as a K-pop singer, debuting as a member of the international sensation Girls' Generation in 2007. After going solo in 2014, she launched the successful fashion line Blanc & Eclare. Jessica has been featured on the covers of magazines worldwide, and her brand now spans many platforms, including film and television.

© 2020 by Coridel Entertainment